THE ITALIAN AFFAIR

THE ITALIAN AFFAIR

MILFY

First Edition: Great Britain, 2024
Copyright © 2023 by MiLFY

All rights reserved. No part of this publication may be reproduced, stored or transmitted in any form or by any means, electronic, mechanical, photocopying, recording, scanning, or otherwise without written permission from the publisher. It is illegal to copy this book, post it to a website, or distribute it by any other means without permission from the author, except for the use of brief quotations in a book review.

This novel is entirely a work of fiction. The names, characters, and incidents portrayed in it are the work of the author's imagination. Any resemblance to actual persons, living or dead, events or localities is entirely coincidental.

MiLFY asserts the moral right to be identified as the author of this work.

The author published a previous version of this story in a serialized form online. The current novel represents an expanded and revised version of the original content.

Designations used by companies to distinguish their products are often claimed as trademarks. All brand names and product names used in this book and on its cover are trade names, service marks, trademarks and registered trademarks of their respective owners. The publishers and the book are not associated with any product or vendor mentioned in this book. None of the companies referenced within the book have endorsed the book.

Cover Photograph by Roland Helerand
Cover Design by Dragoslav Andjelkovic

ISBN: 9781068607097 (Paperback)

This novel is intended for 18+ Mature Audiences only and contains explicit language, sexual content, and adult situations: adultery/cheating. If these subjects offend, please skip this book.

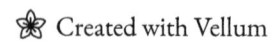

✼ Created with Vellum

PRAISE FOR THE ITALIAN AFFAIR

The Italian Affair just got me hot and bothered... Love all the details... **Food, sex, wine, Italy.** Does it get better than that? What I wouldn't do to have a quarter of what Sabina and Gianmarco have.

Have you read it? You should...

— MONALISASMILED, EDITOR OF *THE SCARLETT LETTER*

I love so many things about this... especially how the main character is so open about her sexual needs. She **never plays games, never holds back,** always tells him exactly what she wants without fearing rejection—which she sometimes gets. That is **so refreshing in erotic literature!** She is a great protagonist that we **can't help but love and identify with**. And that is the heart of good storytelling.

— REEF BABY

I feel as though you have somehow gazed into my past and **written this specifically for me, understanding my passions**, catering to my tastes, and offering what gives me the most pleasure. An exquisite encounter—marvelous, delicious, and **decadent!**

— SLEV

First, I love the **historical details**, making the story breathe with life. Second, even though Sabina is insatiable with Gianmarco at all times, she is a lady: **elegant, cultured, and refined**. I was excited by the fact that she's **so high society, but yet so *basic.***

— AT-TN

Well-written, intriguing story told with just the right mix and attention to detail, whether food & wine, geographical & historical or **sensual & erotic.**

— AVA GAVI

I became enthralled with this **wild, sexy, tale of love & lust**, and how the two connect as human beings... Loved the story! It's a beautiful work.

— WAYNE SCHARPHORN

What a ride.... **a rollercoaster of emotions!**

— HEATHER

A hedonistic, bohemian, sexual foodie's delicious drive through Italy. I **devoured every morsel of this forbidden love affair,** one succulent page after another.

— MORDRED

Well written, full of **adventure, love, lust, history, suspense and twists.** Sabina is a refined sensual lady who wants to revive what she had. She is very refreshing that all she does is asks for what she wants or needs. Sabina meets Gianmarco at a restaurant where he is her waiter. As they flirt with each other it turns into a relationship that they both receive much from. Really enjoyed the time they had together. **Most women would love to have some of what they did.** Would recommend to others.

— ROSE S.

I am a romantic man, but culture tells us we need to be more romantic to woo women: poetry, flowers & wine, dancing & drawing, plus candlelit bedrooms with satin sheets.

In truth, both sexes enjoy receiving these tokens of love; however, romantic gestures performed by women are rarely depicted in traditional romance novels. And why would they?

Men aren't reading them!

The Italian Affair is clearly **a great exception that breaks from the norm,** and that's why I find it so compelling. Sabi showers her man with all sorts of romantic gestures—I lapped it up!

Believe me, **this is not your ordinary romance novel!**

— RHOBEAU

For My Beloved

A FLOWERGRAM TO YOU

My Dear Reader,

It seems trite to say I have always been a hopeless romantic, but I am!

At thirteen, I had a serious crush on a boy with beautiful black curly hair who ran as fast as the wind. He was shy yet friendly, and how his eyes of electric blue shone when he smiled!

Unwise to the ways of the world, on Valentine's Day, I sent my mystery crush an anonymous flowergram. With a name and fifty cents, a high school club member delivered a fresh carnation with a note to the lucky student in the second period.

After lunch, I saw him walking in the hallway toward his locker, surrounded by friends. He was smiling, holding the prize from his secret admirer against his mouth.

Dreaming I was that blossom and his lips were on me, I dashed a love poem during the fifth period, not paying attention to the fearsome and ferocious Ms. Bissell or her lesson on English literature. Surely, she would understand that I was composing a literary magnum opus, channeling the grand bard himself in the name of... *love!*

I intended to hand the note to my crush and reveal my identity after school. Unfortunately, I missed my chance, wondering, was it the hand of Fate intervening? Goal-bound and determined to connect, I found his telephone number in the white pages.

I dialed and hung up at least a dozen times before letting the call go through, my palms sweaty and my voice cracking. "Hi, Bobby! I wrote something for you. May I read it to you?"

"OK," he said, and I did.

Silence, then a polite thank you. I was so grateful he didn't laugh. Bobby was honest yet gracious, a gentleman even at a young age. "I'm sorry. I don't feel the same."

He hung up, and at the sound of the end-call dial tone, I wished I could have died. I threw away my poem, my first public composition, and stifled my voice.

After telling my best friend about my embarrassing fail, Rebecca thought we needed an adventure. Escaping the sweltering heat, she showed me the broken back door of the local dollar movie house and snuck us in.

In its day, the Lorenzo Theatre was a beautiful Art Deco motion-picture playhouse where townspeople once wore black ties and gowns to catch an evening show. By the 1980s, she was no longer magnificent. Frayed at the edges, the once-plush burgundy velvet seats with the carved walnut armrests were lumpy and creaky. If one sat the wrong way, a spring would have poked one's behind.

But in that darkened dream palace on that fateful afternoon, I was transported, watching the unforgettable 1968 Franco Zeffirelli production of William Shakespeare's *Romeo and Juliet*. Never before had I seen such lush costumes and stunning landscapes that I fell in love with Italy and the play. And to my lovelorn thirteen-year-old self, Leonard Whiting's Romeo became my fantasy dreamboat!

My first sweet taste of Italy was in Taormina, living with the Sicilians, learning their lyrical Italian language, and falling in love with their sumptuous food and slow, authentic way of life.

Fast forward a few decades, and I was older, married with children, but none the wiser. Still determined to return to *la dolce vita*, I found a way for my family to spend six months immersed in Italy's *sweet life*, and after proving our sincere desire to respectfully learn everything about their great culture, many kind and generous Italians from all walks of life befriended our family, opening their hearts and homes to us.

One gloomy day while motoring around the enchanting little towns scattered throughout Italy, we happened upon a beautiful, well-renowned Michelin restaurant in the mountains. Typically, one needed reservations to dine at such an exclusive establishment, but it was early, and they had just opened for lunch. Feeling emboldened at the rare opportunity before us, we grabbed the chance for some indulgence, asking if there was space for our family, myself, my husband, and our precocious four-year-old daughter, who shyly peeked out from behind my floor-length skirt and beamed a warm smile at the proprietor, showing him her anthropomorphic, hot-pink toy helicopter.

He bowed his head to be at her eye level and smiled back, twirling the plastic propellers with his finger while buzzing his lips, making my Little One giggle at her newfound friend. Italians loved children and would move heaven and earth to make them happy. Perhaps my daughter had won him over as he welcomed us to his restaurant with open arms.

The waiter assigned to our table spoke perfect English. He

was so playful toward my child and attentive to me. His soulful eyes sparkled whenever he passed by, and it felt like dark clouds lifted the more he engaged with us. Who was this magician?

"Gianmarco," he said with a smile.

I did not realize how influential that afternoon adventure would become. Inspired by the kindhearted Italians we had met, I picked up my pen and found my voice again in an unlikely pairing unfolding in my mind; an American mogul's wife and a simple Italian waiter, star-crossed lovers, finding passion and adventure in the land of romance I love.

Ever the romantic, I had always hoped for a happy ending for the original star-crossed lovers. In my heart of hearts, I wish for Gianmarco + Sabina to find a happily ever after, at least for now.

And so, dear Reader, *The Italian Affair* is my flowergram to you.

Will you say, "No, thank you?" Or, will you give me a chance and say, "Sit with me, and tell me more! I want to listen."

I truly appreciate your reading to the end. And if you feel my little culinary travelogue filled with risqué seduction has touched you, share your thoughts and follow me. I would love to sit with you and hear your voice too!

With love and gratitude,

M

UNFORGETTABLE

I

PIG BUTTER

Friday, October 27, 2017
Ristorante Mirabella
La Guardia, Italy

A cool late autumn breeze blew us into Mirabella, a secluded summit hotel that overlooked the Gran Sasso Mountain range within the Apennines of Abruzzo, the wildest, most untamed region of Italy. But as soon as we entered the exclusive restaurant's foyer, we were warmly greeted with that famed Italian hospitality.

My heart was beating faster as the opportunity to put my foreign language lessons into practice had finally arrived. With a nervous smile, I blurted out to the welcome staff, "*Buongiorno,*" and they smiled graciously.

"*Good morning.*"

As I spoke, sounding nothing like the locals, my cheeks turned a hint of self-conscious rouge.

Unamused, my husband, Cyril, rolled his eyes and said nothing; however, Kally, our precocious little daughter, was all smiles. She was a joyous, fun-loving girl like me, always ready for adventure.

The reserved maître d' tipped her head slightly. *"Benvenuti, signor e signora Skye, e la tua carissima bimba!"*
"Welcome, Mr. and Mrs. Skye, and your cute baby girl!"

She gestured toward the sunlit room. "Please, this way to your table." We eagerly followed her through a grand glass-enclosed dining hall surrounded by spectacular alpine views. The guests casually chatted at their tables; nary a child was in sight.

Their language was so lyrical, and though I didn't understand the passing conversations, I loved hearing Italians speak—as if they were singing, with their cadence and rhythm like melodious poetry falling from their lips.

Nestled in the corner of the dining room, an army of servers presented us with menus, a church Bible-sized wine list perched on a pedestal, and a little upholstered footstool set at my side to hold my enormous black leather handbag.

Now that was different—a seat for my purse to feel welcome! They've thought of everything here. *As much as society moves forward, I hope this Old World etiquette will remain forever.*

An antique wooden highchair waited at the table for our wiggly little Kally. Restraining her in those belted and buckled contraptions was always challenging. Upon our settling in, her tiny fingers stretched for the delicate crystal chalice, tipping and spilling water on the crisp, ivory linens.

Drip, drip, drip…

Droplets slowly fell, pooling onto my lap.

Peering at me over the top of the wine bible, Cyril shook his head in disapproval for my lack of parental discipline toward our daughter. I sighed heavily, wondering if we had made a mistake coming to such an elegant place. However, having a relaxing glass of Montepulciano d'Abruzzo wine would be a most welcome reprieve.

A bearded waiter approached us, ready to take our order. Overwhelmed by the daunting array of choices on their extensive Italian-only menu, I nervously asked him, "Do you speak English?"

In a polite, reserved voice, he said, "*Sì, signora*. A little."
"Yes, madam."

"Thank you." I sighed with relief because we had dined at an excellent little restaurant in Pescara the night before, where only Italian was spoken. The menu went on for pages and pages and was incomprehensible to foreigners.

Though I had studied an online language course every day for three months prior, I was still hopelessly lost. And rolling those darned Rs was next to impossible for me, no matter how many hours I practiced the Pimsleur CDs nor how much wine I drank!

Like a magician, our charismatic waiter enchanted us all by paying extra special attention to my little Kally in such a playful way, indulging her every demand. He grated a tower's worth of Parmigiano-Reggiano cheese onto her plate of housemade pasta until she said, "Stop!" He knelt tableside to speak to her at eye level, patiently answering every one of her silly questions. Since she wore her favorite pink headband with the dainty little kitty-cat ears, he nicknamed her *Little Pink Kitten* and liked to mischievously tweak the sparkly ears as he passed our table. But with the teasing, he also delivered delicate pink flowers plucked from the garden and handed them to her on each return.

As a youngling, it's easy to have one's existence treated as an afterthought, especially in an adult-centric venue like a Michelin restaurant. But not that day, and not with him!

He was such a thoughtful, attentive gentleman, making my Little One feel as special and important as any other guest in that room. Perhaps he sensed instinctively that the way to my heart was through my beloved child, and he had won me over, gaining not only my respect but also my affection.

With my anxiety alleviated and feeling more relaxed, I asked how the tasting menu worked.

Delivered in fluent English with only a hint of the most charming Italian accent, he gestured to the menu selections and said, "You can choose anything on either side of the menu, *signora*. We can also substitute if you wish. We can add white or black truffles to any dish. We also have a *foie gras* course."

Cyril had a stiff tongue, and foreign languages did not come easily to him. He pointed to the menu. "What's this? *Ag-nellow. Castrate-oh. Alla grig-leah?*"

My hand raced to my mouth, trying not to chuckle aloud as I heard my husband mangle the pronunciation.

"*Sì, signore. Agnello castrato alla griglia.*" The spoken words flowed musically from his flexible Italian tongue. "Grilled aged lamb. And yes, castrated. It's very tender and particularly delicious."

"Old, castrated mutton!" Aghast, Cyril shook his head. "No way!"

Guiding us through the menu, everything our waiter recommended sounded tempting. But I knew it was too much to eat in one sitting, especially since Cyril and I had snacked on some tasty *porchetta* at the Friday morning street fair. That herb-infused pork loin was stuffed in a pork belly and roasted until the skin turned into crackling. Feeling like reckless children set free in a candy store, we indulged in scrumptious, wretched excess.

My husband usually liked to be the master of the ship, giving orders, but for now, he allowed me to choose what we would have for our lunch.

Standing over me, our waiter watched as I traced my pointer finger along the left side of the menu. "We'll take all of this." I paused and turned to him, suddenly struck by how handsome he was. After handing back our menus, I winked at him and added in Italian, "*E il castrato.*"

"And the castrated."

Upon hearing my selection, he grinned at me, raised his eyebrow, and, ever so slightly, shook his head, knowing my husband would not approve. "Very good, *signora.*"

Could he possibly be teasing me about being bad by calling me "good," taking note of my stubborn streak?

"*Signore,* would you care for any wine to accompany the meal?"

"We'll both have the wine pairing," Cyril said, handing back the wine tome.

"That's too much wine for me. I don't want—" I objected, but Cyril cut me short.

"You'll get used to it." His standard patronizing pronouncement whenever he believed he knew me better than I knew myself.

"Fine," I answered tersely, smiling awkwardly as I turned to our waiter. I did not want a public fight over something trivial.

"Thank you," he said, giving me a sympathetic look and bowing his head before exiting the tense scene.

Moments later, he returned with a rich, golden aperitif wine to accompany our pre-course. "A little *amuse bouche* as a starter, made entirely from our black pigs, compliments of the chef!"

Perhaps it was the aromatic scent of the warm, freshly baked bread he set before us, paired with a one-inch-high cylinder of butter resting on a smooth riverbed stone and adorned with a single, dainty pink chive flower floating on top, that tricked us into feeling hungry. But we were ready.

The butter was snow white, like lard, but the texture was not greasy. It was soft, fluffy, salty, and sweet. And the taste? Oh, so heavenly! Like nothing I've ever had, before or since.

The first bite released a sigh and a moan; it was mouth-wateringly luscious.

I caught our waiter's eye from across the room. With a raised eyebrow and a smile, I invited a challenge to see if my suspicions about the dish were correct.

Cyril exhaled impatiently. "What now?"

"I have a question about this curious *butter*."

"Sabina, why must you insist on drawing attention to yourself? Can you not just eat food and enjoy it without needing to perform an autopsy on it like a coroner?"

I turned away and ignored his comment.

When our waiter approached the table, I said assertively, "There's butter in this!"

"No, none." He confidently smiled back.

"What! But how?" I demanded to know how I could be so wrong!

"Centrifuged, then roasted garlic and herbs from our garden. That's all. No butter."

It was a confusingly divine substance. Oh my God! The way it melted in my mouth and bathed my entire tongue with all of that flavor and aroma transcending beyond butter.

I couldn't stop! I greedily ate all but one pat of it.

Clearly, our waiter enjoyed watching me devour this succulent serving, scraping every last morsel from the stone with a piece of their still-warm bread roll.

As he whisked the now-barren rock away, I had my hands and arms outstretched, not wanting to let go. "Gimme that stone back, please. I want to lick it some more. I think I see a tiny bit that I've missed!"

He laughed heartily and told us the Italian word for getting every last morsel. I wish I could remember. It was said so quickly. *Strappata? Scarpetta? Scarpe?** He even spelled it out for me. If only the recitation of our alphabet sounded the same!

Alas, the moment had passed, and I was left lost in translation but enlightened by this incredible discovery of Mirabella's *pig butter*.

THE AFTERNOON WAS warm but still breezy, and our waiter invited us to have dessert and coffee on the veranda. He brought over two slate flats with beautifully arranged *mignardise*, a sweet final indulgence: one he placed before Cyril and me, and the other, set before his Little Pink Kitten. It was evident she adored his attention and devoured all four tiny, delicate pink macaron cookies in the blink of an eye.

I looked up and saw him grinning as I snapped pictures; diners taking food porn pics at this Michelin-starred restaurant must have been a common sight. He extended his palm to me and offered to take our family's picture. I smiled, nodded, and handed him my phone.

---

* *Strappata? Scarpetta? Scarpe?* = Torn? Little shoe? Shoes?
The words that Gianmarco told Sabina were *fare la scarpetta*, which means *to make a little shoe*, or the act of forming a piece of bread into a shoe to scrape every last bit of sauce from one's plate.

Capturing a decent family photo was easier said than done with my wild child; our adorable, mischievous little Kally was not cooperating. Hamming it up by sticking her tongue out and being a general goofball, she stole the show in every shot. This released the most adorable laugh from our waiter, trying valiantly to steady the camera.

Cyril soon grew tired of posing for the waiter, and the fun photo shoot ended. I small-talked with our *photographer* as I knew the meal was almost over and I didn't yet want to go.

"Do you live here in the village?" I asked.

"No, I live just over there." With his thumb, he pointed behind his back to the beautiful Apennines.

Rising from the table, I stood beside him, closer than necessary. I followed his finger, indicating a spot from across the distance of the Maiella Mountains, searching for Gianmarco's hilltop home.

Turning to cast my eyes upward to catch his gaze, I said, "How beautiful!" He looked at me with a broad smile, his teeth perfectly straight and white, framed by a splendid jaw.

While gazing into his soulful, enigmatic eyes, I had to ask. *"Come ti chiami?"*
_{"What's your name?"}

He smirked, sounding surprised to be asked. *"Io?"*
_{"Me?"}

"Yes, of course!" At the very least, a name, please, thought I. *If eyes are the windows to the soul, mine would reveal how intrigued and attracted I am to you!*

"My name is Gianmarco."

"You have two first names, like Gianni and Marco?"

"Almost." He chuckled. "It's only one, but with three syllables. Jon-Mar-Co." He corrected my pronunciation. "But my friends know me as Marco."

"That's quite a mouthful, but I much prefer Gianmarco. Unique, like you!"

"When Mamma calls me by my full name, I know I'm in trouble!" he bantered.

"Maybe I am *trouble*, as I'd rather call you by your long mouthful!"

He shook his head, laughing and blushing.

I had a thing for deep voices, and my God, his was so profoundly sexy, rich, and velvety smooth like molten chocolate. It jarred loose a reminder that it had been a long time since my husband had given me a good fucking. A glance at our waiter had me blushing at my wicked thoughts; I would have loved to hear him humming into my pussy. But before my mind completed the picture, I turned off the illicit idea. After all, I was a married woman.

Before saying goodbye, I extended my hand, allowing it to slip into his. Leaning forward, I kissed his cheek in a friendly Italian fashion. His body tensed at the intimate brush of my lips as though I had crossed an invisible boundary.

But then he relaxed and reciprocated the gesture by kissing my other cheek. As we pulled away, we noticed our hands were still clasped, a silent connection that spoke volumes. A shared grin spread between us. I blushed, feeling a rush of warmth flood my cheeks, and lowered my gaze, momentarily overwhelmed by the lurid images dancing in my head.

At our parting, my eyes lingered on his mesmerizing brown eyes. Yearning, I wondered what this man was like beyond his station as a waiter in a starched-gray uniform. "What days do you work here?" I asked, knowing I needed to see him again.

"I'm here all the time," he said with a sigh and a half-shrug. There was no innuendo laced in his answer. Instead, it sounded more like he was trapped in a job he would rather not have, with no choice but to serve. Dressed in a more stylish uniform and tasked with less hazardous duty, no doubt, but conscription all the same.

A sadness brushed over me, and I sensed that there was much more to this man than what he allowed to show on the surface.

Ever the professional gentleman, I watched as Gianmarco crouched down to Kally's eye level to hug her goodbye like a dear friend. His kind gesture and genuine care for my daughter warmed my heart and made me smile.

"I'll come back before we leave Italy," I told him, delivered as the promise I meant.

My mind was already racing, looking for an excuse to return. I tooled my husband's arm and suggested inviting our architects to Mirabella for lunch in thanks for all their time spent looking at land and evaluating potential properties for us to restore. Cyril thought it was a great idea since he loved the food, and its Michelin status fed into his ego nicely.

In reality, all I wanted was to see Gianmarco one more time, and now, with hope in my heart, I drummed the air with my fingertips, waving a final farewell to him. "*Arrivederci!*"

"*Until we meet again!*"

2

THE SPACE BETWEEN OUR WORDS

One month later
Friday, November 24, 2017
Ristorante Mirabella
La Guardia, Italy

The day before our return flight home, my sandaled foot crossed the threshold of Mirabella's front portal, and my heart raced with anticipation, beating like a rapid drumroll, nineteen to the dozen. I pressed my lips together to contain my excited smile, silently praying that my astute husband would not unravel the true purpose of our return.

To my dismay, as I surveyed the room, *my* charming waiter was conspicuously absent. Reality settled in, and a profound sense of disappointment washed over me, casting a shadow on my spirits. The fragile wisp of a thread I had spun with the

Italian was cut before it could be woven, leaving behind a lingering ache of what could have been.

At the table, Kally entertained the architects by building soaring structures from a mountain of hollowed-out bread slices, remnants from the soft interior she gobbled down with gusto.

Despite her young age, Kally recognized the restaurant and eagerly scanned the room for her newfound friend. Perhaps, she was expecting Gianmarco to pop up and surprise her with more freshly picked flowers or secret sweets. But still, there was no sign of our tall, handsome waiter.

When I casually inquired about Gianmarco's whereabouts, the new server simply shrugged and babbled quickly. Our Italian architects translated and discovered *our friend* was on leave for a month, convalescing after spending time at the hospital.

A deep frown creased my forehead, and my disappointment morphed into worry. But I couldn't do anything about it; we were leaving for America the following day.

The corners of my mouth rose slightly as an idea popped into my head. Even though I only knew his first name, perhaps there was a way I could touch him one last time.

The following day
Somewhere over the Atlantic

THE NOVELTY of transatlantic air travel had long since lost its shine for Cyril and me. However, for our little Kally, everything about it was still new and exciting, beginning with the attentive agents at the check-in and playing in the dedicated children's area in the First Class lounge with the TVs and the giant monitors for the game consoles, to settling in with her favorite stuffed animals. After boarding and watching the wings at lift-off, feeling the plane lurch as it fought the turbulence of the storm clouds above Heathrow, and then punching through to sail on clear blue skies, Kally's enthusiasm never waned. With a belly full of a good supper, a darkened cabin, and cruising comfortably aboard the Virgin Atlantic V-LUX airliner taking us home to California, Kally dozed comfortably in her pod.

I, on the other hand, was in a decidedly different mood. During dinner, with the clinking and brushing sound of the stainless steel cutlery against the china, I savored each bite, turning over the memories of the much-needed male attention I had received from the hunky and *younger* Italian waiter. The amorous toying was the catalyst to a craving I had ignored for too long—I wanted a man's hungry touch, and I wanted it now.

I peered at my husband, already back to work, arched over the laptop, eyes darting across the screen, and the hurried *tappity-tap-tap* of his fingertips striking the keys.

A scandalous idea crossed my mind. Was a mile-high milestone still possible for us?

"Scoot over so I can sit by you, Cy." It had been a long time since I had called him *Cy*, and even longer since he had called me *Rina* in return.

Short for *Sabrina*, he had mistaken it for my proper name when we first met as freshmen in the same foreign language class at university. I thought he was too cute to torture with a heckling, so I suppressed my grin and politely corrected him.

Quick on his feet, even when sitting down, he recovered by saying *Rina* sounded like *Reina*, meaning *queen* in Spanish. Cy always viewed himself as a boring engineering nerd, but not me. I knew he could be a throwback romantic when he tried. Those were the days when he was my king and we were young and in love. When we had Eve, our first child, more than two decades ago, we still found time for each other, even if it was only to cuddle.

"No. You have your own assigned seating. Sit there." He nodded in the direction of my pod.

I didn't budge from hovering over him and held my stare.

"What do you need?" Cyril asked without taking his eyes off the screen. "You know I have simultaneous projects with pressing deadlines."

"A little love from my husband, I had hoped."

The only sound in the cabin, other than the hum of the engine, was the clicking of keys on the keyboard. He stopped typing, and I held my breath as his fingers hovered over the letters. Had he understood the message I was sending?

Whatever brief thought crossed his mind quickly passed; his *tap-tap-tapping* resumed, the flame of desire reduced to a wisp of smoke.

"Don't bother stopping work on my account. I can see you can't spare thirty minutes to fuck your horny wife."

Annoyed and exasperated, he sighed. "Didn't you pack your vibrator in your hand luggage? Maybe you can—"

"I need *more* than that."

"I don't. Not anymore." His eyes were transfixed, but not on me. "I'm too old for that sort of foolishness. And so are you."

"That may be so, but I'm not dead yet."

He looked at me. "I didn't say you were."

"You didn't have to." I folded my arms and exhaled my disappointment. "Don't I turn you on anymore?"

Turning away from me, more interested in finishing his

project than our conversation, he resumed his work. "My dick is not a faucet you can just turn on and off."

"Why not? It used to be."

Noticeably uncomfortable, he shoulder-checked for eavesdroppers. "Do we have to talk about this right here?"

"OK, if not here and now, then when can we talk and fuck?"

"Check my calendar and make an appointment." He dismissed me like the help.

I raised my chin, angling my eyes toward the overhead luggage bins, fighting gravity to keep tears from escaping. I had made appointments in the past, and our meetings were often delayed or postponed. Something more important always seemed to come up—*more important than me.*

With one final salvo, I pleaded, "I miss you, Cy!" But my words were ignored. I felt small and humiliated, begging for crumbs of affection from my husband. "Never mind."

I headed to snuggle with Kally in her pod, where I knew I was still loved.

Later that same day
Point Reyes, California

WE HAD HARDLY SET foot inside Sierra Mare, our family residence, when Cyril abruptly left me to unpack while he headed straight for his office. The loud slam of the door indicated he did not want to be disturbed.

With a jet-lagged Kally napping in her room, I had time alone to reflect on our two-month holiday. I had hoped the romantic Italian vacation might have rekindled my husband's libido.

It had not.

But I knew *someone* who was interested. Reliving that afternoon at Mirabella with Gianmarco, I thought of how he had looked at me, and it made my heart soar. Those emotions were bottled up inside, and I needed to find a way to release them. Though Cyril was right about my being older, I wanted to know if I still had the sex appeal to make a man interested in me.

I opened the photo app on my phone and smiled, scrolling through the pictures he had taken of us. I loved the one of Kally sticking her tongue out. I could still hear his joyful laughter in my mind. It was so endearing.

And so, disregarding all logic, I retrieved a leaf of ivory linen stationery from my writing desk and picked up my gold-nibbed fountain pen. Setting the notes I had made on the plane beside the paper, I began my letter to the sexy Italian waiter.

Ciao Gianmarco! We came back to see you, but you weren't there. I was worried when I heard you were at the hospital....

With the letter completed, I stared proudly at my beautifully crafted calligraphic writing.

Driving to the post office in my *Chelsea Chariot*, what my husband nicknamed my Range Rover, I hesitated at the mailbox. Prone to overthinking, I wondered if it was wise to send this.

For once, I refused to give voice to my anxiety. What was I so worried about? We were both adults, and I would have been flattered if I had received a note like what I had just written.

Throwing caution to the wind, I pushed the envelope through the mail slot. It would probably get lost in the haphazard Italian post anyway. Regardless, I smiled and felt content, not regretting for one moment that I reached out. Truthfully, I knew a reply was unlikely, and a letter to an Italian waiter from an older, married American traveler would be taken with a grain of salt. I fully expected my penned words to be the end of our brief, flirtatious encounter.

But I was wrong.

Forty-three days later
Sunday, January 7, 2018
Sierra Mare

THE POSTE ITALIANO mail service had a reputation for being slow and not the most reliable. But they came through since my letter was delivered to Mirabella after New Year's Day. My heart nearly exploded when I saw Gianmarco's text through Facebook Messenger. Touched by my affectionate words and flattery, he must have felt compelled to reply. He said he recognized me by my cover photo, which he had taken of our family at Mirabella.

We became Facebook friends, messaged each other often, and shared pictures of our worlds and families. My cover story to Cyril for communicating with the waiter was that I was learning Italian from a native, useful for when we next returned to Italy.

Not to be left out, Kally also sent her newfound friend, Gianmarco, colorful drawings, short notes, and random questions, allowing her to practice her art and penmanship skills.

For Gianmarco, our correspondence provided an opportunity to maintain his English skills—not that he needed it, as he was already quite proficient, having worked abroad at his uncle's Italian deli and wine shop in cosmopolitan London for two years prior. And though he was often busy with work, Gianmarco made the time and frequently wrote to Kally, sending her hearts and gracious words of encouragement in the language we shared.

As for me, I was held to more serious Italian tutorials, but I looked forward to every opportunity to engage with him: from texting him good morning greetings, sometimes with pictures, to which he sweetly replied, *Che bel risveglio!* to evening farewells, answered with *a domani!*

What a beautiful awakening! to evening farewells, answered with *until tomorrow!*

On Valentine's Day, Gianmarco sent a text wishing us a happy Valentine's, sharing the news that he was now a sommelier at another Michelin-starred restaurant in Pescara—Tutto Mare. He was incredibly proud of this, and I answered back that he had every right to celebrate this achievement. I offered my congratulations, promising to accept his invitation to visit him. Or maybe, *he would call on me in America*, he teased. My heartbeat surged upon reading that message, and my face felt flushed at the idea of seeing him again.

On his birthday, Kally and I made a card with a recording of us singing Happy Birthday to him and sent it to his workplace. Gianmarco loved it so much that he posted it on Instagram. He tagged and messaged me, overjoyed by our surprise, saying it was the highlight of his birthday. I was surprised but honored that he shared us—the eccentric Americans—with his Italian friends and his world.

Six months later
Sunday, August 5, 2018

WHILE WINDOW SHOPPING at the Corte Madera Mall, Kally found a vending machine that dispensed temporary tattoo stickers. I reminded her that her father neither approved of tattoos nor of those who sported them. But she begged me, saying it was only fake, and she wanted to send a picture to Gianmarco, just like the fuzzy Facebook photo of the snake tattoo we saw on his bicep.

How could I say *no* to my ever-so-cute, pleading child? I never could. And feeling mischievous, I smiled inside, knowing it would tweak Cyril if he found out what I allowed; however, it would be another fun opportunity to reach out and send a pic to our playful Italian pen pal.

Bursting at the seams, Kally chose an adorable cat surrounded by hearts. It was the last cute sticker tattoo, but she really wanted to get me one too. Unfortunately, the only other choices were between a giant red fire engine and a menacing flying black bat.

I politely declined but promised she could choose a tiny one for me next time.

At home, she wet her faux tattoo and applied it to her bicep, excited to be like Gianmarco. I texted him a photo of my Little One flexing her temporarily inked arm.

SABINA
Look at Kally's tattoo!
She says she wants to be like you

GIANMARCO
🖤🖤🖤
Tell her mine are fake

LOL She will never believe you

Ahahaha

> Forza

> Why Forza?

> Be strong

> You can do it

His following text left me confused and lost for words.

> When will we see each other again… you and me?

I wondered, was he drunk or lonely, asking me this unexpected question? I knew he loved my adorable Kally, but I thought we were just friends, although I continuously fantasized about and hoped for more.

> I don't know… but I think of you often

He replied instantly.

> How do you think of me???

My hands were shaking; my heart was beating so fast that blood rushing to my brain made me feel lightheaded and unable to think straight.

I sighed and placed my phone on my nightstand. I didn't want to lie by denying how I truly felt about him, but at the same time, I didn't feel brave enough to tell him the whole truth, worried that things would change between us if I did.

Three little blips flashed on my screen as he waited on the

other end. I couldn't leave him hanging; he knew that I had seen his message. I took a deep breath and picked up my phone.

With trembling fingers, I tapped back a non-answer.

> I'm afraid to tell you

> Dimmi

> Please tell me

> I only have good thoughts about you

> When I think of you

> I feel like I am next to a warm fire on a cold winter's day

> Do you want me?

> If you do then say it

> Tell me you want me

> Dimmi dimmi dimmi che mi vuoi

"Oh God!" I gasped, silently reading and rereading his words, *dimmi che mi vuoi... tell me you want me.*

I buried my head in the crook of my arm, excited but worried that things were moving too fast. *What should I tell him?*

> Sorry, I need to go

> Talk soon

My mind was spinning with lurid thoughts and wild scenarios, and I needed solace to think. I took a shower, knowing the powerful hot spray pounding across my neck, back, and shoulders would help wash away the tension and, with any luck, my doubts as well.

Though cleansed and toweled off, I was still wet with thoughts about him. Addicted to his attention, I wanted to keep playing. Turning over my phone from my bedside, I smiled, seeing that he was still active online.

I had paved the way for this; my flirty letter had provided the key, and he had opened the door. There was no closing it now.

> I can't deny the truth
>
> It's true
>
> I want you

> Ti voglio
>
> I feel the same
>
> I want you too

To help soothe the guilt, I justified this liaison by believing Gianmarco and I were merely two lonely people looking for a connection. No longer just friends, our texts became more sexually charged. Soon after crossing that boundary, we exchanged intimate photos. Sexually frustrated at home, I wrote stories of what I would do to him, and he, single and alone, shared his fantasies of what he wanted to do to me. Countless times I gave thanks and cursed the 6,000 miles between us; it was only that distance that kept me from physically betraying my marriage.

After a year of long-distance flirting and sexting, I ached to finally touch him with more than just my words. I wanted to wrap my arms around him. I wanted our tongues to meet. I wanted to feel him inside of me. I wanted him to punish me for going behind my husband's back again and again and again. Finally, a few days before Christmas, we all went to Italy, arranging to meet on Kally's birthday.

Saturday, December 21, 2018
Bernardo Cafe at Pescara Beach
Pescara, Italy

GIANMARCO WAS EVEN MORE handsome in person than I remembered. It was an unforgettable morning for the three of us at Pescara Beach. Kally wanted us to all be together on her birthday, including Daddy, so I invited Cyril, even if only for twenty minutes. However, her father was not interested in joining us for coffee. I was pleased because it meant I didn't have to lie about who I would see that day.

We had a lot of fun on my Little One's birthday. After a delicious Italian breakfast, Gianmarco showered us with gifts. I received two of his favorites: a Bellavista Franciacorta Saten sparkling wine from Veneto and a Montepulciano d'Abruzzo from Tenuta Fiore, which he told me was also his papà's favorite. He gave Kally a whimsical, sparkly kitty-cat hat, and she put it on immediately.

Afterward, we walked hand in hand down to the shore. Sitting on the sand, little Kally climbed onto his lap and demanded a picture, whereupon Gianmarco taught us how to take perfect selfies. Feeling camera shy, I scooted out of the frame.

On the beach, Kally and I chased Gianmarco, trying to tag him, but his competitive nature denied us. We built sand fortresses for mermaids and laughed while stomping the structures to smithereens with our bare feet. Laying on top of the razed destruction, we made sand angels, and I joyfully listened to Gianmarco and Kally sing her favorite rock songs.

Before we knew it, two hours flew by like nothing, and it was time for our friend to go to work. While Kally was digging a tunnel in the sand and running around like a whirling dervish in a sandstorm, I enjoyed a loving embrace with Gianmarco. Next, he turned to his Little Pink Kitten and scooped her up to cradle her in his arms. My dear Kally kissed him goodbye twenty times over his whole face! She giggled with glee as Gianmarco gave her a tender kiss on the forehead. Though he didn't have children of his own, he was loving and attentive toward my baby. *He would make a wonderful father—a true family man.*

Later that night, we dined at Tutto Mare, the restaurant where Gianmarco was no longer merely a waiter but was now a sommelier.

3

CROSSING THE LINE

Eight hours later
Saturday, December 21, 2018
Ristorante Tutto Mare
Pescara, Italy

Standing over me at the table, I felt as fragile and delicate as a freshly baked chocolate soufflé threatening to collapse at his touch. Yet I was enamored with him, my eyes transfixed, enthralled at watching his every nuance. He was so near that the sweet spice of his cologne and the faint scent of his manly perspiration wafted across my nose.

As usual, I was expecting nothing more than the mundane company of my husband, but with Gianmarco as our waiter, the evening suddenly became magical.

I raised the pomegranate soda to my lips to mask my delight

at the sensuous show before me. The tangy-sweet quencher trickled down my throat as my eyes skipped over his marvelous mouth dancing through the Italian alphabet. His lips pursed and curled to form perfectly circular Os; his voice box drum rolled with each R; and at every L, his tongue flicked behind his teeth, clacking like the heel of a stiletto on a ballroom floor.

I felt my entire existence had paused, and even my very heartbeat was held captive as he looked at me, waiting to take our order. When his radiant smile graced his lips, it felt like sunrise across a calm sea. Warmed through, I smiled back at him without a care in the world, bathing in the light of that moment.

Cyril, a big drinker, was already making headway on the complimentary sparkler, the first of his standard two to three bottles of wine with dinner. On the other hand, I had chosen to be more careful. Well aware of my tolerance, I dared not surpass my limit of two glasses, not with Gianmarco so close to me. A third would have dissolved my inhibitions, making me wet and open to anything.

As soon as I laid my eyes on him leaving the kitchen, my need returned; I wanted him. Whether it was in the bathroom or anywhere else, it wouldn't matter. If he wished to have me, I was ready to be his.

I had already had wicked fantasies about fucking Gianmarco at the restaurant where we met a year ago. Visions of his muscular arms lifting me onto the tile ledge of Mirabella's restroom, his face pressed into my chest, his hands tearing my top open, and his fingers brushing over my nipples danced in my head. And with our lurid communications over the past five months, I was practically vibrating in my chair.

That primal desire returned in the first blink of his chestnut-colored eyes. I pressed my thighs together, suppressing my want for him to have me. Fast and hard, dirty and secreted, I wanted Gianmarco with more lust than any man before him, including my husband, Cyril.

Of course, these were still only dreams—forbidden and unlikely to come true. So, I swallowed them with the last of my pomegranate mixer skipping on my tongue.

Slightly bent at the waist, he leaned toward me, asking me if I wanted a cocktail. "Perhaps my specialty—a dirty gin martini?"

I instinctively leaned closer to him, close enough to breathe him in. Shooting him my most sensuous gaze, I whispered, *"Sono ubriaca, Gianmarco!* What can be left to drink when I am already drunk on you?"

"I am drunk, Gianmarco!"

Already buzzing from the mere sight of him, though not a drop of alcohol had passed my lips, I extended my submissive hand toward him. Feeling his palm accept my fingertips, I squeezed his hand to curl into my palm's embrace.

His darting glance at Cyril and Kally, then a knowing look toward me, told me he hadn't misread my signal. Momentarily deepening his gaze to mine confirmed he understood precisely what it meant. But was what I wanted, and what could happen, even possible?

Despite my husband and daughter sharing the table with me, I was in the mood to *play*. I told Gianmarco, "Let's do something crazy tonight! Are *you* ready for a challenge?"

"Noooo!" he responded, feigning protest with an exaggerated look, which made my Little One giggle at the tall Italian man acting afraid of her mama.

I pressed on. "Trust me. It will be fun! I promise."

He drew a deep breath in preparation for facing my trial; it should have been clear to him by now that I was not the usual customer.

"Since I hear this is your last weekend at Tutto Mare, I want you to revisit your favorite dishes and curate an unforgettable dinner, choosing Italian wines to match. And I don't want Tutto Mare's standard offerings—I desire Gianmarco's tasting menu. The sky's the limit!" I commanded.

At first, he was hesitant, probably because he wasn't often given a request like this. Soon, a smile emerged, followed by a twinkle in his eye as the gears of his mind turned.

Walking to the wine cabinet, he opened drawer after drawer, revealing bottles resting horizontally, his *troops* at the ready.

I watched his reflection in the mirror. Examining each *sentry* with such concentration, he ran his right hand over the glass bodies and gently caressed them, considering the best attributes of each.

His hand paused on a bottle of white wine. Returning to our table, he presented us with an Etna Bianca Donnnafugata from Sicily. I asked him if he had been to that beautiful Italian island, and he said he hadn't yet. But he confidently affirmed that this wine's exquisite minerality would pair beautifully with *his* menu.

So far, the best part of that evening was seeing him thrive in his element. I was quite proud of how much he had grown, from a simple waiter I met innocently enough not so long ago to becoming a superb sommelier. His excitement was palpable, from the spring in his step to his radiant smiles all evening long. The upcoming move to Lumos, his new restaurant in Milan, clearly fulfilled his ambition.

Indeed, our fabulous guide surprised us with a superb feast! The accompanying wines he selected paired sublimely with each course: the innovative grilled octopus soup, the perfectly al dente lobster risotto, and the ethereal, dreamy pink finale. Gianmarco's menu was a perfect highlight of our annual Italian vacation.

My lips curled into a delicious smile at my thoughts. *Now, if he could only find a way to fulfill my secret fantasy, this adventure in Italy would be truly unforgettable!*

During a lull, after he cleared the table, I shared an unrequited wish: to learn how to make ravioli as ethereal as we had eaten at the Michelin-starred restaurant where we first met.

With a wink, he said, "This I can deliver, *cara amica mia!*"
"my dear friend!"

Gianmarco whipped out his cell phone and called his brother Niko, who remained at Mirabella as the senior sous chef. With each rich, sensual syllable he spoke, I committed to memory the sound of his Italian voice, so I would never forget. In a few rapid sentences, my hero arranged a private lesson for me before the end of our trip.

Glorious, confident, and bold, he was engaged in a personal phone call on the dining room floor, in full view of the patrons, while looking at me. Command in control, he seemed utterly sexy, working to satisfy my fancy.

I looked into his eyes, yearning to tell him what was in my heart. First, how he had touched me through our messaging over these past months, communicating our growing desire for one another despite the long distance. And last, the joy and appreciation for our time together here and earlier at the beach. I was grateful for all he had done for me, and now I felt an overwhelming sadness that this was the end.

It was now or never.

"Gianmarco, you were amazing tonight!" Blinking away the sparkling tears welling in my eyes, I spoke quietly in Italian, ensuring my husband would neither understand nor hear the words I had been dying to express—I would miss his sexy Italian voice. *"Mi mancherà ascoltare la tua voce affascinante e vedere il tuo bel sorriso."*

"*I will miss hearing your charming voice and seeing your beautiful smile.*"

He blushed and lowered his eyes, trying to hide that stunning smile of his, one that would haunt me long after we parted.

I had touched his soul; message received.

My heart was pounding, and I was terrified of having Cyril see right through my thin facade. It took all my strength to stop what I yearned to do—gently caress his beautiful, bearded face and kiss his sweet lips.

I waited for Gianmarco's response.

Gazing into each other's eyes, neither one blinking for what seemed like an eternity, I searched for non-verbal clues that he felt the same way. Validation arrived with a provocative private glance that said much more than the polite *thank you* that his mouth uttered.

Both of us sensed the boundary we so desperately wanted to cross but could not. He subtly tapped the side of his foot against mine. Unable to do anything more, we let the moment pass.

Again, it was time to go.

We had drunk too much to get behind the wheel. In consummate professionalism, Gianmarco called us a taxi to safely deliver my family to our penthouse apartment overlooking Pescara Beach.

Gianmarco graciously escorted us outside. Without warning, Kally leaped into the air, back toward him. He intercepted my Little One like a football, cradling her in his strong arms. She hugged his neck and planted big kisses on both cheeks, which she had learned was the quintessential Italian goodbye.

Once more, I caught myself staring at him; he approached to deliver my farewell.

Towering over me, I could smell Gianmarco's sweat, making my knees weak. As I raised myself on tiptoes to kiss his cheek, I missed and ended up marking his pristine white collar with my pink lipstick.

How bold of me to reach for his neckband, attempting to erase the blemish with my thumb but only smudging it worse. "I'm sorry!" I murmured.

So close were we that I could feel the vibration of his words forming at the base of his throat. "No problem," he replied with a forgiving smile. But before returning to the restaurant, he leaned in and whispered, "You've certainly left your mark on me."

I nearly fainted as he closed his hand over mine.

Then I watched him leave while standing by the curb with my family. Suddenly, an overpowering impulse sent a jolt of adrenaline coursing through my body. I clenched my legs together, wincing, as I knew I couldn't hold it in any longer.

"I have to go!"

Cyril glanced at me with a furrowed brow, unaware of the true nature of my desperation. "Can't it wait?" he huffed, oblivious to the pressing need that consumed me.

"No, it can't," I replied, my voice strained as I struggled to catch my breath. This was my only opportunity, and I couldn't let it slip away.

Leaning down, I kissed Kally on the nose and whispered, "Stay with Daddy. I'll be right back." With my heart ripping through my chest, I dashed back through the main doors of Tutto Mare.

I was crossing a line, pushing the boundaries of our connection by rushing back to the restaurant. Spying my Italian infatuation's broad shoulders, I called out, "Gianmarco! The toilet, please!"

I could feel his smirk before he turned to face me, and when he took my hand and led me down the corridor to the washroom, nothing would ever be the same again.

Once at the door, like a deer caught in the headlights, I couldn't move or let go. Entranced, I could only stare into his beautiful chocolate-brown eyes. There was so much I wanted to say, but my head was spinning in circles. When I opened my mouth, nothing came out.

Given a second chance, I laid my hand on his collar and reached up to kiss him. Softly, at first.

He didn't flinch as our lips met, allowing my soft kiss.

His lips parted, and he kissed me back, his tongue meshing with mine. I breathed in the air he had exhaled—air that was inside him. I felt my heart touch his soul.

I knew now that the words he sent me were true. He felt the same, and his desire for me was genuine.

As I folded my arms around his neck, my fingers laced together, and I felt the heat from his body flow into mine. Standing on tiptoes, I raised my lips to his ear and whispered, *"Ti voglio!"*
"I want you!"

"Ti voglio anch'io!"
"I want you too!"

"I've thought of nothing but you and that morning at Pescara Beach." I let my confession spill into the open. "When we said goodbye, I sensed you wanted to kiss me. But you didn't. I was confused as you pulled me in closer, embracing me so tightly that I could hardly breathe. I would have given you anything you wanted then and there."

He looked at me with sorrowful eyes, his fingers brushing loose hair strands behind my ear. "There was no time."

"I know. But now...." I looked up at him, and my naughty smile offered a silent invitation. My eyes pointed toward one of the two doors and back to him.

His eyes widened; he hitched an eyebrow and grinned lasciviously at me. I squeezed his hand, and with a frenzy that only a few private minutes could afford, we burst through the men's bathroom, locking the door behind us.

I HAD NEVER BEEN in a men's lavatory before, and this one was clean and furnished in black slate and chrome. It smelled of rich sandalwood and mint. Except for the halogen spotlight over the sink by the mirror, the room was a glowing man cave.

I craved to see my waiter naked and pushed him toward the sink. He backpedaled until he hit the wall, his muscular form bathed in the seductive glow of the soft, white light.

As we kissed more passionately, our eager fingertips searched across each other like the blind reading braille. Pressing my face against his chest, I took in the scent of his cologne—a heady mixture of spice, cedarwood, and baby powder. This hunk of a man smelled like a summer forest and resonated with power and gentleness.

My fingertips pushed between the buttons of his shirt. I needed my hands on his bare skin and curled his shirt into my fingers, ready to tear it off.

Closing his hands over mine, he said, "No time!" I knew he was right; we had only mere minutes.

His palms caressed my shoulders, and his nimble fingers

slipped down the straps of my dress, causing it to fall to my hips.

Exhaling with a shudder, a sigh of longing escaped him as he caught sight of my black lace brassiere and panties; his hands cradled my jaw as he kissed me again.

An uncontrollable shiver ran through my body as he trailed a thick finger between my shielded breasts, barely registering that he had unsnapped my bra. Goosebumps burst across my skin at the tickle of the cool air against my exposed, protruding nipples, hungering for his touch.

"WOW! I love your enormous pink nipples!"

"Do they titillate you?" I shamelessly shimmied my unsheathed breasts before him, blushing at my wolfish forwardness.

"Oh, yesss!" he responded with guttural approval. "You are a delight, sweet Sabina!" His hands clasped my butt cheeks, pulling me tight to his chest. "I love every part of a woman, but I *adore* a lovely ass!" The tenor of his voice was like a reverberating bass, drumming through to my bones.

Making sure not to neglect any part of me, he cupped my breasts, rolling my hard nipples against his palm. I was putty in this Italian stud's broad hands as he caressed, squeezed, and cradled me.

Swooning with pleasure, I adored how he manhandled me, forgetting my body insecurities as his unbridled desire made me feel so sexy. His feverish touch and groping were more attention than my breasts had ever received; not even my husband had ever revered them so. It drove me wild how he sucked and bit my nipples, making me wetter than I had been in a very long time.

I could feel his hardness beneath his trousers, pressing against me. Undoing his belt buckle, I unzipped his pants and slid my palms down the sides of his hips. Reaching for his black briefs, I tugged them down to his knees, releasing his throbbing, veiny cock standing at attention.

I gasped, bit my lip, and purred. "Oh, Gianmarco! What a beautiful beast you have!"

"The better to fuck you with, my dear," he answered with wolfish gurgles of mirth. Immersed in sinful joy, I laughed with him.

His sense of fun encouraged me. "So, what do you do when a sexy customer gives you a hard-on at work?"

"Sacrifice and soldier on," he answered with fun-loving confidence.

Matching my playful candor to his, I said, "No need to sacrifice here, soldier boy! No blue balls on my watch tonight!"

He chuckled at my exuberance, his smile beaming.

Kneeling on the cold tile floor, I grabbed his thick, throbbing cock and swallowed him. Then, flicking the tip with my pointed tongue, I cupped the entire cockhead in my mouth and sucked his adorable little triangle of skin at the base of his head.

"Don't stop!" he growled. The sound of his throaty plea brought a smile to my face.

Relishing the weight of him on my lips, I giggled as I washed the underside of his shaft with the flat part of my tongue. Using one hand, I fondled and cradled his balls; with the other, I groped his firm ass while looking up at him. "My God, what a body!" I uttered as I mouthed his tool.

I loved giving long, deep, slow blowjobs; his cock was already throbbing, ready to explode. I would have loved nothing more than to worship him and swallow his sweet cum straight from the source, but the moment did not offer the time.

"As much as I love tasting you, I need you to fuck me. Right now!" I commanded.

"Happy to oblige!" He lifted me to my feet with his powerful arms, spreading my legs apart. With no time for elaborate ceremonies, he pushed the string of my thong aside to probe my dripping slit. His finger slipping inside was heaven; my legs failed me when I watched him slide his honey-dipped digit across his lips.

"Now, my salacious one. Are you ready for a challenge?" He threw back the same teasing touch I posed to him at the dinner table.

Intrigued by his query, my eyes widened, my pupils dilated, and my heart jackhammered.

Even the blind could see that Gianmarco was an Adonis. The man exuded so much sexual energy that I couldn't help but stare at him with lust. Framed by his bold, black eyebrows and long, thick lashes, his bedroom eyes radiated with charm and dominance. His nose was perfectly symmetrical. Warm and inviting, his lips rested behind his well-groomed beard. And flashing his dazzling pearly whites, his naughty, bad-boy smile sent my head spinning.

Yet, Gianmarco was such a man that I could be deaf and fall in love with only the melody of his sensuous voice. If he were a sonorous Stradivarius, my core would be the cello strings for him to pluck.

With a tantalizing whisper, he breathed his secret desire, which twirled in my ear, sending electric sparks down to my toes. My body had been aching for him, ready for him all night, and he knew he could have me in any way, anywhere, anyhow. Even if I wanted to, I couldn't stop.

"Yesss!" I nodded, struggling for breath.

Turning my body to the mirror, we gazed at our reflection. At that instant, all limits and boundaries vanished. Half-naked before each other, we were a man and a woman engulfed by lust.

From behind, he kissed between my shoulder blades and up my vertebrae, landing at my bare nape. It was thrilling to watch him watch himself *play* with me. Rubbing his hands across my body and breasts, groping my ass and pussy through the silk fabric, made me tingle at his intoxicating touch. I swayed my hips and ground my ass against his groin to the same tempo, slow dancing together to our private, sexy song.

"Take me!" I begged.

He grabbed my hips and folded me over. I hiked up my skirt and steadied myself against the sink. Leaning over the edge, I raised and wiggled my ass, parting my legs wider, inviting him to enter.

Accepting my invitation, he moved my thong to the side. I stifled a scream as he impaled me with his bare cock. With every thrust, I moaned louder, losing control. I couldn't help myself because it felt glorious to see him sliding in and out of my drenched tail.

I was a voyeur and reveled in watching his reflection in the mirror as he fucked me from behind. My skin was tingling, my ears were ringing, and my heartbeat was so loud that I heard it thudding in my head. His powerful drive was almost too much to bear, but I wanted *more*. I wanted to give as good as I got.

With one hand against the wall to steady myself, I pushed back to meet his every thrust. Clamping down, I tightly squeezed my pelvic muscles around his rock-hardness, releasing a pulsing wave within me.

My eyes closed as I savored the climax, letting the sweet, overwhelming sensation take hold. My skin tingled, and I whimpered in absolute ecstasy, "I'm cumming!"

He was close and growing even more enormous with each

stroke. I watched his face in the mirror. With his eyes shut, head falling back, and mouth wide open, I could tell my lurid lover was also on the edge of ecstasy.

Tightening my vulva like an iron vise locked around his magnificent cock, I took control. "Cum for me," I commanded, throwing my hips back harder.

His torso shuddered as he thrust and thrust until he orgasmed, injecting his welcome hot load into me. Spent of his passion, he finally relaxed into me.

My entire body, arms, and shoulders felt exhausted and sore, burning in a good way with the pleasurable pain of euphoric exertion.

Finally, I released my grip on the sink, laughing as we collapsed onto the floor—well and truly fucked.

"You are fucking amazing!" I declared.

"Yes, I know. *Unforgettable!*"

Caressing his beautiful, bearded face, I sang the words from that same song, escaping from my trembling lips. *"Unforgettable, that's what you are..."*

We smiled and giggled like naughty little kids, wiping the sweat from each other's bodies with the fancy bathroom hand towels from the fancy restaurant.

Glancing at his watch, Gianmarco smirked and slapped my ass. "You'd better hurry. Your taxi is about to arrive!"

With his trail of warm cum trickling down my thighs, I grinned at him like a vixen, stuck a finger inside myself, and brought it to my mouth to taste his precious gift. "Mmm," I purred with delight, finally knowing the taste of his creamy deliciousness.

Shaking his head, he looked at me and laughed. We dressed each other hurriedly, and before exiting, I kissed him goodbye, hard on the lips.

I could already feel myself missing the music of his sweet, warm laughter.

THE CAB PULLED up to the curb just as I returned to Cyril and Kally. Stepping out of the taxi, the driver opened the door, apologizing for keeping us waiting. I lowered my eyes and smirked. I wasn't sorry he was late in arriving.

My beloved Kally ran into my arms, giving me a giant bear hug that shocked my sweaty, overheated body. The girl was sopping wet from playing in the fountain outside the restaurant, and now the front of my dress was wet and soaked clear through. I looked down and saw that my erect nipples were now visible. In my haste to return, I realized I was without my bra.

For a moment, I worried about Cyril noticing my faux pas, but true to his indifference, he didn't look. He never did.

Dropping my head to hide my blushing smile, my poor husband had no idea how genuinely wet and naughty his wife had become.

On cue, Gianmarco called out to us from the restaurant entrance. He was holding a paper parcel tied with an elegant silver ribbon. "I apologize for the taxi being delayed. But please, for my Little Pink Kitten, accept this box of special biscotti from me."

Bending to one knee, Gianmarco smiled at little Kally. Without hesitation, she grabbed the parcel, jumped onto his makeshift horsey-thigh, and fiercely wrapped her arms around his neck, almost throwing him off balance.

Steadying Gianmarco's arm to keep him from toppling over, I sighed as his body leaned into me—one last touch.

He smoothed the fine hairs on my Little One's forehead.

"When you go home, change into dry clothes, sit by the fire with some warm milk, and eat these, my favorite Italian cookies!" Cupping his hand around her ear, he whispered, "These are not for sharing! They are only for you, *la mia gattina!*"

"my little kitten!"

My dear daughter's eyes lit up, and she meowed like a pleased kitten for her dear friend.

Gianmarco stood up, shook my husband's hand, and thanked him for coming. Cyril entered the cab with Kally as I turned to Gianmarco and smiled affectionately, thanking him for his kindness and attention.

He grinned and bowed slightly, closing the taxi door after me. With a final wave, I caught him winking at me; I followed his fingers, pointing at his trousers.

My hand instinctively flew to my chest as my heart skipped a beat.

Dangling from his pocket was the black lacey strap of my abandoned bra!

Milan:
Madness in March

4

MEET UP IN MILAN

Almost three months later
Sunday, March 10, 2019
Sierra Mare
Point Reyes, California

Though it was merely one glorious illicit quickie in a restaurant bathroom, the thought of seeing him again, in real life, thrilled me. So, I threw caution to the wind and texted him an invitation.

SABINA
> Hello Darling!

GIANMARCO
> Ciao Sabina!

> How are you and my Little Pink Kitten?

We're all good

Very busy as she's back in school

But she misses you

I miss you

> Me too

I'm in Milan next week

Want to meet up for lunch?

> I'm off Sunday afternoon til Tuesday night

Perfect

My train arrives Sunday but I have an early morning appointment with an overeager estate agent near the Duomo cathedral

He has a long list of villas to restore he wants to show me

I should be done by 3:30 pm

> You are alone?

Yes

Cyril is too busy empire building at home to bother coming

> It's funny
>
> This was supposed to be OUR project to resurrect our dead bedroom
>
> Except it's all just ME again
>
> Alone
>
> Oh well
>
> It is what it is
>
> But I don't want to be alone
>
> In Milan
>
> Or anywhere

> I'm here!

> Thank you
>
> I appreciate you so much

> Prego, mia bella!

A radiant smile illuminated my face as I stared at the words he texted, *mia bella... his beautiful woman*. Me.

> Meet up afterward for a late lunch at a restaurant?

> No
>
> Come to my place
>
> It is not far from Il Duomo

> I'll cook
>
> I have a surprise for you 😀
>
> Me too
>
> I can't wait to see you again 😊
>
> See you soon 😊

Setting the phone down on the table and looking at my travel documents on my writing desk, I could already feel Gianmarco's warm skin as I lovingly ran my fingertips over the ticket and the destination—Italy.

One week later
Sunday, March 17, 2019
Milan, Italy

LIKE A CAGED TIGER, I couldn't wait to escape the confines of the pushy realtor's meeting, which had already gone overtime and kept me from the actual appointment I longed to be at. Finished with my obligation to my husband, I bolted out of that office.

Finally freed, I rushed to meet my Italian lover, unwisely running the last five blocks in my pumps, hoping not to break a heel or twist an ankle from prancing over the ancient cobblestone streets. Cursed with the worst sense of direction, I was lost and late, sure that I had passed the same supermarket twice! It didn't help that I often confused right from left.

But I was close.

I leaned on the wrought-iron gate to catch my breath, then rang the intercom button with the name *G. Romano* beside it.

Bzzzz!

The Italian on the other side of the intercom inquired, *"Chi è?"*

<small>*"Who is it?"*</small>

Hearing that familiar deep, sexy, baritone voice booming from the call box made my heart jump. "It's me, Sabina!" I replied breathily into it.

I heard a loud mechanical *clack!* which unlocked the security gate. "Come on up!" He invited me in.

Once I spotted the glass elevator, in the center of the complex's charming garden courtyard, I dashed toward it and pushed the UP button. Impatiently, I tapped my foot while staring at that illuminated green triangle, willing the elevator to fetch me, but it wouldn't budge. Since it was taking far too long, I opted for a quicker solution and sprinted up three flights of the apartment's industrial metal stairs. When I reached my destination, I noticed that the elevator car was still stuck on the top floor.

Panting and a hot mess, I leaned my hand on the light-terracotta-painted wall to collect myself. As soon as I rang the doorbell, I held my breath and waited at his doorstep. I glanced down at the lush, two-foot-tall potted plant beside me, laden with little red peppers growing amongst the leaves, and smiled. I had no idea he had a green thumb!

I heard footsteps approaching from the other side of the door, and when it opened, unable to contain my thrill, I squealed, "Gianmarco!"

My Darling welcomed me with open arms, Italian style, with hugs and kisses on both cheeks and the biggest, most beautiful smile I had ever seen. The scent of his cologne, intoxicating and heady, hit me.

"I'm so happy to see you! It's been so long," I whispered.

"Yes, I know," he said, melting me in his embrace.

"Mmm," I murmured. The moment I had ached for arrived —our first passionate touch—a ravenous, deep, wet, welcoming French kiss.

But my belly gave away a different ache as it growled like a famished wolf in winter, reminding me of the lunch he had promised. Shrinking, I bit my lip and tried to pull away, but his forceful arms pinned me by his side, in that perfect space tucked in under his arm. I loved how small and safe he made me feel in his embrace.

"Hungry, Sabi?" He teased me with a naughty smile.

We giggled together.

"For you, always! But there's a yummy, rather distracting, mouth-watering smell of garlic drifting from your kitchen."

"Our simple but delicious lunch; my favorite: garlic, olive oil, spicy peperoncini chilis, pasta, and a secret ingredient."

"Secret ingredient?" I asked, smiling. I adored surprises.

"Pane grattugiato." His Italian rang like poetry to my ears.

"Toasted bread crumbs?" I inquired.

"Sì."

"Well, now I'm intrigued. It sounds delish! I can't wait to try it!" I said, then handed him a little present. "I almost forgot! A housewarming gift for you, but I'm unsure if it will go with what you're making for our very late lunch."

"Thank you!"

"I'm sorry I was so late. My appointment ran overtime, and then I got lost."

He lightly kissed the tip of my nose. "No problem. So, are we going to be neighbors?" he joked.

"Not yet." I chuckled. "I didn't like anything on offer. He has more listings he wants to show me tomorrow, but I want to spend that time with you since it's your day off!"

"I go back to work Tuesday evening, so there's time in the morning. I could even come with you as your translator, if you like?"

"That would be lovely! Thank you, my Darling!" I hugged his chest tightly. "Well, are you going to unwrap your present, or what?"

Opening the gift bag, he smiled and cradled the wine. *"Grazie, Sabi!"*
"Thank you, Sabi!"

He chuckled, glancing at his coffee table, which held the same bottle I had just gifted him.

"Prego!" I replied as I gave him a peck on his cheek.
"You're welcome!"

"You're so thoughtful, Darling!" I playfully nudged his ribs with my elbow. "My favorite, Bellavista Franciacorta Saten!"

"Mine too." His hands grabbed my waistline and yanked me into another embrace. With a kiss to my forehead, we laughed at each other's intentions of gifting the same bottle to each other!

He offered, "A glass to start our wonderful evening?"

"I'd love one, thank you!"

With our glasses filled, "Cheers!" we toasted in unison.

"Sabi, come here! I want to show you something."

Holding hands, he led me toward the largest window in the apartment.

A breathtaking view overlooking the city lay before us. Like a silent movie, the busy streets below moved without sound. Unlocking the window's lever, he let the din, of the centuries-old yet thoroughly modern metropolis, pour into the suite. We leaned over the edge of the sill and enjoyed the refreshing, cool breeze rushing past our faces.

All I could muster was, "Wow!"

"It's small, private, and close to work. Plus, I have a stunning view of my new city!"

"It's lovely, and you look so happy here. Perfect for you!"

A proud smile broke across his handsome face.

I raised my champagne glass again and offered a new toast. "To the spirit of Gianmarco's new home, I thank you, *Home*, for keeping my Darling safe and giving him shelter and rest."

He smirked while shaking his head. "Wow, Sabi, you silly girl. No one's ever blessed my place before." He squeezed my hand and kissed my crown. Leading with wine in hand, I followed as he showed me the rest of his apartment. It was so neat and organized, unlike my messy life. *I should take lessons from you, my clean and tidy neatnik!*

My eyes scanned his room and fell upon his shrine. He lowered his gaze, casting his eyes in embarrassment. "It's my malady—an indulgence I cannot afford, but do so anyway."

I placed my hand on his jaw and kissed his cheek in acceptance of all that he was. *To me, you are perfect in every way.*

His obsession with perfumes was displayed on sparkling, modern chrome and glass shelves, all neatly aligned. Front and center was Dior Homme, the first of many in his designer fragrance collection. I unscrewed the black stopper off the elegant rectangular crystal bottle filled with a dark amber liquid. The aroma floated up my nostrils, tickling them with familiarity. "Ah, I know this one! You were wearing this that time we, um—"

From his blushing smile, I knew he remembered it, too.

Nuzzling his chest, I smiled naughtily back at him. His unforgettable scent of citrus and cedarwood made me gasp as I recalled our exquisite, frenzied moments in the restaurant bathroom. The memory of my singular act of adultery that occurred months ago rushed back to me as though it had happened yesterday.

As I returned his beloved bottle to its station, my eyes caught the gold of a fancy Rolex. Sparkling clean with its bezel facing forward, it made me think of an Italian Medal of Military Valor waiting to be worn.

I noted, "Fancy vintage watch!"

Gianmarco smiled, his eyes glinting with pride, as he carefully lifted the timepiece and deposited it in my palm. "It was a gift from my father. Given to him by *his* father, *mio nonno*, when we marked the same age."

Turning it gently in my hand, I marveled at its simple elegance. "It's a beautiful family heirloom," I said, sensing once again, just as when he doted on little Kally, Gianmarco's respect for heritage.

"Sort of. Not really from my family, but from my grandfather's friend, who gave it to him during the war." He paused and shrugged. "It's a long story."

"I have time," I said, smiling while cradling the watch. "Tell me, please? I want to know everything about you." And this was true. For reasons I hadn't yet unpacked, I felt an almost irrational desperation to understand the totality of this gorgeous, enigmatic hunk standing before me.

As if lost in memories, Gianmarco's face softened as he began his tale. "It was World War II when Mussolini allied Italy with Germany as the second nation of the Axis powers. My grandfather's best friend, Noè Moretti, was an Italian Jew, although he was raised Catholic, like all good Italians. They were rounding up the Jews, and his people were desperate to leave Italy, but the borders were closed. They saw the writing on the wall, so my grandfather, Gianni, tried to help the Morettis escape. His good friend's father gave him the only thing they had left of value—this watch.

"My grandfather said he would keep it safe. Promising to return it when the war was over, he reassured his friend that they would see each other again. I'm sure *signor Moretti* knew the likelihood of that occurring was slim to none, but they had always hoped."

"How old were Gianni and Noè?"

Gianmarco's gaze fixed on the treasure resting in my hand. "Can you believe it? Only twenty-one. So young, with a life still full of promise—until the war."

I ran my fingers over the watch's surface and then looked at Gianmarco. "*Carpe diem*," I murmured under my breath. A solemn appreciation dawned on me: *life is fleeting, and we should make the most of the time we have.*

"*Mio nonno* survived, but he never heard from Noè again. And so, Grandfather Gianni gave the Rolex to his son—my father, Marcello—and my father gave it to me, marking a rite of passage in my life."

"Did they ever find out what happened to Noè and the Morettis?" I asked, heartsick at hearing how the war story profoundly touched Gianmarco's family line.

"No. Like the other countless innocents taken, they disappeared from the face of the Earth."

I nodded and handed back this precious memento. Returned to its place of honor, Gianmarco adjusted it, ever so slightly, so that it was perfectly straight.

Right below was a small wooden folding triptych of Mary, Joseph, and baby Jesus, as well as a charming black-and-white portrait featuring three fellows.

"That's a splendid picture! Which one of these gorgeous lads are you?" I asked, peering closely at the sketch.

"None."

"None?" Another curiosity about this man—a family portrait without him.

"May I?" I reached to lift the picture frame from the shelf.

"Of course," he replied, grinning as he pointed at the mischievous toddler.

"You've met the adorable rogue on the left with his finger up his nose. That's my baby brother, Niko. He's still a sous chef at Mirabella. You haven't met my younger brother, Antonio, on the right, who's chosen a field outside the restaurant trade. He's an officer in the Italian Navy. And the one in the middle is our beloved papà, chef extraordinaire, and ringleader of our gang." The pride in his voice was evident. Yes, this man valued his roots greatly.

"Everyone looks so happy. I bet he's a fun dad!" I pointed to the parental face. "You said Marcello, right?"

"Yes, and he's a good father."

"So, you're the firstborn and named after Papà!"

"Actually, it's a combination of my father's and grandfather's names: Marcello and Giovanni. I never met *mio nonno*, but his nickname was Gianni. Hence, *Gianmarco*," he explained.

Setting the picture frame back on the shelf, I turned to my Darling and tapped a finger along his arm.

"Ah, full circle!" I said. "Now I understand, Gianmarco."

"Yeah, but I like plain *Marco* better."

"Oh, no! Not for me. I particularly love the way *Gian-mar-co* rolls off my tongue. It's so rhythmical that I could do a striptease while chanting it!" Like Marilyn Monroe, I exaggerated every syllable, rolling my shoulders at him and swaying my hips to the same three beats. "It's unique, like you. The only Italian men I know are called either Luca or Francesco."

His smiling eyes followed the curves of my undulating body. "Oh, my! Yes, I *like* that!" He laughed as though it may have been the first time anyone had sung and danced to his name in such a provocative manner.

"But your moniker, *Gianmarco*, is quite an honor and a legacy to uphold, following in your forefathers' footsteps. It's clear to me how much you value your lineage. It would be a sin to go with only *Marco*."

He took a sip of wine and nodded. I thought I detected a touch of sadness in his soulful eyes. "We may not always agree on everything, but yes, of course, I love my family—my rock, my life preserver. They're here for me, just as I'm here for them—in Italy, blood always comes first."

I placed my hand on the side of his beautiful, bearded face. I wanted more of this man than I was allowed. "I can see that. You're lucky to have each other. I'm sure the legacy you will carve out for yourself will make them proud."

As he clasped my hand and folded it into his, I knew I had touched his heart. Closing his eyes, he gently pressed his lips to my knuckles; like the professional wine connoisseur that he was, he savored the scent of my fingers. "Your hand smells of fragrant rose petals! If you were a wine, I'd swear you were a beautifully perfumed glass of Gewürztraminer from Alsace."

Love radiated from my heart at his compliment. Gianmarco believed he was a simple man, but poetic charm fell from him as effortlessly as pouring wine, and like having a flute of bubbly, it left me feeling flushed and a little giddy. After the last sip, my cheeks tingled from the alcohol and the warm affection of his company that had spread through me.

"Thank you. You make me feel so beautiful. And what a

great nose you have, master sommelier! You're right. The rose is from my French hand cream."

With a sultry smile, I handed him my glass, my fingers lightly grazing his chest as I did so.

"You're welcome!" Gianmarco said as he accepted it, his hand lingering upon mine for a moment. Looking into my eyes with a mischievous glint, he asked, "So, how was the train ride? Not too long?"

As his fingers rested on the small of my back, barely above my derriere, a hint of his brazen thoughts became evident, indicating that he desired an escalation to our intimate exchange.

Smiling provocatively at him with liquid courage coursing through my veins, I said, "I was thinking about you the whole way."

He leaned in closer, his voice low and seductive. "How were you thinking of me?"

I was reluctant to answer the first time he asked me that question in a text message. But not now. My eyes eagerly roved to the waistband of his faded blue jeans, which rested snugly on his hips. I took a deep breath and sighed.

That was what I wanted.

But how much and how quickly should I reveal to my lover that I touched myself and fantasized about being in his bed whenever I closed my eyes and thought of him? The way I pretended my finger was his finger, playing with my nipples and clitoris, twiddling it like a mini joystick in a way that drove me wild.

I blushed crimson as hot blood rushed to my face.

He knew.

"Only good thoughts of you, always. Well, maybe some naughty ones too."

"Aren't those the best kind?" he teased.

I lowered my eyes because I didn't want him to see. Not yet. More was hidden behind my wicked smile, but holding back was my prerogative.

He grinned, raising his eyebrow at me. Gianmarco had the most expressive, thickest, darkest, and blackest eyebrows I had ever seen!

I leaned into his torso and gazed at his gorgeous face. "I can't believe you're right in front of me. Is this a dream? If it is, please don't wake me. If I may, I want to linger here with you for a little while longer."

He smiled and cradled my neck, rubbing my bottom lip with the pad of his thumb. Almost a foot taller than me, I had to stand on my tiptoes like a ballerina on pointe to reach him. Then, as graceful as a Trumpeter swan, he lowered his head for a sweet and gentle kiss.

I parted my lips slightly, and his neatly trimmed mustache tickled my nose, but it was *nice*. Inside his delicious mouth, I explored the straightness of his perfect teeth. My hand held onto his collar, steadying me. It was pure heaven cradled in his brawny arms, and I knew he wouldn't let me fall. I leaned back to catch my breath, staring in awe at him. My words fell across his lips. "You have no idea how much I want you."

His eyes were greedy and sparkling with sexual intent as he clutched my hips and grabbed me forward, rocking his pelvis into mine. "Can you feel me?"

"Yesss!" I was already breathless as my thighs pressed against his erection, swelling through his pants. We moaned in harmony as my palm traveled up and down, fondling and stroking his hardness.

"I want you the same way, Sabina."

5

INTIMATE REVELATIONS

Wrestling him out of his navy blue shirt, I finally discovered what I was denied at Tutto Mare. Drawing back the stage curtains revealed his sexy, well-toned, muscular body, and I was amazed by the silkiness of his beautiful skin. With my hands around his chest, I pulled him closer and buried my face into the soft, curly hairs upon his breast, breathing in his heady, woodsy scent.

My eyes flared to discover that Gianmarco sported even more tattoos on his sculpted arms and shoulders, secretly hidden under his sleeves! I had never felt inked skin before, and it fascinated me. My fingertips followed the intricate design of the Celtic band encircling his bicep. What ornate artwork adorning such an exquisite, rugged body—all mine tonight!

Like a cat marking her master, my lips traced a delicate path of butterfly kisses, gently gliding up his arm until they reached the intertwined reptiles inked on his upper right bicep.

Curious, I mused aloud, "Blue snakes?"

"Don't you recognize *Il Biscione?* The Blue Vipers? Inter Milan's mascot for the football team I support?" He sounded slightly amused that I didn't understand the significance of Inter's emblem permanently emblazoned on his pelt.

"Oh, a soccer team," I said, nodding but not actually knowing much about the difference between football and soccer.

"Not just any team!" His mouth was agape. "They are the best of the best, the champions of the *Serie A* League!"

"No, but I—" Shaking my head, I smiled like an idiot, biting my lip in embarrassment.

"No problem," he said, smirking. "We will remedy that by teaching you later." He leaned forward. "In the meantime, I'll educate you about something else."

"OK, *maestro*. Let the class begin."

Peeling me out of my skin-tight dress, he stopped to admire the red and black satin and lace brassiere I bought for him, see-through, of course, because I knew how much he loved it when my nipples played hide and seek through the mesh. He smiled, gazing with adoration at my breasts.

He placed his hand under my chin, raising my face so our eyes met. Such gentleness in his gorgeous eyes! His hands flew toward my balconette bra to caress my bosom, whereupon he greeted it with a breathy kiss. *"Eccola! Bellissima!"*
_{*"Here she is! Beautiful!"*}

"Thank you." I tipped my head to the side and blushed, beaming that he found me beautiful. "I like that."

It seemed ridiculous, yet I was still self-conscious about how small my bosom was. And I struggled to comprehend how

Gianmarco found me attractive at my age. I saw myself as rather unremarkable, but I wasn't about to let my insecurities inhibit me. Like a good student, I was ready to obey my teacher, willing to be schooled and punished in equal measure.

"You're the first man who has ever admired them so!"

"I love your boobs *and* pink nipples, Sabi!"

I giggled. "You know, breasts without nipples are pointless!"

He roared with laughter. "You're funny!"

"Thank you, again!" Cupping my hands under my petite pair, I offered them to my grinning lover. "Since you're so fond of them—they're all yours, love!"

Reaching behind me with one hand, he unsnapped the clasp of my bra, and it dropped to the floor.

I imagined a myriad of Italian girls he had bedded and wondered how I measured up. "It seems you've had much experience doing that maneuver!"

His lips curled into a smug smile as he goosed my cleavage with his whiskers, drawing another giggle from my throat. "Maybe." The way he looked at me with lust made my spine tingle and flood my frilly knickers.

"Aahhh!" I wailed as he squeezed and rolled my nipples between his fingertips like coiling a cigarette into shape; my tips darkened and became more erect at his touch.

Massaging my right breast, he dove in and mouthed the other one, sucking hard, and I didn't care if my husband saw my lover's mark. Cyril wasn't attentive and hadn't seen me naked in a very long time.

On the other hand, Gianmarco knew what I liked without saying a word, moving from playful discovery to forceful possession.

"Now tell me your naughty thoughts of me on the train, Sabina."

My heart melted whenever he said my name. I loved hearing him say it in that charming Italian voice as much as I loved his gentle touch upon my bare skin.

"Train or no train, I fantasize about you constantly. You are so unbelievably sexy, even more so in real life."

He grinned at my confession, and drawing that look from him only encouraged me.

"Do you know that just thinking about you makes my pussy gush?" I whispered.

"Oh, yeah?" He pressed his lips to kiss me on that spot right behind my ear.

"Mmm," I purred. "When I see you, I want to tease you, strip for you, and fuck you. Hard!"

"Me too," he growled into my neck as his paws dug into my bottom.

"I dream about you licking my kitty, making me cum and squirt until I cry out."

"Mmm-hmm!" He nibbled my earlobe, delighted at my revelations.

"And I want to make *you* gush from that steel rod of yours!"

He gazed into my eyes as he stroked my cheek with the back of his fingers. "Well, how will we do that, my dear Sabayon?"

SOMETIMES, it was Sabi, short for Sabina, and sometimes Sabayon—these were the endearing nicknames that Gianmarco, my Italian lover and connoisseur of fine cuisine, called me. Drawing inspiration from the world of French delicacies, he playfully bestowed upon me a name that captured the essence of *me* when we first started playing and texting online a year ago. To him, I became like one of his favorite sinfully delicious desserts, Sabayon, a luscious custard made with egg yolks, sugar, and sweet Marsala wine, whipped over a fire until saucy, then eaten hot.

Truth be told, my first time sexting was awkward, and it surprised Gianmarco at how inexperienced I was, given that I was much older than him. I had only known plain *vanilla* sex with my husband, Cyril, my second and last boyfriend.

I felt timid and embarrassed about sharing pictures of my hairy vagina. But my lover wanted to see me—all of me—not only explicit photos but also clips of me masturbating with my fingers and sex toys. With an unavailable husband, my virtual paramour enjoyed guiding me on how to pleasure myself.

He also shared with me how he liked to touch himself and work his glorious tool. Feeling emboldened, I asked him if he could make a little movie for me to replay when we couldn't play together online.

"No problem," he said.

Lying alone in bed at night, I replayed his video. Putting my headphones on, I cranked up the volume to shut out the world and hear only the sound of his breath filling my ears. I parted my legs and slipped my curved purple vibrator into my wet slit. Glued to the screen, I smiled while watching him lie face-up on his bed, rhythmically stroking himself from base to tip and back again. I followed his hand, softly stroking my labia to the same tempo, listening to him say my name, and hearing him whisper all the dirty things he wanted to do to me.

When his breath hitched, I knew he was close. Then, I closed my eyes and buried my slick toy, pumping it even deeper while circling my clit faster and faster. Biting on my bottom lip, I pressed down harder with my fingertip, moving my engorged pearl from side to side, and as I peaked, I shuddered, swallowing my moans to silently cum with him. I missed him so much, and seeing his luscious cream gushing like an exploded milkshake from his cockhead had become my favorite way to fuck myself when we were apart.

Near or far, my lover's desire and adoration for me undoubtedly changed and taught me to be open and see the beauty he saw in me. I may have been fifty and looked forty, but Gianmarco made me feel thirty.

"Sabayon, where were you just now?" He called me back to Earth while stroking my cheek with his knuckle.

I blushed and lowered my eyes while repeating the question he asked of me. "How will I make *you* gush from that steel rod of yours?"

"Yes?" He waited patiently for my reply.

"Well, for starters, I want to kiss you and be kissed by you. Everywhere. How I want to see and touch your veiny, engorged cock. I want to put it in my mouth, suck him, make him bigger, feel him grow hard, touch my tonsils, and swallow every drop of your juice!"

He threw his head back and exhaled. "Oh, yesss!"

"I'm dying to taste your sweet cum straight from the source. May I?"

Pleased with my confessions, he smiled smugly, like the cat that ate the canary.

"And I want to 69 with you. You eat me as I eat you. What's it called in Italian?"

"The same."

"And when you're there, I want to watch your cum spurt out of your head like a fountain, bathing your entire cock with your spunk!"

"Mmm-hmmmm!" His long sigh raised goosebumps across

my skin. Grinning, he playfully teased me more by gently tracing the outline of my mouth with his fingertips, tickling them. I licked my lips and tried to suck his finger, but he retracted it just out of reach. "You wanna suck my finger?"

Closing my eyes, I nodded. "Yes, please."

"Tell me more; then you can have *more* than my finger."

Though I pursed my mouth and bit my bottom lip, he knew that, only with him, I was an open book and would tell him all of my dirty thoughts.

He probed, "Anything else? It was a long train ride to Milan."

"I want to straddle you, impale myself onto your cock, and ride you hard."

"And then?"

"I want you to grope my ass and guide my hips. I need you to ram my cunt into your balls!"

"Yes, my good girl! Keep talking to me."

"I love how you play with my breasts, gripping them between your teeth and playing with my nipples, pulling and twisting them, making my pussy wetter and tighter for you."

He closed his eyes and growled as I reached for the bulge growing in his trousers. Mischievously, I pressed my palm against that perfect tent.

"I can't wait for you to explode inside me so I can hear your loud moans mixed with my aroused screams, so the entire building knows what we're up to!"

"That can be arranged," he said. "I didn't know my little minx was an exhibitionist!"

With an appreciative smile on his face, hand in hand, he led me to an area of his apartment I had yet to explore.

I stopped at the doorway; like his living room, it had a window that overlooked the cityscape. Everything was orderly and spotless, with nary a speck of dirt on his polished hardwood floors.

My eyes glanced at his double bed, with its ornately carved wooden headboard, noticing that the bedding was fresh and tightly tucked-in, made with military corners, such that if you were to toss a coin onto the nubby, tan bed cover, it would have bounced. I grinned, pleased that the frame looked sturdy because it was about to take a pounding, like my wet pussy.

He walked over to an antique bedside table lined with clear glass votive candle holders, like at an altar. One by one, he lit the beeswax candles. The shadows and light from the flickering flames bathed the room in a warm, soft glow.

"Come!" he beckoned, extending his open palm. The glance he gave me melted me into the floor. My heart pounded. I was shaking, feeling faint with excitement and trepidation. I strode toward him, accepting his hand.

"Tell me what you want," he commanded.

"I want you, *all* of you," I answered obediently.

He kissed the side of my neck with his wide mouth, pressing the flat of his tongue behind my lobe, making me purr with delight. Working his way up, he nibbled and traced along the curve of my cartilage. His breath tickled as he exhaled and revealed his intimate secret desire.

I bowed my head low; he grabbed a pillow and threw it onto the floor.

Following his command, I licked his chest and sucked his nipples. I heard him sigh as I circled one with my tongue, just as he had done to me. Next, I trailed kisses down to his belly, my eyes fixed upon his, as I knelt on the cushion, my face at cock-level.

My palms traveled up and down his muscular thighs, my

fingers massaging them along the way. One hand pulled down the zipper; the other snaked around to grab his ass.

He roared with laughter when I slapped it.

I gazed up to meet his sparkling eyes, digging my hands into his waistband to pull his trousers down. But before removing his black briefs, I kissed the unmistakable bulge tenting in his shorts. He shut his eyes and groaned as I mouthed his crotch, breathing hot air onto his fabric-sheathed cock.

Inching lower, I reached for his balls and nuzzled them open-mouthed through his underwear, breathing in the ambrosial scent of his sweat.

But the suspense was too much.

"My God, how I want you!" I cried out.

We slid his tight briefs off his hips together and let them fall into a twisted mess at his feet.

His cock sprung to life, defying gravity. My hands could not resist caressing him. My lips could not resist brushing against the smoothness of his mound.

"You are so sexy, Gianmarco!"

"Yes, I know." We laughed together at his confident, cheeky reply.

Holding his throbbing monster, I kissed him, head first. Then, with my flexible tongue, I flicked and traced along every inch of his shaft.

"Yesss," he hissed.

My lips formed a snug cockring encircling his girth while my saliva lubricated the breadth of his hardness.

"Aaahh!" Deep, exhilarating groans burst from his chest the more suction I used on the downbeat, encouraging me to stay the course.

His smooth balls brushed against my chin. I threw my head

back as he fucked my throat while gobs of spit dribbled down my chin.

"I love it!" he declared.

Dribbling juices from between my hams, too, I pulled back, giggling as I spoke with a mouth full of cock. "I'm so horny for you!"

He grinned. "Where do you want him?"

Disengaging, I licked my lips and laser-focused on him like an insatiable lioness, ready to tackle her prey. "Oh, how my dripping pussy longs for you!"

He hoisted me up, placed his hand behind my neck, and laid me on his bed. Using the tips of his fingers, he glided them down the length of my tingling body.

Suddenly, he gripped my ankle and jerked me toward him.

"Eek!" I shrieked in surprise.

Splaying my legs, he blessed me with kisses from my shaking knees to the tops of my writhing thighs. I sighed at his power and submitted to his control.

He pulled off my soaked panties, hurling them somewhere into the room. With only two fingers, he caressed my slick labia and slid those same fingers inside me, making me squeal and squirm with delight.

Kneeling on the cushions by the edge of the bed, he buried his head between my legs, his mouth landing on my mound. Gently, he lapped my full pearl with the flat of his tongue. I shuddered as he sucked and devoured me into blissful, rolling waves of ecstasy.

His beard against my freshly waxed pussy was so stimulating. His chin hairs tickled and scratched my softness so much that he had to pin me down with his free arm to keep me from wriggling away and thrashing about as if a thousand volts of electricity were passing through me. It was so unbearably pleasurable, the way bitter fought sweet. The sensation was almost too intense, verging on torture. "Too much, Darling!"

"OK, but hold still. I wanna taste your sweet honey." He drove his tongue deeper, down and up, flicking my clit with a flourish.

"Fuck me, please!" I panted like a bitch in heat.

He stood up; using his powerful arms, he pulled me by my feet and hooked my ankles over his broad shoulders. With my knees pressed against my shoulders and my upper thighs crushing my bosom, he leaned into me and slipped himself into my slit.

Shocked at his substantial girth, I gasped for air. I longed for him to explode, filling me with his warm, sweet cum.

"Sweet Jesus! I love how you fuck! Aaahh, so hard!" I moaned.

"Mmm," he moaned along with me.

"You're hitting me so deep that it's almost too much for me in this position. But so good! Don't stop!"

Overwhelming pressure built within; my feet burned hot, but he pounded me harder, his momentum unbroken. His face grimaced as he exerted himself, but he wasn't slowing. If anything, he was ramping up the pace even faster. Finally, my entire body shuddered and gushed, as if pushed over the edge, like water over a weir.

"Ahh! I'm cumming... I'm cumming.... Cum with me!" I exhaled as the crashing waterfall of this exquisite orgasm left me breathless.

I clamped my pussy tight around his cock. Matching his tempo, I caught, released, tensed, and then released, pulsing my pelvic muscles to match his every thrust.

His eyes closed, and his lips curled into a perfect circle. His entire body stiffened, and his breath quickened as his pelvis bucked over and over again. I heard his low, guttural growl as he gushed forth his gift.

"Cazzo! Mi sto per venire!"
"Fuck! I'm about to cum!"

There was so much cum mixed with pussy juice. A perfect sex cocktail poured out of me, drenching his balls and dripping down his oh-so-lovely, long legs. His body, glistening with sweat, fell on top of me.

Having subdued my beast, I languished in victory. I was a swirl of emotions, full of joy, ecstasy, and desire, fulfilled. Cradled in his arms, he made me feel so young and alive that I was beaming in the afterglow.

I brushed my cheek against his soft beard, tracing the tip of my nose against his full lips, and I stared into his mesmerizing eyes. His warmth radiated from the grinning, satisfied smile on his sexy, gorgeous face.

"You make me smile, Gianmarco." I sighed, releasing the final embers of sexual bliss. "You make me smile."

6

TRULY MADLY DEEPLY

"Do you know I find it incredibly sexy to watch a man cook for me?" I said as I leaned back, my fingers interlaced behind my neck, my legs crossed and extended, propped up on the adjacent wooden chair. "And the view from here of your gorgeous ass is whetting my appetite!"

Turning with a smile, Gianmarco didn't miss a beat. "I come from a long line of experienced chefs with gorgeous asses, passed down from generation to generation."

His effortless charm drew a chuckle from me. "I see."

"You wanna see my *bare ass?*"

"Mmm!"

"Oh, Sabi! If I wasn't starving and we hadn't just fucked, I'd *take* you on that kitchen table." His tone carried the mix of a threat and a promise.

I rose from my seat and sidled behind him, enfolding my arms around his waist. "I'm so hungry that I could eat you!"

The scent of the dried, pheromone-laced sweat from his back made me growl like a feral wildcat. I rubbed my face against his body and nipped at his skin.

"Ouch!" He spun around, grabbed me, turned me to face the counter, then slapped my bottom, eliciting a gasp from me.

Fueled with bravado, I grabbed hold of him and rolled my hips. Facing each other, pelvis to pelvis, I gyrated, arousing him and making his cock grow again for me—tenting through his boxers.

"You're insatiable, Sabayon. I'm not as young as I used to be," said my Italian heartthrob.

With a pout, I turned away from him like a reprimanded, spoiled toddler.

Grabbing me in a hug and cradling me in his arms, *that voice* sent chills right through me. "Sabi!" He looked directly into my eyes. "I want you as much as you want me. But if you want me to last, I need to eat something before we can *play* again."

I declared to him with dewy eyes, "You'll never be old to me!"

THERE WAS a significant age gap between us. It was an immutable and undeniable fact with every platinum hair that sprung from his chin and mingled with the black of his beard. Even at mid-thirty, he was no longer a spring chicken. But at fifty, neither was I.

Deciding to use playfulness to address our common issue, I focused on his passion. "You know, Darling, fine wines only get better with age." I winked at him.

When he rubbed his nose against mine, I knew everything was OK between us. He opened a bottle of red and offered me a glass. "Speaking of wine, try this!"

After swirling the glass to let the wine breathe, I took a sip. "Yummy! Soft and full of fruit. What is it?"

"Don't you recognize it? The Montepulciano d'Abruzzo from Tenuta Fiore is the same one I gave you at Christmas."

"Ah, yes, of course! It's lovely." I gladly took another sip. "Where can I buy this?"

"Papà sells it at his restaurant in Abruzzo, which is connected to the winery."

"That's a shame! Too far for a day trip from Milan. Perhaps next time?"

He nodded, a mischievous smile dancing on his lips. With a flourish, he leaned below the counter, his movements akin to a magician conjuring a wondrous surprise. As if by magic, his hand emerged, presenting me with a sealed bottle from his secret wine cabinet. "A gift for you!" he exclaimed, his eyes sparkling with delight.

I pressed my lips to his bearded cheek, savoring the warmth of his gesture. "Thank you, sweetheart! You never cease to amaze me with your thoughtfulness!"

Pointing to the bottle, he proudly explained, "Though this wine is made from Montepulciano grapes, it tastes and feels as incredibly fine and floral as a delicate Pinot Noir, perfect at any age."

Once again, my Italian wine connoisseur had a palate that astounded me.

"Well! Cheers to Montepulciano and us!" I said, tipping my glass for more.

"Shall we?" He directed me to the galley, where he rolled up his sleeves to begin the show.

Standing by his side, I watched his every move, taking in his culinary mastery. Gianmarco was as much a savant in the kitchen as in the bedroom.

As steam rose from the pot of boiling water on the stove, he opened a box of dried bucatini and slid the contents into the salted water. While the long, hollow pasta cooked, he mixed the roasted garlic and olive oil with a pinch of the dried peperoncini flakes. The pores of the red-hot Italian peppers burst open in the hot oil, and the heady aroma of the melange permeated the air. Incorporating the *al dente* pasta into the sauce, he saved a little of the cooking water and swirled it slowly into the pan.

"Why do you put the pasta water back in?" I inquired.

"It's already salted, which adds flavor, and the starch from the pasta water thickens the final sauce." My grinning chef smiled, pleased to teach me another Italian lesson, this time in traditional country cooking.

For the final step, he added a fresh, chopped peperoncino pepper that he proudly harvested from his potted plant outside.

"Ooo, spicy!" I pursed my lips, worried that two peppers would be too much.

"Relax. I'm only using a tiny one. Trust me, Sabi. I promise that it will be a spicy, but well-rounded dish." He winked as he added, "Like you."

"My, oh my, Chef! You're as smooth as olive oil!" I rubbed his firm bottom hidden under his boxers.

His eyes darted to my panties while teasing me with his words, "You know me; I do prefer things... *smooth!*"

Then he kissed me deeply, and I wanted him to keep going, but the sauce started popping and sizzling. I sighed as I pulled away. "Looks like things are getting too hot. You better not burn my promised lunch, or I'll be mad at you!"

He chuckled, then grabbed a handful of *pane grattugiato*, tossing everything in the pan together.

"Isn't adding bread crumbs a Sicilian thing?" I inquired.

"Nope. It's an *Italian* thing!" He corrected me. "It gives both texture and flavor, making it an excellent substitute for grated cheese."

He offered me a forkful. "Here, try it!"

"Wow! You're right. It's salty enough that you don't miss the cheese. And the taste of the roasted red garlic shines through, alongside the olive oil and that unmistakable vibrant kick from the dried peppers combined with the fresh one. Adding even a speck of Parmesan would mute the bright flavors. Simple, yet fantastic!"

"Exactly!"

"Who showed you how to make this? Mamma?"

"Not sure," he mused. "My parents, like many from Campania, are excellent cooks. Did you know it's the birthplace of pasta and Neapolitan pizza?"

"A chef *and* a historian! They've taught you well!" I took a large taste of his fantastic vino. "And your papà's wine is a perfect match."

Using a large serving fork, he twirled the pasta into a ladle and poured it onto our plates, which I had only seen done by master chefs on cooking shows—a skill he undoubtedly learned from watching his father, the chef extraordinaire. "And what service!" I complimented him.

Gianmarco smiled proudly and handed me the beautiful, perfectly plated dish, along with a fork and a spoon.

Before diving in, I rubbed my hands together, excited to feast. "How wonderful! It looks so professional!" It may have seemed trivial to cook and serve a simple pasta dish, but the effort meant so much more to me. Gianmarco's gesture of care and affection was as sweet as the touch of his lips to mine.

I was captivated, watching him expertly twirl just the right amount of spaghetti onto his fork and effortlessly glide it against his spoon. With the slender tail of the noodle elegantly dangling, he showcased impeccable dining etiquette with refined grace.

On the contrary, my method must have seemed uncouth to him. I put too much on the fork so that I had to masticate my giant wad of pasta, which was almost a choking hazard, needing a gulp of wine to help wash it down.

He observed me, too, as I savored everything to its last strand. Finally finished with his plate, Gianmarco wiped the glistening sauce from my mouth with his napkin.

"I just realized that it's you who watch others, *nosh!* Not the other way around. I love watching *you* dine so elegantly!"

"Your observations on life are sometimes so silly. Definitely different from everyone else's!"

I touched my napkin to the corners of my mouth as he had done. "Thank you. I'll take that as a compliment!"

Gianmarco brought a slice of cake to the table. "Dessert?"

"Why, there's an *S* on it!" I said, delighted by yet another surprise of his spoiling me.

"It's an Austrian Sachertorte, one of my favorites, made of dark chocolate and apricot jam. They write *Sacher* in chocolate; that's why there's an *S* on top," he said with an amused shake of his head.

"Is that *all* for me?" I giggled, my hands clapping joyfully and my hips wiggling in my seat.

He stared at me with his piercing brown eyes and sighed. "It is rich." He paused, sliding the plate toward me, then added, "I thought we could share, but if you want, you can have it all."

Embarrassed by my gluttony, I bit my lip and decided to recount a funny story about a picnic outing with friends to deflect attention away from my greed. "And when it came time to eat, they handed me a large foil cylinder, which I thought was *my* lunch. I unwrapped it, but before I could bite into it, my friend stopped me and said, 'Um, that's for all of *us!*' You see, when I looked more closely, my foil-wrapped burrito comprised a dozen tiny ones. They were all stacked together and wrapped as a single, giant super burrito. What can I say? I'm a girl with an enormous appetite!" I threw my hands in the air.

As I told my story, Gianmarco's eyes widened in disbelief. Now at its conclusion, his uproarious laughter infused the room, filling me with joy to hear his deep, throaty laugh.

Blushing cherry-red, I slid the dessert plate between us, cut the cake with the fork, and fed the first mouthful to my Darling.

I BARELY NOTICED the sun transitioning to evening as the afternoon slipped away. Despite having eaten just three hours ago, my stomach grumbled, and I started feeling *hungry* again. Though the pasta was perfect, the portion was a little smaller than I was used to.

"Gianmarco, you've been here for a bit, and I've only been here twice, but I'm not impressed! I've yet to find an amazing authentic Italian pizza in Milan, Darling."

"Another challenge!" He smiled, seeming to enjoy them. "Are you still hungry?"

I threw him a wink. "You know me. I'm insatiable!"

A naughty twinkle appeared in his eyes. "In that case, you need to meet Marì."

"Marì?" I asked. A crack in my armor, a faint hint of suspicion and jealousy, trembled in my voice.

He squeezed my hand as he smiled his biggest smile at me. "Trust me. It will be fun! I promise."

Those were the exact words I used to challenge him the first time we *played* together at Tutto Mare. I couldn't say *no* because I had no limits with him. I was his toy, his *needy-greedy* good girl, and his happily obedient servant; he knew it.

FINALLY, after tidying up the dishes and ourselves, we settled on the couch, where I curled up onto his lap. The warmth from his body and the comfort of his closeness lulled me into a restful power nap.

When I awoke, his fingers were gently stroking through my hair, and for a moment, I had to remind myself that I wasn't dreaming. His gaze met mine, and a smile tugged at the corners of his lips. "If you're ready for an adventure, come with me, and I'll introduce you to Marì."

Feeling a mixture of nervousness and excitement bubbling within me, I reached up to cup my Darling's face. "Mmm, I'll go anywhere with you, love!"

Before we shut the front door, I rose on my tiptoes and pressed my lips against his in a long, lingering kiss.

Just then, my phone chimed; I glanced at the screen.

> CYRIL
>
> Contact me when you have a moment

"Hmm... It doesn't sound urgent. I'll catch him later," I said, dismissing the interruption without hesitation.

Concern flickered in Gianmarco's eyes. "Are you sure?"

Surging with renewed confidence and anticipation, I grabbed my lover's hand and led him out the door. "Yeah, let's go. I'm eager to meet this Marì!"

7
MARÌ

Hand in hand, we descended the stairwell to his apartment's underground garage; the clack-clack-clacking of my heels against the cement floor echoed in the expanse. In the far corner, sandwiched between a concrete pillar and two neon-orange traffic cones, sat a luxury black panther on wheels, sparking questions in my mind. Despite Gianmarco's working-class background, he had a taste for the finer things in life: exquisite wines, designer perfumes, and now, an elite motorcycle. The closer I looked, the more I realized how little I knew about this enigmatic man and his world.

"Oooh, is that an Italian *riso-rocket*?" I teased.

"Rice rocket!" He smiled and shook his head at my naïveté, nipping the tip of my nose as he burst into fits of laughter. The sound of his melodic reverie reverberated against the cavernous walls. "Not a Japanese sport bike, silly Sabi."

Embarrassed, I stifled a sheepish smile, pretend-pushing his shoulder with my own. "But still, it looks like it could fly!"

My Darling gave me a devilish wink. "Maybe... in the right hands!" He paused, fingers tracing in the air the sleek lines of this magnificent speed machine. "This is a Ducati!" Then I giggled when his hand playfully squeezed my ass. *"Bellissimo!"*
"So Beautiful!"

I half-smiled at his playfulness but took a step back, pulling on his arm as he approached his beautiful but scary motorcycle.

"I've never been on one before," I admitted, my voice tinged with nervousness. "And *this* is so new! I imagine it's like riding a bicycle, only faster?" I asked innocently, unaware of the difference.

Sensing my hesitation, he lovingly cupped my cheek and flashed a grin, then slipped the snug spare helmet over my head. "Nah, it's nothing like riding a bicycle. And it's not new; I take great care of the things I love." With careful hands, he tightened the straps of my helmet. *"Non preoccuparti, ragazza mia!* I've been riding motorcycles for a long time, so you'll be safe with me."
"Don't worry, my girl!"

"OK." I gulped down my fear. "But are places still open at this hour?"

"Of course!" His voice brimmed with amusement. "Welcome to Milan, the other city that never sleeps!"

He looked so alluring in the tight-fitting leather gear that I longed to steal a kiss, but he abruptly lowered my visor, concealing my face.

Undeterred, I grinned and playfully bumped the front of my helmet against his. Through the tinted glass, the world appeared darker, but I caught a glimpse of his mischievous, sparkling eyes and enchanting, seductive smile.

Gianmarco mounted his motorcycle, and with his gloved hand, he motioned for me to hop on behind. Feeling exhilarated, I pressed against him, holding on for dear life as he raced us through the winding streets of Milan. "Woo-hoo, this is so fun!" I screamed with glee. My goodness, how my cheeks hurt from smiling so much! And though our words were lost in the roar of the engine, my arms, wrapped tightly around his middle, vibrated from his joyous laughter.

We whizzed by Porta Venezia, the two massive neoclassical marble buildings beautifully illuminated at night. Historically, these were one of three gateways into the city of Milan.

After parking the bike and removing our helmets, the unmistakable smell of rising dough and baking cheese pulled us to his beloved pizzeria. Leading the way, Gianmarco extended his arm with a sweeping gesture. "Welcome to Marì!" he announced, beaming as if delivering the punchline of a joke.

"*Stronzo!*" I huffed. "Letting me stew in jealousy over a pizza parlor!"
"Asshole!"

"Come here and kiss your favorite *Asshole!*" He bellowed with laughter, grabbing me into an embrace. "You have nothing to be jealous about." I pretend-pouted and surrendered to his teasing humor.

Coddled in his arms, we waited in line to order. My roving eyes were as large as the pizzas made here, utterly mesmerized by the sensory overload of the space—loud, frenetic, unstructured —an unexpected departure from Gianmarco's quiet and controlled demeanor—except, of course, when he unleashed his primal instincts in the bedroom.

One wall was spray-painted with the pizzeria's logo of a woman with vibrant red lipstick. In contrast, other surfaces remained in their raw, unfinished concrete state, with dozens of books attached by their spines and splayed open. Book jackets hung above, suspended like artwork above the ceiling's chicken coop wiring. Vintage leather valises dangled from a metal grate, frozen in mid-air. A pink and green jukebox blared 1980s love songs. And amidst it all, a pristine avocado-green Vespa scooter was parked in the center of the room! I couldn't decipher if the eclectic mix was random chaos or deliberate genius.

Inching forward, almost our turn at the till, Gianmarco turned to me and asked, "What do you want?"

I was caught off-guard by his choice—the cognitive dissonance between my Darling's refined style and the disorganization of this place. Folding metal chairs matched with chipped Formica tabletops? That he found joy in a chaotic world, starkly contrasting with his usually orderly, Michelin-starred lifestyle, was a surprisingly unique facet of my lover, uncovered.

I looked at him and the pizzeria with fresh eyes; there was so much more to Gianmarco to explore. And in that moment, with a mischievous smile, I leaned in closer, whispering, "I want you!" I surprised him when I licked his lips like a delicious, dripping, creamy gelato cone, locking eyes with him and conveying a look that explained I wasn't joking. "Bathroom? Finger me!" I bit his earlobe. "I'm already so wet for you; I want to squirt your hand!"

He raised his left eyebrow and met my carnal gaze. He kissed two of his fingers and touched my lips with them. "Naughty Sabayon, behave," he said, reigning in my lust.

I grasped his hand, wanting to suck his fingers. But instead, I closed my eyes and chastely kissed them. Reluctantly, I obeyed.

Pulling closer, I leaned into his chest as he softly kissed my ear. "I'll do that and *more* to you. At my place."

I looked up at him and smiled. "I like *more*."

"Yes, I know." His fiery gaze branded my soul.

I took a deep, calming breath to compose myself, mentally pivoting to focus instead on the chalkboard menu, handwritten in Italian. "Isn't *Quattro Formaggio* your favorite?"

"Four Cheese Pizza was at Tutto Mare. It's different here, so I'll choose something else."

"What wine would you recommend with it, master sommelier?"

He laughed.

"What's so funny? I don't get it."

He kissed the bridge of my nose. "There are no wine flights or tasting menus here."

I blushed since I don't often frequent pizza joints. Nonetheless, Gianmarco hugged me, tucking me under his arm, accepting me for my quirky self; he chose a pizza for us to quell my cravings.

Since the pizzeria was too hot and crowded, Gianmarco led me by the hand to wait outside for our order.

My legs felt sore and shaky from our earlier sexual exertions, so I sat down on the sidewalk, and he joined me.

"Tell me, Darling, why is this your favorite place?"

From the doorway, he pointed to the red and blue shirts that lined the service counter. "Do you see those? They are the actual shirts worn by famous AC and Inter players who've *eaten* here!"

"A-C?" I shrugged.

"Woman, do you not watch *calcio?*" he asked incredulously. "We're *Nerazzuri!* We support Inter Milan! Those are our team's sacred black and blue jerseys!"

He slapped his right bicep twice, reminding me of Inter's mascot, the tattooed blue snakes emblazoned upon his skin.

A realization dawned on me as I heard the passion and awe in his voice. I smiled at him, thinking he was *starstruck by footballers.* This was a holy shrine of soccer shirts, akin to religious relics.

"You're so fiery about football! I'd love to watch you watch a game. Is there one now?"

"Sabi, it's half past eight on a Sunday night. Games are usually played on Saturday, and you have to spend the whole day going there and watching; that's if you can even get tickets."

"Oh!" I pursed my lips, embarrassed. Again, how strange that I knew him intimately yet, outside the bedroom, I knew so little about his world! But I wanted to change that.

"When you come back in the autumn, I'll take you to a home game."

"I would love that very much, my Darling."

Just then, a nostalgic smile crossed my face when *Crazy For You* played on the antique jukebox, filtering out through the open door.

I bopped and swayed to the music, rolling my hips and shoulders and shimmying my chest at him. "It's so corny, but I love this song!"

"Me too," he said while humming.

"You know this ancient tune? I danced to this at my high school prom!"

"Sure. It's by Madonna and one of her biggest hits too!" he replied. Adding, "Do you know her grandparents are Abruzzesi from the town of Pacentro?"

Unaware, I shook my head and bobbed it side to side to the beat, astonished that he would be a master of music trivia too.

"Yeah, no, I love *all* types of music!"

I looked dubiously at him. "You *love* cheesy 80s love songs? Yeah, right."

He grinned. "I love cheese! Especially on pizzas!"

I laughed even louder at my fun-loving man.

Moved by the moment, my unpretentious partner stood up and extended his open palm to me. "Dance with me?" His eyes shimmered with anticipation.

My eyes grew wide as I noticed other patrons smiling warmly at us. Blushing self-consciously, I felt I might have already become a spectacle.

"Sabi." He waited.

Looking up, I met his earnest eyes. How could I resist that beautiful, inviting smile?

With my chest aflutttering, I slipped my palm in his, feeling the strength of his grip. He guided my hand to rest on his well-built shoulder, and with my other hand, I gently traced the contours of his muscular arm, intertwining my fingers behind his nape. Hip to hip, we swayed, his hands locked and rested at the small of my back as we danced on the sidewalk of Milan.

I thought he was joking, but he sang along in his deep, sexy Italian voice. *"Crazy for you..."*

Laying my head on his chest like the prom queen dancing with her king, I let the thrum of his voice and the beat of the music carry me away. In that embrace, I surrendered to the moment, feeling the warmth of his body enveloping mine, creating a world where only the two of us existed.

"Gianmarco! Gianmarco!" When I heard his name being called out as our order was ready, my stomach growled a reply.

He laughed, teasing me. "My hungry girl with a big appetite!"

"Uh-huh!" I grinned, leaning into his truthful assessment.

"I'll get our food. Stay here and save our spot," he joked, referring to our claimed piece of *precious* sidewalk.

I nodded and beamed at my sexy lover.

While waiting for his return with our feast, I retrieved my phone to check the time. I gasped in surprise at how late it was and thought I should reply to my husband's text by calling him.

"Hello, Cyril! What can I do for you?" I spoke while watching my Darling jostle his way to the front of the disorganized queue.

"Why didn't you call when I texted you?" Cyril asked in a brusque tone.

"You didn't make it sound urgent," I said nonchalantly.

He exhaled loudly into the phone. "Where are you?"

"I'm having dinner. What's up?"

"Kally was hysterical, wailing for her mother."

Panic rose in my voice. "Why? What happened?"

"A little accident and an emergency room visit—"

"What? An accident! Why didn't you call me from the hospital?"

"I can never reach you by phone. You either turn off your ringer or ignore your calls." Cyril was correct; I found being constantly notified by phone distracting.

"I want to talk to her and see if she's OK."

"Your daughter is taking a nap. They gave her a sedative. I'm not going to wake her. Do you know how long it took to get her to calm down?"

"Cyril, I need to know what happened. Tell me."

"She was being her normal rambunctious, unruly self. She knows the rules; she's not supposed to climb trees without supervision. Nanny was sick, so I was looking after her."

"Really? And she fell out of a tree. Where were you?"

"I could ask *you* the same question."

"You know exactly why I'm here; I came here to look at the land and palazzo you're interested in. But obviously, I'll have to postpone tomorrow's appointment since Kally needs me."

"I told you, she's fine. The doctors X-rayed her arm, set her bones, and put it in a cast; it will be weeks before it's healed." Then Cyril commanded me. "I want you to see the properties. You're already there."

"No," I said. Unlike when my lover, Gianmarco, commanded me, I had no intention of obeying my bully of a husband. "I'm coming home tomorrow. My baby needs me!"

"Your baby? She's five, for crying out loud! You've always put your and Kally's *needs* over mine!"

"You *need* this land? Really? You *need* this villa? What you need is to be a good father to your daughter."

There was silence on the other end. I took a deep breath to calm my irritation with my uncooperative spouse. "I can come back anytime. The palace and that land have been on the market for years. It will still be there when I return."

"Fine. You do what you like. You always do anyway." Cyril hung up abruptly.

"Arghhh!" I shrieked through my gritted teeth. Steam was pouring from my ears, and I pouted because I didn't even get to see my little Kally on the phone.

"Sabi, are you OK?" Gianmarco asked, returning with a pizza box and setting it down on the sidewalk with our beers.

He tenderly caressed my back with a soothing touch. "Come here," he whispered, opening his arms and enveloping me in his embrace. He cradled my jaw with his broad hand, gently wiping away the tears that cascaded down my cheeks.

I had no idea how long he had been standing there, silently listening, but from the loving concern etched on his face, I was certain he had absorbed every word. "Did you catch all of that?" I hung my head in shame for my outburst, rubbing my temples, since I now had a massive, pounding headache.

"It was impossible to miss," he replied with compassion in his voice.

As I glanced around, people averted their gazes; once again, I had made a spectacle of myself. Sobbing uncontrollably, I hid my face in his chest. "I'm so worried about my baby."

"*Ay, Sabi, cara mia,*" he said, rocking me softly. I loved it when he called me *my dear* in Italian, but it did nothing to soothe my raw emotions this time.

"Cyril never listens to me. He doesn't hear me, then he judges me."

Gianmarco wiped the tears trailing from my cheek with the tab of his thumb. "You know, Cyril is right," he said softly. "Kally isn't a baby anymore."

"Are you siding with him?" My eyes narrowed into slits. I needed to know he was on my side.

"No need to bite my head off," he said tenderly. "Just stating facts."

His choice of words disarmed me, and despite my mood, an unexpected smile crept across my lips. "I'd never bite you down there," I said, softening my tone.

"You better not, dear Sabayon!" Then we both chuckled.

"It sounds like her father looked after Kally, and her arm will heal!"

A tear streamed down my face.

"*Come mai, carina mia?* Why are you still crying? My Little Pink Kitten will be fine."

"*How come, my dearest?*"

"If I were there, she wouldn't have fallen out of the tree and broken her arm." I blurted out the words, laden with guilt.

His face turned serious. "Listen, you can tell me to mind my own business, but it sounds like Cyril is there for Kally, and her arm will heal! I'm sure she will be fine. It's not your fault. You can't watch her 24/7. Accidents happen."

"But I feel so guilty! What kind of mother am I? I'm here having fun with you, and she's suffering!"

He shook his head. "No, you're not just here for yourself. You came on assignment."

"Yeah, I'm disappointing my husband there too."

"He'll survive. But you're right about the land; things move slowly here in Italy."

"Good." I smiled. "So, I can see you again." I lowered my head and sighed, realizing I had one less day with my beautiful lover. "I'm sorry to cut my visit short."

"No problem. We still have tonight." He reassured me that everything was still OK between us.

"I wish my husband were more understanding. Like you!" I gazed up at him through my teary lashes.

"But if he were, then you wouldn't be here with me now, would you?"

I nodded and laughed. "You're right. You're always right."

"No, I'm not. I make mistakes all the time, sweetheart."

"Me too."

"Taking risks and living to tell about them is something all kids learn. You push it too far, and you can get hurt. But you learn you can heal."

"I never took big risks, broke an arm, or went to the emergency room!"

He raised his eyebrows. "No, but what you're doing here with me now—*is*."

I nodded. "Yes, you're right." I hugged him but quickly

drew back. "Yeah, I know! But other than Kally, no one loves me at home. I need you in my life, Gianmarco!"

"I need you in mine too."

"Please keep holding me!"

He wrapped me in his arms and squeezed me tight. I was so close to him that I could feel his tummy grumbling.

"You hungry?" I teased.

"Starving!"

He looked at me, and I looked back at him. "Me too!"

Though the sun had almost set, it was still too warm to eat our second dinner inside the packed restaurant. Instead, we dined outside, *al fuori*, sitting on the sidewalk, enjoying our cold beers, the only alcoholic beverage they served.

"Good?" he asked.

"OK, you win!" I conceded as we clinked the necks of our glass bottles together. "This is by far the best, authentic Italian pizza ever!" My entire body was beaming at him. "Thank you for another amazing dinner!"

He smiled. "Welcome."

I reached for another slice and smiled, marveling at the simple perfection my hand beheld. "The crust is light, thin, airy, and beautifully baked in the wood-burning oven. And I hate burned pizza crust; you might as well be eating from an ashtray! Oh, and the fresh toppings are plump, colorful, and taste as good as they look." I took a bite and closed my eyes. "Mmm, it's delicate despite the mass of cheese on it. I'm impressed!"

Gianmarco grinned, pleased with my complimentary analysis.

"Do you find it irritating when guests ask endless questions like, 'There's butter in this? Are you sure there's no butter in this *pig butter?*'" I winked at him, and he laughed.

My Darling found it entertaining how I analyzed food,

remembering how I grilled him at Mirabella. In particular, I challenged him on that dreamy-creamy spread, but he confidently held firm.

That was when I first noticed him as more than a handsome face with a hard body. I craved to kiss his luxurious lips and stare into his smoldering, sexy eyes... among other things.

He kissed my nose again. "You're too funny!" And we laughed again.

Using his tongue like a napkin, he licked a bit of cheese oil from the corner of my mouth. "You are a messy girl!" He shook his head in mock disapproval.

I knew he was teasing, yet I was insecure since I knew what a neatnik he was. "Do you like messy girls?"

"I like you very much because you are messy—especially *in bed*, my Sabayon."

"Do you know that whenever you call me by my sexy nickname, my pussy salivates like Pavlov's dog?"

"Yes, I know," he said deadpan while holding a wicked smile.

I gazed at him with wonder. "I don't understand, but I'm a wild animal around you! Why is sex with you so fucking amazing?"

"It's how you look at me; I know you desire me so, and that makes me want you even more!" His velvety voice melted me.

"You've changed me for the better. You make me feel so incredibly sexy and happy! Thank you, my love!" I whispered, and he tenderly pressed his lips to mine.

I laid my head on his shoulders and gazed at his luminous face, lit by the last warming rays of the summer's sunset.

He had a dreamy, faraway gaze. "That sky, fiery orange-red... reminds me of my home."

"Gianmarco, are you happy here in Milan?"

He kissed my forehead. He didn't want to say it, but I felt his non-verbal response was not a simple yes or no.

After a long swig of his beer, he stared at the empty pizza box, stained with patches of oil and crust crumbs. "I don't know." He seemed hesitant to say more.

Still, I waited, my silence urging him to elaborate.

"After my great disappointment, I needed to start somewhere new to better my life. There are more opportunities here. But I am alone, without my family or friends."

I could have offered words of encouragement or asked him about his *great disappointment,* but I didn't want to interrupt him because I needed to hear what he had to say. I leaned into his chest and listened, hoping he would open his heart to me.

"My world is small, therefore, I only have small dreams," he said in a quiet voice, but immediately went silent. Perhaps he was afraid that revealing his secret wish aloud might jinx it.

I reached for his hand and brushed my cheek against the word *HOPE* tattooed on his right inner wrist; tiny leaves were intertwined around the red and black block letters. I didn't know its significance, but I chose to believe it symbolized who he was—a proud Italian from Abruzzo. *Forte e gentile*—strong and bold like the block letters, yet gentle like those delicate, tiny leaves. Gianmarco's tender side was there. You only had to dig a little to uncover the beautiful gentleman that he was.

"Tell me your hopes and dreams. I want to know."

He gave me a tiny smile. "I have one small wish for a place of my own," he explained. "I want to run a little champagne bar where I add a special Italian wine to it and serve aperitifs, unusual gins, and tonics."

"I love your unique concept! It would be a perfect place to apply all that you've learned as a sommelier. Thank you for sharing your dream with me." I felt so honored to learn of his aspiration.

"But this dream is not for me." The confidence in his voice faltered. He stared at the ground as if speaking to his shoes.

Not understanding, I asked, "Why?"

"Italian bureaucracy!" His raised shoulders almost touched his ears. "So many rules to open and run a business! So much money to start!"

"Must it be in Italy?"

"No, not necessarily." He looked up at me with curious eyes.

"May I suggest something?"

He nodded.

"Your English is near-perfect. You could open your bar anywhere: in London, Edinburgh, Stockholm... It isn't easy, but it can happen. I believe in you!"

I didn't care who heard me; with stars in my eyes, I sang to him the song, *The Way I Am*, bursting from my heart, for if he were falling, I would catch him.

I had touched his soul as he kissed my lips, ever so softly that he melted my heart and soul. I kissed him back with all the love that I had, trying to wash away the sadness, the loneliness, and the self-doubt in his troubled heart; in return, I felt my troubles melt away too.

"*Home*, tonight, I wanna make love to you."

May the Sun Never Set in Milan

8

LOST IN TRANSLATION

About three months later
Sunday, June 2, 2019
Gianmarco's apartment
Milan, Italy

Barefoot in the kitchen, clad in nothing more than a dark blue T-shirt, the long, black fabric ties of the apron dangled like seductive seams from silk stockings cascading over my bare legs. Finishing my culinary surprise for Gianmarco, I bent over to wipe off the sauce splatters from his pristine floor, giggling as my tiny sheer panties rose to my hips, exposing more of my cheeks, which was a good thing since we both liked *more*.

I heard the click of the front door opening and glanced at the clock above the stove. Mr. Punctual was right on time. With a sly smile, I decided not to turn around just yet. I wanted

Gianmarco to catch sight of me from this vantage point, knowing how much my ass-loving Italian adored seeing his American lover in such a provocative state.

It had been much too long since our last encounter in Milan; the three months felt like six, and I had thought of him daily. Tonight, I was determined to surprise him and blow his mind, starting with his tongue.

I had prepared his favorite cocktail using the intensely floral Edinburgh Gin 1670, distilled with flowers harvested from the Royal Botanic Garden.

This elixir exuded an aroma reminiscent of my favorite citrusy perfume from Spain that instantly transported me back to memories of hot, sultry summer days where a mere spritz on my skin would rejuvenate me, leaving me feeling fresh, light, and as vibrant as a gin blossom.

I positioned the new bottle and mixed drink on the bar, facing the door.

By now, the ice was melting, and a slight coating of condensation glistened on the glass rim. I heard him laugh and pictured Gianmarco smiling, holding my calligraphic cursive note while reading, *Drink Me!*

"Different. *Ma non c'e male,*" he said from across the room.
"*But not bad.*"

Tilting my head, I did a happy little shimmy with my hips. It was his recipe, and I must have made it precisely to his liking.

I surreptitiously peeked and saw him remove his suit jacket and hang it on the back of a chair before facing the stove again. Footsteps approached the kitchen until they stopped.

"Mmm... *Buona!*" I smiled at his verbal stamp of approval.
"Mmm... *Good!*"

But was it for the aroma of the ragù or from the sight of me barefoot and my barely veiled ass on display in his kitchen? I hoped he would love the dish and the derriere; both were for him.

"Ciao Sabi!"

His deep, sexy Italian voice painted a giant grin across my face before I even turned around.

"Hello, Darling! How's your day?" I answered as if it were routine, waiting at home for him to return from work.

Glancing over my shoulder to meet his gaze, I beamed my biggest smile at him while stirring the rich ragù—Massimo Bottura's recipe with beef cheeks simmered low and slow.

"By the look on your pleasantly surprised face, you forgot I was coming, didn't you?"

He took a large swig from his glass and ignored my teasing question. Charmingly cheeky, he winked at me, smiling with a mischievous grin.

Gianmarco adjusted his navy blue tie and patted his chest. He looked so sexy, wearing his form-fitting wool trousers and pressed white dress shirt. "I wore your gift to me because I knew you were coming."

"You remembered!" I smiled, misty-eyed.

"Of course. For my birthday last year, along with that singing card you, my sweet rose, and my Little Pink Kitten made for me," he said before taking a long draw of the gin concoction, "and which you sent to the *restaurant.*"

I wondered, had it been difficult at work for my lover? I assumed it was, but I knew the difference between an unwinding drink enjoyed as a refreshment and an uninhibited one used as a numbing tool to cope. Gianmarco's clenched-jaw slug of alcohol seemed like the latter, a knife to cut loose from the thorns of his day.

He toasted, *"Salute!"* before tossing back the last of the liquor.

"Cheers!"

"Not every day can be a winner, my Darling," I told him, then set the wooden spoon down, slipping the lid partway over the pot.

He moved to open the ice box, but I shut the door quickly.

"No-no-no!" I wagged a finger at him. "No peeking!"

"What are you hiding, Sabi?"

"I have quite the boozy lineup planned for tonight."

"Oh, yeah?"

I nodded.

"Hand me the ice, will you?" He wiggled the empty tumbler in his hand at me. "I feel like another drink. Want one too?"

"No, thanks. I'm a lightweight, but I'll take a tiny sip of yours."

"No problem."

"Hey!" I grabbed his arm and looked into his eyes. "I'm here now to listen to your troubles or anything else."

"Yes, I know. I love that you're here for me." He smiled and kissed my forehead before turning back to the bar, where he set about making a second drink.

When he returned, I reached for his replenished glass and tasted his concoction.

"Very nice," I said, gazing at him. "But mine is better." I winked, and he laughed loudly as he set his drink on the kitchen counter.

I opened my arms to beckon him forth. "Come here, sweetheart. What's up?"

It felt like Gianmarco needed some loving acceptance as he slipped behind me, leaning in to hold my waist. One hand glided to my nape; the other skimmed over my curves to the small of my back. Burying his face into the crook of my neck, he delivered a kiss that he knew brought sensual shivers to my core. Holding me to his body, I arched into him. As he kissed me softly, caressing and teasing my mouth with his tongue, I was awash in pure pleasure and desire for him. "Mmm, that kiss of yours is felonious! You take my breath away!"

How does he do it? His kisses are so magical that I would pardon him of all sins, even before he commits them.

A charming bad-boy smile snuck across his face. "What's on the menu?"

I was unsure if he was asking about dinner or taunting me since his hand slid down to give my ass a firm squeeze.

"Want a taste?" I giggled, not sure if I was offering myself or the ragù.

Dipping the wooden spoon into the sauce, I placed my other hand below it to catch any errant drips. Blowing lightly upon it, I presented my work to his mouth and awaited the verdict.

He smelled, tasted, and licked his lips, looking pleasantly surprised. With his palm up and his arm extended a foot from his body, he bunched his fingers together as if yanking them down from the air, leaned into his Italian accent even though he spoke English perfectly well, and said, *"Mmm, it's-a-good, but not as good as Mamma's!"*

Feigning insult, I huffed and blew all the air from my nose. "Hmm, if you weren't such an irresistible Italian, I'd slap your ass with this spoon. I know my place. Italian men love their mammas first and foremost, above all other women."

His deep, warm laughter enchanted my heart.

Raising his shoulders and pushing them forward, he threw his hands in the air and, with a typical Italian gesture, said, *"Ehhhh!"*

I pecked my genuine, full-blooded Italian man's lips, saying, "I love you, *Asshole!*"

He reached for his G&T, grinning in mock shock. "You love my... *asshole?*"

"Yes, every part of you, you sexy thing!"

"*Eccellente!*"
"Excellent!"

He smiled brightly before finishing the cocktail. With his fingertips pinched together at his lips, he blew me an appreciative chef's kiss.

I puckered my lips, ready and waiting. "I earned only an *air kiss* after slaving in the kitchen all day for you?"

He playfully swatted my bum.

"Ah!" I yelped, then giggled in surprise.

"Better?"

"Mmm, I do love it when you give my ass attention. But why is my ragù only *good?*"

"Oh, Sabi. Do you always have to win and be the best?"

"Yes, I like to win. Teach me."

I watched his gorgeous frame pace across the kitchen like a tiger, tapping his finger on his lips and lasciviously staring at me in contemplation.

"Hmm, what should I teach my Sabayon tonight?" he asked the room.

"Don't *Sabayon* me. I'm very competitive. I want to know how Mamma's ragù is better than mine!"

"Ask her!" he chirped. "Here, let me phone her!" He whipped out his phone and dialed.

"Gianmarco!" I shrieked, aghast. "No! Listen, what could I say to her? 'Hi, you don't know me, but I've been fucking your son, and he says I should learn how to make a proper ragù from you. Show me your secrets so that I can WOW the pants off him, please!' What do you think she would say to that?" I stabbed the sauce-stained wooden spoon in the air toward him.

"Your words would flatter her!" He chuckled. "And then she would tell you, *'That's-a not how you getta his pants down!'*"

My smile morphed into a straight face. "Until she finds out what I am."

He arched a jet-black eyebrow. "And... *you are?*"

"Seriously, I'd love to learn how to cook from your mamma, but..." I hesitated, unsure whether to go on. "I don't think she would approve of me."

"You judge her, and you don't even know her!" His black brows knitted together in irritation.

"I'm a mother, too, and if my son told me he was having an affair with a married woman," I exhaled sharply. "I would not be happy. You are her firstborn son. She has such high hopes for her favorite, and perhaps a woman like me is not what she had in mind!"

I had so little time with him, and I didn't want to waste it by fighting. So now I was deflecting as I put the spoon down and turned away from him, heading to the living room.

"Sabina, look at me!" His irritated voice was rough and raw, on the edge of anger. "Are you *not* happy being with me?"

I turned to face him. "I love being with you, body and soul. Know that I regret nothing that happens between us. No one else makes me feel so young, sexy, and alive but you." I paused and whispered my great fear. "But I don't deserve to be this happy—with you."

"Why not?"

"It's complicated. Not only am I already married with a child, but I'm probably the same age as your mother! I'm a cradle robber, worse than Prometheus stealing fire from the gods, with eternal punishment as the price for my sins!" I held back the dam of tears, threatening to break.

"My mind judges and condemns me because I know what I'm doing is wrong. But to the depths of my soul, it feels so right to be with you. Hell be damned, my heart wants what it wants, and I don't know how to give you up!" The warmth of my heart ran cold, sending my body into aching shivers.

Collapsing into the corner of his couch, I wrapped my arms around my knees, folding myself into a tiny ball that was small enough to get lost in the crease.

I sobbed.

"And I thought I had a rough day," he murmured. He sat beside me, unfurling my hands to wrap his arm around my shoulders, cradling me like a baby in his lap.

He soothed my grieving body with the gentlest touch from his tender hands, caressing me from my back to my shoulders, along my rib cage, beyond my hips, and ending at my ankles. He wiped the tears streaming down my cheeks with his giant thumbs.

"Oh, my poor, dear Sabi!" His baritone voice hung words in sweet tones of cherry red. "You fell for a poor boy. Unlike you, we make do and maximize every ingredient to extract the most flavor from what we can. It's what I'm used to—my comfort food—Mamma's ragù."

"I only want to make you happy," I said, pressing my body deeper into his warm furnace. "As happy as you've made me!" Reaching for his left hand, I kissed the word *HOPE* inked on his inner wrist.

He cradled my face with his hand. "You make me so happy. But I'm a simple man. I'm not used to that kind of love. You overwhelm me with your generosity, Sabi. I'm almost embarrassed by it."

"Overwhelmed and embarrassed by my generosity? I don't understand."

"I feel like..."

"Yes? Tell me."

"Like you're trying to buy my love."

"I know your love is not for sale. It's that... I need to feel needed and appreciated. My husband has everything and doesn't need or want me anymore." I sniffled and took a deep breath. "Plus, I love spoiling you since you love my surprises. Or, at least, I thought you did. I'm much better at giving than receiving; it's how I show my love."

"I know you mean well, but I'm not a thirty-year-old *mammone** living with his mother. I moved to Milan to be independent and make something of myself." He exhaled deeply. "I'm looking for wild sex with you, not a mother to baby me."

"But what do you think people will say when they see us together? I'm old enough to be your fucking mother," I snapped back. "And, by the way, no one would mistake you for being a mamma's boy. You are many things, but a *mammone*, you are not!"

He looked into my eyes and gently touched his chin with the tip of his fingers, then flicked them away. *"Ma che cazzo me ne frega di quello che pensano gli altri!"*
    "I don't give a shit what other people think!"

I found myself crying again, but this time with tears of joy that he didn't care what others might think of us; that we were misfits didn't matter to him. Surely, my teary eyes were ugly, red, and swollen, and yet Gianmarco kissed me on my wet,

---

*   *mammone* = adult man who lives with his mother or parents

puffy eyelids. His lips were like butterflies landing on dewy morning flowers; his pure sweetness liquefied my heart.

"You look and fuck like you're my age, my Sabayon." His words rolled hot and sexy against my ear.

A blush rose in my cheeks as a rush of arousal swept down to my toes. "You make me feel like your age, my Darling!"

I reached for his hand with another confession. "I'm sorry. When I went shopping for you today, I didn't know you felt that way about my gifts."

"Yeah, I see a mountain of packages on my groaning counter!"

Embarrassed at my exposed, wretched excess, I pointed at the treats from his hometown that I knew he would enjoy. "Fresh, thin, handmade square-edged *chitarrina* egg pasta, a small wheel of sheep milk Pecorino cheese aged in hay from Abruzzo, a fresh loaf of crunchy Italian bread, lots of salami, antipasti, and *pizza dolce* for dessert, and more!"

"Thank you. All my favorites! And you, who get lost so easily, found everything here in Milan! You are amazing!"

I gasped, second-guessing myself about whether I had gone too far. "You mean, you like my gifts?"

"Of course! And where did you find my cake? I love it!" All smiles, he beamed like a joyful little boy on Christmas morning. "But after today, no more extravagant gifts, OK?" The inflection of his voice made it a gentle command rather than a question.

Feeling emboldened, I smiled guiltily. "Does that include birthdays and Christmas? No gifts on Easter and Valentine's Day, too?"

He extended his index finger, looking at me seriously. "You know what I mean."

I nodded and obeyed. Almost.

. . .

FINDING *PIZZA DOLCE*, a specialty from his hometown, was a challenge. When ordering it from a bakery, I didn't realize how massive this multi-layered chocolate and vanilla tower, filled with almond marzipan and buttercream, would be! Customarily, they served it at huge Italian weddings. No wonder the bakers at the *pasticceria* shop laughed when I told them the dessert was for two people.

The sponge cakes' unique, bright red layers came from soaking them in *alchermes*, an ancient liqueur invented by the nuns of the Order of Santa Maria dei Servi in Florence. They extracted its bright crimson color from the crushed bodies of cochineal insects, like ladybugs.

SMILING, I knew I had hit the mark with the extravagant dessert. "A girl has to keep the mystery alive, keep some things secret, and mix things up. But, I may tell you if you're good."

With a naughty twinkle in his eyes, he licked my ear. "You know, and I know, Sabayon, that I'm beyond good!"

I blushed at his playful but truthful words.

"I like it when you mix things up. You are fascinatingly different! I've never met anyone like you before," he said.

"You too!" I grinned from ear to ear, overjoyed at our mutual fascination for one another. "You're unlike anyone I've ever known," I said, thrilled with myself, with him, and with us.

In the mood to party, I suggested, "Shall we have some vino? There's a Rosé in the fridge you might recognize."

Upon opening the refrigerator, Gianmarco whistled when he spotted the chilled bottle of Cerasuolo d'Abruzzo Rosato.

"Wow! Cerasuolo from Azienda Agricola di Ventimiglia! What's the occasion?"

His misty eyes were as large as giant wheels of cave-aged Parmigiano-Reggiano cheese. Resting in his hand was a rare bottle, the best Cerasuolo in Italy. Stunned by the gift, he spoke to the bottle, reminiscent of Hamlet holding a skull and reciting Shakespeare's famous soliloquy, "To be or not to be."

"Do you know that Cerasuolos are made from red Montepulciano d'Abruzzo grapes, also known as a winemaker's dream grape?"

I shook my head, happily absorbing his vinicultural insights.

"It's so flexible that it produces fantastic, bold, fruit-forward wines like California Cabernet Sauvignons you can stand a fork in. But it's versatile enough to craft soft, rounded reds as smooth as the most refined French Pinot Noirs, like the Tenuta Fiore I gave you the last time you visited me in Milan."

"Yes, of course. Thank you! I loved that bottle you shared with me. It was a soft, smooth, rounded red." When I repeated his words, I had to bite my lip to keep a straight face since he was being perfectly earnest in his detailed description. But oh, the salacious thoughts running through my mind! I blushed at what I wanted him to do to me and my smooth, rounded bottom—for his broad hand to slap it until it was tingling and bright red!

I pinched my arm to focus on the pureness of his words.

"But a Ventimiglia Cerasuolo, like this one, is special. Made from rare, red-fleshed Montepulciano grapes, it is vinted like white wine, producing a fantastic blush Rosé. *Signor Ventimiglia* is the master of perfectly blending the rich fruit flavors against its striking mineral acidity, ensuring a perfectly balanced palate."

"I'm glad you like it." I smiled, pleased that he genuinely appreciated my gift.

"But of course, this particular vintage is extraordinary!" He caressed the bottle as if it had a beautiful ass. Although, if this wine were a live woman, I might have been jealous, as he looked like he had fallen in love with her body.

"When you asked me what the occasion was, I should have answered, 'You are, my super sommelier. You're the occasion!'"

I gazed into his gorgeous browns, and he shook his head, raised an eyebrow, and half-laughed. "Now you're really overdoing it!"

"Forgive me, I can't help myself," I said, brushing my lips against his soft beard, "but you're worth it. You are as special to me as this wine is to you! And the way you're staring and stroking this Rosé, it looks like you'd have kissed her and gone to bed with her, if she were one of your *ragazze!*"
"*girlfriends!*"

"Ahahaha!" he roared. "Thank you for the gift, dear Sabi!" Then he embraced me while kissing me on the nose and whispering teasingly, "*Tra tutte le mie ragazze, tu sei la mia preferita!*"
"*Of all my girlfriends, you are my favorite!*"

I shook my head and grinned; I suppose I was the one who brought up the idea of *girlfriends*. "So, how do you say *cheeky bastard* in Italian?"

He mimed turning a key over his lips. "*Non te lo dico!*"
"*I'm not telling you!*"

"Oh, come on! Why won't you tell me, *bastardo?*"

He grabbed me by the waist and kissed my ear, whispering, "*Per te, sono il tuo bastardo furbo!*"
"*For you, I am your clever, cheeky bastard!*"

. . .

POP!

Gianmarco opened the bottle of Cerasuolo, inspected and sniffed the cork, then poured a smidgen into his glass. He swirled it, evaluating the wine's dark pink blush as the glycerol legs cascaded into a starburst pattern. Like tears running down the sides of his glass, they reflected how rich and buttery the wine could be.

Closing his eyes, he placed his perfectly symmetrical nose on the rim of the glass. He inhaled, searching for ethereal fruity, herbal aromas, like melon and peaches, that the vintner had captured at the time of bottling.

Taking a sip, he let the unctuous liquid roll around his mouth, settling on all the parts of his tongue: sweet, acid, bitter, and mineral content. I knew he was committing the flavors and textures of this wine to memory.

I loved seeing him in his element. He once shared with me that wine on his palate summoned colors and images, the way an artist painted a panorama onto a blank canvas, as if he were touched by an inspiration others could not sense. Lumos, the fancy, ultra-modern Michelin restaurant in Milan, was certainly lucky to have hired Gianmarco. They could not have chosen a man better suited to be their sommelier.

"Nice!" A singular approval from my gentleman of few words other than when he was rhapsodizing about viniculture. Approving my choice, he poured me a glass, then filled his own.

Drinking wine was an enjoyable experience, but I didn't understand the subtle nuances of the art of tasting it. Either I liked it or I didn't, but I could appreciate Gianmarco's passion for it. I echoed his words after taking a sip. "Nice!"

His next sip was not analytical, but one of pure enjoyment.

His shoulders relaxed, his eyes softened, and his smile grew.

Even though I had received my warning, I was goal-bound and foolishly handed him another surprise. "Please don't hate me, but I mentioned there's more," I said, chewing on my bottom lip.

"Sabi—"

"You said, 'After today, no more.' So, technically, it's still allowed. The last one for today."

"More, huh? Hmm." He feigned disapproval by shaking his head.

Like a puppy caught gnawing her master's shoe, my expression shifted from pleasure to shame. I lowered my head in supplication, hoping the punishment would not be severe.

He opened the parcel and looked confused. It was an unlabeled bottle of wine wrapped in an Italian newspaper. "Thank you. But what is it?"

"You're welcome!" I added cheekily, "It's a bottle of wine!"

"OK, and—"

"And it's an invitation, of sorts."

No smile; his reaction was tepid, so I jumped into further explanation. "This fantastic Malvasia dessert wine is from a single cask, made only every few years. It's bottled and served exclusively at Ristretto, the esteemed Michelin restaurant in Taormina, Sicily.

He listened intently without blinking.

"This gift is only the first part of your surprise. You don't have to drink it tonight, but I'm sure it would pair brilliantly with your cake."

"Invitation?"

"Given what you've just told me, I'm afraid to tell you the second part. I never want you to be angry or upset with me."

"Tell me everything," he commanded.

Contemplating my words before letting them escape from my lips, I took a deep breath. "I know how much you love the wines from Sicily, and you mentioned you've never been. Wouldn't it be a fantastic experience for my sommelier to savor his favorite Sicilian wines in person? Imagine tasting the rich, inky Nero d'Avolas and the minerally, crisp, and fruity Etna Biancas in their terroir."

He was silent but pursed his lips.

I should have stopped, but I was buzzing and bursting at the seams with the hope that an adventure with me would also excite him, which is why I continued, albeit unwisely. "If you could get the time off, I'd love for you to join me in Taormina as my guest. It's known as the jewel of Sicily. My favorite time is autumn, when the weather is still warm and lovely. With the end of cruise ship season, the best restaurants sit open, free of tourists."

He looked down at the floor but met my eyes when I said his name.

"Gianmarco, play with me? Be silly with me in Sicily, and let's pretend we are children again! You can be the fireman you told me you wanted to be as a boy, and I can be the treasure hunter of my childhood dreams."

A half-smile emerged from the corner of his mouth.

"I'd love to show you the stunning mosaics at Piazza Armerina. They are similar to your hometown's recently uncovered underground mosaics, which you were so excited about."

He rubbed the side of his temple as if attempting to massage away a looming migraine.

"If we're lucky, we could watch the fire erupting from Mt. Etna's volcano. And even if it's dormant, I want you to see this spectacle, where millions of sleeping ladybugs huddle among the crater's steam vents, trying to keep warm, oblivious to the lava hidden just below the cap." My heart forced me to plead. "You mean the world to me. Let me share my world with you while we still have time."

He closed his eyes and steepled his hands beneath his chin, searching for a response to my proposal. The silence made my ears ring as blood rushed to my throbbing head. Terrified of rejection, a sudden shiver ran down my spine. "I fear your answer because you're frowning right here." I touched the space between his dark, striking eyebrows, where now a deep furrow existed.

"My dear Sabina." He drew a long breath and reached for my hand to kiss it. "Because it's a gift today, I would love to try your Malvasia with the *pizza dolce* after dinner."

I raised his hand to my cheek, kissing his soft skin. "This is more than about the gifts, isn't it? Talk to me. I'm listening."

He clasped his hand over mine and squeezed it. "I am thankful for everything you do for me. Truly, I am. I don't want to insult you, but you know I cannot accept the trip." His reply sounded flat and formal, suppressing hidden emotions.

"Overwhelming?" I winced as I said that dreaded word, my eyes searching his expression for the truth.

The sparkle in his eyes disappeared. "Yes. Too much."

I sighed regretfully as he let go of my hand.

"You knew it was excessive." The kernels of anger were noticeable in his tone.

My stomach flipped. Feeling his disappointment in me, my heart sank like a dead weight falling into the abyss. "Please don't be angry. Upsetting you was never my plan. I love spending time with you, and I thought you would enjoy going somewhere fun and new with me." Tears welled in the corner of my eyes. "My offer was made with love; that was the intention, not pressure."

He leaned forward and touched his forehead to mine, so

that we were now eye to eye.

"I'm sorry," I whimpered. "I went too far."

His eyes closed.

I clasped my hands together in prayer and raised them to my heart. Tears escaped from my clenched eyes.

He embraced me. "I have already forgiven you."

Though I could not see his face, my neck was wet from his tears.

"We come from different worlds, you and I. You are a starry-eyed girl with a charmed life who dreams of unicorns and chases rainbows. Your love knows no limits, and your heart knows no bounds."

He cradled my face with both hands and kissed my forehead. "You know that my dream is to make something of myself, become someone important *first*. One day, I will take you to Taormina, and we will visit the volcano, see the mosaics, and drink amazing Sicilian wines together. *Ma in questo momento, sono nulla!*"

"But right now, I am nothing!"

"No! It's not true!"

"I am *nothing*, and I have *nothing* to offer you!"

"STOP! Don't say that!"

He stared at his empty hands searching for answers. "I don't understand what you see in me." Then he raised his head, and with dewy eyes staring into mine, he asked, "Is it only for sex?"

"Sex with you is a life-altering, mind-blowing, fantastic experience. You're the best I've ever had, like an addictive drug that should be illegal."

He shook his head, snorting in disbelief.

"But you're more than that to me." I reached out to hold his hand to connect with him. "You know I can't just fuck anyone. I need to like them as a person. And I like you so very much!"

He squeezed my hand back. "I like you very much too."

"From the first day I met you at Mirabella, you intrigued me. You're an enigma, so different from everyone else!"

He shook his head again. "*Me*, an *enigma?*"

"Yes, you! I saw you as a man beyond your station, not just a waiter in a starched gray uniform. I hoped to one day know the real Gianmarco."

"And do you think you know *him?*"

"Yes! I see *you*. I know you don't share your emotions freely, and I'm grateful for the times when you're vulnerable. Trust me, please! Let me remove a brick from your protective wall so I can peer in. Share more of your life with me, like right now."

"Tell me. What do you see?"

"You can tell a lot about a man's character by his actions. You *are* a modern-day knight, though you don't have the armor. It's not what a man wears outside or how much he owns that makes him valuable, but the heart he has inside that counts!"

He smirked and shook his head again.

I slapped his upper arm. "Don't shake me off—it's true! In our messages and texts, those bits you revealed told me volumes. You've rescued rain-soaked, abandoned kittens, found homes for them, and volunteered at an animal shelter even when you're tired or busy. You're always kind to the homeless and the poor, empathizing with them so much that you ran for political office because you believed you could be a champion for your fellow disenfranchised Italians!"

He listened still.

"I hear you when you fight for what is right and shine a light on injustices, whether in Abruzzo or Milan."

"Sabi," he sighed, uncomfortable hearing me recount his

accomplishments.

"Beloved, you are a knight, but you just don't realize it! You're a good man with a heart of gold, and that's why I've fallen in love with you. Not only for what you are, but for who I am when I am with you!"

As he lowered his eyes, I placed my hand on his gorgeous face and lovingly kissed his forehead.

"If my opinion means anything to you, then know that you're already so important to me and many others. One day, I hope you see what I see in you."

"If I am a knight, I am also a beast, and I could never bear it if I hurt you," he confessed.

I frowned. "How would you hurt me?"

"The way I desire you... Oh, Sabayon!" he sighed. "You haven't seen all of me yet, and I'm afraid that if I let myself cross that line—"

"What? Tell me!" I shook my head, and my steely, determined eyes flashed. "Show me your worst! You underestimate yourself, and you underestimate me. I'm not easily scared away."

9
Hurts So Good

He stared at me with eyes narrowed into slits, sizing me up. "Sabi, have you tried having pain with your pleasure?"

Unfazed, I playfully replied, "Shall we start dinner now, or...?"

He turned quiet, not responding to my question, as I did not answer his.

"Gianmarco?" My voice wavered since I couldn't read what was on his mind.

When he finally replied, it carried a sinister, icy tone. "You've been naughty, Sabayon."

My eyes widened as I chewed on my bottom lip to suppress a smile. No man had ever looked at me that way, like a hungry panther stalking his prey. Waiting all day for him, my pussy was dripping with anticipation. He wanted to *play*. Rough.

"Someone needs a spanking," he growled.

I backed away in mock fear and watched as Gianmarco lowered his shoulders, his hands spread wide across the back of the couch. He looked like a German Shepherd waiting for his toy to make a move, staring at me with wanton desire; a dewy sliver of wetness lined my slit.

"I want your ASS, Sabayon!"

Panting, I stood between my sexy beast and his furniture. "Anal, for dinner? Sorry, sir. It's only ragù and cake on the menu tonight."

"I'm hungry now, but not for food!"

Playing hard to get, I squealed with glee as I attempted to escape. Unfortunately, I wasn't quick enough as he lunged for my hand and yanked me toward him. Lifting me by my torso, he slammed my body onto the sofa. Compared to his muscular mass, I weighed nothing; he overwhelmed me with ease.

Though I tried to push him away with all my might, he easily pinioned my wrists above my head with one hand. Growling at him, I bared my teeth and snapped at his arm but missed.

He opened his mouth and sealed it over mine, roughly stabbing me with his iron-like tongue and fucking my maw. I tasted traces of Cerasuolo and kissed him back, sucking off his tongue as hard as I could.

Moving up, he trapped my squirming hips under his. Then he pinned my shoulders down by spreading his forearm against my chest. Grabbing my long, dark hair with one hand, he twisted it like a rope around his wrist so tightly that I could hardly move my head.

I struggled to wriggle away, but he was too powerful; his limbs were as thick as my thighs. With one hand clamped over my wrists and the other using my hair like a leash, I was at his mercy.

Leering at me with wild eyes, he huffed into my ear. "Everything we've done before was just playtime, Sabi. Now we're really gonna fuck." Gone was the suave sommelier, replaced instead by an animal consumed by pure lust. "I'm gonna fuck you so hard, you'll feel like I'm breaking you in half!"

His savage words uncaged my passion. "God, I hope so!" I purred, looking back at him with carnal fire.

Finding my strength, I thrust my hips up, grinding my pelvis against his, my tongue slicking a wet trail all the way up to his neck.

"Now, are you *gonna* fuck me or just talk about it?" I dared him, and a wicked smile formed on his lips as his eyes ignited with desire.

With my feet pushed against the sidearm of the sofa, I arched my back. Reaching for his groin with my hips, I thrashed about, twisting and thrusting my pelvis up again and again. With each hit, I could feel his hardening cock knocking against my throbbing clit. This lewd response distracted his focus enough to liberate a hand from his seemingly unyielding grip.

I grabbed his ass and yanked, willing him deeper into me, desperately yearning for his naked body to fuse with my bare skin as if we were one. My fingers fumbled, unable to unbutton his shirt. Still restrained, I begged, "Help me!"

He let go, and feverishly, I worked to release him from his clothes. Unwinding my hair from his clutch, he single-handedly whipped off the tie, and I watched the navy blue, woven silk number with the tiny white chevrons, snake through the air.

Grabbing a fistful of the borrowed blue T-shirt from his closet, Gianmarco swiftly tore it from my body; the friction from his balled-up paw left hot burns across my skin. Looking down at me, he raised his shoulders and paused again, admiring my sheer black and midnight-blue bra. He drew a fingernail tantalizingly around my aching pink nipple that threatened to pierce the lace.

"Aaahh," I exhaled as goosebumps flashed across my breasts and my tummy fluttered with uncontrolled spasms.

He examined me and raised a dark, expressive eyebrow, calculating whether the outfit was another purchase I had made especially for him. "Another unrequested gift for me, is it?"

"No, I bought this for *me* in your favorite football, um— Inter Milan's team colors." This was, of course, a lie.

He knew the truth and laughed malevolently. "Ah, still so naughty, Sabayon," he snarled at me. "Lying to me, even now! As much as I love *our* new bra, I want you naked; I'm gonna fucking ravish you tonight!"

His promise sent a taser jolt of electricity shooting down to my pussy, making me instantly drenched.

"Yesss!" I hissed.

Slap! His hand flew across my face.

The sting from his palm unexpectedly striking my cheek startled me. He leaned over and gently caressed my jawline, placing his thumbs and forefingers around the sides of my lips. "Yes. *Sir*." Gianmarco enunciated, and I realized that *this* was the game he wanted us to play.

In the next instant, he flipped me around and splayed me across the tops of his thighs. Muffled moans of protest and arousal emanated from my mouth as he buried my face in the cushions of his couch. With his elbow against my back, he pressed into me as I squirmed like a prisoner. Finally, I felt the clasp of my bra rip open, and I gasped, whimpering, "Thank you for freeing me, *Sir!*"

His hand ran along my spine toward my behind, but he paused when he noticed my crotchless knickers. From the living room mirror, I caught his reflection, salaciously grinning with pleasure. "What have we got here?"

"A surprise—from your slut." I laughed at my reply.

His hand smacked my ass, and my butt cheek scorched from it. "Try again!"

"A-a, surprise from your slut, *Sir!*" I sputtered between gasps.

"Mia troia!" He roared with laughter, sounding even more delighted than a minute ago. "I'm happy to see you learn quickly, my salacious one!"

"My slut!"

Exploring further with his two fingers, he discovered an opening concealed within the sheer lace. He breached my pussy, slithering and pushing his fingers inside. Far from gentle, his every strike smacked hard against me, but soon, the sting of pain turned to bursts of pleasure.

I wanted *more*; I wanted it harder; I wanted everything he could give. I thrust my pelvis into the slams of his knuckles against my mound, and I felt myself becoming slicker and wetter with my hot nectar now pooling around his fingers still within.

"Mmm, that's so good," I moaned in delight. "I could cum this way. But I can't lose it just now. I want to cum with you; cum on your stiff cock, Darling!"

"You have no idea what you're in for, my dear. Are you ready to *play*?"

I nodded, panting, aroused, and excited by his words. "Yes, I'm ready, *Sir*."

First, he caressed my bum softly; then, he slapped it repeatedly. Hard. I yelped a scream and uncontrollably shook as the splendid shock waves thrilled my pussy.

He flipped me over—a compliant rag doll was I. Now facing him, he sat me on his lap to straddle him.

Burying his face in my chest, he exhaled with long, drawn-out breaths, bathing my breasts in warm sanctification. Like God's kiss, he anointed each with his sacred lips, nuzzling and grazing them with his abrasive whiskers. His rough touch was heavenly, as though the Pope himself had blessed them with a leather whip.

His mouth hummed, "God, I love your boobs!" Gianmarco was unbelievable. Time and time again, he had said some variation of "I love your tits!" And the way he looked at them with such reverence was not a pickup line but a truthful confession that flowed from his lips, which I believed.

I loved this man so much because he accepted me for who I was, just as I accepted him for who he was.

Our wild eyes met; I leaned in and purred my confession into his ear. "You are incorrigible. But, so am I."

"Yes, I know," he smiled, wickedly pleased at my admission.

I swallowed hard, remembering how timid I was when we first began. Since then, I had changed and grown for my lover, as he revealed to me the rough sex he wanted, which I didn't realize until he opened my eyes that I wanted it too.

"Beastly, the two of us," I said. "I see your dark side, and you see mine. It scares me, but it excites me."

The wind from his words collided across my neck. "Oh, my sweet Sabayon. We've only just begun."

10
OUR WICKED, WICKED PLAY

Almost midnight

Lucid and surreal, fantasy and reality existed together and shifted positions where we lay naked after showering. I cuddled with my illicit lover, stroking his muscular thighs with the same hand that bore my wedding band. In the silence of our post-orgasmic bliss, I traced hearts upon the surface of his skin and asked myself, *Am I a terrible wife or merely a woman finally awakening to her true self?*

Tingling from head to toe, I was buzzed and high off Gianmarco. A few hours earlier, I was thoroughly ravished by my lover, who gave me the most satisfying, vigorous, moaning, groaning, fun fuck session on that same sofa. In the sinfully delicious afterglow, he fed me morsels of cake.

I turned to him. "Darling, I've been reading a controversial erotic confessional, and I'm curious. Hypothetically, if this were our last time to *play*, what other deliciously devious, *filthy fornications* would you do to me?"

"*Filthy fornications!*" Gianmarco coughed out the words with bursts of laughter, trying not to choke.

He judiciously sipped his Malvasia, the unctuous dessert wine I gifted him. With profound regard, he answered. "I'm not sure you're ready for the kind of *filthy fornications* I like. It's dark and violent, more than you have dared to indulge in, my dear Sabayon."

He fed me another forkful of dessert.

"More than tonight's wild escapades?" I swallowed hard, taking a sip from his glass.

He took another bite, savoring the *pizza dolce's* rich flavor, licking his lips, and looking at me in a wicked, wicked way. "Much, much *more*."

"I might surprise you with what I imagine, *signor Romano*, when my mind wanders." Now, I was the one with a lewd smile. "You're an outstanding teacher, my paramour, inspiring me to explore where I've never gone before."

He toasted, "Happy to be of service, *signora*." Then he offered me his glass, and I downed the last of his Malvasia. The warm, liquid courage coursed through my blood.

"Do you know what I fantasize about doing to you right now?" I whispered as I licked his ear.

Curious, he smiled and shook his head while raising one of his thick, dark eyebrows.

"I think we want the same thing with each other, but a variation on a theme."

I reached for my purse and pulled out something blue.

"Want to *play?*" I waved my big, blue butt plug at him. When I pushed the button, it vibrated like a jackhammer.

He laughed heartily when the toy glowed neon blue. "In you or me?" The casual reveal from my uninhibited lover sent an unexpected tingle to my nipples.

"Whatever you want. No limits." I gave myself to him, displaying my willingness to be *his* in every way, to venture beyond my Sabayon flavors, and to please my man.

"I wanna push it in your ass and fuck you with it—full on." His voice rumbled with desire.

Unveiling my next prop, I dangled a pair of silver handcuffs. Banging the cold metal restraints together, I twirled the keys around my finger. I bit the side of my smirk and asked, "You like?"

"For later."

I put them away. "Your wish is my command." Looking at him sideways, I slathered the plug with anal lube, handed it to him, and smiled.

"Bend over," he commanded.

I obeyed.

I knelt on his sofa, the front of my hips pressing against the seatback, feeling the soft cushion yield beneath me.

Leaning forward, I swished my tail in his face.

He laughed at my playfulness as he followed behind, pressing his groin against me. Reaching for my bum, his hand gently caressed the side of my hip.

As he pulled off my panties, I took a deep breath and concentrated on relaxing the muscles that ringed my butthole. With the strong fingers of his free hand, he cleaved my cheeks and moved the sex toy into place. I braced myself, gripping the top of the sofa's back.

"Oh, my!" I exclaimed as the bulbous plug crossed my threshold.

Fiddling with the controls, he found a setting that made my whole pelvis thrum. Swallowing my groans, I breathed deeply, exhaled slowly, and tried to control myself from almost cumming; my pussy pulsed to the rhythm of the vibrator's tantalizing crescendo.

Though still leaning against the sofa's back, I pushed away and straightened my torso, twisting my neck to face him. "I feel so dirty with it inside me—like I'm your whore!" My words felt as slick as my wet slit.

He grabbed my hair and pulled my head back, spinning me around so we were face-to-face. My fiery eyes widened and transfixed upon his. Neither of us seemed to blink.

"You wanna be *la mia troia*, Sabayon?"
"*my whore*, Sabayon?"

I rubbed my nose against his soft lips and nodded.

"Yes, have your way with me, your *troia!*" I commanded, and he pressed his lips to mine. While kissing him full on the mouth, I sucked and entangled my tongue with his.

He sat us onto the sofa, and with his hands on my ribcage, he dropped my pussy onto his sheathed cockhead, tenting through his boxers.

"Now take control," he commanded.

Smiling mischievously, I wrapped my hands around his nape while circling my hips and rubbing my pussy hard against his cloaked erection, pressing my pelvis snug against his, to ride him as if I were fucking him in hard strides, which made his eyes roll to the back of his head.

Willingly, I obeyed, pushing him onto the couch and playfully lording over him. Like a lioness with paws weighted on his shoulders, I lowered my head and nuzzled my nose over his hairy chest, scenting him while breathing him in. I skimmed his pecs with my hungry mouth, worshiping him down his belly and beyond.

"Your hard body is so perfect, Darling!" I purred as my lips adorned his body with kisses.

"May I taste your perfect pussy?"

"Mmm, music to my ears!" I swung my leg over his torso, planting myself on all fours to face his feet. Arching my back, I waggled my glowing blue bum closer to his face.

He laughed. *"Eccola!"*
"There she is!"

Touching my pouty, pink pussy, he parted my labia with his fingers in search of my clit. When my lover found her, he gently sucked my pearl while his tongue traced circles, round and round, as if licking the milky glaze off a donut hole, making me squeal and squirm with delight.

"You're amazing!" I quivered and panted, laying my cheek upon the soft fuzz of his legs. Now, my eyes rolled to the back of my head. "Oh God! If you keep going, I'm gonna cum!"

Spurred by my explicit remark, he devoured me by curling his tongue into a cup to create suction. "Ohh-aahhh," I wailed as he lifted the hood of my engorged clit, pressing the flat of his tongue against my pearl, polishing and burnishing it with long, slow strokes with such force that I shook and writhed uncontrollably. Then he stilled his tongue but soon began sucking and bobbing his head up and down as if he were giving *me* a *clit* blowjob! It was challenging to stop from climaxing with his exquisite torture and a buzzing vibrator up my ass, pushing and edging me forward.

"Squirt me!" he commanded as he furiously tongue-fucked me with his thick taster. In and out of my slit, he bore into me. My pussy seemed to have a mind of its own, clenching and gyrating, thrusting and grinding itself hard against his hungry mouth and nose. I knew I was almost there; the blood rushed to my burning feet, my legs stiffened, and my knees quaked. With the final flick of his tongue, my whole body shivered as I came, drenching his gorgeous face.

From the fathom of my belly, unintelligible cavewoman grunts echoed in the cavern of my throat. "Unghh-ugh-aaah!"

A warm, sweet tide of longing relief crashed through my body. Dizzy from the headrush as if flying through a void, my eyes lost focus, and I felt peaceful, floating freely in time and space, yet sentient in body and mind.

"Goddamn! That is one fucking amazing tongue you've got, lover!"

He grinned at my proclamation of his impressive sexual prowess.

Encouraged by his smile, my eyes twinkled full of mischief. "My turn to make you cum!"

"Is that a challenge?" he said as he licked his grinning lips.

My eyes roved to the unmistakable contour bulging through his boxer shorts. I lifted my pointer finger to my mouth and ran it along the bottom edge of my lip, sighing, "Look! *Gran*-Marco is calling me. Your big boy wants me to release him from his cage, suck, and then swallow him until he spurts."

He roared with laughter at the flirty nickname I had just christened his member. "You're putting words in his mouth—ahem, my cock!"

We laughed.

While on top, I spread my knees wide apart so that our bellies touched. Pulling down his black briefs freed his beautiful, luscious, mouth-watering erection. "I love how your cock springs to attention!"

"Boing-boing!" he said, giggling with me.

When our laughter subsided, I stared at his glorious, veiny cock and shook my head. "My God, you look so sexy when your pubic hair has grown back in from not shaving for a couple of days!"

"My Sabayon, so sexually hungry and eager, yet still endearingly naive." He grinned impurely at me.

"OK, I don't have much experience, but I'm learning because I like what I see." I salaciously stared and drooled at him, biting my bottom lip. "I just love how you look!"

"Thank you."

"I'm so horny for you! My pussy throbs at the sight of your thickness! May I suck on you, please?"

"Be my guest." He snickered. "But first, taste my balls."

"Mmm, I would love to fondle and kiss your lovely silky sac, bursting full of cum—all for me!"

"You're so adorable!" He shook his head and chuckled.

I was not flexible enough to reach them in this position, so I spun around to face him. Holding onto his muscular thighs, I buried my nose between his plums and inhaled the sweet, earthy scent of his sex while nuzzling and licking his balls. I loved how the soft, curly hairs on his sac tickled my eyelids. I cupped and massaged his balls with my left hand while my right hand stroked his shaft up and down.

His beautiful cock glistened with pre-cum, and I could not resist taking him. My lips clamped tight around the groove under his cockhead as I sucked hard on the entirety of him. Like a sable brush tracing figures on the canvas of his flesh, my tongue twirled all around his head, desiring to lick his snake eye clean. "I love your flavor! I want more, please!"

Then he spread his legs wide and reached for his sac. Squeezing both balls with one hand made them pop toward my face, teasing me and reminding me of his request.

I giggled like a surprised little girl. "Of course, Darling! How could I forget your lovely, lonely pair?" I answered, smiling broadly, happy to oblige his request.

His ballsac looked so pink and smooth when he pulsed his fist, pulling the folds that covered his balls taut. My jaw dropped in awe as I marveled at how I could see the distinct contours of his crown jewels through his thin, transparent skin.

I placed his soft, hairy boulders in my mouth—one at a time—since they looked too big to fit together in one mouthful.

Sucking on the first one, I pulled it toward me, circling my tongue and polishing him until he was soaking wet with my saliva. As I repeated the tender, loving care with the other, he sighed and moaned, making me smile because I was addicted to hearing his deep, guttural bedroom noises. The volume of his groans was like my barometer, telling me how much fun he was having. His pleasure was my pleasure.

"Mmm, your balls are so yummy! Creamy with a hint of sea salt and sweet butter rolls, like an exquisite, late-disgorged sparkling wine from California."

My sommelier roared with laughter. "The outrageous things you say!"

A scheme formed in my mind. "Come with me."

My eyes grew large, and I tittered because it felt funny as I walked. "Good lord, I'm waddling like a duck with a giant, double magnum cork up my ass!"

He couldn't contain himself from roaring with joy as I led him by the leash of his stiff cock to follow my blinking blue butt. I took Gianmarco to bed, but before he lay on his back, I swatted his firm, sweet ass and said, "Not yet, lover boy. You first—on your hands and knees—doggy."

He raised his eyebrow, curious as to what game was afoot.

Moving behind him, I positioned my knee between his legs and spread them. Kneeling on the mattress, my hands rubbed the sensuous contours of his firm ass.

I held onto his hips and dove down, my nose delving into his rear. My dear neatnik, impeccably clean and tidy, had figured out what I was up to as he jerked forward and clenched his cheeks.

"Sabi, what are you doing?"

I caressed his perfect, toothsome ass, dying to sink my teeth into his hot flesh. "Mmm, you're so sexy!" I nipped one cheek.

"Ouch!"

"Sorry, Darling. I can't help it. It's so hard to control myself around you."

I drew his hips toward me, rubbing, massaging, and kissing his tailbone to relax him, and then I continued south.

"I love your ass! It's like a mouth-watering, perfectly ripe peach, and I'm dying to take a bite and eat you!" Pressing my hands against his cheeks, I spread them slightly and stuffed my face into his inviting ravine.

"You naughty minx! So, that's what you have in mind!"

"Mmm, may I?"

"Well, it's a good thing you scrubbed me clean in the shower after we fucked!"

"Mmm-hmm." With his permission, I went lower, kissing him until my lips softly touched his adorable starfish. I opened my mouth to let the tip of my tongue tickle it. He pulled away, yet his moans and groans told me he loved it.

"Do you like that?" I inquired. "Because your messy, naughty minx desires to taste your unadulterated flavor!"

He laughed between gasps.

I slipped my hand between his muscular thighs and caressed him up and down, from balls to knees and back again.

"Let me pleasure you, please? I know you want this."

"Aaahh!" He breathed out a deep exhale.

"I want to do this for you and only you." Diving in again, my face nuzzled his tasty, finger-licking-good tush.

"Sabina, wait! I like getting rimmed, but I've never," he said, spinning around to face me.

I mock-pouted, then pursed my lips at my kinky lover. "Trust me, Darling. I'm not going to peg you. I just want to taste you and stick my tongue in your ass." I purred at him. "Might your Sabayon possibly be filthier than her *filthy fornicator?*"

"Yes! I concede, dirty girl. You're fucking filthy like me!"

He captured my middle, locking me into a tight embrace. Wrestling back, I showed him my raw strength. I had spent too many years waiting to get what I wanted. Now, I would take it.

I smacked his ass hard and bit him. When he flinched, I pinned his thighs back and introduced the tip of my tongue to his hot ass.

Gianmarco yelped as he pretended to run away from me, eagerly clambering onto the mattress. On hands and knees, he rested his head upon a pillow as his teasing, seductive ass swayed beautifully in the breeze.

I crawled behind him and caressed his sweet cheeks, burying my head into his crevice. He giggled again as my long tresses tickled his tush. Then I reached up for his cock between his legs to stroke his thick shaft with one hand while rubbing his smooth balls with the other.

"You look glorious like this, sweetheart! Your beautiful, veiny cock and those full, heavy balls. Mmm, and yes, I love your asshole, too."

He shook his head in disbelief. "Sabi!"

"In fact, I love every damn part of you!" I offered him my cock-and-ass worshiping services. "May I pleasure you now?"

"Yes," he sighed, and then I felt him relax as he willingly slid his knees apart.

"Thank you, my Darling," I purred.

With both hands, I spread his cheeks wide and buried my face into his bum again, kissing him with my lips. When my tongue pressed against his pucker, I heard him take and release a deep breath, which egged me onward.

Like a kitten lapping up a bowlful of milk, I licked him with light brush strokes from the top of the crack to the very bottom. Kiss, lick, kiss, lick, up and down; my tongue was a paintbrush; my saliva, a hot varnish. Reaching around, I caressed his wet balls with my free hand. Then, like cranking the throttle on his motorcycle to give it more gas, I gripped his throbbing cock and twisted it while I stroked him up and down.

His legs shuddered; I must have been doing something right. He huskily breathed as I continued to rim and circle his tight sea star, round and round, followed by quick feather flicks.

"Is that the way you like it? Or would you prefer I lap you harder with the flat part of my tongue, rubbing you more forcefully, like this?"

"Aahhh, yes!" He panted, sounding like he was out of breath from running a marathon. "Everything like that!"

I loved giving my lover precisely what he wanted. With the point of my tongue, I tickled his nether hole, slipped it right in, withdrew my tongue, and slid it even further.

"Oh, Sabayon!" he groaned as I bore deeper, pushing and tongue-fucking his asshole while I groped his cock.

Dang, how I melted whenever he growled my sexy nickname! "God, your cock is the biggest ever! Oh, how I want to swallow your sweet cum!"

"So good!" he howled.

"Or should I French kiss you and let you taste your heavenly *crema* too?"

"*Sì-sì!*"
"Yes-yes!"

"Deep throat, Darling?"

"Yesss! In your mouth. Now!"

I slid to the foot of his bed, placing a pillow to cushion my knees. My mouth was wide open as I threw my head back, licking my lips in anticipation. "Fuck my throat! I know you want to."

He smacked my face with his rigid cock. Startled, I laughed in surprise!

Opening my mouth wide, I swallowed all of him. He was more than a mouthful that I was almost choking. Throwing my head back lengthened my throat, stopping my gag reflex.

I held onto his hips as he thrust his cock deep into me, his balls banging against my wet chin. I loved being suffocated, though I had to time my strokes to the thrusting tempo to breathe.

A river of spittle ran down my neck, flowing between my cleavage. I withdrew to take a deep breath.

"Don't stop, please!" he implored.

"Your wicked whore wants you to fuck her hard with your double-delicious cock!"

With immense strength, he lifted me back onto his bed, turning me over on my hands and knees. Between my legs, I reached behind, pumping his smooth shaft, making it throb at my touch.

He rubbed my ass, then slapped it; rubbed my ass and

smacked it again. I shrieked with delight with every strike. All the while, he was teasing me by pushing on my butt plug and rubbing his hard cock against my wet pussy. I moaned even louder. "I know I already came, but my pussy desperately aches for you to be inside."

"Is my dick big enough for you?"

"I'm a small gal, and you're too much for me, but I want you all the same. Fuck me, please!"

But instead of his cock, he stuck one finger in and out of my dripping pussy, then two, making his digits swing dance inside me.

"Oh, you are so soaked!" He marveled, extracting his fingers and tasting my freshly squeezed pussy juice, smacking his lips together.

"I know," I mewled.

"Mmm, but I'm not sure you're ready yet!"

He put his hand over mine, taking control of his hard cock.

"Please, Darling! You're driving me wild!" He tortured me by rubbing the tip of his cock against my entrance, penetrating me just a little, and sliding in and out. "I want *all* of your hardness! *Now!*"

"You mean like this!" He roared, grabbing my hips, pulling my ass toward him, and mercilessly ramming himself into me.

I screamed with shock and pleasure as his wide girth filled me up. He teased me even more. Driving me from behind, he pulled out until the tip of his cock was parked at my gape. Quivering and shaking, he pounded into me again and again. It was almost too much.

"I'm so close. I want to cum with you, Darling."

"You wanna cum *again? Say it!*"

"Yes, please, God! Yes! I *wanna* cum *with you!*"

"Not yet for me, angel," he whispered. "I wanna fuck your tight little rosebud and cum in your ass."

I was beyond excited. I trusted him, and I could not stop now. He pummeled harder and faster, every thrust hitting deeply, making us both moan together in pleasure. The second orgasm's contractions were much stronger than the first. I was panting so hard I could barely speak through the blinding pleasure, feeling lightheaded as blood rushed to my brain. My head and pussy were throbbing in unison.

"I'm cumming, Gian-*ahhhh!*" I squirted on him again.

A torrent gushed out of me, running down my legs and past my knees. I was giggling, embarrassed that I had drenched him even more than the first time when I climaxed on his face.

He laughed and kissed me down the spine.

"Wow! Second orgasms are so rare for me, Darling. Goddamn, you're still rock-hard! You look like you could go for thirds, but I can't take any more. You're incredible!"

He grinned as he pulled out of me. "My turn!"

I gasped as he yanked the butt plug out, lubed up his cock, and slowly, inch by inch, impaled my throbbing asshole. "Oh, slow—slow! *Slo—Ohhh!*" I winced as he pushed himself into me. He was so much bigger than the plug, almost too much for my tender rosebud to take.

"Aahhh, you are so tight! I love it! I wanna take your tiny asshole and break it."

Whether asking or telling me, "Anything you want, I'm yours." Gianmarco didn't need my permission because I was already his. I gave him my heart, body, and soul a long time ago.

Exhaling deeply, I gulped, panting and screaming with every thrust. It burned, but it was so good.

He stilled himself to ask, "Are you OK?"

I nodded, trying to find my voice, muted in pleasure. "Oh, yes! Do me like I'm your whore! I know it's what you want."

Looking back, I saw him close his eyes as he tensed his body. With gusto, he thrust quicker and harder. Panting and moaning, he made guttural, grunting, growling animal sounds I had never heard him make before.

"Cazzo! Sto sborrando!"
"Fuck! I'm cumming!"

I could feel him cresting into an orgasm, engorging and pulsating. Then he relaxed and leaned his entire weight on my back. He was so much broader and stronger than me that my knees gave way. I could not carry his weight, and he fell on me.

Down we went, onto his bed. My belly was cold and sticky from my cum on his messy, wet sheets. I gasped again as he slowly pulled out. He turned me over to face him, spooning and hugging me so tightly that I could hardly breathe.

Kissing him softly on his lips, he saw tears crossing over the bridge of my nose and trailing down the side of my eye. He caught one with his fingertip and looked worried.

"Did I hurt you?"

"No, I'm fine. Just tears of joy." He kissed my tears away. I was smiling at my lusty, sexy Italian. Nothing in my life made me as happy as seeing him happy, and right now, my Darling was fucking elated!

I closed my eyes and breathed him in, tattooing his sweet scent of sex and Dior into my very soul. I savored every second with him as if the world were ending and this was the last time we would *play* together.

Euphoria flowed from my mouth. "Wow! You're so fucking amazing! So incredibly sexy! God, I love how you fuck!"

He smiled proudly, and his face beamed as if he had just won an Olympic gold medal. I felt so cherished and secure as he enveloped me in his strapping arms! He looked deeply into my eyes—with those gorgeous, mesmerizing, soft brown eyes of his—awash in sexual bliss.

He traced kisses from my eyelids to my nose and lips ever so softly. Our mouths opened, our tongues met, and gently, they intertwined. Never had I ever been closer to him than right now. He didn't need to say anything. I saw it in his eyes. I melted at the way he looked at me.

Connected, here in this moment, I felt his love in his tender kiss.

II
LOST

Monday, June 3, 2019

Sunrise. A bright, golden beam of light streamed through a window, illuminating the dust, which glinted like diamonds. It was so bright that it pierced my eyelids, startling me awake. In my arms was a sight equally penetrating as I basked in the delight that last night was real—not a dream.

My bare leg lay folded over his hairy thighs, and my cheek rested on a pillow of his left breast. While my arm draped across his chest, my fingertips felt compelled to brush the soft, fine hairs carpeting it. While gazing into his beautiful, gentle face, I noticed one of his gorgeous eyes was open.

We were the only two in his apartment, yet I whispered, "Good morning, Darling. You look so peaceful. I didn't mean to wake you so early, especially after our rather energetic evening!"

He smiled and hugged me with his sculpted biceps wrapped in blue and green Celtic bands. A vivid contrast to my ivory skin pressed against him.

"It's hard to sleep next to you and not want to touch you."

"No problem," he said. "I sleep so soundly that not even an earthquake can wake me."

His comedic comment made me laugh.

"Breakfast, then?" I inquired as my fingers walked across his stomach.

"Too early!" he groaned. "We Italians aren't big on breakfast."

"Come to think of it, you guys say *pranzare*—to lunch and *cenare*—to dinner, but how interesting that there's no Italian verb for *to breakfast!*"

He roared with laughter. "It's *fare la collazione*—to make breakfast."

"*Grazie, Professore Romano!* And that's quite a mouthful, but it's not its own unique verb!"

"Another funny observation about life from my one and only, Sabi!" That endearing sound of his laughter melted my heart and filled it with joy.

"Thank you!" I blushed. "I love how you make me feel so special. And to spoil you, shall I pop into the cafe downstairs and get you an espresso? I hear you drink ten cups a day!" His ability to consume coffee forever astounded me.

"Stay here with me." Even his half-sleepy bedroom eyes beseeched me not to go.

"Of course!" I rolled on top, straddling him, embracing his whole body, tucking my hands underneath his neck, and nestling my head below his whiskered chin.

"I wish I didn't have to go," I said with a lump in my throat as I spied my packed valise in the corner of the room by the doorway.

He combed the stray hairs caught between my lips, gently caressing my face. "I love..." he hesitated. His eyes were misty. "That you came to visit me twice already since I moved here six months ago."

I lovingly kissed his tender lips, then smiled naughtily. "There are still two hours before I have to catch my ride."

He mimicked the same naughty smile. "What do you have in mind, Sabayon?"

Stretching each minute of our remaining hours together, we swam in the warm sea of our passion and need for each other.

11:00 am

I HATED goodbyes and missed my lover already. Sitting in the Italo First Class train compartment on my way to catch a plane home, I stared outside the windows; the urban sprawl was becoming more rural as the locomotive sped away from Milan, leaving my heart sad and empty. Unwilling to sever our connection entirely, I reached out to him with my fingers by sending him a text.

SABINA

Hello Darling!

GIANMARCO

Ciao Sabi!!

> You were fan-fucking-tastic this morning and last night, all night long!

😏

> Are you at work now?

Not yet

> I'm curious

> Which do you love more, soccer or music?

> Let's say you could only have one

> Which would you choose? 😇

You know that football is my passion

Even more so than

> Sex? 😏

You're too funny

Music

I was typing MUSIC

You're sooo bad Sabayon

> Yes, I know

> I heard a rumor

> You like bad girls that do naughty
>
> Dirty things to you and with you
>
> In bed

🩶🩶🩶

> Even when I'm bad
>
> I know you forgive me
>
> And love me anyway 😇

😳

> Spank your messy Sabayon some more

You're lucky I'm not on the train with you now

I would do that and more

> I always want MORE with you
>
> Crave what I can't have
>
> I want you
>
> All of you
>
> Even though I know I shouldn't
>
> That's why I'm so bad
>
> So incorrigible

> Because your incorrigible ASS would be mine right now!!!

> I'm excited dripping just thinking about you fucking me HARD

> Show me !!! 😜

I gasped and giggled. A passenger glanced at me with disapproving, suspicious eyes.

> God, how I want to do that for you

> But I'm on public transit

> I could get arrested for indecent exposure

> Do you want me to be an outlaw by giving the stranger on the train opposite me a peepshow?

> Of me playing with my erect nipples poking through my shirt

> Shoving my hand under my skirt

> Pushing my wet panties to the side

> Fingering myself so I can sext you pictures?

> I love outlaws!!! 😈 💚

> You're out of control!

> Ahahaha

> What's so funny?

> Look at my Facebook profile pic

I booted up the Facebook app, and there he was, wearing a blue button-down shirt, staring into the screen, smirking with his comment, *la faccia dell'ingestibile.*

> OMG! What a perfect picture!

> Ahahaha

> You do have the face of the unmanageable!

> But… you're really FUN!

> Yes I am

> Not sure how I'll manage away for so long

> Without you

> Then come back!!!!

> I wish I could

> Because I miss you already

> In the bathroom 😊

> Show me how much your wet pussy misses me

> So demanding!

SHOW ME, PLEASE!!!

I miss la mia bella figa

♥♥♥♥♥♥♥

It was endearing how he called my beautiful pussy, *la mia bella figa.*

I glanced down the corridor, seeing a long line of passengers waiting to use the toilet.

> There's quite a queue for the toilet
>
> I can't sext you there
>
> It's so bumpy on the train
>
> At best I'll be able to send you one fuzzy picture before the other passengers start banging on the door wondering what the fuck I'm doing inside

Ahahaha

You and I are loud when we cum

They'll know

> Exactly!
>
> You know that YOU are the only one that has that effect on me!

> Besides, you were just breaking my drenched pussy less than an hour ago

> Your figa looks the same

> Red and swollen and dripping with lust

> Getting hot and bothered

> Fantasizing about grinding against you right now

> My sexy thing!

> Next time make a video or take pictures

> As many as you like

You wanna make a sex tape with me???? 😏

> I have no limits with you

> I trust you 🖤

🖤

> Oh, and send me a copy

> So I can watch us again and again and again

> 😇

Ahahaha

> When will we see each other again you and me???

I don't know

But I want to see you again too

So much

> My dick is big for you now!!

Show me!!

He immediately messaged me a delectable dick pic, the head of his cock glistening with his pre-cum.

🤍🤍🤍

Wow! What a thing of beauty!

I never tire of seeing Gran-Marco!

I can almost taste you

How I miss my favorite

Love love love your big bold beautiful cock!

I haven't even left Lombardy

Yet I feel like jumping off at the next station and taking the first train back to you to fuck your brains out

My phone rang, making me jump in my seat.

I hardly ever answered my mobile, usually letting it lapse into voicemail. I was terrible with telephone calls and even worse on live video chats. Cyril joked that if he were dying on the side of the road, I would be the last person he called for help because he could guarantee I wouldn't pick up, even if it was a life-or-death emergency.

It was weird that I preferred texting or email because it gave me time to reflect before answering. But I couldn't ignore Gianmarco since he knew I was online, so I accepted the video call.

"Hello?" I reflexively answered, even though I knew who was calling.

"Sabayon, keep talking like that, and I'm gonna ruin both our plans."

"How so?"

"Have you thought that maybe they don't need you at home as much as you think?"

I wondered where my lover was going with his loaded question and became suddenly aware of my thumping heart. "Are you saying *you* need me more, Gianmarco?"

"Can't you stay a little longer?"

"And what am I supposed to do about my husband? Or, did you forget I'm already married?" Remembering Kally, I swallowed hard, feeling guilty. "My child needs her mother."

"Yes, Kally needs her mamma's love; but I'm not asking for forever."

"Tell me you need me and want me more!" I studied his eyes intensely, waiting for confirmation and craving him to crave me.

"Sabayon, you're the one who has forgotten when you gave yourself to me. You did so already, belonging to another man. Can't you see how haunted I am by you?"

"You're haunted?" His revelation caught me off guard.

"Yes!" he said. "With your every breath, rising and falling, I think about you all the time."

His hand reached for my face on the screen as if to place a wayward tendril behind my ear.

"When I run my fingers through your long, dark hair, I confess that I have terrible thoughts of accidents that could befall your husband... so you can be free."

Gazing into my eyes, it was as though I could feel him raising my chin with his two fingers beneath my jaw.

"I look at your delicate face with your soft sleeping smile and wonder, am I just an escapist distraction for a season? Or do you need rescuing and shelter from a loveless life?"

His poetic sincerity was surprising yet unmistakable. I rested my hand upon my cheek, imagining I was leaning it into my poet's palm, aching to touch him.

"Or, perhaps you are waiting for a grand romantic gesture to convince yourself to follow your heart's desire rather than your obligations?"

His introspective tone seemed different. I had become accustomed to his fun flirting and bold innuendos that hung in the air between us as thick and juicy as ripe Montepulciano d'Abruzzo grapes hanging on the vine. But instead, my beautiful, brave knight was exhibiting cracks in his armor. Was I hearing insecurity in his words for the first time, or was there something more?

Moved by his words, I reached for my earlobe and rubbed it, wishing he were kissing and nibbling me there.

"Oh, Gianmarco! I adore you—no, it is beyond adoration—I'm addicted to you! Your baritone voice thrills my ears and casts a spell over me. I love the way your broad hands hold me as though I were a delicate honeysuckle, tipping me into your mouth to have as big or as little a sip of my nectar as you like."

Licking my lips, I threw him a wicked look, imagining I was sending my playful hand to his waistband to explore *more*. "You have the body of a god! To me, you are—"

"Your sex toy. That's what I am to you! Am I right? An Italian stallion you keep in your stable until you have the urge to ride me again—every three fucking months! You say you want *more* with me! *Well?*"

I couldn't believe it. He was sore and jealous, revealing a layer of desperation I did not expect. "Well, aren't *I* your sex toy?" I threw the question back at him. "I've never asked you directly if you had other lovers, since we're more like friends with benefits. But am I not only one of the many mares you stud in your stable?"

Silence followed his heartfelt and wounded words. It was a pregnant pause, but who would birth the terms of our reconnection? I didn't know.

"Darling, I love being with you, but it seems I'm the forward one in this relationship, chasing you. Maybe I wasn't paying attention, but I didn't realize how deeply you felt about me. I'm sorry if I've hurt you; truly, I am. But, to be fair, you knew this was the situation. I care about you and appreciate you so much, but my home is with my husband and daughter. I was honest and transparent from the beginning."

I heard those words as I said them, but they sounded hollow because, the fact was, ignoring him was impossible. He wasn't one of many; Gianmarco was the only one I was in love with. Still, I didn't say those three little words now because I didn't want to scare him off by coming across as desperately affectionate or too needy, even though that was precisely what I was.

But I loved *playing* with him, especially after so many years of neglect in my sexless marriage—I needed him. Yet I could see how unlikely a confirmed Italian bachelor and a much older married American woman with a small child could work.

My head was spinning in confusion. Young, sexy, naturally flirty, and spoiled for choice for sexual partners, why would he choose me? Had he met someone else at his restaurant, turning this all around, hoping to spook me and push me to disengage with him?

He was quiet. Too quiet. I felt he was lining up his conscience to cut me loose.

"You're a devil! Do you know that?" I snapped back at him. "Don't think I don't see what you're up to! You want to send me off feeling crushed and guilty on top of being heartsick and wild for you!" My jealousy and insecurity were rising to the surface. If he was burning with rage, now, so was I.

"In reality, you're saying all this to trade me in so you can be free of me and frolic with other women. Party with a plethora of long-legged, double-D cleavaged paramours half my age!"

The air hung heavy and tense in the vast space between our phones. I could hear him breathing on the other end of the call, but he offered no words while I swallowed sobs.

Finally, he cleared his throat and spoke in a raspy, scorched-throat rumble. "If that's what you believe, then you don't know me. I've misjudged you and acted the fool. Go home."

My jaw sagged. "What?" My heart was in my throat, my shoulders shook, and tears welled in my eyes. "Darling, perhaps I could take the next train back and steal a few—"

"No, Sabina. There is nothing left to say. Go home to your husband and forget me as soon as you cross the border. Just as you had planned."

The line went dead, and he was gone.

Whiplashed, I couldn't make heads or tails of what had

happened. I had gone from having my cake and eating it to nothing but crumbs left on my plate in the snap of a finger.

The only thing I knew was that I had hurt the love of my life, and the stress of being responsible for another person's pain left me sapped of energy and my heart heavy. I rubbed my temples to dull the pounding migraine. Closing my eyes, I lay my head against the cool glass windowpane, praying for absolution.

As we began pulling away from the next station, the deep lullaby hum of the electric train lulled me to relief.

* * *

12
RESCUE ME

"Antonio!" Gianmarco bellowed into his phone while tapping his feet nervously on the tiles. "Pick up the damn call!"

Still half-asleep from an afternoon nap, his younger brother answered the phone with one hand, wiping the sleep from his eyes with the other.

"Gianma?" he asked in a raspy voice. "Is that you, bro?"

"Listen, I don't have time to explain, but I need your help."

Antonio sat up, fully awake. He could count the number of times his older brother asked to bail him out on one finger; the direct plea was serious.

"Does cousin Mario still run that dealership?"

"Of course. Why?"

"Good! I'm running out of time. Tell him it's a family emergency; say whatever you need to, but I need a fast ride. NOW!"

"Gesù Cristo! Gianma, is this for real?"
"Jesus Christ!"

"Sì! Ho bisogno di te, fratello mio."
"Yes! I need you, my brother!"

"I'll make the call. But they're all fast. Which one do you want?"

"The fastest! We don't have time to waste."

* * *

Leaving Milan not a half hour later, the brothers rocketed down the Autostrada A14, the powerful automobile pressing their backs into the custom leather seats as hard as they pushed ahead. Even if they ran all the horses in the blood-red Alfa Romeo Giulia Quadrifoglio, hitting its top speed of 191 mph, the brothers would be hard-pressed to intercept her.

Flipping the finger-toggle gear shifter and dropping into fourth, Antonio scanned the road ahead. "How much is Sabina ahead of us?"

Gianmarco glanced at his watch. The exquisite timepiece from Sabina ticked away. The mahogany calf leather straps held the bronze case snugly against his skin. Its face, a galvanic, anthracite sunray dial, showed clearly through the sapphire crystal lens. As much grief as he had given Sabi over her spoiling him with her generosity, his love of fine timepieces made this a gift he couldn't refuse.

Congestion was building, and at the turn toward the bridge, they saw a line of red brake lights flickering.

"We have no choice, Antonio. We have to try the country roads. Look at the snarl of traffic ahead!"

Antonio gripped the steering wheel and exhaled fiercely. "If we miss her in Lombardy?"

"Then on to Tuscany!" A determined look sat on Gianmarco's face. "We'll chase her to Sicily if we have to—Now, GO!"

Shifting gears, the younger brother veered the luxury sedan onto the A14's right shoulder and shot straight to the next exit.

From the outskirts of Milan to Florence, the route would take a typical driver about three hours on back roads and crosscuts. However, Antonio the Naval Aviator, wasn't a regular driver, and this Alfa Romeo wasn't an ordinary car.

* * *

Sabina sat by the window seat, soaking up Italy's stunning landscape. Though she was moving toward her necessary destination of California via Florence, Rome, Naples, and finally Sicily, Sabina's heart remained behind in Milan.

Leaving this beautiful country full of stately vineyards and villas, friendly, passionate people, and her Italian love pulled tears from her heart.

Much of the landscape was familiar to Sabina, having summered for several seasons in Italy with her husband, Cyril. The couple had decided to make Italy their second permanent residence, which was why she was there in the first place.

Cyril had put her in charge of finding an Italian palazzo to restore. Purchasing one was not as simple as it would seem. Still, building on Italian soil was a nightmare of a quagmire from which Sabina had yet to extricate herself. At the end of this bittersweet sojourn, Sabina was returning home to California empty-handed and barren-hearted from abandoning her lover.

A dilemma greater than her house-hunting now lay in her lap. Her husband sent her to find them a home where they could enjoy the second half of their marriage together. Instead, Sabina had charged into a romance that might be the love of her life.

The truth of the affair became more apparent to her with each passing mile. What began as pure physical attraction, which she had pursued rather wantonly that first night at Mirabella, had turned into something more. She was sure her Italian stallion felt the same way, making this sudden separation even more bittersweet.

* * *

Closing her eyes, she drifted off to sleep, her mind replaying the sugary and savory memories of being his. The lulling, rocking motion of the train lowered her mind into a trance of the lust she had been swimming in since giving herself to the dashing sommelier in his restaurant bathroom.

It was all a rolling highlight reel of erotica. His mouth sucked and teased her lips; his large hands cloaked her small breasts while his agile fingers pinched and rolled her hard, tingling nipples. His signature scent, Dior Homme, was tinged with his manly perspiration, and the lingering aromas of a decadent kitchen steamed into his skin. And finally, his big, beautiful, pulsating cock!

Moans escaped Sabina's pursed lips as she slumbered in dreams of sexual bliss. Her hand moved on its own accord as she shifted in her seat. Hidden inside her jacket, she slipped her manicured fingers beneath the waistband of her skirt, coaxing their way down until they rested over her panty-less entrance.

A small tuft of fur kept neat and trimmed was the crown overtop her jewel. And so she dreamt on—her fingers feathered her clitoris and labia, their tips dripping with nectar—Sabina's sex had a memory bank of its own. Blissfully, she relived the sensation of being stretched wide open, filled deep, and fucked by her lover's thick, meaty cock.

How willingly she let her paramour handle her like a desperate whore. So happy was she to take his pounding and thrusting and be an eager vessel to drink in every drop of his luscious cream.

Muscle spasms shot through Sabina's thigh, jolting her ass off the seat as the dream memory delivered Gianmarco's loving discipline, punishing her for being a marvelous slut for his cock and rewarding her for being a dedicated and attentive lover.

Sabina giggled in her sleep, overcome with happiness. Her mind's eye watched her Italian hunk, smiling like a boy winning first prize. She begged and rejoiced for his cum to cover her body and adorn her head like a crown. Sabayon was his queen, and she made sure Gianmarco felt like a king.

When an elegant silver-haired lady took the vacant seat opposite, she could not have imagined that this lovely, demure, equally elegant, younger woman, fast asleep in the chair across her, was in the throes of ecstasy—lost in the lucid dreams of being a willing submissive for a handsome Italian man and his thick, velvety, mouth-watering cock.

As the woman watched the princess' legs twitch, hips bucking in the seat, she could not have known the scenes Sabina's mind was replaying—the act of having her thighs tossed open, her lover's teeth clamped around her nipples, and his wonderful, throbbing cock slowly opening her tight, tender, succulent rosebud.

The newly seated traveler was ready to shake Sabina by the shoulder to rouse her when the daydreaming lass shifted and rolled over, exposing her cute little bum. Smiling with shock, the woman turned to look away as the siren's skirt rode up. Revealed was a bare bottom and a hand nestled between her legs, with three glistening fingers stroking her own pussy.

Shaking her head, the voyeur mused, "I've heard of sleep-

walking, but I've never witnessed sleep fucking yourself." Nevertheless, this raven-haired lovely was clearly in dreamland, and whoever she was with was giving her rapturous attention.

With the steamy sex show and the sun blasting through the window, the temperature was rising in the cozy train compartment. The woman looked on as Sabina moaned and licked her lips; mouth wet and open in supplication; tongue darting and flicking in and out as if reaching for an imaginary, forbidden fruit floating invisibly just in front of her angelic face.

Aroused, the older woman couldn't help but run her tongue across her own lips. Stealthily, she unbuttoned her trousers, eased her zipper down, and, behind the shelter of her oversized purse, slipped a finger down over her own dripping pussy. Tracing slow circles over her nub, she masturbated while watching the sleeping beauty fuck herself to a dream-soaked orgasm.

After both women enjoyed a sweet, sexual climax, Sabina's breathing calmed, and the older lady adjusted the vixen's clothes to cover her. Then she joined the satisfied, smiling princess in an afternoon nap as the train rolled on toward the next stop—Florence.

* * *

"Signora, your ticket, please?" asked the conductor.

Sabina had woken only minutes before the train slowed to a stop. She hadn't expected any issues or delays, even though Italy was famous for running on a schedule sometimes void of reason.

With the conductor leaning on the back of the bench, Sabina dutifully dug into her purse to produce her paper ticket, fully anticipating a courteous apology for the disturbance after she handed it to the young attendant. Her fare was to carry her to the ferry and then to the last stop in Sicily.

His amiable smile dropped as he checked her slip.

Sabina held her hand out for her proof, but when nothing touched her outstretched palm, she looked up.

"Would you come with me, please?" he asked.

"Go with you—where?" she asked.

"Signora, you have reached your destination. Your luggage will be waiting for you on the platform."

"What!" Sabina answered in shock. "There must be some mistake. I paid for passage to Sicily!"

"No. I'm sorry, signora," he said. "If you like, you can extend your journey at the Customer Service desk."

Puzzled and more than put out, Sabina snatched back the stub. Her eyes shot to the block letters naming the destination. The conductor seemed correct; her passage ended at Florence.

Still trying to straighten it out in her head, she followed the conductor to the end of the car. Graciously, she accepted his hand as he assisted her from the train.

"How long before this train departs? I need time to sort this mess out to continue to my final destination."

"But, of course, you will have much time since the next train to Sicily leaves at 7:00 am; you should arrive by dinnertime tomorrow."

"Tomorrow!" Sabina put her hands on her hips. "We have a problem. I need to be in Sicily by tonight!"

The conductor shrugged as his smile disappeared. "You have money for a taxi and a hotel. No problem." With a curt bow, he added, "But this train, she will go on without you."

Without giving her a chance to argue, the man turned on his heel and vanished. Sabina sighed, resigned that she had either made a foolish error or been swindled; both were possibilities.

Still, she had to admit that, with her head in the clouds and her legs in the air for most of the tryst with her illicit lover, Sabina was surprised she hadn't booked passage to Timbuktu.

***

A voice, heavy with Italian inflection, called from behind. "Scusami, signora. I hav-a your bag, yes?"
"Excuse me, madam."

When she turned to aim her ire at the next person to rub her up the wrong way, she gasped and stood with her mouth agape, utterly speechless.

Wearing a victorious grin, Gianmarco stood, holding her valise.

The sound of the speaker blaring the final announcement for the Milan-bound train drowned out any words they might have said. Suddenly, Sabina was startled for the second time by the sight of a man rushing toward them.

Huffing and puffing breathlessly, Antonio clasped his big brother's hand and warned, "Listen, don't make cousin Mario hunt me down. You have until tomorrow night to bring her back, or we will both be walking with shorter legs!"

Antonio smiled and winked at Sabina. "I'm talking about the car, not you!" he said before bolting past them to board the train, ready to roll him back home.

Sabina approached her lover warily. Her mind was calculating how these two brothers could have pulled this off. First, smuggling themselves to Florence before her arrival, and next, getting her evicted from her seat. The answer could be only one thing, and from the very start of their affair, Sabina had asked, and he had sworn he was honest with her.

"Darling, I won't say I'm disappointed to see your gorgeous face again so soon, but I don't like to think that I'm looking at a liar," she said with an icy tone. "You told me your family has nothing to do with the Mafia!"

He smiled with a grin that could convince a Juventus fan to wear an Inter Milan jersey.* "You asked me if we're Mafioso, and I answered truthfully, no, we are not."

"So, how do you explain this? And don't you dare call me foolish or crazy by telling me that I only bought a ticket to Florence, or I'll smack you where you stand!"

Gianmarco regarded his fierce lover—this gorgeous, cultured, educated, married American woman with whom he had fallen haplessly in love. And much like the conductor, he shrugged his shoulders. "You don't need to be in the Mafia to stop a train and exchange a ticket with a sleight of hand—only a family who has been their lifelong neighbors."

Sabina tried valiantly to suppress her smile, but failed. Stepping toward her luggage-laden lover, Sabi raised herself on tiptoes to meet his mouth, delivering a soft kiss on his marvelously luscious lips.

"Darling, what if I had refused to get off the train or made such a fuss that I exposed the trickery being played and was allowed to go on to Sicily? Then what, signor Diavolo?"

"Mr. Devil?"

Pulling her into his chest, her wickedly sexy devil lover answered, "Ah, yes. Unfortunately, I understand the ferry to the island was having some mechanical issues this evening. I am afraid many angry travelers would have to spend an extra night on the mainland."

She smiled in wonder at her man.

---

* Juventus and Inter are rival football teams from Turin and Milan, respectively. Both teams are usually at the top of the Serie A League at one time or another. Gianmarco supports the International Milan Football Club, known as Inter/Inter Milan.

"Such is life, Sabayon. These things happen." He mirthfully licked the tip of her nose.

She giggled at his playful tone, forgiving his treachery with another kiss.

Hand in hand, they promenaded to his sleek, sexy Alfa Romeo. Before she could utter a word, he pulled her into his arms and took a deep, delicious taste of her mouth. "Let's hurry! We can talk over supper. I made reservations!"

* * *

Florence was a culinary mecca, with exquisite restaurants within a stone's throw in any direction, no matter where one stood. Sabina could easily have spent a week indulging her taste buds, savoring the tantalizing flavors, exploring the city's decadent Bacchanalian delights, and yet still have craved more.

Standing head over heels amidst this vibrant gastronomic scene, Osteria Firenze rose as a beacon of innovation. Renowned Michelin-starred guest chefs from across Italy showcased their dynamic contemporary menus, making it a place where gourmet excellence converged. Tonight, Osteria Firenze would become the first stop of their evening.

After selecting the tasting menu for the table, the pair swooned over their delicious first course: a lovely bowl of Almond and Olive Soup with Artichokes, Bergamot, and Juniper-scented Lobster. The unique combination of flavors, from the nuttiness of almonds to the brininess of olives, the sweet-earthiness of artichokes, the citrusy notes of bergamot, and the aromatic touch of juniper-scented lobster, presented a highly complex and layered taste experience.

Gianmarco was awed by the second course: Warm Salsify Salad with Prawns, Pine Nut Cream, and Smoked Mozzarella

Milk. The greenness of salsify, coupled with the sweet umami of the prawns, bathed in the pine nut sauce and infused with smoky undertones from the smoked mozzarella milk, created an intriguing mix of tastes and textures, perfectly balancing delicate and indulgent elements.

As they reveled in the chef's ingenious combinations, neither was willing to address the elephant in the room—Sabina's expected return to her husband in California.

Distracted, Gianmarco's eyes sparkled upon the arrival of the Lehengut Riesling Renano Alto Adige Val Venosta DOC, a minerally, bone-dry white wine from the northern Italian Trentino-Alto Adige region. This adventurous sommelier had heard about but not yet tried this exclusive, intensely floral, perfectly balanced wine, carrying notes of apricot, peaches, melon, and lemon peel.

For Sabina, the simplicity of the third course was mind-blowing: delicate capellini pasta simmered in a velvety porcini broth, garnished with unctuous, golden-orange just-caught sea urchin uni, and sprinkled with marinara mussel powder. The melange offered a taste of the ocean so fresh and clean it was hardly there, leaving nothing on the tongue but an idea of the sea followed by a shadow of rainforest treasures.

Then came Gianmarco's turn to indulge in the next course: Salami Tortellini in Saffron Cream, Pistachio, and Chamomile. The splendid pasta pillows, adorned with pistachios, gently floated over a pool of floral saffron-chamomile cream. This exquisite dish brought together the richness of the filled pasta and the fragrant nuances of the delicate sauce, creating a captivating harmony of flavors.

The finale was the chef's homage to her mother's Southeast Asian heritage: Sautéed Lumache on Polenta Cream with Chicory and Coconut Sauce. This startling fusion combined the *sweet, earthy flavors of the delicate snails with the creamy texture of polenta, juxtaposed against the bitterness of chicory. The addition of a coconut sauce introduced a tropical and slightly sweet element, enhancing the blended complexity of this bold yet subtle offering. The incorporation of gastropods added a surprisingly whimsical touch for gastronomists.*

By the end of their main courses, neither worried about anything other than the promise of an early morning stroll to explore the city and climb to the top of Cattedrale di Santa Maria del Fiore's dome, where they would be rewarded with breathtaking panoramic views that stretched over the picturesque rooftops of Florence. From this vantage point, they could see landmarks such as the Palazzo Vecchio and the Arno River.

Astonishingly, packed to the gills with no room for more, Sabina and Gianmarco opted to skip the desserts. However, they agreed that every one of the chef's creations did not disappoint in either artistry or execution.

Before the thoroughly sated pair departed, Gianmarco and his friend, the maitre d', kissed cheeks goodbye. He also gifted Sabina an elegant box of house-made chocolates, a sweet remembrance of the couple's unforgettable dining experience.

With their hearts brimming with anticipation, they bid farewell to Osteria Firenze, eager for the enchanting night that Gianmarco had assured Sabina was only the beginning. No matter how things turned out with her beloved, she felt like a girl again, awash in the tides of summer love.

As they stepped out onto the streets of Florence, the air was crisp and carried the faint scent of blooming giaggiolo, purple Florentine irises, growing wild along the banks of the Arno.

The moon hung high in the night sky, casting a soft glow over the cobblestone paths that lay ahead. Hand in hand, they laughed *and whispered as they wandered through narrow alleys, searching for their next destination.*

Gianmarco once again dazzled Sabina at the opulent and historical Palazzo del Marchese di Donatello. Their palace suite had them nestled in a room with the Arno River at their front and the Cathedral of Santa Maria at the rear.

Sabina gasped as she entered their ultra-romantic paradise for the night. She felt like Juliet when she jumped onto the mattress, bouncing on the trampoline of their four-poster curtained canopy bed. Draped and swathed in elegant ivory and baby blue gauze silk linens, it was a bed fit for royalty.

Gianmarco marveled amusedly at how beautiful and young-at-heart his fun-loving Sabi truly was.

Like on a balcony on high, she extended her hand, inviting her Romeo to join her silliness, and he did.

There, they lay side by side on the sumptuous silk covers, gazing at the ornate, blue-frescoed ceiling. At that moment, Sabina felt her heart soaring, sailing straight through the roof, flying with her beloved, and touching the brilliant Florentine sky above.

The night was still young, and so, in their soft-soled shoes, the pair of star-crossed lovers explored together the city by night, stumbling upon hidden piazzas adorned with ancient statues and vibrant flowers, where they disappeared into the labyrinthine Boboli Gardens behind the grand Palazzo Pitti.

Like teenagers immune to the laws of man and indifferent to the rules of nature, they dashed and giggled through the garden's winding paths. They dodged and laughed some more, chasing each other around the fountain of Bacchus, depicted riding a giant turtle, until they fell onto the grass and into each other's arms, exchanging stolen kisses and playful glances. Time seemed to stand still, and nothing else mattered except the love they shared.

Under the Tuscan moon, they coupled, their bodies bare and as beautiful as the marble sculptures populating the gardens, cherishing each other with as much reverence as those Roman antiquities.

Sabina and Gianmarco made love as timeless in its perfection as the 16th-century botanical oasis created by the Medici family at the peak of Italian artistic celebration.

As the night grew deeper, they found themselves by the riverbanks of the Arno, where the moon's reflection danced upon the water's surface. Listening to the gentle lapping of the river, he led her over the Ponte Vecchio Bridge as the final point on their tour—the fenced cage protecting the sculpture of Cellini, the famed Italian goldsmith. There, Gianmarco pressed a tiny key into Sabina's palm while slipping a padlock through the fence.

"Kiss me, Sabayon. When we close this and you throw the key into the river, it will lock our love forever."

Pausing their embrace, they latched the bolt to the fence, and with a bursting heart and eyes holding back tears of joy, Sabina turned the key to secure the lock. Staring into her beloved's brilliant eyes, she smiled and tossed the key over her shoulder. The quiet plop of the metal hitting the water bonded their love to one another forever.

I FELT a tap on my shoulder and opened my eyes to see a uniformed man standing over me. Startled, I was not on a bridge, embraced in my lover's arms, with the full moon staring down at us. Instead, I was ensconced in my train seat, with the sun streaming through the window. I stared up at the train conductor, shell-shocked and disoriented.

"Excuse me, where are we?" I asked.

"We've arrived at Stazione Firenze Santa Maria Novella."

"What?" I yelled in surprise. "I've only just arrived in *Florence!*"

I could feel the fatigue in my feet from traipsing around the city with my Italian guide. Yet here I was—seated on the train still.

Closing my eyes, I remembered our fight and recalled the line my lover told me when we first became intimate: *Io sono solo...*

I am lonely and alone...

I held back my tears, feeling that sentiment profoundly; I must not cry.

Craning my neck, I noted I was the last one left in the compartment.

"Yes, madam," the conductor replied, retrieving and handing over my valise from the overhead shelf. "Please, madam. You must leave now." He gestured toward the exit.

Still a bit shell-shocked, my feet refused to move.

A binging sound warned that the doors would soon close. The conductor raised his shoulders to his ears and chuckled. "Unless you intend to return to Milan with us?"

I shook my head while gathering my belongings. Then I thanked the conductor, who nodded farewell as I stepped onto the concrete platform.

Staring at the departing Milan-bound train, I pondered my next move. *Should I hop back on and surprise my lover in his apartment?* I checked my phone. No messages. *No, he would be at work by now. It's too late—for us.*

I forlornly cast my eyes down, hoping no one would notice my silent tears.

"It was only a dream, a fabulous fantasy. Not real." I lamented aloud as I followed the other travelers marching toward the terminal exit. In my heart of hearts, I wished the brothers had pulled that daring stunt to sweep me off my feet and rescue me.

Since it was much brighter outside the station, I donned my shades and waited for a cab to take me the last 2.5 miles to Florence Peretola Airport—a plane ride home to California awaited.

Suddenly, a sleek black Ducati pulled up to the curb.

"Need a ride?" asked the helmeted stranger in near-perfect English.

I smiled, recognizing the motorcycle and the deep, sexy Italian-inflected voice.

"You're crazy! What are you doing here?" I said, astonished at his bravado.

Gianmarco raised his visor. *"Sì, sono pazzo!"*
"Yes, I'm crazy!"

His playful, mesmerizing brown eyes sparkled at me. "Crazy for you!"

I laughed, remembering Marì, the pizzeria where we danced unabashedly on the sidewalk to that same-named song in front of other diners.

"Stay with me, Sabi. I need you!"

"But what do I say to my husband, who's waiting for me on the other end?"

"You know, Alitalia is perpetually late. Planes malfunction; flights get delayed and canceled at the last minute."

I giggled.

"Italians are constantly striking for one cause or another," he added.

We laughed together.

"A lot can happen in one day," he teased.

I grinned. "A lot can happen in a dream!"

He furrowed his brow as a perplexed expression crossed his face. "What?"

"I had one hell of a sexy dream about you on the train! It was so rich and vivid—I was sure it was real!"

"Oh yeah! Tell me."

"For some bizarre reason, I dreamt I was going home via Sicily, but you intercepted me at Florence."

He nodded and listened.

"You wanted to sweep me off my feet and rescue me like this, but you were driving an Alfa Romeo Giulia Quadrifoglio, a highly snazzy sports car."

"Wow! When you dream, you dream *BIG!*"

I stepped toward him, gazing into his gorgeous eyes. It was a wonder how they looked almost blue with the azure sky's reflection. "An angel must have inspired me, whispering sweet nothings into my ear." I winked at my love. Incredibly happy, I was laughing and smiling so much that my face hurt.

"Well, if I ever have to speed to rescue you again, I'll use that beast."

"Oh, and you took me to Osteria Firenze."

"Funny you should say that, Sabi. I know the sommelier there, and he owes me a favor. A huge one, and I'm gonna *collect* tonight."

"You're not a Mafioso, are you?" I whispered under my breath.

"Sabi, if I revealed my secret life to you, I'd have to kill you," he deadpanned.

"You're kidding, right?"

"Silly girl! Not every *ragazzo* is a *Mafioso!*"
"Not every *boy* is a *member of the Mafia!*"

Yet he smiled a naughty, knowing smile. I laughed nervously, not wanting to know.

He winked. "Plus, I kinda like you."

"*Like me!* Is that all you *feel* toward me?" I grinned, amused by his teasing.

"Yeah!" He smiled wickedly at me. "You're OK." He shrugged.

"You did all this and blew off your job because you *like me, and I'm OK?*" I said, feigning insult.

"Uh-huh!" He blushed, and now I smiled a knowing smile at him.

Just then, a taxi cab pulled up behind him and honked the horn. Gianmarco's bike was illegally parked in the taxi rank. Rude gestures and words were exchanged between the men.

Gianmarco held his extra helmet out to me, his eyes pleading.

I shook my head and smiled. How could I say *no* to my beloved? That word seems to have escaped my vocabulary where he was concerned. I grabbed the helmet, secured it on my head, and hopped on board to mount his bike from behind.

And then he rocketed us out of there!

Closing my eyes, I held tight, wrapped my arms around his broad chest, and pushed my pelvis against his firm ass. I leaned the side of my helmet against the back of his butter-soft, black leather moto jacket, infused with the scent of his favorite cologne.

"When you hung up on me, I thought I had lost you. God, how I've missed you, my Darling!"

He reached back to pat-pat the side of my butt with his leather-clad hand, and I knew he had forgiven all.

As we passed the Ponte Vecchio bridge, I asked him, "Do you have an extra lock?"

"A bike lock?" He shook his head, confused at my cryptic words. *"Non capito, amore."*
_{"I don't understand, love."}

I smiled, remembering my fabulous, impossible fairy tale of a dream.

And yet, it was not a dream. Perhaps now Gianmarco believed he was a knight as I told him he was.

"I love you!" I shouted at the top of my lungs, above the motorcycle engine's roar, because I wanted the universe to hear.

He laughed while yelling back his reply. "Yes, I know!" He didn't need to say it with words, but with his grand romantic gesture, I knew he loved me too.

CYRIL'S ASSIGNMENT

13

TURNING POINT

Almost three months later
Saturday, September 7, 2019
Sierra Mare
Point Reyes, California

Almost midnight. I soaked in my sensuous sanctuary, a white clawfoot tub full of warm water. The soap bubbles clung to my neck like a strand of iridescent Mikimoto pearls. Candle flames threw a sunset glow over the bathroom, and the sweet, honeyed aroma from the melting beeswax transported me to a beautiful memory of my lover, not so long ago. In that moment, aroused in my liquid cocoon, I touched myself the way he did, squeezing my submerged legs together as I sighed and wished he were here by my side.

Desiring a visual of him, I dried my hands on a white cotton towel draped over the edge of the bathtub before reaching for my phone. Scrolling through my gallery of photos, I found the racy pic he sent while I was on a train home. A guilty smile crept from the corner of my mouth. I must be more careful about hiding this incriminating evidence. It would be an abrupt end to my playtime if my husband were to stumble upon the truth—and probably my marriage. But I couldn't bring myself to delete these few priceless tokens. He was worth the risk.

Bing!

My heart jumped when I heard the familiar text alert on my messaging app. I glanced at the time; it was about eight o'clock in the morning, Milan time, and my Italian lover must have just awoken.

GIANMARCO
Ciao Sabi! 😘

SABINA
Good morning, Darling!
I was just thinking about you 😘

Me too

My brother Antonio is getting married

Come with me

I take it your whole family will be there?

Yes

Sounds rather intimidating

> No problem if you don't wanna go
>
> You know I 🩶 being with you, but…
>
> ????
>
> I'm scared
>
> Why????
>
> You know why
>
> Tell me
>
> Mamma
>
> I don't want to embarrass you
>
> Ever
>
> We need to talk
>
> CALL ME!!

My heart sank to my stomach when the phone rang for a video chat request before I even had a chance to reply. We primarily texted, so it must have been important for my lover to call me at home. Had it been any other time, it could have compromised our secret and my safety, but I decided to let it go. It had been so long since I had heard his lovely voice, and I would hate to upset him.

"Hey, Sabi," he said while gnawing the side of his thumbnail with his front teeth.

The bathroom was cavernous, and sounds echoed against

the hard marble surfaces. To not awaken anyone, I whispered, "Good morning, Darling. It's always good to see you."

He squinted as he peered into his screen. "Where are you? It looks dark there."

I placed my index finger over my lips and answered in hushed tones. "Shh, everyone's asleep, and I'm taking a relaxing bath before heading to bed."

His whole face beamed as he tried to contain his booming excitement by speaking in a quiet voice. "Mmm, I wish I could join you, Sabayon!"

"You did!" I giggled. "Well, in my head. But I wish you were here in person. Care to *play* with me, Darling? I miss you!"

"Me, too, which is why I was so excited to ask you to come with me when I found out about a wedding in my family."

I could have been coy and toyed with him, but he looked so earnest.

"Thank you. I love that you thought of me. But is it *wise* to introduce me to your family at such a special event?"

"Sabina, are you ashamed to be seen with me?" He furrowed his brow as my question bristled his ego. "Because I am not ashamed. Not of you, not of us."

I sat up in the tub. "Not at all. Walking arm in arm with you on an adventure is one of my favorite things to do." I hoped my tender words would reassure him.

He shook his head in confusion at my reluctance. "Then, what is it?"

"Your parents have such sway over you. What if they find out I'm married?"

I tilted my head to one side and stroked my phone screen as though it were his cheek—tears pooled in my eyes. I couldn't forget a friend's warning that all affairs have expiration dates. "I don't want to lose you. Not yet."

"Ah!" he sighed, finally understanding my insecurity. "You're worried Mamma will not approve."

"Of course, I'm worried!" I whisper-shouted. My eyes instinctively swept to the door. Cyril was not a deep sleeper, but luckily, his bedroom was far from my bathroom, so I continued, "Her gorgeous, talented, charming son has himself wrapped up in an affair with an older, *married* woman! Mothers disapprove of that sort of thing, believe me!"

"Remember when I told you at Marì how I love my family, but we don't always get along?"

I nodded.

He gave me a guilt-ridden smile. "Well, I don't always listen to their advice."

I shook my head. "Even if it's for your own good?"

"I want you, regardless of what they think."

"But I would never want to cause problems. Family is too important to you, Darling."

"Italians are passionate people; fighting is in our blood. But we always kiss and make up afterward." He laughed.

I bit my lip, still unsure. "I'm afraid I may be walking into a lion's den."

"So, who do you think will be at your side?"

His gentle tone soothed my flighty nature. My anxious body relaxed, and my shoulders lowered in reassurance. "You."

"If you keep hanging out with me, you're gonna bump into them at some point. Anyway, at weddings, everyone is on their best behavior."

I laughed; his voice and calm confidence charmed me once again.

"Come with me to Sicily! It will be fun and exciting. Go on an adventure with me! Please?"

"I'm afraid it will be too exciting!"

We chuckled together.

"Let's behave around my family and in my world. Afterward, we'll go wild in yours. Just the two of us, however you like—no limits."

"Hmm," I said with an impish smile. "Do you mean I'm allowed to spoil you or surprise you in any way I please?"

He pointed a scolding finger at me. "Sabi, you promised!"

"Are you aware that my motto is *wretched excess is barely enough?*"

Like an upturned pendulum, he oscillated a finger of disapproval. *Tick-Tock, Tick-Tock.* "Remember, no extravagant gifts."

"Only a moderate amount of excess." I pinched an imaginary inch with my thumb and forefinger. "Enough to have some good, clean fun, like in this bathtub with me right now." I wiped the bubbles off my chest and flashed him my soapy pair.

He roared with joy. "How I love your boobs!"

I giggled when he put his paw out and scrunched it like he was squeezing one of my breasts in midair.

"Thank you, Darling!"

Now, he was the one suddenly wearing a naughty smile. "But... I prefer messy, dirty fun with you."

I blew him a kiss. "I bet you do, you sexy thing!"

"Ahahaha!"

"So, when is your brother's wedding?"

"Autumn. Mid-October."

"Where? In your hometown?"

"No, Sicily."

"Oh." I pouted, remembering he had rejected my invitation to be my guest in Sicily not so long ago. Searching for another excuse, I said, "I was looking forward to attending a soccer match with you in the fall."

Ever the consummate salesman, he knew how to sweeten

the pitch. "No problem. Football season runs until May. More time to play with me later in Milan."

We both knew the hard truth of my situation. "Unfortunately, I can't actually run away with you whenever I want, though I realize I make it seem that way. I can only get away once every few months, and even then, I have to convince Cyril of the urgency for me to go." But I hated to disappoint Gianmarco; he had such a hangdog expression. "Are you *sure* you want me there with you?" I gracefully offered him one last chance to back out.

Gianmarco placed his hand on his heart like an honest scout. "Absolutely, yes! I wouldn't have asked you if I didn't want you to go with me." His kind words warmed my heart.

His mood turned, and suddenly, he was playful, sticking his tongue out, panting like a canine, and pulling an angelic puppy dog face, instantly melting my resolve. The only thing missing from the picture was a happily wagging tail.

I placed a hand over my lips to stop from laughing out loud.

Then he grinned at me. "We always have fun in the end."

"In the end!" I repeated, rolling my eyes at him.

He flashed me his gorgeous, irresistible, wicked grin. "My favorite place!"

"I could pinch your cheek, Darling." I met his double entendre and raised him.

"Oh? Yes, Sabi, but which one?" He winked.

I lowered my eyes and blushed. "You know I can't say *no* to you."

"YES!" He pumped his fist in the air as if Inter Milan had just scored a goal.

To confirm we had sealed the deal, *Sir* spoke with a gentle dominance, his words landing somewhere between a question and a command. "Meet me in Sicily."

Titillated, I submitted willingly. "I will be at your side, *Sir*."

"Good girl, Sabayon." He smiled joyously, ear to ear. "I can't wait!" He kissed two fingers and placed them on his screen. "Good night and sweet dreams."

With a press of my lips to my screen, I bid him adieu. "Have a good day! Talk soon!"

Sweet dreams were on the horizon for me tonight.

Knock-knock!

It was my husband's morning wake-up call.

Half-awake, I rubbed the sleep out of my eyes with the back of my hand. "Hello, Cyril."

"Good morning, Sabina."

"Mmm, it's Sunday!" I whined as he threw the curtains open to let in the sun.

"The early bird gets the worm!"

"I'd rather be the second mouse that gets the cheese!" I put a pillow over my head, trying to block out the oppressive sun.

"Wake up, sleepy head. I have to talk to you about something important—about Italy."

A pulse of terror made my heart skip a beat as I wondered if I had been found out. I took a deep breath and smiled innocently at him, trying not to show my guilt.

Even on Sunday, my husband was dressed in his tweed jacket and slacks with a crisp white cotton dress shirt, his *casual* attire when he worked from home on the weekends. He said it put him in a business mindset.

It was the difference between us. Cyril was a strategic planner who embraced organization and tidiness. My husband made his bed as soon as he rose. Mine stayed rumpled for days. I was happy ignoring anything resembling structure, preferring to lounge around the house all day in my silk dressing gown if I had the chance.

"I just got an email from our Italian architects. Given my requirements, they located three prime properties they wanted me to consider. When can you return to Italy to view them?"

"Family trip?" I nonchalantly inquired.

"Strictly business, a few days at most. Plus, Kally has school."

"Pre-school. She might find the trip exciting and educational," I offered. Kally had not seen Gianmarco in a while, and she made him a gift I was supposed to send to him; it would be fun for her to hand it to him and be together again, even for just a few days.

"You can handle this scouting expedition on your own," he said, shrugging off my veiled excitement.

"Fine," I said as calmly as I could muster, though I was beaming inside. "Let me check my calendar." The one I had to check was my lover's work schedule, since I would hopefully be seeing him sooner than planned.

Cyril was about to exit my bedroom when he turned and added, "One property has a vineyard next to Ventimiglia's. It's on the small side—a postage stamp-sized lot—and quite expensive for what it is. But maybe we can acquire the adjacent lots over time."

"OK, I'll look for a flight now." I pulled my laptop from under my bed and opened it to text Gianmarco.

SABINA

Hello, Darling!

How are you?

GIANMARCO

Ciao Sabi! I'm good

You and my Little Pink Kitten?

> We're great
>
> But I'm excited

Oh yeah?

Tell me

> I have a surprise for you

Surprise?

> Want to see me again next week?

HELL YES!!!

When and where?

> How about next Sunday?
>
> Meet me in Pescara?

I would ride 5 hours straight from Milan to see you for even 1 hour!!

> WOW! Now that's dedication
>
> LOL. But I'm hoping for more than one hour 😁

Ahahaha

> Is my Little Pink Kitten joining us?
>
> I miss her

She misses you lots and lots

But unfortunately, no

> What's happening next weekend?

Cyril is sending me back alone to look at 3 properties in Abruzzo but I don't like to drive since I get lost easily

Can you come with me?

> Of course
>
> Yes I would love to drive & cum with you 😇

LOL. You're so funny, sweetheart

Thank you for being there for me

> No problem

Meet me at the hotel where we had Kally's birthday breakfast

> I know the one
>
> But I have to leave by mid-morning on Tuesday to work the dinner shift

> Won't you be dog tired after driving so much?

Nah, I love riding my bike!

> I'm so excited to see you again!

Me too!

> Talk soon

I emailed our architects to arrange a meeting with the realtor to see the properties one week from Monday. Within minutes, I received a reply confirming a morning appointment at their office. Overcome with sheer joy at the thought of seeing my Italian lover again, I immediately booked a ticket to Pescara Abruzzo Airport for Sunday evening, texting him the details of our rendezvous.

GIANMARCO
🤍

He instantly replied.

14

A PLACE FOR US

One week later
Sunday, September 15, 2019
Incanto Hotel
Pescara, Italy

Standing on the balcony of my hotel room, sipping a tall glass of cool, sparkling mineral water, I eagerly awaited my lover's return. Gazing out to the horizon, I watched as the golden glow of daylight gradually faded. A breathtaking display of warm, fiery-red and vibrant orange hues streaked the evening sky—Nature's stunning masterpiece painted against the endless blue backdrop of the Adriatic Sea.

In that moment, I felt a sense of liberation, dressed in the lightest, softest baby blue cotton sundress adorned with delicate white polka dots. It swayed gently in the sea breeze, mirroring my newfound freedom. Venturing to Italy to be with Gianmarco renewed my spirit; to match my fresh and excited mood, I indulged in new lingerie sets.

Tonight, I chose a black and gold push-up quarter bra with a band of metallic mesh stretched teasingly tight over my perky nipples. I knew they would not remain chained for long once I was in his embrace, but I yearned to present him with something tantalizingly novel, exclusively for his eyes only.

Knock-knock-knock!

My heart fluttered happily at the sound of knuckles rapping on wood. I peered through the spy hole and flung the door to our room wide open.

"Gianmarco!" I shrieked with exuberance.

He dropped his satchel, seamlessly catching me mid-jump as I wrapped my arms and legs around his muscular frame. Then he flashed his million-dollar smile. "Well, hello, Sabayon!" Each time he playfully uttered my innocently wicked nickname, I couldn't help but gasp, my knees weakening.

With his mesmerizing eyes focused on me, I felt like a perfectly grilled, meltingly tender, medium-rare Wagyu beef steak he longed to devour. The scent of his heady cologne filled my nose, and the response to breathing him in was Pavlovian—I was soaking wet and desperate—dizzy as if the air suddenly lacked oxygen.

Wrapping me in his great, big arms, he leaned closer, pressing me against the door. With one fluid motion, he reached behind and secured the lock, sealing us off from the outside world.

Draped over me, he nuzzled my neck, his lips planting kisses along my shoulders and spine. The heat from his fine Italian body melted my skin.

At first, we were by the door, and I thought, surely, he

would take me standing up. But his eyes narrowed, and I felt his sugar turn to spice as he set my toes on the floor. Threading my arms under his, I drew him closer to me. "I need you!" I begged. "Here, against the wall!"

Gianmarco smiled wickedly before dragging me away, raising the dress over my head, and throwing it into the air. His eyes widened bright in appreciation, and a low, appreciative whistle escaped his lips as he took in the sight of the bra. I gasped as he unclasped and yanked it off my chest with such force that my petite breasts bounced with the aggressive undressing.

Then he knelt before me, curled his strong fingers around the mesh waistband, and ripped the tiny, sheer panties off my hips, sliding the remnants down my gams and over my heels.

His lips trailed love bites down my tummy and then my mound until his hunger met his meal; my knees buckled when his mouth swallowed my pussy. It wasn't a kiss or a lick but the plunge of a gourmand diving into his favorite feast, and I wanted him to feed until I burst.

With his whiskers glistening from my nectar, Gianmarco rose, picked me up, and kissed me. I loved tasting myself on his lips and tongue, feeling my wetness messily cascading down his chin.

I wrapped my legs around his waist, my soul rejoicing at being so completely desired. I buried my smile into his neck as he carried and deposited me onto the table, squealing as he pushed me backward. The counter's cool surface felt soothing against my bare skin.

"This is how I like you, my Sabayon, naked, spread, and ready to be served," he said as he nudged my legs apart.

Titillated, I teased him, "I feel like an *amuse bouche* for my Italian gourmand!"

"Oh, my temptress," he said with a salacious taunt. "Your beautiful pussy pleases my mouth, but I am dying to devour all of you!"

As Gianmarco slipped his fingers beneath the band of his boxers, my eyes sparkled in anticipation. I bit my lip, nodding and purring for him to keep going. "Oh my!" I gasped with schoolgirl delight when my lover stripped bare and his cock, already hard and throbbing, popped free of his restraints.

"Mmm," I moaned as I leaned back on my arms and spread my legs wide for him, begging, "Eat me!"

He draped my gams over his shoulders, then dove in. A primal groan escaped my mouth as his tongue swept across my exposed kitty, obliterating any remaining reserve I might have had—I was his to ravage however he pleased.

With light licks, he flicked around my labia. I tried maneuvering my hips to help him reach my clit, but surprisingly, he moved his tongue away.

"What are you doing, Darling? You're missing your target!"

"Nuh-uh," he mumbled, shaking his head. "Relax," and he continued using long strokes to trace the outline of my slit.

To help move things along, I reached for my pearl, but he grasped my hand and kissed it, placing it by my side. Then he raised the hood of my engorged clit, barely tongue-tickling the surface, driving me absolutely wild.

I bucked my hips, driving myself harder into his face, but then he disengaged and started kissing my inner thighs, moving away from my furrow.

"Where are you going? And why are you teasing me, Darling?"

"You know you love it!"

Squirming beneath him and panting, "I do. But I want *more!*"

Rotating his right hand so it faced palm up, he slowly inched forward, placing his ring and middle fingers at my entrance, and stopped. "You mean... like this?"

"Mmm... *more,* please!" I begged.

"Wicked girl, always wanting *more!*" He slipped into my pussy and curled his double digits into a soft hook to stroke up in a *come hither* motion. "Does your kitty like that, Sabayon?"

I sank into his fingers and miaowed. "Oh, yes!" I purred. "She loves it so very much!"

Slowly, he swirled them inside me and lowered his head, tongue tickling my pearl again to the same tempo as he ran his fingers along the soft folds of my G-spot.

I was aching and dripping for him like a wild cat in heat. "I'm so wet, Darling. Make me cum!" I growled.

"Uh-uh," he mumbled, then he slipped his left thumb into my juicy asshole, his thick finger pulsing, pushing in and out, while his tongue clit-licked and flicked for all he was worth.

My entire body throbbed, my clit pulsed, and my nipples ached. Shaking and convulsing, I felt my rosebud pucker; cresting the wave of release, I yelled, "Ah-ahh-ahhh! Don't stop!"

Pushed over the precipice, I was overwhelmed by a tsunami-like orgasm crashing over me, such that my thighs shuddered and my juices flowed like a stream. Struggling to recover, I asked my lover, "Oh my God! What the *hell* was that?"

He smiled triumphantly. "Was it good?"

"Fuck, YES!"

"Venus Butterfly," he bashfully whispered. "It's old school, but I heard about it and wanted to try it with you."

"Old school, huh?" I joshed. "Well, whatever the fuck it's called, thank you! That was *amazing,* sweetheart! We should definitely do it again!"

My Darling chuckled and placed his hand on his chin, moving it from side to side as if trying to readjust his jaw. I suspect it was tired and sore from all that wonderful, *filthy fornication* he gifted me!

Sweaty, spent, and thoroughly relaxed after that blissful oral caressing, I drew him in for a deep soul-kiss. "Now it's your turn, love."

Gianmarco's hands curled beneath my knees, pulling me off the counter. No sooner had my tiptoes touched the tile when he turned me around, yanked my hips backward, and felt his girth entering me from behind. That moment of being deliciously spread open was heavenly. I sighed with longing as he buried himself further inside.

"Mmm, Darling!" I hummed. "You fit me like a glove."

"That's because your pussy was made for my cock," he said with *that voice* that thrummed into my soul. I felt his teeth nipping at my nape as he breathed into my ear. "He's been dying to feel your deliciously wet hug."

Gianmarco's unbridled desire for me felt like the first blissful time we *played*. Such a lover, and he was all mine!

His solid heat stroked inside me with long, deep, firm thrusts while his hands cupped my petite pair, firmly squeezing my breasts in his broad hands.

My wetness pooled like a reservoir, waiting to burst over the dam. I reached back and curled my arm behind his neck, my fingertips caressing the smoothness of his shaven scalp. I couldn't wait but didn't want to cum again without him.

"Give it to me, Darling. Your hungry kitty needs your cream!" I panted, my legs shaking once again. Thrusting my hips back, I heard that marvelously noisy slap-slap-slapping of my ass against his thighs. Feeling my restraint begging to yield, I cried out, "Cum with me! Please?"

Gianmarco growled. His hands curved up and over my shoulders, pulling me back into his body. His muscular thighs flexed and tightened as he buried his cock deep inside. With a final, solid plunge, I could feel his balls spasming against my tingling, freshly waxed skin.

The surge from his hot cum released tidal waves of euphoria I had kept at bay. He held me as we came together with cries, grunts, and moans. Freshly filled, I giggled with delight upon feeling the rivulets of our passion running down my thighs.

Spent, he leaned onto my bare back. Panting, he confessed, "Oh, my Sabayon, you are a wonder! *Adoro scoparti, mia innamorata incredibile!*"

"*I love fucking you, my incredible sweetheart!*"

"Right back at you, babe!" I felt the same.

Tenderly, he turned me around; his drained, semi-erect cock, hanging heavy and thick, rested against my still-throbbing pussy. Droplets of our cum splattered onto the floor between our feet.

"Are you sated, Sabayon?"

"Never. I always want *more* with you!"

He laughed, spooning and cuddling me, brimming with the joy of pleasing one another, until we caught our breath.

"I've been driving non-stop, then you gave me a real ride! Now I'm starved!"

"Well, shall we order room service?" I asked while tracing the Celtic maze tattooed around his bicep.

"Nope!" he said. "Tonight, I wanna go out—with you on my arm!"

"Of course, I'd love for us to step out and play! I feel so alive when I'm with you, my Darling."

Smiling, Gianmarco brushed a finger across my neck. "I know a place around the corner that's still open."

. . .

DRESSING QUICKLY, we took the elevator to the ground floor, my hands and fingers entwined in his. Vibrating with happiness, I snuck a kiss on his cheek just before the doors parted. We felt like two kids sneaking out. I had to be careful since this city was more like a small town, and traipsing around hand in hand with an Italian, a man who was not my husband, might raise eyebrows.

We walked on air through the red-tiled lobby with the colonnades. A pair of stone lions guarded the entrance. As we approached the double glass doors and stepped onto the red carpet, we jumped and laughed in surprise at the roars emanating from the big cat statues' mouths.

On this beautifully warm mid-September night, we strolled under a full moon along Pescara Beach to a little restaurant called La Pesca, where they served the best home-style seafood dishes in town.

I grinned when Gianmarco stopped at the front door. "Great minds think alike, Darling. I know this place, too. And the funny thing is, I was planning on taking you here tonight!"

He chuckled.

Sandro, the waiter at La Pesca, had become my friend, having visited this establishment at least once a week while our family was vacationing in Pescara last year. No matter how crowded the restaurant was, Sandro made sure a table would always be available for me. Tonight would be no different.

Gianmarco, my perfect gentleman, opened the door and let me enter first. We faced a giant, crystal-clear aquarium with colorful little fish darting around the green fern fronds and coral fingers embedded in the rocks.

Sandro greeted me, *"Ciao Carissima!"*

"Hello, dearest one!"

As our fingers met, a warm blush crept over my cheeks when Sandro delicately raised my hand and pressed a tender kiss onto its back, leaving a lingering trace of warmth. Sandro and I had our own language, a quiet one where words were often replaced with hand gestures and smiles, bridging the gap between our limited English and Italian fluency, making our "conversations" all the more interesting.

I leaned in to kiss both of his cheeks. *"Ciao Sandro! Come va?"*
"How's it going?"

"Bene, e tu?"
"Good, and you?"

I stepped to the side to introduce Sandro to my friend when he said, *"Ciao Marco!"*

My jaw dropped. "You already know each other?"

Gianmarco smiled. "It's a small town. I know every waiter in Pescara."

"Anch'io!" Sandro nodded, and we all laughed together.
"Me too!"

I was grateful that Sandro did not ask about my husband or daughter, but I detected a half-raised eyebrow. I blushed and smiled weakly. He nodded once, silently acknowledging that he would be my secret keeper.

Since the restaurant was already full, we were offered an outdoor patio table. A beautiful breezy night, with the sound of the gentle waves lapping the shore in the background, provided the ideal setting. There was enough moonlight to see the line of breakers paralleling the coast, sparkling in the distance. The fresh, briny smell of the sea and the aroma of the seafood dishes wafting from the kitchen made my mouth water.

Sandro came back with our menus. The first time I was here

was with my husband and child; we were clueless about the offerings, all in Italian. Despite the language barrier, our family returned many times and was surprised that they always remembered our favorites. With Gianmarco translating by my side, he could finally unlock the remaining Rosetta Stone of La Pesca's menu for me.

I told my Darling I felt like celebrating, and he knew I wanted him to order *wretched excess*. While he studied the menu, I studied him. He looked impressed, pouring over the seasonal menu and nodding his head at times.

From my purse, I retrieved a small, wrapped box and placed it on the table beside him.

"What's this?" Gianmarco asked.

"A gift from Kally."

"May I open it?"

"Of course! She made it for you."

Gently removing the tape from the homemade wrapping paper of painted hearts and flowers, Gianmarco carefully smoothed it out and smiled at Kally's handwriting. *FOR GIANMARCO!!! I LOVE YOU!!! LOVE KALLY!!!*

"She's working on her capital letters and punctuation at the moment. Exclamation marks are her favorite," I told him.

"Tell my Little Pink Kitten it's perfect! I love it!"

"Kally misses you, and she wanted to be here and give you this gift herself, but Cyril said, no."

Gianmarco pursed his lips and nodded in understanding. Lifting the lid from the box, he found another piece of her artwork and cradled it in his palm. He stared at the fragment of her arm's plaster cast and, with his finger, traced the colorful smiling cat faces with long black whiskers and red hearts and rainbows Kally had drawn.

Dewy-eyed, he asked, "Her arm is strong again, no?"

"Yes, it's as good as before, except for a small scar on her forearm."

"Good." He nodded quietly, touched by my Little One's gesture. "Tell her it's beautiful and that I miss her very much and will treasure this gift from her always."

"Show her." I took my phone from my purse and pointed the camera at him.

Gianmarco pressed Kally's colorful wrapping paper against his chest, placed her hand-decorated plaster cast onto his lips, and kissed it.

I showed him the picture I had captured. "Thank you, my Darling. Kally will be so happy to see how much you love her."

He reached over and leaned his head on my shoulder. I cradled his face in my hand and kissed his wet cheek.

When Sandro returned, my Darling ordered the hot seafood starter, which came with grilled wild, hand-harvested razor clams and a delectable simple soup of ground chickpeas, shrimp, and fish broth, flavored with rare bright yellow, red-tipped fronds of saffron from the Italian Navelli Plains, all processed into a silky rich, golden soup. Gianmarco added the squid risotto, made with glossy Carnaroli arborio rice grains cooked perfectly al dente, mixed with squid ink, crab, and chopped parsley. The finale was crepes stuffed with scampi bathed in a cream sauce and finished on a salamander grill.

Since there was no wine list, Gianmarco asked what wine pairing he would recommend with the dinner. Sandro said he didn't drink but mentioned that many diners had been pleased with the Contessa Passerina from Le Marche, the region north of Abruzzo.

My sommelier's eyebrows rose so high in shock that I worried they might shoot off his head! Gianmarco handed back the menus and agreed to try a bottle.

For a small establishment, their menu offerings were abundant, and everything was made fresh and crafted with love. At the end of our gastronomic feast, I asked my fellow foodie, "What do you think of La Pesca, and which dish was the standout of the evening, Darling?"

Gianmarco dabbed the side of his mouth with the white linen napkin before answering. "I've been here before, and it is always fantastic! But my favorite was the seafood garbanzo soup at the start! You can taste all four equally proportioned ingredients harmoniously blended, such that the sum of the whole is greater than its parts. And the white Passerina was the perfect wine match. Its fragrant grapefruit flavors had just a slight hint of sharpness from the citrus. Sublime! The only thing that could have improved the wine is if the winemakers had turned it into a sparkler in the first place. Now that would have been incredible!"

I smiled proudly at Gianmarco. Not only did he enjoy wines, but he also had a discerning, refined palette that he could imagine how a wine could be made even better.

"You are no ordinary sommelier, my Darling. That was my favorite, too!" Cautiously, I inquired further. "And the service?"

He grasped his chin with his thumb and forefinger in contemplation. "Too attentive."

I wrinkled my brow at his comment.

"I was a waiter, Sabi, and I know attentive service when I see it."

"And?" I wondered where he was going with this. *Could my lover be feeling slightly jealous?*

"I also know Sandro, and I see that he likes you very much." Gianmarco downed the last gulp of wine from his glass.

I blushed. "We're just friends."

"Hmm. Well, Sabayon, you introduced me as your *friend* too."

"But you are my *favorite!*" I reached for his hand and squeezed it. "Beloved, there's no one else but you!"

He squeezed my hand back and smiled; we chuckled together.

Too stuffed for dessert, we asked for the bill. In the end, we thanked our friend for an excellent meal and said goodbye with kisses on both cheeks, promising to return another day.

THE WIND HAD PICKED up and was surprisingly chilly for a September evening. So, instead of following the shore, we returned to our room. It had been a long day for both of us—my two international flights from California via Rome to Pescara, and his working a full day in Milan and riding for miles to meet me here. We made for the hotel and went straight to bed.

Cuddling beneath a thin sheet, our hearts and tummies content, we fell asleep, gently snoring in each other's arms.

15

ECHOES OF THE PAST

Monday, September 16, 2019

Jet-lagged and discombobulated, I woke up with a start. "Where am I?" I smiled when I realized Gianmarco was still by my side, slumbering like an angel. I wish I had time to wake him gently with a good morning romp, but we had overslept and now only had an hour to shower, change, and make it to our appointment with the architects. There was no time to order room service for a light breakfast, only a quick grab of an espresso at the cafe downstairs before taking off on his bike.

As he was securing my helmet, my thoughtful and caring man grasped a handful of my wet locks and said, "Sabina, your hair!" He shook his head in disapproval. "You really shouldn't go out with it sopping wet."

"Oh, Darling, that superstition only affects Italians!"

"It will be the death of you!" He warned me as he adjusted the straps.

"Then, remember how much I love you when I'm gone!" I teased.

"You know, you're tempting Fate." He pursed his lips, shaking his head again.

"You're my lucky charm, sweetheart. I feel immortal when I'm with you!"

"You. Are. So. Sweet." His eyes sparkled with a hint of sadness. "I would fuck you so sweetly if we had time."

Hearing his words turned me on instantly, forcing me to squeeze my legs together and breathe slowly, trying to control my sexual urges, which threatened to come to a boil whenever I was around my lover. "Oh, Darling. I'd like that very much. If we didn't have the appointment, I would have dragged you back to our room and fucked you senseless!"

"Yes, I know. So would I." His words made my pussy ache. I instinctively crossed my thighs to clamp them shut and control myself around him.

"Can I, at least, kiss you?" I asked hopefully.

He checked his watch. "Nope!" Then he hopped onto his bike. "Mount behind me!" I bit my bottom lip and giggled because that was exactly what I wanted to do. But I was a good girl and obeyed, holding onto his torso tightly so I wouldn't fall off.

ZIGGING and zagging between the cars, leaning into him with every turn, my speed racer got us to Claudio and Francesca Teatino's home/architectural office with a minute to spare.

Unfortunately, they were in a rush to reach the airport at

Pescara since they received an emergency call regarding the building site of their Greek island hotel project. They apologized profusely for postponing our appointment.

"We tried texting and calling last night, but no one picked up," Claudio said. "We canceled the meeting with the realtor too."

I checked my phone, and sure enough, there was a text message and a missed call. I didn't want to disappoint Cyril again by going home empty-handed. "Is it possible for us to just drive ourselves to the sites and look around, to see what we think of them, to see the towns and their surroundings?"

Claudio and Francesca looked at each other and thought that was a good idea. They buzzed their secretary to retrieve the files on the properties of interest.

A woman entered the foyer with a folder with photocopies of the three locations. *"Buongior—"* She stopped her greeting when she saw me.

"Buongiorno," I replied, extending my hand for the file.
"Good morning."

Gianmarco was silent. Perhaps he felt uncomfortable around my architects.

"Would you care for a coffee?" the secretary asked.

"No, thank you." I glanced at her, lifting my eyes momentarily from the papers. "Darling, coff–?" Oops, I stopped dead in my tracks, realizing my term of endearment had slipped out. I hoped no one noticed.

Strangely, he never normally turned down a cup. I noticed his usually friendly face was blank. "Are you OK?"

He didn't answer my question but instead pulled his keyring from his trouser pocket, nodding toward the exit. "Shall we go?"

The girl scurried to the door, holding it open as we headed to our vehicles. Again, the architects profusely apologized.

"No worries. I'll report my recommendations to Cyril, and we can go from there."

"Of course," Francesca and Claudio said in unison before dashing away in their Fiat station wagon.

Gianmarco strapped his helmet on; next, he secured mine. "Where do you wanna go first?"

"Hey, what happened back there? Are you upset about the architects canceling at the last minute?"

"No. I'm fine. Let's finish Cyril's assignment, so we can have lots of time to *play* after."

"You bet, babe!" I placed my gloved hand in his. "I think the *palazzo* is the closest to us. Let's check that one out first."

He gave me the thumbs up.

Snuggled behind my sexy Italian, Gianmarco engaged his Ducati and zoomed us out of there.

THE FIRST PROPERTY on the docket was the palazzo in the mountain village of Casoli. The palace was fortified with high stone walls and an intimidating entryway; a small portal was cut out of the massive double wooden gate. The rusted lock was broken, allowing us to push the gate open and peer in.

As the fresh breeze and light entered the space, it blew back a cloud of dust that hung in the heavy, dank air of the closed-in room. The place smelled as abandoned as it looked, musty with the sour scent of decay. It seemed unbelievable that this ruin was once a grand, gleaming castle.

The entryway alone was an impressive 100 feet long. And the flooring consisted of a Penrose pattern of black marble stars tessellated around white diamond tiles. Twenty feet above our heads, the sunlight penetrated through the expanse of the transparent glass sunroof.

The sunbeam from the skylight allowed us to see until the end of the hallway, where an iron gate opened to a lush, hidden jungle. This intimate private garden was a desirable and rare feature of this property, given that this palace was in the center of a crowded old town. The only other green space was a small public park, shared by the whole community.

Standing beneath the dilapidated ceiling, the dust and heat of the enclosure gave me an overwhelming urge to step into the open air. Investigating on my own, I pushed open the iron gate of the conservatory. Upon entering the expansive space, I immediately felt cured of claustrophobia. I approached the pavilion next to a fountain in the secret garden.

To my astonishment, its frame, made of solid black oak beams, hardly looked aged at all. Whatever resin the carpenters used preserved the structure from degradation. But what was more shocking was that the air felt cool and pure under the canopy of the ancient trees. Goosebumps sprang up along my arms and neck, yet the touch of my fingers to my neck felt the dampness of perspiration.

The fountain's centerpiece was the marble statue of a forlorn young girl. But as I looked closer, the sculptor had carved a determination in her eyes. Crystal-clear water still trickled down her outstretched arms, running from her upturned palms into the basin below. I dipped my fingers in and felt that it was as cold as a mountain stream. As I followed the ripples, I saw something afloat on the other side: a blood-red handkerchief with white stitching, half submerged.

The earlier chill seemed to have abated as suddenly as it appeared. Now the suffocating heat and humidity rolled back over me. My forehead beaded with sweat, my cheeks felt hot, and my neck pulsed. After retrieving the kerchief, I dunked it back into the water and wrung it in my hands. Despite dabbing my forehead with the cold cloth, I felt no relief. Suddenly, the entire place closed around me, and the need to flee overcame me.

Worried I was suffering from heat stroke, I dunked the hankie into the basin once more, squeezing it lightly to wash my face and neck to stem my dizziness.

Calling to Gianmarco, I hurried down the stone path, through the gate, and back into the house. To my relief, my Darling appeared immediately, and with one look, I could tell he was alarmed at my state. "*Sabi, che succede?* You look pale."

"*Sabi, what's happening?*"

"I don't know, sweetheart, but I felt incredibly dizzy in the garden."

He caught me before I stumbled, almost fainting in his arms. "I think we should go."

Suddenly, a raven flew through a gaping hole in one of the broken stained glass window panes. It was chasing a mouse scurrying through an obstacle course of broken marble tiles and hillocks of roof plaster lying heaped on the floor. The pursuit heightened my anxiety, and I silently wished for the rodent's escape and sighed in relief when it did. As though the bird heard my thoughts, it twitched its neck and peered at me with cold, black eyes before it took off again.

Our eyes followed the hunter as it swooped back and glided through the crumbling house, landing in the salon. The baby blue and white plaster ceiling had magnificent hand-painted frescoes of floating angels dancing in the sky. A few cherubs were missing where the paint peeled off due to the high humidity in the room.

"What a shame!" I mused aloud. "I'm sure the original

owners sunk a fortune building such a palace. How could something so magnificent have been allowed to fall into such a decrepit state of disrepair?" My knees felt shaky and unsteady, mirroring the crumbling state of the palazzo itself.

"Are you OK? Do you need me to carry you?" said my concerned hero.

"Thank you, my gallant knight. I can manage with you by my side." I leaned on him as he took my hand and led us back out the portal of the double wooden doors.

OUT OF NOWHERE, *Nonna,* an ancient woman, hunched over, dressed in a long black skirt and a black shawl over her head, came up from behind and tapped me on the shoulder. Startled, I jumped into Gianmarco and nearly shrieked. She giggled and gave us a friendly, apologetic smile, revealing her lack of several teeth.

Gianmarco spoke to venerable Nonna, telling her I was interested in restoring the property. Since the door was unlocked, we went in and had a peek.

Nonna quickly made a sign of the cross, crying, *"È un luogo maledetto infestato da un fantasma."*

"It's a cursed place haunted by a ghost," Gianmarco translated.

Intrigued, I asked him to delve deeper into the meaning of Nonna's words. She began recounting the palazzo's murky history, which my Darling expertly interpreted for me:

> *"The Denaro* family once owned this grand palace and controlled all the land in the village. The Duke who presided*

---

*   Denaro means money in Italian.

over it was an arrogant, mean man who felt justified in charging usury rents to his impoverished, sharecropping tenants. He grew rich while his renters suffered.

"One fateful day, he fell into a twisted obsession with the youngest daughter of one of his tenants and offered her father a chilling deal—to work the land rent-free in exchange for the girl. Disgusted by the proposition, her papà defiantly spat in Duke Denaro's face.

"Feeling entitled to his revenge over the slight, the sadistic nobleman, cloaked in the darkness of night, commanded his henchmen to abduct the maiden.

"Tied up to one of the posts in the gazebo in the secret garden, the Duke flogged and then raped the girl repeatedly. Afterward, he burned her arm with a D, the same mark he used to brand his livestock. Without remorse, he threw her beaten and scarred body onto her family's doorstep.

"The town was outraged at the Duke's heinous crime, a flagrant violation of a poor, innocent girl. That night, the townspeople gathered and raided his palazzo. They strung him up by his neck, intending to hang him. The hobbling girl he defiled was at the front of the murderous mob, and they wanted her to have the honor of kicking the chair out from underneath his feet. The crowd was chanting for justice. She raised her hand, silencing the crowd."

"'Have mercy!' cried the Duke."

"'What is your life worth?' asked the girl."

"'Everything,' Duke Denaro begged. 'I will give you everything!'"

"She paused and nodded. Decision made, she looked her rapist in the eyes. 'We will spare your life in exchange for all your land and palace. But never return, or we will not be so merciful.'"

"The Duke readily agreed, skulking away into the dark. Without the Duke's choking, iron fist, the town prospered. The only blight in the village was the disgraced Duke's crumbling palazzo. Many had tried to refurbish it, but every owner had failed. Permanently abandoned and left to rot, its stones held the bad karma left behind."

After my Darling finished translating Nonna's words, she reached for my hand. Although etiquette and respect dictated my accepting her touch, the appearance of her skin, thin and yellowed as onion paper, made it a forced effort. Her hand felt, at once, frail and leathery; the veins trailing from her wrist looked black-blue and sinewy. I held her hand gently, nodding at her smile, but found myself unable to gaze at her for more than a moment as her fingers clutched mine.

When I felt her grip lessen, the shawl she wore fell around her shoulders, revealing a *D* burned into her bicep.

Nonna gave a sudden burst of Italian and looked me squarely in the eyes. Her other hand clamped over mine, and though I could not translate her words, I understood it was a plea.

"Don't buy it, Sabi," Gianmarco said while crossing himself. "Nonna is warning you that evil hovers over this place."

Never had I agreed with a statement more readily. Upon feeling relief, my composure returned. "I'm not an engineer, but even with my untrained eyes, it looks too far gone to salvage. Plus, if the town feels the way Nonna does, they'll want to keep it intact as a reminder of the sin and toll of loving gold. And the fact that the underdogs won is a beacon, the townspeople's source of pride, for their triumph over greed."

Gianmarco closed his eyes as he kissed my forehead.

"I will listen to you and heed your warning. Please reassure Nonna that I have no interest in this place."

He didn't need to translate my words. I could see that Nonna understood what I meant when she cupped Gianmarco's hands and kissed them. I gasped when she did the same to mine because it felt like an angel had kissed my soul.

Nonna beamed at me. Slowly, she hobbled away.

Moved by her story, I buried my head in Gianmarco's chest. He kissed the top of my crown and wrapped his arm around my shoulder. I turned back to ask what had happened to the girl.

"Where's Nonna? Where did she go? I wanted you to translate one final question for me."

"She was moving slowly. She can't have gone far." He craned his neck to see if he could find her, but Nonna wasn't anywhere nearby.

Quickly, he ducked inside, turned back, and shook his head. "I think she's gone." He shrugged, equally bewildered as I.

"Vanished, like a ghost," I murmured as a nervous shiver ran down my spine. "Rest in peace, Nonna," I whispered while crossing myself.

We left without another word spoken between us until we reached Gianmarco's bike, both silently thankful we had a fast exit away from there.

16

OASIS

The next estate we evaluated was a little vineyard with a little house in a little town called Atri. It was adjacent to the famous vineyards of Azienda Agricola Ventimiglia, so we knew the soil was good, but the shack was a scraper, a write-off.

My husband would not like this style. It was not grand enough, more like a micro-cottage with a hobbyist garden, and the plot was too small to grow enough of the grapes that Cyril would want to cultivate.

On the other hand, I smiled at my sommelier, who was beaming, enamored by the fantastic, breathtaking views before him. The quaint cottage, situated atop a little hillock in the middle of a valley and surrounded by vineyard land as far as the eye could see, felt like it could become a wine lover's paradise.

The owner noticed us walking around the perimeter and invited us onto his property. Passing the rows of mature vines, we could see the man's joy as he proudly regaled us with wine-making stories. Every year, this man and his father harvested these grapes and crafted beautiful wine from them. He lamented that he was getting old and had hurt his back recently, so last year was the first time he hadn't produced wine in decades.

We asked if we could try the grapes since there were still some berries on the vine—not quite raisins, but not plump like they should have been at harvest had they been adequately cared for. The man picked a bunch for us, and we sucked the juice from the berry, then popped another into our mouths. We chewed the thick skins between our teeth, avoiding the giant pip, tasting the tannins that would leach into the free-run juice when pressed.

The brix, or sugar content of the juice, and the taste profile of the fruit from these thirty-year-old vines were outstanding. Their sweet, rich flavor would make an excellent, bold, fruit-forward vino. But only half the land was planted with the Montepulciano d'Abruzzo variety. The other half was grafted with Trebbiano d'Abruzzo. Unfortunately, the Trebbiano was ordinary, and more than forty percent of those vines were dead. Most would have to be ripped out and replanted with new rootstock. The others could be T-budded with cuttings from the same Montepulciano grapevine canes, but it would take another five years before the new vines would be mature enough for harvesting.

We asked the man about the neighboring vineyard properties. He said that *signor Ventimiglia* had them locked up in long-term contracts with the promise that he had the right of first refusal if they wanted to sell their land. Having Gianmarco translate for me, I asked why he hadn't sold his lot to the Ventimiglia family.

The man smiled. "I guess they didn't think it was worth what I priced it at; they didn't see its value."

I told him I didn't think he actually wanted to sell, did he? And he laughed while tapping the side of his nose because I had figured out his ploy, but his wife hadn't.

He said to Gianmarco, "Your wife is brilliant."

My Darling smiled proudly. "Yes, she is." He winked at me, and I bit my lip to hide my glowing smile.

The man admitted he didn't want to sell his father's land, so he priced it way above market value, hoping no one would bid on it. "My wife is a school teacher, and she is tired of living in the country. She wants to move to the big city and have an apartment by the sea to retire there. But the only way we could afford that would be to sell my father's legacy. What a choice!"

We thanked him for his time. I told him I saw the value in his land but would not bid on it; although, I'm sure if Cyril wanted this and the neighboring properties, he could have out-negotiated even the Devil. When my husband wanted to own or control something, he was relentless.

With a big smile, the man showed his relief and ran to the cottage to collect a gift. The bottle of wine he wanted to share with us was the last vintage the man and his father made together.

He waved goodbye as Gianmarco and I walked hand in hand back to his motorcycle.

On the main road, we spotted an inn called La Bosca. The parking lot in front was populated with mainly Fiat econobox cars. Since it was almost noon, we decided to investigate where it seemed like the entire town was hanging out to have lunch.

At first sniff, without even looking at the menu, we smelled a winner. The ragù, made from game meat and garlic, smelled tantalizing. We spied a rare treat—Ventimiglia's Cerasuolo *vino sfuso*—on tap. The restaurant made a bulk wine purchase of this recently-made, unaged, and unbottled wine, and we ordered a carafe to accompany our meal. It was amazing how much fruitier the wine could be without any French oak aging program applied to it.

Lunch started with an antipasto platter of specialty salamis and cheeses from Abruzzo. My favorite was a cured, stubby, housemade sausage with a surprisingly soft interior. The other starters included local Pecorino cheeses made from sheep's milk in varying stages of aging. Most Pecorinos were hard, grating cheeses. We were served a young one that was still soft, almost like Cheddar cheese, but with a great, rich, sweet, and nutty flavor.

Next was the *lepre* pasta dish made from wild hare. Larger than a rabbit, it was rich and flavorful but not at all gamey. Al dente housemade pasta mixed with the rich hare ragù was to die for! We could still see the finely chopped brunoise of carrots, onions, and celery since the mirepoix was not cooked to the point where it dissolved into the sauce, leaving enough texture and a nice bite to the veggies. And for dessert, since there was a wedding in the other dining room, the restaurant made *pizza dolce*, my Darling's favorite dessert, and we inquired about ordering one serving.

Our server returned with a coffee and a complimentary slice, saying the newlyweds agreed to share—a gift from them to us—and wished we would invite them to our future wedding. Gianmarco smiled, and I blushed.

After the tiny but rich espresso, Gianmarco patted my behind and, with a smile, told me he was off to fetch more. The glint in his eye told me my man had a plan. While waiting, I asked for the bill and thanked our hostess for the amazingly economical yet soul-satisfyingly delicious lunch.

When Gianmarco mysteriously returned a quarter hour later, it was with a satchel stuffed to bursting and a cloth bag clinking of glass.

Spying the unlabeled bottles in his tote bag, I asked, "Don't tell me you managed to bargain for some Ventimiglia Cerasuolo *sfuso?*"

"Maybe." He smirked. "And I certainly won't tell you how little I paid!"

"Honestly, Gianmarco! That poor innkeeper will think we're a pair of Roma on the loose! I do hope you paid him fairly!"

He shrugged and raised the wine carrier. "I paid him the price he asked for, which was almost nothing. But *this!*" He shook the ballooned satchel. "*This* cost a small fortune! But one has to expect to pay handsomely for a picnic with a princess."

Responding with a shriek and an excited clap, I leaped to his side. "A picnic! Are you truly taking me on a picnic after our massive lunch?"

"Sabi, we have seventeen hectares to preview; of course, we must have a picnic!"

After a huge meal, southern Italians typically took a break for *il pomeriggio,* the afternoon nap. Still, we decided to power through and view the final property in Abbateggio, not far from the restaurant.

When we arrived, the land's beauty, with a river running through it and horses grazing in the fields, left us in muted awe. The plot was in the middle of the Majella National Forest, situated between the two mountain ranges of the Gran Sasso and the Majella Mountains. It was named so because it looked like a beautiful, reclining woman in profile. The tallest peak was attributed to her breast, and the lower, rounded mound to her wide hips.

Italians were so creative; how they adored women! I told Gianmarco that I thought *this* was the property to bid on. I could envision the house—a modern build designed by our architects—in the middle of the land next to the brook. At sunrise, we would awaken to the view of two mountain ranges while drinking an espresso on the patio, with the belled sheep tinkling away as they traversed the path to graze on another field.

By late afternoon, we had toured as much of the parcel as we could on a motorbike. However, the roads ran to an end, and the raw terrain was no place to ride. Leaving his Ducati in the shade of a chestnut grove, we trekked on foot in search of the perfect place to picnic.

Following what looked like a well-worn shepherd's path, Gianmarco and I walked hand in hand, smiling more than speaking. It was nearing three o'clock when both of us began to feel the pangs of hunger for a snack and for each other.

As we crested a small hill, the sight on the other side stopped us in our tracks. Encircling a spring-fed, sparklingly clear pond was a grouping of mature olive trees. And distinct from the sea of their lush green canopies, an ancient wooden fruit tree stood alone, dripping with bright orange orbs, like translucent paper lanterns perched on the tips of the branches, dancing in the wind.

"*Dio mio!* I can't believe it!"
"*My God!*"

"What is it, Darling?"

He pointed to the cluster of trees in the distance. "Look at how thick the trunks of these rare old trees are! I'd guess they were planted over a hundred years ago. See how the ground around the trees is covered in black? Those trees are bursting with mature olives that have fallen and are ready to be harvested. And that one," he pointed to the tree with the orange fruits, "tiny *kaki*, ripe and translucent! Incredible, since it's still early in the season!"

"*Kah-key?*" I asked.

"Persimmons! You wouldn't expect to find that here since they're grown mainly in the south, like Sicily and Campania, where my family is from. Someone from a long time ago knew the delights of eating this fruit, brought it here deliberately, and cultivated it. And that pool, here, in the middle of nowhere?" Gianmarco looked on with disbelief. "Is this a mirage? Tell me you see the same thing, Sabi!"

Giggling at his exuberance, I reassured my lover of the sight before us. "I see it, Darling. It's like an oasis, isn't it?"

He wasn't exaggerating. By the wide girth of their trunks, these trees were planted at least a century ago. I had seen forest groves looking old, gnarled, and unhappy, but these trees looked resplendent, vibrant, and full. If these trees had a voice, they would have been singing arias.

"I've had persimmons before, and I find them chalky. What makes *kaki* so special to you, sweetheart?"

"Ahhh. You've never experienced a perfectly tree-ripened one, have you?"

"No."

"Come with me." He pulled me along with such enthusiasm that I had to keep my eyes pinned to the ground to avoid stumbling over the rocky terrain. Gianmarco rushed us into the shade of the abounding branches. A delicate olive bouquet floated around us with its fruit hanging everywhere.

I plucked a black olive from a branch and was about to eat one when Gianmarco stopped me. "Raw olives are too bitter to eat without first curing them in a salt brine. But this," he plucked a plump persimmon for me, peeling the thick skin back, revealing a soft orange purse of delight. "Like this." He bit into its flesh and began turning in circles. *"Mamma mia! È come baciare il seno di una donna!"*
   "Oh, Mamma! It's like kissing a woman's breast!"

Sauntering toward me, he finished with his arm outstretched in a bow, offering it to my lips. I giggled when he placed it in my hand. It felt like a squishy water balloon resting in my palm.

"Bite, eat, and tell me what you taste!"

I couldn't help but smile watching this city-slicker sommelier transform into a farm boy when let out to play. Being a good playmate, I took a bite and closed my eyes, seeking to discern the nuances of this delicate fruit. Almost immediately, flavors danced across my tongue like notes in a song. "Wow! Silky without a trace of chalk! But it's almost like a perfectly summer-ripened peach crossed with a fruity honeydew melon. And, oh my!" Pressing it against my lips, I took another bite, and the juice dribbled down my chin. "Is that...? No, wait, there's something else. Caramel?"

I opened my eyes to see Gianmarco nodding and smiling at me.

"This tastes incredible! And the texture is like soft, sleek custard."

"Pssh! Way better than custard! I have enjoyed many tastes in my life, but I got a hard-on the first time I ate one."

"What!" I exclaimed, my eyes widening in astonishment.

"No, really! That texture is the closest thing to my favorite —fresh, slick pussy!" He gazed at me and licked his lips like he wanted to eat *me*, sending an electric pulse straight to my toes.

"Does mine feel like that?" I blushed, confessing, "I've never eaten *one* before."

"Oh, yessss! You should try yours sometime."

I snorted. "I'm not that flexible."

"Oh, but you are, Sabayon! And adventurous too. We should try *one* together, one day."

I laughed nervously and gulped, unsure if I was ready for his *ménage à trois* fantasy. I pointed to the fruit dangling above me since I was too short to reach it. "They're truly remarkable! Would you pluck another one for me, please?"

A devilish smile crossed my lover's face as he stepped toward me. "I see one that's perfect!"

As he pressed us against the tree, the rough bark grazed my back. I seized his hips and drew him into me. He released the buttons from my buttonholes, and with my hands entwined around his head and neck, I tugged him even closer, French kissing his soft, luscious lips.

Cupping his broad hands around my ass, Gianmarco raised me while I wrapped my legs around his waist. He perched me on a rough, solid branch, and I shrieked when my butt teetered on the edge.

"Trust me, Sabi. I've got you! I won't let you fall."

I nodded and anchored my hand to his nape. Adjusted so I leaned securely against the trunk, he lifted the hem of my skirt past my thighs and smiled. "Were you in such a rush this morning that you conveniently *forgot* to wear panties, Sabayon?" he teased.

I bit my lip and blushed. "Nope! I hadn't forgotten, Darling. I'm exactly the way you like your *kaki*—ripe, juicy, and ready to eat!"

He bellowed with delight, slinging my bare legs over his shoulders and spreading my knees wide. The man began devouring my pussy as though I were the most succulent persimmon he had ever had. "Yum! The same remarkable texture as *kaki*, for sure!" I giggled at his delightfully sexy comparison.

Running my fingers over his bare scalp, I wrested his head harder into me, writhing and bucking my pussy over his mouth as he brought me to a resounding orgasm.

When he pulled away from my thighs, his smile glistened with my nectar, making me smile.

I hopped down into his arms and kissed him deeply in appreciation. "Mmm, that was magnificent! Thank you, my love!"

Suddenly, a strong gust blew leaves and rained ripe olives down onto our heads. We couldn't help but burst into laughter together.

"My goodness! I feel like an olive. Much more of this pressing against each other on a tree, and I'll be made *extra virgin*, for sure!" I teased.

Gianmarco smirked while extracting stray olive leaves that were tangled in my tresses. "Mmm, and I'll be the one to hand-press your precious, ripe fruit with my hard millstone!"

Pulling myself onto his frame, addicted to his lips, I moaned another kiss into his mouth. "Yes, please! I want that! Cock-pressed by you every day of the week, lover! Now lay me in that grass and fuck the hell out of me!"

"Yes, ma'am!"

Seeking a less rocky surface, we shed our clothes with impulsive abandon, flinging them in a haphazard trail as we made our way toward the clearing. We were a blur of bodies intertwined, consumed by our impetuous fire. By the time he was done with me, sweaty, sated, and covered in grass, the sun had traversed from one side of the mountain range to the other.

Amazingly, Gianmarco had barely softened. His beautiful cock remained engorged and glistening. I wanted to taste his saltiness, breathe in his sweet, sweaty balls, and feel him back inside me. I couldn't get enough of him. I wanted more and more of this man—his cock, hands, lips, and *that* voice—each with the power to penetrate me, body and soul. "You truly are an Italian stallion! It seems there's no tiring you out! I've lost track of how many times you've made me cum, but you look ready for *more!*"

Those beautiful lips curled into a smile. "Oh, Sabi, you know I always want *more* with you, but if we stay under this sun much longer, we'll turn as dark as those olives!"

Before I could react, my lover scooped me into his arms, turned, and sprinted down the slope to the pond.

"Noooo! Gianmarco! Don't you dare!" I screamed, but his laughter filled my ears. When I felt him leap from the bank and launch us into the air, I closed my eyes and pulled tight into his chest.

The shock of the cool water hit every nerve ending, all at once. As we bobbed to the surface, with my Darling laughing uncontrollably at the mop that was now my face beneath my drenched hair, I couldn't help but join in his laughter.

With the water colder than I expected, my body erupted with goosebumps, and my nipples jutted out like hard gumdrops.

"I love to taste many things, but your tits are my favorite to have in my mouth!"

Holding my ass like a platter in his enormous hands, he devoured my breasts, and I felt his stiff cock bobbing against my mound.

Kissing his neck delivered his salty tang to my lips. I leaned in, nicked his earlobes with my teeth, and traced his ear with the tip of my tongue. "Do you think your big boy, *Gran*-Marco, has enough left in him to fuck my ass?"

A grunt and a growl were his answers as he pushed us through the water to the slippery clay bank. Laying me on the earthen bed, he kissed my nose and walked away without a word, leaving me perplexed.

Within seconds, he was back, holding a bottle from our picnic. He opened it, biting the cork with his molars and spitting the stopper onto the ground. Grasping his erection in hand, he doused his cock with olive oil, then eased himself slowly into my rear.

Our eyes locked on each other as I nodded, permitting him to push further.

I loved feeling his thickness and the slow submission of my muscles. I whimpered when my sphincter relaxed, and I swallowed his entire length inside my canal. It was raw and primitive—the sun baking us from overhead, the fruity scent of the olive trees wafting across us, and the cool, slippery clay beneath, coating my skin.

"Cum on me, Darling!" I commanded. "I want you to paint me with your seed. Out here in the wild, in this perfect spot to build a home, spill all over me and this soil, marking this place as ours—forever."

Water beaded across his bronzed skin, and sweat dripped from his nose as he fucked my ass deep and strong; the smacking of his balls against my cheeks was the only sound in our lover's oasis.

Pulling out and slipping back, Gianmarco held onto my shoulder with one hand while he jerked his cock to its furious finish with the other. Spraying my body with arcs of cum, he jettisoned his load all over my breasts, tummy, and neck.

Pleased with our pleasure, I rose from the mud bank and lay across his chest as I pushed back into the water. Lingering like a mermaid in his arms, we swam, rinsing our bodies and feeling born anew.

If I could only stop time, I wouldn't have to return home tomorrow, and this *assignment* would never end. Until my last breath, I wanted to always remember this perfect day and this picture-perfect picnic... with *him*.

Meet Me in Sicily

17
BEST MAN

About a month later
Sunday, October 13, 2019
Catania, Sicily

The mid-October morning air hung hot and muggy. The Sicilian humidity sapped my energy as I exited Catania International Airport. Dust from the ongoing terminal construction clung to my damp skin as I walked away from the stifling concourse.

After an exhausting international flight, I stood outside with the sweltering sun beating down on me. My body felt like a used candle on the verge of melting into the cracked, gray pavement beneath my feet.

My heart soared when I spied my dashingly mysterious *partner-in-crime* for the weekend waiting at the arrivals curb, dressed in his tailored black tuxedo that hugged the shapely outline of his muscular body like wet latex. He spotted me despite his devastating brown eyes hidden behind his black metal-rimmed Aviators. When he flashed me his patented killer smile, I was a goner.

"You look like a sleek Italian James Bond in your tux, Darling!" I raked my eyes over his drop-dead gorgeous six-foot frame.

He flushed with pride when I told him I loved his sexy style.

"I've missed you so," he sighed as I stood suspended under his lustful gaze.

In his warm hug, his fingers skimmed between my exposed shoulder blades, his hand racing down toward my derriere, squeezing firmly through my puffy satin skirt. I bit my bottom lip to stifle a gasp.

My cell phone pinged, and I became distracted by a text. I snuck a peek at him and grinned.

He looked at me sideways. "What?"

It was difficult to hide my euphoria. I had a massive surprise in store for him—bigger than a breadbox!

He raised a profound black eyebrow. "Sabi, you look like the cat that ate the canary!"

I was ecstatic, giggling, and trying to hide my guilty face behind my hands.

"Tell me!"

He grabbed me into an embrace from behind and tickled my tummy. I screamed with glee and tried to wriggle away from his powerful grip, continuing to shake my head and purse my lips closed.

Like downshifting thunder, a faraway noise approached—a blazing fire engine red convertible parked in front of us.

Gianmarco peered at me over the rim of his shades.

The driver stepped out of the vehicle. "Mrs. Skye? Mrs. Sabina Skye?"

"Yes," I answered, straightening out my dress.

"Passcode, please."

"*Argento.*"

The driver handed me the key. "Your car, ma'am."

"*Argento?* Your passcode is *silver?*" Gianmarco muttered.

Slipping my hand into his, I smiled mischievously at my Darling but left it a mystery.

With knowing eyes darting between me and *my husband*, the valet grinned and, before he headed back to the airport terminal, said, "Enjoy!"

Gianmarco whipped his sunglasses off, blinking to clear his vision and get a closer look. "Is that Ferrari 458 Spider really for us, Mrs. Skye?"

"It's not a Ducati, and it's not an Alfa Romeo Giulia Quadrifoglio." I handed him the key fob, winking. "But I think this will do, *Mr. Skye.*"

Looking as excited as a mega-millionaire lottery winner, Gianmarco stared incredulously at the red remote, adorned with the iconic Ferrari yellow and black emblem, resting in his open palm. "Less than an hour in Sicily—no extravagant gifts, eh?"

I was well aware I was disobeying his rules. But his gorgeous smile had not left his face, and I knew the car would be too marvelous a treat for even my fiercely independent Italian to deny. "It's technically only a rental, Darling; unfortunately, you don't get to keep it."

He laughed and shook his head. "The problem with fucking smart girls is that if there's a loophole, they'll find it."

"Did you mean smart, fucking girls, or fucking smart girls, Darling? I want to make sure I'm the right one."

He chortled. "OK. You won this round."

"I didn't know this was a competition. I thought we were on the same side. You know, Team Gianmarco?"

He smirked, still in disbelief at the outrageously fun start of our trip.

"Top up or down, my captain?"

"Most definitely—down!"

He opened the car door for me, then hopped into the driver's seat. Sliding his sunglasses back on his pretty face, he beamed his perfectly straight, iridescent smile at me.

"Damn, you look mighty fine, *signor Romano!*"

He posed and winked at me. "Yes, I know."

I sighed, and like the starstruck paparazzi, *click-click-click* went the camera shutter of my phone.

Gianmarco left me breathless.

SHIFTING his focus from posing to driving, he took a deep breath before pressing the red ENGINE START button, which beeped several times before the beast came to life. Giggling like a giddy schoolboy, he jumped for joy upon hearing the sexy, deep roar of its awakening.

After adjusting the mirrors, he caressed the sides of the leather steering wheel with the prancing black stallion crest emblazoned upon it. He giggled again as he rimmed the LAUNCH button with his pointer finger, eager to try out all the gadgets at his disposal.

Toggling the vertical paddle shifters, he slipped the car into gear.

When I showed him the image of what I had captured, the biggest smile I had ever seen blazed across his face.

"I love it! Send it to me so I can post it!" He laughed, and I smiled at his approval.

"I'm ready to ride my Italian stallion!" I teased him. "Are you?"

He bounced his eyebrows up and down at me. "Vroom-vroom!" he said as he punched the accelerator, and off we went!

Whooping and yelling at the top of his lungs, he downshifted to race his rocket down the Autostrada A18, Sicily's major north-south coastal motorway.

He squeezed my thigh and threaded his fingers through mine. "Thank you! Thank you! Thank you!"

I kissed the smooth surface of his hand before resting it on my lap. "You're welcome." No other words were necessary to declare my utter happiness.

"I can't wait to *play* with you tonight, Sabayon." Raising my hand to his lips, he kissed my knuckles and sniffed them. "I love how you always smell like a fragrant bouquet of roses!"

Gianmarco was so unintentionally romantic! I reveled in the idea that my sommelier experienced the world through his nose.

Because I was with him and he was with me, I couldn't stop smiling, feeling like the luckiest girl in the world!

OUR DESTINATION WAS about an hour away, on the outskirts of Syracuse. Unfortunately, I was more interested in enjoying the white, pink, and red oleander flowers flanking the motorway.

Rather than watching the GPS and helping him navigate, I stared at the beautiful golden hills of the Sicilian countryside; my daydreaming got us horribly lost! I apologized to him for my poor job as a copilot.

"No problem. *C'è una vita sola!*"
"You only live once!"

Gazing at my beloved while rubbing his thigh, I mused at how right he was. *You only live once. That is why I'm here with you now, my love.*

"I'm having a blast driving this sexy beast! Besides, we are on an island with only three main roads. How lost can we get?"

I smiled at his carefree mood. Sitting beside him, watching him savor the best of what life could offer, nothing made me prouder than knowing I was the one making him happy.

Gianmarco was so different from Cyril. It was nerve-wracking to travel with my husband, who mercilessly poked fun at my lack of a sense of direction. But not my lover. To him, ending up lost was not a mistake to point out but an adventure to relish!

"Tell me about Antonio," I inquired as if I were nervously cramming for a test—meeting the family!

"He's my cool younger brother who gets along with everybody; although, he can be a pain about planning and punctuality."

"You mentioned he's in the Italian Navy."

"An officer. It suits him since he's always loved visiting new places."

"And Valeria. What do you think of your future sister-in-law?"

"I like her. She's nice. Pretty."

"Are you guys close?"

"No, I only see her when Antonio brings her home for the holidays. She likes to cook, and she fits in with the family."

"So, how did Antonio and Valeria meet?"

"Guys don't talk about that kind of mushy stuff. We wanna know if she gives *good head* and if she swallows!"

"No-no-no! I do *not* want to know intimate details about your brother's sex life!"

With a wry smile, he added, "Oh, and if a chick's tits are real."

"You're so bad!" I punched him in the shoulder, and he laughed some more.

"It's true. Ask any guy, and they'll tell you the same thing."

"Seriously, do you know how they met?"

"They began dating when they were classmates at university. They fell in love and stayed up north because that was where the jobs were."

I knitted my eyebrows together in confusion. "So, why is the wedding in Sicily?"

"Her family's Sicilian," he explained, "and if they held it up north, many of her grandparents and older relatives wouldn't be able to attend because they're too old or sick to make the trip."

"Wow, I love how Italians are so tight-knit."

"I don't know about every Italian family. But for us, *la nostra famiglia*, our family is very important, especially for the older generation. They've sacrificed so much to make things better for us. I wish I had known my grandparents; they died before I was born. So, having a wedding where it's easier for the old ones is a small thing."

"But what about their friends in the north? Do you think they'll make the long trip to southern Italy?"

"No problem. It's easy enough to come to Sicily; afterward, they get a side vacation on the island. Like us." He squeezed my knee, and I smiled.

We rounded the corner, passed the church, and arrived very late.

"We're here!" Gianmarco announced.

He parked the car, but before we unbuckled ourselves, I

gripped his thigh with panic in my eyes and a frown that etched my forehead like parallel worry-waves on the sand left by a receding tide. "Do you think they'll like me?"

"I know you're worried about meeting my family, but everything will be fine." He took my hand and kissed it. "Italian weddings are fun! Good Italian food and wine, some dancing, and fantastic sex afterward, depending on the partner!"

"I'm hoping for that last part!" I smiled.

Bouncing his eyebrows, he said, "Me too, Sabayon!" Then he reached across and kissed me. In a collision of passion, our mouths melded together, tongues dancing in a velvet embrace. When he pulled away, the taste of his wet kiss lingered on my lips, leaving me breathless and craving *more*.

I sighed and crossed my legs, trying to control the growing arousal. "You bastard, getting my engine fired up like that!"

"Save that for me for later!" teased my gorgeous lover.

We smiled in anticipation.

Casa Caradonna
Siracusa, Sicily

As soon as we exited the car, a flustered man approached. "Bro, I need your help! We have a big problem."

Gianmarco briefly introduced me to Antonio, a taller version of himself with the same mesmerizing Romano features reminiscent of their shared heritage, except for the brother's gray-green eyes adorned with golden flecks of hazel, resembling the shimmering surface of the sea when kissed by the noonday sun.

Antonio, the Naval Officer before me, was athletic, clean-shaven, and sported a military regulation haircut—unlike *bedhead Antonio*, with his wind-swept curls that cascaded in waves, as in my daydream on the train to Florence.

I felt like a fifth wheel while the brothers became engrossed in an animated discussion. Gianmarco frowned and turned to me to explain that they were short-staffed for the party because many had suddenly come down with a fever. "It's too late to cancel the wedding, so everyone is helping out; even our parents are in the kitchen, prepping." My Darling informed me that he had agreed to pitch in and manage the event.

Being loyal and supportive of his family was of the utmost importance. I tried to hide my slight disappointment at the turn of events. So, I gave him an understanding peck on the cheek and straightened his tie. "Your brother is so lucky you're here for him. You're truly the *Best Man* for this job, Darling."

He cradled my face and gently kissed my lips. I blushed at his public display of affection in front of his newly-introduced brother.

Antonio politely apologized as he whisked away my date so they could attend to their duties. I watched them disappear into the house, Antonio's arm draped over my lover's shoulder, leading him away.

18

THE FAMILY

I wandered around the beautiful grounds of the Caradonna family's grand, three-story terracotta, brick, and plaster villa. The original structure of Casa Caradonna was more modest and was built by Valeria's great-great-grandfather, Federico Caradonna, in the 1870s, around the time when Northern and Southern Italy united.

The Caradonna ancestral home sat adjacent to the cathedral, Il Duomo di Siracusa, and was currently an *agriturismo*, a holiday farm house, where the family hosted lavish 150-person events. With an ancient olive grove and head-pruned old vines surrounding the villa, it was the perfect setting for a romantic Southern Italian country wedding.

Today's event was more personal for the family. I was sure everything would be beyond perfect for their beloved daughter,

Valeria Caradonna, and their future son-in-law, Antonio Romano.

Just then, an adorable group of children appeared from nowhere and surrounded me. With excited chattery, they ushered me back to my sports car, where the gang of innocent youths begged and pleaded for permission to climb inside the luxury speedster.

Gianmarco liked children and had a hidden, playful nature. Still, I was unsure if my neatnik would approve of what I suspected this unruly gang would do to *his* pristine Ferrari.

But he was currently busy and none the wiser, so I decided to let them in. I intended to dust and wipe down the interior, lest he find out what I had allowed.

One child grabbed the sunglasses off my head and planted them on his face, strutting like a rock star. Another jumped into the convertible and pretended to drive it, pounding on the horn and making everyone peal with laughter.

So many rambunctious youngsters piled into the two-seater. I took pictures on my phone, now that the Ferrari looked more like a carnival ride than an elite automobile. When I showed the kids the shots, they giggled and laughed raucously.

Out of the corner of my eye, I noticed a shy, skinny boy disengaged from the pack. The young man shone with a beautiful olive complexion beneath close-cropped, glossy black hair. With his thick, dark eyebrows, a smooth, symmetrical nose, and stunning eyes, one gray-green and the other a hazy, milk-white, I was sure he was a Romano. He was what I imagined my Darling looked like as a child. Beautiful.

He stood away from the others, wearing a blue and black striped Inter Milan football jersey, leaning against an ancient olive tree. His aloof demeanor reminded me of my shy Kally and how Gianmarco, our then-waiter, charmed her out of her shell when we first met him at Mirabella.

I walked over to the young man and crouched down to meet him at eye level. "*Ciao!*"

In a shy voice, he replied, "Hello!"

"You speak English!" I smiled with delight.

"Yes. I learned in school," he proudly informed me.

"Well, you speak it very well!"

"Thank you."

"You're welcome."

"What is your name?"

"Luca."

I extended my hand to him, and he shook it like a grownup. "Pleased to meet you, Luca. I'm Sabina."

"Pleased to meet you, Miss Sabina."

"Just Sabina. Hey, Luca! How would you like to play in my fancy car with the others?" I offered.

"No thanks."

"Why not?" I asked, surprised by his reply.

With a shrug, the boy delivered an *eh*, the quintessential monosyllabic answer, when an Italian didn't know or want to say.

I pointed to the children using my vehicle as a jungle gym. "But aren't those your cousins?"

He shook his head with his hands on his hips. "I don't know any kids here."

"Me neither. We're in the same boat, you and I." I smiled and offered a warm laugh.

"No, I'm not from here. I'm a Romano from Naples!" He proudly informed me.

"Oh, I see! So, Antonio and Gianmarco are your cousins?"

"Second cousins. Our papàs *were* first cousins."

Were? I knew I shouldn't pry, but wasn't Gianmarco's father, Marcello, still alive? What happened to Luca's father?

"A Romano! No wonder you look so handsome, Luca!" I said.

"I get that a lot!" he said with a bit of swagger. "We Romano men look alike."

I chuckled.

"Except I have more hair!" He giggled, running his fingers through his thick black mane.

"Hey! I think bald men can be incredibly sexy!" I laughed, amused at my conversation with a kid! Italians were such confident flirts, even at a young age.

I had a serious chocolate addiction and always carried a secret stash in my purse. "Do you like chocolate?" I opened the round tin and offered him some.

"Yeah, thank you!" He nodded appreciatively, and I smiled, happy to discover that food, particularly chocolate, was the key to connecting with another Romano.

"You're welcome!" I popped a piece in my mouth. "May I *lean* next to you?"

He nodded, gesturing to a free spot by his side.

"Why do you look so sad, Luca? A wedding is a happy day!"

He stared down at his shoes, the fine dust clinging to the worn leather. "It's my birthday."

"Happy Birthday, Luca! How old are you now?" I said, raising my voice an octave, hoping to cheer him up.

"Nine!" He put out nine digits to emphasize the milestone.

"What would you normally do on your birthday?"

His eyes looked into the distance, smiling dreamily. "Eat cake and ice cream."

"I'm sure we'll get to do that later."

"Play games—"

"Like what?" I asked my new friend.

"Tag, as well as Hide and Seek."

"Let's play that now. I'm in heels, so I'm going to be really slow; I'll be *it*."

The boy looked at me with a wide smile. "Really?"

"Run, Luca!"

He laughed and ran toward the Ferrari. Naturally, the other kids wanted to join in the fun and hopped out of the car, much to my relief.

I tripped and fell on a patch of dry grass poking out of the parched landscape. I sighed, certain that the back of my dress was sandy from the encounter. The kids piled on top of me; I hugged them, and we all laughed merrily.

A soccer ball appeared, and the kids started kicking it around. When Italians see a ball on a field, it's instinctive for them to begin a match. The children screamed and played together, including happy Luca, who looked back, smiled, and waved at me.

Drumming my fingers in the air, I waved back and blew him a kiss.

Of all the luck! Turning toward the house, I slipped on that same patch of scrub, and I was in the dirt again. I shook my head and snickered at myself.

As I looked up, a gorgeous, bearded Italian man with a magnificent smile and sparkling eyes offered me his hand. Under the cuff of his shirt sleeve, I glimpsed a barbed-wire tattoo encircling his wrist.

"Thank you!" I graciously accepted his help, dusting my backside as best as possible.

"Ciao Niko!" I kissed him on both cheeks, Italian style.

"Ciao Sabina!" He reciprocated.

Mirabella was where I met Niko Romano when he fulfilled

a favor arranged by his older brother, *Gianma*, the nickname Gianmarco's family gave him. Though tired, Niko was so generous with his time, giving me a private demo on how to make the most delicate, ethereal pasta ever!

I wasn't sure it was allowable, but Niko, the sous chef, revealed the restaurant's secrets to me. The first tip was the perfect proportion of the thrice-milled, super elastic, *Triplozero* '000' flour: 1kg to 300 grams of egg yolks and 200 grams of egg whites.

The second trick was letting the dough rest overnight in the refrigerator to relax the gluten, making the final rollout easier.

Lastly, instead of a moistened pastry brush, the cleverest trick was using a spray bottle filled with water to lightly mist-seal the pasta layers together.

The tips were utter genius!

Afterward, Niko generously shared with us the finished burrata-ricotta ravioli, along with a substantial jar of that unctuous saffron sauce to go with it and enjoy later.

I smiled at seeing my friend once again. "I'm so happy to see you! How are things at Mirabella?"

Niko grinned at me. "Very good, and I'm glad to see you too. How goes the ravioli making?"

"Thank you for the master class! You inspired me to make it at home. Mine are not as good as yours, but I'll keep trying."

"It's difficult to recreate what we produce in a commercial kitchen at home."

"I covet your amazing industrial pasta machine."

He smiled and gave the same Gianmarco chuckle. The sound of his deep, throaty laughter balmed my lonely heart.

Emboldened, I winked at him, saying, "Or maybe I need another private lesson!"

"For you, anywhere, anytime." The intensity of his gaze touched my soul. I lowered my eyes and smiled.

"I can see why my big brother is smiling more these days!"

A drop from the same cup of charm flowed through the Romano bloodline like wine. Feeling the warm raindrops of his compliments, I stepped into the shower. "Why?" I asked.

"My serious brother is like our cousin Luca. Both seem aloof, like they don't care, but they do. But your smile and playfulness have a way of disarming men, Sabina. You bring out the child in us!"

I blushed. My eyes were enormous, shocked with embarrassment. "You were watching!"

"We all were. We saw your kindness toward Luca, coaxing him to drop his guard and act like a kid." Niko gestured to the sea of faces peering through the windows and doorways, looking our way.

"I think security cameras are unnecessary in Italy. Every eyeball is watching!"

Niko treated me to more of his warm laughter, sparkling, happier, and freer than my guarded Gianmarco. Yet Niko's sultry brown eyes were as devastating as his brother's!

"Oh, no! That means even *Mamma* was watching!" I clapped both hands to my mouth. "Oh God! Did she see me trip and fall? Twice? I'm so nervous about meeting her."

"She's just as nervous, but she won't show it. She's like Gianma. Poker face."

We laughed.

"Niko, are you a groomsman at the wedding? You look quite charming in your tux, but I'm not sure the girly apron complements the outfit."

"Ahahaha! Yes, I am. I don't know if you've heard, but Papà, Mamma, and I volunteered to be prep chefs for the big feast since they're short on helpers." Niko beckoned me with his hand. "Come with me and meet the family."

"I was hoping to make a better impression—look at my dress! I'm *filthy!*"

"You look beautiful! No one will even notice. Maybe the color and the design—"

"Is it too much?" I placed both my hands on my face, worried.

"Black for a wedding makes a bold statement. And the cut—somewhere between nightclub and funeral."

I laughed nervously. "Hmm, I was shooting for *Breakfast at Tiffany's* elegance in the afternoon, but without the hat."

"Don't change a thing. I like your sophisticated style!"

I blushed again. "You're too kind." I paused before we entered the doorway into the kitchen. "Niko, may I ask you a question, please?"

"Of course."

"You mentioned that Luca pretends like he doesn't care. Does he feel like an outsider, a misfit, because of his eye?"

"Yes, I think so. Luca was a happy boy until the accident left him partially blind. His body has healed, but he carries a wound deep inside." Niko pointed to his heart.

"I know I'm not family, and you don't have to tell me since it's none of my business, but what happened?"

"Luca and his father, my uncle, were inseparable. Luca survived a tragic car accident, blinded, but it took his papà's life."

"I'm sorry."

"It remains a heartbreak for us, Romanos."

"Thank you for confiding in me."

"You're welcome. Maybe you'll be one of us someday."

I smiled at his kind words.

"Are you ready to meet the family?"

"No!" I answered with a dry swallow. "But, yes, I suppose I should."

Niko extended a gallant arm, and I weaved mine through his. Being in the comfort of his care quelled my fears.

ENTERING the hot and steamy galley, the smell of a wonderful banquet flooded my nose. Niko, like an experienced dancer, knew not to lead too quickly. I stepped in quietly and absorbed the atmosphere in the room.

With a sunflower and lemon theme, the kitchen felt warm and inviting. Scattered along shelves and tables were vibrant Sicilian Maiolica ceramics, interspersed with colorful hand-painted tiles of the *Trinicaria*—the three-legged lady painted on the squares in bright yellow and green—symbolizing the united Kingdoms of Sicily and Naples.

Italians tended to have large extended families. The kitchen was its heart, where you would most likely find them together. Everyone here was busy working, from the siblings and cousins to the nieces and nephews, the aunts and uncles, and even the grandparents. Three generations from each side of the family operated as seamlessly as a well-trained brigade.

We approached an older couple in the kitchen. The woman was the mirror image of Gianmarco, except with a full mane of hair.

"Mamma, Papà, I present Sabina, Gianmarco's girl from America."

I smiled since it had been years since I had heard myself referred to as *someone's girl*. And though my accent was tragic, we exchanged the standard Italian greeting of *piacere,* because I was genuinely pleased to meet my Darling's parents.

Papà Marcello Romano had a kind, gracious countenance. His broad, friendly smile and big, bushy eyebrows were the most prominent features on his face.

Like his middle son, Antonio, the Naval Officer, Papà was clean-shaven with a receding hairline that had turned gray. He stood like a proud Italian, as tall as his youngest son, Niko. Rather than casting words, his charm emanated from a still, playful gaze. His eyes appreciated his eldest son's catch, and though slowed by time, I sensed Papà Romano still had some *pep in his pipe.*

Mamma Lisabetta Romano, with dyed-black short-cropped hair, looked a decade younger than her husband. It was clear she was a force to be reckoned with as she fussed over Papà's cappelletti, meticulously refining his pinching technique to ensure each one resembled a perfectly formed miniature hat.

Her genetics were so dominant that her sons had her olive complexion and stunning eyes. They looked like they could cut through bullshit like a hot knife through butter, and I could see why Niko referred to his mother as Poker Face.

"Is there something I can do to help out, please?" I inquired timidly, hoping to be useful.

The ladies conferred and spoke rapidly in their native tongue, a tad too quickly for me to decipher. Finally, after witnessing what seemed like a tense hostage negotiation, I received a terse, single-word reply from Maria Romano.

"*Sì.*"

I was assigned the harmless task of shelling beans with the young girls. Excited for the opportunity to practice their English, they fired a flurry of questions at me. "What is your name? Where do you live? What is your favorite food? Can you cook? Do you have any pets? What are your pets' names?"

One bold girl asked, "Do you love my cousin, Gianmarco?"

"Chiara Romano, why can't you be more polite like your little brother, Luca?" Her mother's wagging, bony finger chastised her for her pointed, nosy question. The girl tightly pursed her lips, looking angry and bristling at the comparison to her younger sibling.

Chiara was a chubby preteen with long, tight curls; she wore her brown hair pulled into a big, bushy ponytail. Though she didn't wear makeup, she did paint her nails a shocking neon pink. Besides her thick, dark Romano eyebrows, this girl had her mother's sharp black eyes and thin lips. She donned a tight white T-shirt with a red cola logo imprinted on the front.

Chiara and Luca's widowed mother, Maria Romano, looked like a withered leaf of arugula left on the counter for far too long. Her thin, wavy hair, pulled back into a tight bun, rested low on her nape. She had fierce, joyless black eyes, a narrow nose, and severe lips.

Though it was boiling in the kitchen, she wore a black frock that hung loosely on her skeletal frame. A simple gold wedding band rested on her left ring finger, and a silver necklace, a rosary, hung around her neck.

The chatter died down. I guessed more people understood English than they let on. No one looked at me, but all ears were pricked up, waiting for my reply.

Do I love him? I often ask myself that question, and now I must publicly declare my intentions to his family! How should I answer? "Of course I love Gianmarco! He's so handsome! Doesn't everybody here love him too?"

A series of nods and giggles spread throughout the room, cutting through the awkward tension.

"*Ragazzi!*" Maria commanded like a general. "It's time to get ready!"

"*Children!*"

We finished shelling the last of the beans piled high in an enormous white enameled bowl, and the kids dashed upstairs.

Maria turned to me. "Do you want to change and freshen up, Sabina? You look dusty."

I looked at Niko, and we burst out laughing—our little inside joke.

She looked confused.

I tried to compose myself. "Yes, thank you."

Before exiting the kitchen, I stopped by Mamma Lisabetta's station and admired her work. "Your *gnocchetti* are so perfect, as if made by a machine, such that every little gnocchi are like beautiful handmade pasta seashells."

"*Grazie,*" she beamed, and Papà Marcello looked proudly at his wife.

"I hope you'll please share your recipe and technique with me."

Mamma nodded, and her eyes softened toward me, making my heart jump for joy.

But an instant later, *General* Maria snapped her command, "Come," interrupting the budding connection between Mamma and me.

I obeyed and followed behind.

GENERAL ROMANO INVITED me to change in the spare bedroom downstairs. There was a simple twin bed with a peach-colored floral bedspread. I dared not place my luggage on the new cover, so I opened the valise on the floor, kneeling on the cold travertine tiles to find something more decent to wear.

Staring into the looking glass, I shook my head. I guess the black gown I planned to wear was not OK for the ceremony. Inside my luggage were mainly lingerie, toys, and an even shorter, tighter dress for clubbing and playing with my lover later. A pair of jeans for the plane trip back was squashed near the bottom. The last two items were definitely not appropriate wedding attire.

However, the flirty and flouncy linen dress I was saving for when we were on the beach piqued my interest. It was a knee-length, off-the-shoulder, low-cut number. I hoped it was not too casual or close to the off-white shade of the bride's gown. *Now that would be a worse faux pas!*

After stripping down, I shimmied the dress over my head, looking pleased with myself in the mirror; the bands of my sexy black bra showed through the thin, spaghetti shoulder straps. As I twirled around, a giggle escaped me.

Catching *The General's* reflection in the looking glass, I wondered how long she had been watching me. Quietly, she entered the room. "May I place a shawl on your shoulders in case you get cold in the church?" She demonstrated how to attach the matching headscarf with a pin and then placed it on the bed.

"Thank you, that's so kind." I respectfully complied. Apparently, women should not show their bare heads or arms inside the church. It was sweltering hot, yet we had to abide by these religious customs, no matter how illogical they seemed.

I could not stand the heat, so a quick shower to freshen up was in order. Having survived my initial introduction to the family, I welcomed the opportunity to wash away the stress and ducked into the sanctuary of the bathroom.

19

TWIST OF FATE

Revitalized and clad in conformity, it wasn't long before the stifling humidity flushed my face. Looking for relief from the heat, I found a memento of my last adventure with Gianmarco stuffed in a hidden pocket of my suitcase—an old, red and white handkerchief absentmindedly taken from the fountain of the palazzo's secret garden. I dabbed away the perspiration; the fabric soothed my skin.

As the crimson cloth cooled against my neck, a playful thought crossed my mind, and I couldn't help but blush. If it failed to keep the heat off me, I could always wave it in the air to catch my Italian bull's eye; perhaps he could provide some relief.

Ready to join the church festivities, I encountered an elderly woman descending the stairs. Her arthritic hands gripped the rail with each measured footstep.

"*Salve!*" I respectfully greeted her, though she remained lost in her thoughts, her gaze fixed downward, calculating her every move.

I wanted to be of assistance, but something foreboding kept me from reaching out to take her hand, afraid of touching her weathered skin.

Though I didn't know this reverent Italian grandma, I loudly addressed her, "Nonna, may I help you down the stairs?"

Still, she offered no reply. As we drew side by side on a step, I created space, mindful not to intrude. Fearing that her eyesight might be failing, I instinctively waved the red handkerchief, hoping to capture her attention.

Suddenly, she extended her cockled hand and gripped my still-damp hair. "You should not tempt Fate, *carina fagiolina*," she said in a voice that crackled like old parchment.

Her grip tightened as if she could sense my vulnerability through her touch. "Your lungs are weak and scarred," she continued, her words punctuating the air. "You almost met Death the last time. Venturing outside with wet hair is a fool's errand. To worry less, my child, you must hasten less. He will be there, happier with your hair—dry."

When her gnarled fingers brushed against my face, a strange sensation prickled at the nape of my neck. Her cloudy, cataract-covered eyes seemed to fixate on me, though I knew her blindness should have obscured her vision. It was as if she saw through my flesh, gazing into the depths of my being.

Taken aback, my face turned ashen. How did this *nonna* know I had weak lungs? As a teenager, I almost died of pneumonia. And she called me by the nickname my grandfather gave me—*dear little bean!* I was a rambunctious, energetic child, full of beans, and had difficulty sitting still or following rules, like my sweet little Kally.

An eerie shiver ran down my spine. I had never put much stock in superstitions, but the Old World had ways that were not understood. Worried that Nonna's prophecy might ring true, I returned to the room. Though I couldn't imagine willingly making myself feel even hotter than I already did, I blow-dried my hair.

Dried enough, I turned, hoping to see Nonna and ask how she knew about my past. But looking around, I saw no one in the foyer; she was gone. Goosebumps rippled across my skin, raising the tiny hairs on the back of my neck again. The villa was deserted except for a few remaining workers setting up for the reception party.

The church bells rang, and I had to hurry not to miss the main event. Fortunately, it was next door, so I would not be late, joining the tail end of a parade of smartly dressed guests.

PAUSING at the chapel's narthex allowed my senses to adjust to the sudden contrast from the bright outdoor sunlight to the darkened shadows within; the dimness in the vestibule carried the weight of devotion. Though it had been years since I had attended Mass, the flock never forgets the rites and rituals. My fingers, dipped in the marble font, trailed through the cool Holy Water—still clinging to my fingertips, I made the sign of the cross.

A mesmerizing display of vibrant yellow sunflowers and snowy-white plumerias greeted me as I passed the threshold. The reminiscent, intoxicating aroma made me swoon. My mind drifted to the bittersweet memory of my own bridal bouquet, composed of yellow plumerias and white roses, seemingly a lifetime ago.

When we first married, I was sure Cyril *was* the love of my life. He was my sun, and I was a planet revolving around my guiding star, happily pulled along by his gravity. But in my willingness to surrender everything to him, I lost my inner light. Now, all that remained was a spark of who I was before. Over the years, the space between us grew, and my orbit, addicted to his mass, decayed.

In reality, there was no *we*. It was only Cyril, with my shadow ghosting alongside him. Sleepwalking through life had been more than comfortable as his business partner, wife, and mother of Eve, our firstborn, now twenty-five. But then came the accidental pregnancy of our second daughter, Kally. He didn't want the baby, partly because he didn't believe she was ours—his and mine. His unjustified accusations of infidelity hurt me. There was never another. Only Cyril.

It was the wedge that split us wide apart.

I CRANED MY NECK, searching for a seat, but guests had packed the church on both sides of the aisles. At least 150 people were crammed into the pews, furiously fanning themselves to stave off the heat.

Luca sat in the back, on the groom's side. I smiled when I saw him leaping, beckoning me to join their gang. He had become the ring leader, the big kid looking after the other boisterous children, ordering them to scoot over and make space for me. Although the familiar young faces comforted me and I enjoyed their company, I felt like an outcast—no longer fitting in. My place in the Church had expired long ago.

My eyes wandered, seeking solace within the sacred walls. And there, bathed in the soft hues of stained glass, my gaze found the Crucifix—a poignant symbol of sacrifice.

After years of always being something for others, I now

wanted something for myself. I wanted my lover, who desired me like no other. He was my master and my teacher, helping me find my true self. As crazy as it sounded, being with him was like going home—where I belonged.

And so I defy You and reject Your Commandments. I am an adulteress, unashamed of standing in Your house, witnessing one of the Seven Sacraments of the Holy Roman Catholic Church, although I fear the price that You, the Lord Almighty, will extract from this unrepentant sinner will be high.

Though a shadow of dread passed through my body, my heart held my conviction steady. Loving Gianmarco was worth a fall from grace.

AT THE ALTAR, Gianmarco and Niko scanned the crowd, their eyes searching through the sea of unfamiliar faces. I waved, a gesture that earned smiles and waves from the brothers. Gianmarco, however, turned back to face the altar, his focus unwavering.

Niko's gaze lingered on me, and I felt my cheeks heat up. Did he notice my blushing? Then Gianmarco elbowed Niko; cowed, he turned to face the altar too.

Valeria Caradonna, the beautiful bride, was a vision of loveliness. Wearing an elegant ivory satin and lace floor-length wedding gown, she stood with her parents at the rear of the church. Papà Caradonna's beaming smile was a testament to his joy, while Mamma Caradonna appeared more anxious than her daughter. This new role on center stage clearly unsettled her. Her usual place was behind the scenes, catering such grand events with a practiced hand.

Antonio Romano, the dashing groom, and his parents, *il signor e la signora Romano*, stood gracefully at the altar. Like the Caradonnas, they were in the hospitality business and accustomed to hosting weddings at Fiore, the family's restaurant in Abruzzo. But today, the relaxed expressions on their faces suggested that they were relishing this rare moment as guests rather than hosts.

As the Best Man, Gianmarco's face carried a gravity beyond the occasion. A thousand details swirled in his mind—a choreography of responsibilities he must execute with precision. Beside him, Mamma Caradonna would orchestrate the culinary symphony, while Gianmarco, the maître d' of his restaurant in Milan, would command the front of the house—a role at which he excelled.

As the Mass commenced, the ethereal notes of *Ave Maria*, sung by a choir of angels, enveloped the church. Two joyful families moved gracefully toward each other, converging at the heart of the church's nave. The Romanos, soon to be Valeria's kin, held her hands with tender reverence, kissing her gently on the forehead.

Antonio Romano's eyes blazed with a mixture of adoration and awe as he gazed upon his bride, offering her a simple bouquet of long-stemmed sunflowers tied with an ivory ribbon that perfectly matched her gown's satin.

With clasped hands, the bride and groom floated toward the sanctuary. The brothers, the priest, and the two bridesmaids awaited them there.

Tears sparkled in the corners of my eyes. Weddings were so romantic, especially when performed in the lyrical language of Italian. Like gazing at a star from afar, I watched my lover at the altar and wished I were by his side.

. . .

After the ending Processional, Gianmarco collected me with his brow furrowed in agitation. "Were you flirting with my brother in front of my family?"

I knew he was busy, so I tried to diffuse his disquiet with my most loving voice. "Your brother was friendly and kind. He saw that I was uncomfortable with you leaving me alone and wanted me to feel less like an outsider. I get the sense Niko relates and sees himself as a bit of a misfit too."

"I am the misfit, not Niko! He is the favorite son who follows Papà's every footstep. Yet, even when he strays, the family forgives him because he can do no wrong!" His voice boomed so loudly that people turned to rubberneck us.

I kept my tone calm and even. "Yes, they're both chefs, but they're different. Your father is much more reserved, but Niko is playful, like a giggly boy trapped in a man's body."

"Is that what you want, Sabina, to play with giggly boys?" His harsh whisper burned my ear.

I stopped in my tracks and looked at him. "What's up? Why are you so edgy? I've done nothing wrong. Whatever this is, it's about you, not me."

He said nothing. He was looking intently at something, and it wasn't at me. I followed his line of sight. He stared, transfixed, at the woman heading toward the exit on the other side of the church.

"She looks familiar. Who is she?" I dared to ask.

"You met her at your architect's office."

I narrowed my eyes for a better look. "The secretary, Ro-something?" I couldn't remember her name since she seemed to blend into the woodwork with her nondescript clothing.

He nodded, and I peered more closely at the stunningly toned Italian bombshell with shapely hips, a tiny waist, and a voluptuous chest. "Wow, I didn't recognize her. Are you sure? The secretary wore glasses."

"I'm sure."

"Do you know her? You seemed standoffish toward her when you met."

"Her name is Ravenna. She's my ex."

Those heavy words hit me like a ton of bricks. I stared at him, then at her.

Speechless.

Her black hair was cropped short and shaved at the nape. The top fringe held a band of bleached blonde that fell over one of her eyebrows; the sharp cut of her lightened mane starkly contrasted her dark, suntanned skin. Her nails, painted bright red, matched the color of her tight bodycon dress and the likewise lacquered toenails that poked out of her sky-high peep-toe stilettos.

The woman looked like an enchanting tower of cotton candy floss—hard to resist and cloyingly sweet. But I knew what she looked like without the facade; it was all for show. And yet, Gianmarco was bewitched by the insubstantial spun-sugar rush she offered, which was just a cloud of foam in the end.

"Would you rather have asked *her* to be your date?"

His eyes remained riveted on his ex. "She only wants to talk. She said I looked different. Changed."

I bit my tongue as I surmised the situation. A woman dressed like that doesn't *only* want to talk. Though my voice quavered, I fought back my insecurity. "She finally sees your beautiful side; the one I've always seen is inside you, Gianmarco."

He turned to me at the mention of his name. I saw the pain in his eyes and understood why he rejected the coffee she offered him at the office.

"Seeing her this way again brings up deep emotions I buried long ago."

"Do you want her back?" The words strangled my throat.

He could not tear his eyes from her, and his lack of reply wounded my heart.

"Gianmarco!" The photographer motioned to him.

"Sorry, Sabi. More pictures."

"You're a free man, Mr. Romano. I'm not your jailer." I pecked his cheek and placed my hand on my face, trying to hide the tears that threatened to spill over.

He kissed my forehead and hugged me with one arm before walking away.

20
NIKO

I stared at the green rectangular sign lit above the doorway —*USCITA*—EXIT. Escape. I clenched my fists, my nails digging into my sweaty palms, for every fiber of my being was screaming to abandon this suffocating reality and run far, far away.

Seemingly out of nowhere, Niko approached me. "Ugh, more posing for photos!"

"Shouldn't you be at the photo shoot?" I asked. My voice was unsteady, and I sniffled back the anxiety of impending heartbreak, threatening full-on sobbing.

"Nah, they wouldn't even notice I wasn't there." Niko's words were gentle and soothing, but his eyes showed empathy from witnessing the verbal exchange. "I'm parched! Can I get you a cold drink, Sabina?"

"Thank you! I'd love one... or two!"

Niko returned with two flutes of sparkling wine and invited me to walk with him. While exploring, we discovered a hidden sanctuary. In the middle of this secluded garden was an ancient Roman fountain that looked like it predated the church. We sat on a fallen marble pillar under a grove of mature oak trees and listened to the sound of cascading water, calming my troubled soul.

"Niko?" I asked. "Can you tell me what happened between Gianmarco and Ravenna? He's never mentioned her, but I think it's a deep wound."

He shrugged. "He's not told me, but I heard they fought a lot about many things. Fire and Ice."

"Who was whom?"

Niko looked at me and shrugged again. "Both."

I couldn't help releasing a huff-like laugh.

Before lancing the proverbial boil, Niko glugged his wine, then asked me a serious, pointed question. "How much do you love my brother?"

I put the glass down, wiping away the pent-up tears escaping from my eyes. "A lot."

"Why do you love Gianma?" he gently asked.

Looking up at the night sky, I remembered telling Gianmarco how I felt about him. My voice was full of loneliness, and perhaps he sensed a kindred spirit in me. "Your brother saw my wound, the huge hole in my heart, and without thinking, he courageously jumped through it and healed me from within."

"My brother is capable of good, and love demands you trust him and give him a chance to explain."

This earnest and direct side of Niko was new to me, so I listened without interruption to his counsel.

He cupped my cheek, and I leaned into his comforting hand. "Love is a choice—an act of faith—not an exchange."

I took a large gulp of my wine. "But I don't know if he loves me. He's never said." My voice was quiet, and I could hear the words mixed with fear and hope.

Niko took a large swig that matched mine. "Some men find it difficult to express themselves with words but show it through actions."

"Yes." I swallowed hard. "I saw how he stared at Ravenna—with longing." I gazed into my glass. Surely another tear had fallen into it.

"Like cousin Luca, we all have wounds. Some hide their unhealed ones better than others. Perhaps Gianma's heart has not found closure with her yet."

I peered at Niko, looking for some insight. "How much has he told you about us?"

"Our family is close, but why would my big brother tell me or even want my advice?" With a wry smile, Niko added, "There's an old saying: Complaints flow upstream, shit flows down!"

I gasped at the profane imagery and genius of the statement, laughing and wagging my finger at him. "You may be younger, but you are a wise owl. Hoot more of your wisdom to me, and I will listen because you see everything with those big, beautiful eyes of yours!"

He chuckled.

"He went to talk to *her!*" I gulped half the wine from my glass. "Dressed like that, she is the type of flawless I wish I could be. How could any man resist a woman like that?"

"That look may appeal to a lot of men—but not to me. Tantalizing on the outside, but dangerous on the inside."

I drained my glass to the last drop. "Maybe she's *la ragazza* he truly desires."

"the girlfriend"

"My brother is a good man. Do not abandon him because I know he will not abandon you."

"I don't want him to stay with me because he thinks he's obligated; I'm a big girl and can drive myself home."

"Indeed, I see you are a most competent woman!"

"Right now, I am lost and alone, like a stranger who doesn't belong."

I peered into my empty glass. Torn in two, I desperately wanted to be on my lover's arm, acting demure and beaming inside as he showed off his American girl. Yet, I was merely one more hurt feeling from bolting away in the Ferrari and disappearing down the Sicilian coast.

Somehow, Niko read my mind. "How much do you want to be with Gianma and have our family accept you?"

"So much that it hurts."

"You arrived together, and my brother has introduced you to the family. As you saw earlier, every eyeball is watching you. No matter how much you want to run away, you cannot. It will look bad for both of you if you do."

I turned my eyes to the ground, but Niko lifted my face with his fingertips, his eyes looking intently into mine. "For Romanos, nothing is more important than family, honor, and loyalty. It is everything." My wise young owl offered a final piece of advice. "Do not place a scar where there is no wound."

"Yes, I know," I said, nodding.

"It sounds like my brother is rubbing off on you."

We laughed, breaking the heaviness of the conversation.

With his wine now finished, Niko carefully placed the glass down. His eyes remained locked onto mine as he leaned in, his sincerity shining through as he spoke his truth. "You're not alone, Sabina. Count on me to be here for you."

"Thank you!" In appreciation, I kissed his cheek and hugged him tightly. "I feel better after talking to you. With the kindness of your counsel, you could have been a priest!"

Niko guffawed at my pronouncement. "I'm not sure the church would want me." He shook his head, subconsciously rubbing his wrist. "I'm a rogue, a wild one. I had a checkered past but was given a second chance when I followed Papà and became a chef."

Seeing the barbed-wire tattoo encircling his wrist, I wondered, was that his reminder of an event where he strayed, to which Gianmarco alluded?

"Besides, I love women too much to give them up for the priesthood!" I laughed aloud at Niko's remark, which reminded me of the Romano men's deep appreciation for women.

"Could we have more bubbly, please, Father Niko?" I teased.

He nodded his head and roared with laughter. "Of course, my child! Stay here. I'll get us another glass of courage."

I was still smiling as he left to refresh our drinks. Niko was funny, caring, and sweet. Yet, in my lifted spirits and the effects of drinking the wine too quickly, my mind wandered. For a moment, I imagined a future with *another*... if the circumstances were different.

The instant Niko returned, we both received a text. Mine from Gianmarco; Niko's from his brother Antonio. *Where are you? It's time for dinner.*

We heard the dinner bell ring from a distance, and everyone headed to their assigned seats. We were the last to enter the patio, beautifully illuminated with incandescent globe lights on black wires strung between the ancient olive trees. The sounds of chirping crickets and Sicilian minstrels serenaded us while we dined.

I noticed Gianmarco was already seated at the head table with the newlyweds; the chair beside him remained unoccupied. Before joining the wedding party, Niko walked me to my place and gallantly pulled my chair out. I felt the warmth of his touch as he placed his hand on my bare shoulder.

"Thank you!" I smiled at Niko, then turned to Luca and my other table acquaintances, the older girls I shelled beans with earlier in the kitchen. My stoic lover approached us and nodded to Niko, who turned and left.

Gianmarco stood over me, removed a leaf from my hair, and kissed my crown. As he placed his palm on my shoulder, I gazed up at him and reached for his fingers.

"You look flushed, Sabi. Are you OK?"

"I'm not used to all of this Mediterranean *heat!* Not what I imagined tonight would be."

I saw genuine sadness in his eyes. "Me too." He took my hand and kissed it.

"I miss you," I said as I turned my head and kissed his hand, brushing my cheek upon it.

He skimmed his palm over the length of my long, dark hair. "We'll sit together later."

My mind was still preoccupied with the reappearance of his ex. "Did you talk to her yet?"

"'After dinner,' she said."

He turned to the head table and saw Antonio motioning for him to return. "Dinner service is about to start, and we're first. I have to go back. Are you sure you're going be OK?"

I forced a smile; he was leaving me again. "I'm fine. Luca will look after me." I put an arm around my young companion's shoulder, who looked pleased to be sitting next to me.

Gianmarco ruffled the top of Luca's hair and gave me a tiny smile before walking away.

I remembered how flawlessly my Darling ate pasta the last time we were together and wished I had his etiquette. Suddenly, I realized I had found the perfect teacher! "Luca, can you teach me how to twirl and eat pasta like a true Italian?" I asked with a lilt in my voice.

"Of course!" He puffed his chest proudly, laughing at my strange request.

Hand in hand, Luca dragged me to the overflowing buffet tables laden with the finest local fare Sicily offered. Prepared by the Romano and the Caradonna families, they had worked tirelessly for days putting together an eclectic feast of stunning Italian dishes.

The display was a magnificent explosion of color swimming beneath a mist of mouth-watering aromas. Mountains of fresh seafood were fried and drenched in sauces, sautéed and stewed vegetable platters, and fresh salads.

An assortment of delectable pasta filled the beautiful, hand-painted Maiolica ceramic bowls. I spotted Mamma Romano's *gnocchetti* bathed in a wild porcini mushroom sauce, aiming to make it my first stop. The breaded *arancini*, a marvel of Sicilian cuisine, would be the second. The deep-fried risotto balls, shaped like golden pointy breasts, were bursting with meat, cheese, and ragù; they were to die for!

Jugs of Valeria's father's homemade red Nero d'Avola wine were available at every table. For the little ones, glass carafes filled with diluted wine allowed them to have their own taste.

SCANNING the party for Gianmarco at the end of dinner, my heart sank when I glanced at the head table and saw he was not there. I struggled to push aside thoughts of where he might be since I knew he was with *her*.

I noticed Niko rising from his chair. He passed the table full of flirty, giggly gals in shiny, tight, brightly colored mini dresses. Though these single ladies catcalled and eyed him, he graciously smiled at them but continued onward.

"Ciao Niko! Don't you need to sit at the power table with the bigwigs?" I joshed.

He chuckled. *"Ciao Sabina!"*

"Your groupies of fawning Sicilian lasses are missing you!" Though I teased him half-heartedly, I was hoping he would stay.

He smiled and looked directly into my eyes. "Nah. I'd rather be here at the *fun* table." I blushed, smiling, grateful for his playful distraction.

The children loved Niko's natural playfulness. They climbed onto his welcoming lap while he balanced a bouncing child on each knee. Facing me, he told the kids funny jokes, and they told him even sillier ones. Frequently, he had to translate and explain the subtleties of the puns to me.

I tried to tell my favorite joke, *What is brown and sticky? A stick!* It was funnier in English. Unfortunately, it seemed lost in the translation.

When it was time for the newlywed couple to cut the elaborate, multi-tiered wedding cake, the little ones rushed for a piece. Luca snagged three slices: one for himself, one for Niko, and one for me.

"It looks delicious! Thank you, Luca!" I licked the fluffy frosting off my fork. "I told you we'd have cake later!"

He pouted. "But no ice cream!"

I wrapped my arm around his shoulders and squeezed him. "I'll buy you ice cream later. I promise!"

Eyebrows raised, Niko excitedly pronounced, "Why don't we *make* ice cream instead?"

"Yeah!" Luca's animated face beamed pure joy, as did Niko's.

Sneaking off to the kitchen to rummage for any leftover supplies, we hit the jackpot—a crate of overripe strawberries in the refrigerator, perfect for making Luca's favorite, strawberry gelato.

Luca and I washed and cut the strawberries, pilfering the best-looking berries as a taste test. "One for you, one for me."

Though Niko's hands were busy blending the cream mixture, he called out to us, "Hey, what about me? I must taste the fruit to judge how much sugar to add to balance the acidity."

Niko made *aah-aah-aah* sounds, looking like a hungry baby bird waiting for a wriggling worm. He opened his mouth wide as I fed him a clean, de-stemmed berry. The touch of his wet lips, as they sucked the fruit away from my fingers, delivered sparks. We looked at each other as I wiped the strawberry juice dribbling across his mouth with the pad of my thumb.

I watched him swallow and lick his lips as he savored the moment's sweetness. We both lowered our eyes, and I flushed a little pink.

For some crazy reason, I had always wanted to be a pastry chef and briefly trained to be one. But the early schedules and grueling pace weren't for me, and I dropped out of the program. Now, I had the fortunate opportunity to learn by Niko's side—a true master! Time faded away, and once more, I was a student, attentive and captivated.

Niko began by making custard in a large, heavy-bottomed aluminum pan. First, he heated the cream with the sugar, then drizzled the glossy liquid suspension into the egg yolks to temper them and prevent the mixture from turning into scrambled eggs. Whisking slowly, he thickened the custard over a low, open flame, transforming the scavenged parts into a luscious crème anglaise!

He placed the strained cream base in an ice bath to quickly cool it down. Next, he mashed the strawberries with a handheld potato press, turning the slurry into a soft pink pastel soup, which he poured into the ice cream machine. We waited as the beaters whirred away, slowly scraping the frozen layers from the sides of the stainless steel bowl.

Hot from the oven, Niko lifted the wafer-thin almond cookies with his bare fingers and carefully draped them around the wooden cone-shaped mold to cool.

Finally, the machine stopped. Niko removed the canister and scooped the half-frozen ice cream into a warm, freshly made cone.

With a smile and a bow, Niko presented me with a beautiful work of art crafted by the hands of a master for the muse at his side.

What a gift! The taste was a tantalizing sensation of hot and cold dancing in my mouth.

While enjoying Niko's utterly delectable culinary creation, we sang along to *The Way You Look Tonight* from the playlist on his phone. In our little haven, we laughed and fooled around while taking selfies on my phone. My favorite was the one of Niko and Luca crooning into their cones, pretending they were microphones.

After I flashed them the picture of two silly *mike-cream* cone serenaders, my *Sinatra* pointed to it. "I want that one! Send it to me!"

"How? I don't have your number!"

Niko put his palm out while shoving the whole cone into his mouth.

I shook my head and handed him my phone, giggling at his bird-bill pose as he tapped in his digits.

He extracted the cone from his mouth and returned my phone. *"Bene?"*
"Good?"

Staring at his lips glistening with cream, I stepped to him. With my thumb, I whisked away the excess gelato from the whiskers lining his mustache. My heart was racing as I lowered my eyes and blushed. Gasping for breath, I stepped back and bit my lip. *What the fuck am I doing?*

Composed once again, I forwarded the playful pic.

His phone binged; mine binged soon after.

NIKO
♡

His eyes never left mine as I peered at my screen; my cheeks burned pink. While holding my gaze, his sparkling smile said it all. *Now we are connected.*

THE DOUBLE DOORS BURST OPEN, and Gianmarco thundered into the kitchen with cold fury in his eyes.

The man was livid.

"Ice cream?" I smiled and offered him my half-eaten cone.

"I don't like ice cream," he said through gritted teeth. "Let's go, Sabina." His voice was unwavering.

I shook my head in confusion. "But the party doesn't look like it's over yet!"

His fierce, icy stare was his reply.

I obeyed.

"Ciao Luca. Ciao Niko," I said softly.
<small>*"Goodbye, Luca. Goodbye, Niko."*</small>

Concerned, Niko placed his hand on my arm while glaring at his big brother. "Are you going to be OK, Sabina?" he asked with worry etched across his face.

Gianmarco gave Niko an unmistakable stay-out-of-my-business look. I stepped between them, refusing to be the reason for any family rift.

My wide eyes were saying more, but all that my mouth could publicly utter was, "Thank you for tonight, Niko. I will be fine. A wise owl once told me that love demands trust."

As I kissed Niko's right cheek goodbye, he whispered in my ear, "Did you ever wonder if..."

I tenderly brushed my cheek against his while whispering softly so that only he could hear, completing his thought. "If I had met you first?"

Next, I turned to Luca and kissed his cheek goodbye. "Happy Birthday, dear Luca."

"Thank you! *Ciao bella!*"
<small>*"Goodbye, beautiful!"*</small>

My diminutive Romeo already knew how and when to flatter a woman to make her feel utterly beautiful.

"Are all Italian men flirts?" I teased my dear friends. Luca smiled and nodded, licking his ice cream with an air of confidence.

And Niko confirmed, "Truth, *bella!* We live for a woman's smile!"

Tossing my head back, I laughed heartily at Niko's sweet talk.

I took Gianmarco's outstretched hand and glanced back. Niko looked at me, frowning with worry.

"Shouldn't we say goodbye to everyone else? I don't want people to think I'm a rude American."

"I said goodbyes for us both. I told my family you were ill and wanted to go."

My forehead creased in confusion. "Why did you say that?"

He didn't answer.

"And our bags?"

He pulled me away. "In the car." His mood was dark, different from when we arrived.

His silence scared me.

21

UNSTOPPABLE

Just past midnight
On the road to Taormina, Sicily

He drove the Ferrari at frightening speeds, braking erratically and slinging us around bends along the narrow Sicilian roads. Still burned up from the events at his brother's wedding, he didn't look at me or notice the trail of tears drying on my face as the wind whipped them away. Feeling numb and confused, I dared not speak. The silence between us was obscured by the growling engine and sharp gear shifts, but I held myself rigid and stared out the window. Wishing to be a million miles from here, I pretended not to care, but all I heard was *No More I Love You's* playing in my mind in an endless loop to the tune of my broken heart.

There were no streetlights on the dark country roadways.

Despite the full moon reaching the meridian, it barely illuminated the cracks and potholes in the uneven, crushed gravel and asphalt. Accelerating hard through a poorly cantilevered curve at full throttle sent the powerful sports car spinning out of control. We hit the dune's edge and found ourselves facing the wrong way. Luckily, the airbags did not deploy.

I exited the car, and Gianmarco jumped out too. Slamming the door, he bolted to the rear to catch me.

My body shook uncontrollably. I swiveled to confront him. "I know you're angry, but what the fuck! Are you trying to get us killed?"

"I LOOKED FOR YOU!"

"What are you talking about?"

"You disappeared from the party!" he hollered.

"You saw me at the reception and in the kitchen."

"No, EARLIER! Were you fucking my brother in the bushes, Sabina?"

Through gritted teeth, I said, "I was making ice cream in the kitchen with Luca and Niko!"

Distress and confusion swam in his eyes. "When you first arrived for dinner together, I saw oak leaves in your hair *and* on Niko's jacket."

"Nothing happened," I said slowly and deliberately. "I drank *one* glass of wine with your brother in the garden behind the church. We were only talking." I shot back at him, "I trust you and Ravenna were *only* talking."

He opened his mouth, then shut it. Turning his head away from me, he looked into the darkness. "For so long, I wanted Ravenna to want me again. Tonight, she said that when she saw me at your architect's office, she realized that breaking up was a mistake. She kissed me hard, and I kissed her back."

His words stabbed my heart, and icy venom escaped from my lips. "Well, did *you* fuck *her* in the bushes?"

He was quiet.

"Even if you didn't, you wanted to," I answered for him. Though humiliated and angry, I bit my tongue and dared not say what could not be unsaid; I felt like the village idiot. "All this time with me while still in love with her."

Gianmarco grabbed my hand as I tried to leave; I smacked it away. "Ravenna's waiting for you. Go back to her." My words were icy and sharp. He lunged for me again, but before I could strike his face, he intercepted my wrist and tethered it behind my back.

"LET GO OF ME!" Beating his chest with my clenched fist, I threw my head against his heart. He tried to pin down my flailing arms, hooking his muscular bicep around my neck. He cradled me tightly in an embrace, like a boxer clinching his opponent to stop the body blows. We were so close that his long eyelashes pressed against my temple.

Despite the warmth from his skin against my skin, I shivered. Cold.

I could not bear to look at him and shut my eyelids tight, yet tears escaped. "I love you. Trusted you."

"I could lie to you, but I can't erase my past. Our love story was a hard one to forget. But now, so much has changed that I can't go back." He lifted my chin to see my tear-streaked face.

I jerked my head away.

"Sabina, you say that I've changed you. Well, you have changed me too. When Ravenna said she wanted me back, I wanted to want her," he confessed.

I lowered my crown in defeat and sobbed. Gianmarco nuzzled his face against my hair; his warm breath was like a mist upon my head.

"We used to have so much chemistry together, her and me. It was off the hook! But when I kissed her tonight, she tasted *sour* in my mouth. I don't know if I had changed, or maybe *she* had. But either way, I didn't like how her kiss tasted anymore."

I turned to face him with open eyes, listening to his odd explanation.

He cradled my head and looked into my eyes. "That's when I realized *your* kisses taste sweet, and it's you I want. You, Sabina, I want you!"

I searched his enigmatic eyes for the truth. "I want to believe you."

"After Ravenna left, I was so empty and alone, like being in a black hole. But then you came along and accepted me, broken as I was."

With my arms hanging limply by my side, I turned my head to lean my cheek against his chest. I could feel his strong heart thundering through his shirt.

"When I'm close to you, Sabina, and you embrace me, you fill my emptiness with your kindness and love. When I kiss you, I burn with desire, and I wanna swallow the passion you pour over me." He nuzzled the side of my neck, and I felt his whiskers bristle against my skin. I sighed. Confused, I wanted to embrace him, but my heart still hurt.

"It's you I want," he uttered in a soft plea. "No one excites me or makes me feel as good about myself as you do." He buried his nose in my hair, pressing his lips behind my ear, taking such deep breaths that I felt his hot breath on me.

"I'm sorry," he murmured, releasing me from his clutch.

I stepped back from him and protectively wrapped my arms around my waist, searching for the right words. "I love you so much. Do you know the power you have over me?"

He looked down at the sand. "It scares me how much you love me."

"Why?" I asked. "Why should my love *scare* you?"

His voice was quieter as he continued to look at the ground. "I'm not enough, and I'll let you down." In barely more than a whisper, he said, "I'm afraid if I give you my heart, you'll eventually leave me."

"Like Ravenna?"

He nodded. "Losing her was my greatest defeat."

"Your greatest defeat? The one you mentioned months ago at Marì was Ravenna?"

"Yes. She didn't believe in me and told me I wouldn't amount to much. I wanted to prove her wrong, so I left my friends and family, running away to Milan to show her that I could be successful and become someone important enough for her to love me again. Now she wants me back, but I don't need or want her anymore. I want to be better for myself." Gazing into my eyes, he added, "And for you."

I closed the distance between us. Snaking my arms between his, I drew him toward me, resting my head against his chest and wetting his shirt with my tears. "I don't know your whole story with her, and it's not my place to criticize your ex. I'm probably overstepping my bounds as it is, but that woman should have accepted you for who you were then, not who she hoped you would become."

I looked up and watched as a single tear rolled down his cheek, his silence ignoring its appearance. "Do you want me to tell you everything between her and me?" He sounded like he wanted to confess to a priest and be absolved.

"Only if you want to. But I don't need to know because I'm trusting you again now that you say that she's really part of your past."

"Yes," he said, and I believed him.

"We do not need to say anything more about her," I said, gladly closing the subject, which had already stolen too much joy from us.

He wrapped his body around me like a big, warm bear, pulling me into him so tight that I could hardly breathe. His tears were cascading down my neck.

"My Darling, you are already more than enough for me. I'll never let you let me down because we're on the same team. Remember? Team Gianmarco, my captain! If you lose, I lose."

He's hugging me even tighter, crushing me into him...

"I'm not her. Let me into your heart. I promise I'll never abandon you. I would move heaven and earth to follow you to the gates of hell and beyond."

... as if he has a need to be inside me and never let me go.

Our heartache turned into desire. When our lips met, the passion that burned between us surged like a tsunami, kissing with the reckless abandon of teenagers caught in the overwhelming riptide of first love.

"I want you!" I moaned the words between our kisses.

"I wanna fuck you hard, Sabayon."

The rougher, the better, Darling. Show me I'm yours!" I grinned hungrily at him and grabbed his jacket by the lapels, pulling it off his shoulders and down his arms. He let his coat fall to the ground as he whipped off his black bow tie and undid the top button of his collar.

With his powerful arms, he hoisted me onto the back of the Ferrari. Splaying my legs wide, he untied the side ribbons off my panties. Yanking them out from underneath my bottom, he hurled them into the cabin. I gasped as he groped my breasts and mewled as he dug his face into my aching pussy. His beard scraped my flesh; his tongue stabbed and lashed at my swollen slit.

Ramming two fingers into my gash, Gianmarco finger-fucked me, making me writhe in ecstasy. I ground and pulverized myself against him until I orgasmed, moaning and panting, squirting his palm with my pussy juice.

The next thing I knew, he dragged me off the car and lowered my feet onto the sand. I couldn't wait a moment longer to have him inside me. Unbuckling his belt in a frenzy, I unzipped his trousers and pulled them down. With the same desperation, Gianmarco swiveled me around and shoved me against the rear of the car. Lifting my skirt, he smacked my bare ass so hard that I yelped.

As he twisted the long strands of my hair around his wrist, I eagerly waited as he grasped his raging cock, positioning it at my wet well. I cried out as he drilled into me, though I hungered for *more*. Wanting to dive into him as much as he was diving into me, I drove my pelvis into his groin. His thighs fired like a jackhammer as he pounded me mercilessly.

My lover was giving me exactly what I wanted—a banging so beautiful yet brutal—his every thrust lifted me into the air as he rage-fucked me with savage abandon.

I clamped down on his thickness with the walls of my pussy to hold him, contracting and pulsing around his cock for all I was worth. He yowled like an animal, filling me with his white-hot seed, and then he collapsed onto me, sweaty and spent. How I relished the feeling of him lingering after milking every last drop!

Raising my head, I turned to reach for his lips; his cum,

mixed with mine, trickled down my thighs. I rolled my hips against his groin as we sucked each other's tongues, still seeking to fall deeper into one another.

I grinned when his slick hardness pressed against my ass, and I knew what was next—his favorite.

"Now I want the rest of you!" He teased me by tickling my tight hole with the tip of his cock. "Open up!"

"With you, I am always *open* to *more*," I whimpered, arching my back as my dark rosebud throbbed with anticipation of his cockhead crossing my threshold.

Just then, we heard the sound of a roaring engine coming into the bend toward us. A moment later, the pitch-black roadside became visible in the beam of the oncoming headlights.

With no time to find my knickers, I straightened my dress and went *au naturel* while Gianmarco struggled with his fly. It was tricky to stuff his erection into his trousers, a unique problem that had never before crossed my mind.

"*Cazzo!* The damn zipper is jammed!"

"Let me see." I knelt on the sand. "Turn on your torchlight."

Through his black briefs, I could see the distinctive outline of his male member, so beautifully smooth and hard that I could not help rubbing my cheek against it and giving it a peck.

He sang in jovial irritation. "That's not helping, you naughty girl!"

I giggled. "Sorry, Darling. I can't control myself around you!"

"Focus, Sabi!" Gianmarco snapped. "The car looks like it's slowing down. I think it's gonna stop."

"ARGH! SHIT! It's derailed! And I need to unzip it a little to free the fabric caught in the teeth." I was panicking, my fingers sweaty and shaking. "It's stuck!"

"It's OK. Get up, Sabi. Lemme try."

I stood in front of him to cover his open fly. Gianmarco bent down to retrieve his jacket and bow tie and draped them over his arm to hide his erection, pressing against my bum through our clothes. I wiggled my booty against his bulge.

"Oh, Sabayon! You're gonna pay for that in the end."

I turned and grinned, playfully bumping his crotch with my butt. He pinched my ass hard, making me gasp.

The car, a Fiat Uno, slowed and stopped. The good Samaritan rolled down her passenger window. *"Buonasera, signore e signora. Tutto bene? Come possiamo aiutarvi? La tua auto è rivolta nella direzione sbagliata!"*
"Good evening, sir and madam. Everything OK? How can we help you? Your car is facing the wrong way!"

She pointed out as if we could somehow be unaware that our car was turned the wrong way.

Gianmarco politely replied, *"Grazie ma tutto bene!"*
"Thanks, but all is well!"

I smiled as I entwined my arm with my handsome partner, searching for the correct words to say in their native tongue, a language of love. *"È così bello stasera che..."*
"It's so beautiful tonight that..."

And Gianmarco completed my words, *"Abbiamo pensato di fare una passeggiata romantica lungo la spiaggia!"*
"We thought about taking a romantic stroll along the beach!"

The older couple nodded and smiled back.

"Bene! Che meraviglia essere giovani e innamorati!"
"Good! How wonderful to be young and in love!"

Sticking their hands out the windows as they zipped away, they yelled with exuberance, *"Ciao ragazzi!"*
"Goodbye, guys!"

We waved and bellowed back. *"Ciao!"*

. . .

Hand in hand, flitting away from our car, we laughed until we reached the shore. The moonlight's reflection shimmering on the water was mesmerizing, calming, and peaceful. The white sand was soft and powdery beneath our shoes.

"We don't have to continue to the beach if you'd rather, um —" I said, pointing my head to the dunes beside us.

"Come walk with me, Sabi," Gianmarco beckoned.

"Doesn't this remind you of the first time we met at Pescara Beach?" I asked.

"Nah, this is better!" He smiled and watched the waves lap the shore.

I nodded as he tenderly kissed my lips and slipped his tongue into my mouth, making me melt into his embrace.

Whether it was his super kiss or the breeze on my half-naked body that made me grab the sides of my arms and shiver, my hero came to the rescue. He shook the sand off his jacket and placed it on my shoulders. I rubbed my face against the warmth of his black woolen tux, his unmistakable scent lingering on the lapel.

"Are you not cold, my gallant knight?"

He hugged me to keep me warm. "Only you see me as a knight!"

"You are more than a knight to me; you're a knight in waiting."

He arched his eyebrow. "Waiting, like a waiter?"

"A knight-in-waiting to be a king!" I curtsied to my lord.

He laughed and shook his head incredulously. "Forever a starry-eyed girl."

"Yes, I have stars in my eyes for you, my liege." I smiled and rubbed my finger along the bottom of my lip. My eyes squinted, peering toward the horizon. "That's why I can see your castle in the not-so-distant future."

He chuckled. "My castle?"

"Someday, we'll build Camelot, your dream bar in Milan, sparkling white and clean. Serious business on the outside, but the atmosphere will be fun and playful inside!"

"Are you describing me or the bar?"

"The kingdom one builds is a reflection of one's personality."

He kicked a shiny black stone embedded in the sand into the sea. "Well then, mine will be a flawed bar because I am far from perfect."

"Darling, *perfect* is boring. There's no room for change. Part of being human is that we make mistakes but grow from them."

We linked hands while walking. I nuzzled the smooth surface of his hand against my cheek, murmuring, "We behaved badly tonight."

"Even though I was busy, I went looking for you," he whispered.

"I know that your family needed you. You were so busy managing the details of that fabulous wedding. I hope they thanked you for all your hard work behind the scenes because, despite the problems, you directed everything flawlessly!"

Gianmarco was quiet. I assumed he nodded to accept my compliment.

"Whenever I looked, I found you at Niko's side." I heard the disappointment in his voice, so I stopped and turned to face him.

"I felt alone tonight, and your kindhearted brother stood in your stead for a moment."

"Through the window of the kitchen door..." Gianmarco looked toward the sea when he spoke, perhaps hoping the wind would whip away the doubt uttered from his mouth. "You looked into my brother's eyes and smiled at him the same way you smile at me."

"Did I?" I knew what he meant and attempted to deflect. "Or perhaps I only have one smile."

Gianmarco remained silent with pursed lips, not buying my answer. I walked around his side and saw his face full of sorrow.

Quietly, I confessed, "You're right; I was hiding, brooding like a selfish child."

"Why?" he asked.

"Because I was jealous."

"Me too," he whispered.

"I'm sorry. I wanted to run away. Disappear. I couldn't face seeing you with *her.*" I nestled my head under his chin and rubbed my face against his soft beard. "You asked me to the wedding, to be by your side, but you were somewhere else. I missed you so much that it hurt."

"Yes, I know. But I'm here now." The calming tenor in his voice soothed me once more.

I placed my hand on his beautiful beard. "The Romano men are so handsome, but in different ways! You all share the same enchanting double eyelashes that frame your sultry eyes. And those dazzling, radiant smiles of yours—simply beguiling; it's hard not to be attracted to a Romano!"

He chuckled. *"Ay, Sabi!* I should spank you, naughty girl, for flirting with my brother."

"Maybe you should." I laughed. "I admit it; I was enjoying the attention. It was as if Niko were you for a moment, but *nothing* happened."

His thick, dark eyebrows rose. "No?"

"Nothing," I reiterated. "Niko loves you. He doesn't call you his big brother only because you're older, but because he looks up to you. It was *he* who reminded me to trust you and to hear your side, because you are inherently a good man."

Gianmarco straightened his spine, furrowing his brow in disbelief.

"I love you so much! I would never intentionally hurt you by betraying our trust because I am yours. I gave you my heart and soul long ago because I want only you!"

His eyes softened as he caressed the side of my neck with his warm fingertips, his mouth playfully licking my lips like a melting ice cream cone. I attempted to suck his tongue, but he darted it away from my longing mouth.

I nuzzled his chest and breathed in his haunting perfume. "You're teasing me, Darling."

"You love it when I do!"

I looked up at him, nodding at that truth, as he cupped my face and kissed me sweetly. Gently. Our tongues danced together, reconnecting, but the sudden growl of our stomachs broke the intensity of our passion.

"Mamma mia!" He rubbed his palm on my belly. "How can you be hungry after that massive feast at the wedding?"

I playfully threw the accusation back at him. "It sounds like you are too!"

We laughed together.

"I guess the make-up sex whet our appetites!"

The fun mood had returned as we giggled together and rubbed noses.

"Wanna go back to the party?" He tempted me while burying his face into the folds of my long black hair.

"No, there are too many eyeballs. Everyone will know we like to fuck in the bushes!" I teased him back, pointing out our disheveled state, and he grinned.

He tucked a wind-blown tendril behind my ear. "You know, they do have beds at Casa Caradonna."

My fingers drew figure-eights across his chest. "What if they're fully booked? It wouldn't surprise me with the size of the wedding!"

"Hmph," he grunted with a shrug. "Well, there are always... *options.* In fact, I thought I noticed one of Valeria's hot Sicilian cousins eyeing me," he said without giving a smile.

I focused on playing with his nipple through his shirt, making it erect at my touch. "I can believe it, you sexy thing!"

Continuing to toy with me, he pressed on. "I can eat her pussy while you suck on my cock. Or would you rather—*ouch!*"

I knew he would yelp when I nipped his breast. I pulled back, but he pinned me in his muscular arms.

"But isn't she a cousin now? Wouldn't fornication with her be forbidden in the eyes of God?"

"We're only related loosely by marriage. And God forgives."

I rubbed my lips against his chest on the spot I bit. "That's good to know, given that you like fucking adulteresses."

"I don't make a habit of it. You're the only married woman I've ever fucked, Sabayon."

He raised my chin, and I gazed into his eyes with wonder and awe. "You make me feel so special, Darling."

"That's my superpower!"

I laughed.

"And that's why women fall in love so easily with you," I paused, adding naughtily, "and your Italian *salami!*" My wayward finger traced a path down toward his delectable cock.

He roared with laughter, intercepting my hand and lifting it back to his lips. The kiss on my inner wrist made me drip. Wherever he kissed me, that spot immediately became a newly discovered erogenous zone.

"Darling, I'm curious," I asked him breathily. "Have you ever had a *ménage à trois?*"

"I've had many girls, and I just tease you, but I'm not interested in a three-way. Why?"

"Good! Neither am I, because I refuse to be anyone's sloppy seconds!" I swatted his gorgeous behind, and he grinned.

"OK, let's check into our hotel. It sounds like m'lady needs her own fucking bed!"

I nodded eagerly, my head bobbing up and down with enthusiasm. "Desperately!" I said, my voice caught in a throaty plea. Then I laughed, and he laughed with me.

Jumping into our sexy Spider, Gianmarco drove the Ferrari out of the sand dunes and sped along the coast to Taormina, the Pearl of Sicily. The radio played one of his favorite songs, *Eternamente Ora*. I could listen to Gianmarco's sexy baritone voice singing in Italian all night long, his grinning face beautifully illuminated by the moonlight above.

TOMORROW IS ANOTHER DAY

22

THE SHAPE OF YOU

Monday, October 14, 2019
Taormina, Sicily

In the hush of the late hour, the valet at Villa Bellagio was all smiles, his enthusiasm palpable as he eagerly took the reins of our Ferrari. I couldn't help but stifle a grin as Gianmarco hesitated for a heartbeat, reluctant to surrender the keys to his beloved racecar. Stepping between him and his fancy new toy, I teased, "Are you going to sleep with the car tonight or go to bed with me?"

My Darling chuckled, then dropped the key fob into the parking attendant's hand, whisking me across the red carpet to the hotel's grand foyer. Stately and elegant inside, the fragrant perfume from the three-foot-tall dwarf Sicilian Femminello lemon trees in bloom filled the room.

"*Buonasera!*" I smiled at the dawn of a new day, for us both.
"*Good evening!*"

The receptionist's hand instinctively raced to his mouth to suppress a yawn.

"*Buonasera!*" His reflexive response came as he glanced at the clock and rubbed his tired eyes—it was 1:00 am.

However, the hotelier, with a polished demeanor reflecting the professionalism of Villa Bellagio, politely stepped forward as we approached the main desk. He wore a perfectly tailored suit and greeted us with a warm but reserved smile, an embodiment of gracious hospitality.

"Good morning, madam, sir. Welcome to Villa Bellagio. How can I help?"

"We have reservations for tonight." I chuckled and corrected myself. "I mean, today."

"Splendid! If I could see your IDs, please? It's for the Municipality, in case of *irregularities.*"

"Of course," I said, sliding forward my blue and gold American passport as Gianmarco passed his Italian *Carta di Identità*.

"Thank you." The hotel manager discreetly sized us up, perhaps wondering how to address us—we weren't wearing wedding bands.

He handed back Gianmarco's ID, tucking it into my passport. "Your documents." Nonchalantly, he slipped us our room keys. "We have prepared the honeymoon suite for your arrival. Congratulations and many happy returns of the day, Mr. and Mrs. Romano!"

We looked at each other and grinned. I blushed pink, not used to hearing my name attached to his, but with the acoustics of the empty lobby, it sounded comforting and pleased my ear.

"Only the best for you," I whispered. "Because, *signor Romano*, your juice is worth the squeeze!"

Gianmarco smiled and embraced me, whereupon he kissed my ear. *"No problema, signora Romano."*

<small>"No problem, Mrs. Romano."</small>

Clearing his throat to catch our attention, he added, "The elevator is at the end of the lobby; the attendant will bring your luggage to your room. We hope you enjoy your stay with us at Villa Bellagio."

"Thank you!" we said in unison.

"Is there anything else we can do for you?"

At the invitation, I inquired if the kitchen was still open.

"It is, madam."

"We're a tad peckish. Could you please have a little something sent up to our room immediately? Thank you."

The hotel manager nodded with a half-bow. "Yes, of course, madam."

Gianmarco opened my passport, stared at it, and laughed as he handed it to me. *"Mia moglie!* Now I understand why her passcode for the rental car was *Argento*."

<small>"My wife!"</small>

"Remember? It's my maiden name, *mio caro marito!*" I teased.

<small>"my dear husband!"</small>

He laughed. "Sabina Argento, you have been keeping your Italian heritage a secret from me, *amore!*"

"How I wish! Unfortunately, I'm not actually Italian." I winked with a naughty reply. "But I *love* all things Italian." In a breathy, husky voice, I revealed, "My secret is that I'm only Italian when your meaty *salsiccia* is inside me!"

He roared with laughter and gave my ass a hard pinch—the kind that always made me gasp!

. . .

TRAVERSING across the red and ivory checkered octagonal tiled lobby, we passed luxurious burgundy leather couches and thick Persian rugs. Curved, vintage burlwood furniture, gleaming with polish, graced the space.

We took the antique elevator to our floor while the dutiful porter, following behind, carried our getaway travel bags. Gianmarco slipped the key card into the electronic lock. He halted before we entered. "I've always wanted to do this!"

"What?" I asked, and at that instant, he surprised me by whisking me into his arms to carry me over the threshold. I wrapped my arms around his neck and beamed at his playfulness. "Such a romantic!"

"Shh! That's *my* secret."

I shrieked with glee as he cradled me in his arms, spinning us around and around. He kissed me sweetly when he stopped —he made me dizzy. "Thank you, my Darling! Every day with you is a beautiful, priceless gift." We smiled and rubbed noses. "What do you think of our pleasure palace?"

His gorgeous chocolate-brown eyes lovingly gazed at me. *"Che bello!"*
_{"How beautiful!"}

Filled with gratitude and my heart content, I happily purred and nestled into the crook of his neck.

Our room for the weekend was an elegant suite decorated in fifty shades of cream, from the king-sized bed to the throw pillows and linens.

Feeling too warm inside after riding in an open convertible, I asked Gianmarco to open the Juliet windows to let in the cool breeze.

"To really get a proper sea view, how about if we lounge on

our private veranda instead of trying to squish ourselves over that decorative balcony?"

"What a great idea, Darling!"

Walking backward while taking snaps of my sexy Italian, I exclaimed, "Whoops!" as I almost tripped on our bags that the porter had set by the terrace's double doors. *Our shadow* exited so silently that I didn't even notice his departure.

Holding his klutzy girl's hand, Gianmarco and I stepped outside, and the fragrance from the Sicilian lemon and orange blossoms, permeating the night air, enveloped us. Glancing down, we admired the magnificent vista of the hotel's ornately tiled pool. Its surface glimmered with the reflection of the moonlight and a regatta of fallen, floating petals. Beyond the property was the bay, outlined by the lights of the seaside town of Giardini-Naxos, just south of Taormina.

When I told Gianmarco, "I'm hot, sweaty, and sandy everywhere," his eyes sparkled with mischief. I grabbed his shirt and pulled him toward me. "Want to join me in the shower, Darling?"

"Mmm," he hummed, grinning and nodding as our fingers entwined at the edge of his shirt. Together, we lifted it over his head, exposing his sculpted body. As the fabric slid away, the warmth of his skin met my palms, and I couldn't resist the urge to explore further. My fingers brushing against the soft hairs of his chest sent a rush of desire through me.

"Your turn," he said, a suggestive smile playing on his lips as he gestured toward the hem of my linen dress, skillfully guiding it over my head. Standing utterly bare before him, he inquired, "But where are your panties, Sabayon?"

"Have you forgotten you ripped them off me in the heat of passion and hurled them into the car? It should still be there!"

He snorted amusedly, his voice dipping with playful possession. "Well, that valet better not take them! They're mine now!"

I laughed, the sound mingling with the roguish glint in his eyes.

"Do you enjoy wearing ladies' undies, or are they merely trophies you keep as notches on your belt?" I quipped while unbuckling his belt and unzipping his fly.

He chuckled as his pants fell to the floor. "Again, with the *notches* on my belt!"

"Souvenirs from all your sexual conquests, perhaps?" My lips curled into an impish smile.

He bit his bottom lip, a knowing look passing between us. "You should see my collection!"

I giggled while pulling his black boxers to his knees and swatting his tight ass. "I can believe it, you sexy thing!"

Enjoying the game, Gianmarco stepped out of his underwear, his voice dripping with humor. "*Sì!* A whole drawerful!"

"Which reminds me, love, I need to retrieve my favorite black bra you pocketed the first time we, um—got acquainted at Tutto Mare's restroom."

He shook his head, grinning. "Nope. That's mine now too!"

I couldn't help but laugh. "But I like that bra, and it's not even your size!" Our laughter intertwined, cloaking us in the warmth of shared memories as he playfully tugged me toward the bathroom. Inside, a spectacular sea view greeted us once more.

"No bras and underwear are needed where we're going, Sabayon!" Gianmarco's voice held a promise of the intimate *play* to come.

With one hand, he turned on the hot water tap, and steam poured into the room, misting the mirrors.

"It's too hot and steamy in here, Darling!"

"But I like it that way, Sabayon! Don't you?" he teased.

"No," I mock-protested. "It's so foggy that I can't see a thing!"

"No problem. I *see* you, and you're the only one I wanna see. And feel!"

I smiled at his words of desire for me. Gliding my fingers over his thick, veiny cock, he exhaled deeply as I gave it a firm squeeze. "I love how you feel too!"

Locking my hands behind his nape, I jumped onto him, wrapping my legs around his torso. As he pulled me in closer, I pressed my lips to his, lightly nipping his bottom lip. His mouth opened, and together, he walked us into a rainstorm of warm water cascading from the ceiling-mounted showerhead, which felt like an all-encompassing waterfall.

"I want to make love to every part of your body, Gianmarco!"

When he lowered my toes to the tiles, I caressed his loving arms with my fingertips and pressed my lips onto the Celtic tattoos encircling his biceps. I would never tire of gazing at and running my hands over his well-toned, naked body.

His frisky fingertips skipped over my skin like a flat rock across a pond, sending ripples of electric chills through me.

Melting under his touch, I squeezed the tube of body wash onto a sea sponge, depositing a dark amber liquid onto its craggy surface. "Let me wash the sand away." I spread the foamy lather over his shoulders and neck, scrubbing my way across his chest. I lifted an arm to soap his pit. "Mmm, dirty or clean, you smell like heaven!"

He fought off the reflex giggles as I buried my nose in the crevice, tickling him; my hand slowly headed south. He took the sponge away to cleanse me.

"Naughty girl!" He smacked my ass, grinning because he knew what I wanted, his cock growing larger-than-life in my hand.

My fingers were now free to sensuously roam the solid muscles of his sexy, chiseled torso, which felt beastly beddable beneath my fingertips. Aroused by his wet, unbridled nakedness, my hands could not help exploring *more*.

Sinking down, I knelt on the tiles, dying to give him a sloppy, wet blowjob. Focusing on his frenulum, I licked and flicked that delightfully delicate little triangle of skin under his shiny bell.

He sighed and leaned with one hand on the wall as I enveloped his shaft, pushing my face into his pelvis until my lips touched his base. I also adored juggling his balls with my tongue; my sexy beast growled at the pleasure of my worshipful gift.

Shielding myself from the stream of water, I closed my eyes, moved behind him to massage his well-built butt, and dragged my fingernails across his shapely ass. "I want to eat you."

"Mmm!" was all he could manage in response.

His rounded, sweet cheeks were so irresistible! They were like two loaves of brioche, perfectly plump and golden; I was aching to sink my teeth into their buttery goodness. But I knew he had a fickle-switch that could flip when the fun went too far. So instead, I gently grazed my teeth against his skin.

"Your ass is so sexy!" I squealed, nipping him gently, then immediately kissing and rubbing my flared lips against the same spot. "I love it!"

He laughed.

"Too rough, Darling?"

"Nah, it's OK."

My hands moved to spread his butt cheeks wide. Steadying

himself against the wall, he arched his back as I burrowed into his valley.

I kissed his throbbing, puckered ring and lightly licked it with the point of my tongue in a quick, side-to-side motion. It pulsated on my lips as he groaned and gurgled into the water.

"*Sabayonnnn...*" His ragged breath profoundly exhaled my name as I worked his erection and tongue-fucked his sweet ass.

Needing his manhood in my mouth, I moved my body to face his groin, slipping my finger into my slit and coating it with my pussy juice. Then I swallowed his cock, gently pushing my damp digit in and out of his puckered starfish.

"*Aahhh.... Sìì!*" Gianmarco's roar was music to my ears.

Sucking his throbbing cock with so much suction, I could feel his balls and the seam of skin that separated his stones rising taut against his body.

He grunted and groaned even louder. "*Cazzo! Aaahh! Arrivohh... Sborrahh!*"

    "*Fuck! Aaahh! I'm coming... Cummm!*"

His body tensed as his deluge suddenly arrived, salty and warm on my tongue. He produced so much spunk that I couldn't swallow it all! The rest gushed out of the sides of my smile.

"Yum! I love how you taste, Darling."

"Grrr!" he growled in gratitude for the fabulous fellatio. "I love your filthy mouth, Sabayon!" he exclaimed, and I smiled with pride.

Toweling me off, he tussled my hair into a windblown mess, gracing me with that spectacular smile before raising me in his arms and carrying me to our bedroom.

23
EAT ME. DRINK ME.

When Room Service arrived, the porters must have noticed our sandy clothes and shoes scattered about on the travertine floor. With professional discretion, they set the table and played ignorant of our bathing activities.

Still, I blushed, feeling embarrassed.

Gianmarco frowned at my reaction. "What?"

"The door to the bathroom was wide open the whole time. I wonder what they saw or heard. We're not exactly quiet when we *play*."

"You're so funny, Sabi. The hotel staff knows what goes on behind a closed door." He kissed my nose. "Just like the restaurant waitstaff knows what couples do in their locked bathroom stalls!"

"Gianmarco!" I punched his arm, and he laughed,

mouthing *ouch* as if my loving swat had any effect on his rippling bicep.

He motioned to the tray of cold antipasti, pâté, cheese, cut fruit, and bread spread across the table. Accompanying our nibbles was a bottle of champagne chilling in a bucket. "Ready to eat, Sabi?"

I nodded and headed to the feast, where Gianmarco fed me melon wrapped in prosciutto, and I fed him a piece of crusty baguette with some soft and creamy Gorgonzola Dolce spread on top.

He nodded with approval. "Champagne?"

"I'd love some!"

Draping a linen napkin around the bottle, he gripped the cork and twisted it open with nary a hiss.

"Mmm!" I purred. "Even watching my sommelier work makes me horny!"

He laughed and shook his head. "The things that turn you on, Sabayon! You're so different from anyone I've ever met."

"I've never met anybody like you either, my Darling."

I cut a thick slice of pâté and slathered it on the bread, offering him the first bite. I finished the rest, playfully dropping a hint. "Do you know that bubbly on an empty stomach arouses and relaxes my body, especially my nether regions, making me insatiable for you?"

He flashed a ferocious grin. "Yes, I know." I could feel the hot breath of his whisper against my ear.

"I want to finish what we started at the beach." My hand raced to my mouth, and I blushed at the greed and depravity of the words that escaped. After all, we had just fucked in the shower.

Staring at me, he lifted a wine flute and poured me an extra-large serving—on purpose. I gasped as the golden liquid overflowed the glass, the excess dripping onto the floor. Gianmarco slurped the foamy top to savor every last drop. Watching him indulgently lick the side of the flute with his thick red tongue made me want to languorously glide mine across his lips to savor his taste. I waited until he filled his wineglass, and then we toasted.

Like a young Bacchus ready for debauchery, he laid down in bed, his gaze unwavering as he took a generous gulp of his wine. A sip was all I needed for the effervescent sparkler to rush the alcohol to my brain, putting me in the mood for *more*.

"Come here," he beckoned me forth, luring me closer.

Downing more bubbly, I climbed onto the sumptuous comforter and crawled like a cougar in heat. Inching my way toward him, I paused at his legs and sensuously purred my confession. "I crave you!"

Setting his glass on the nightstand, his voice held the same longing. "And I, you."

His powerful arms grabbed me and tugged me toward him. I lunged for his mouth, my teeth nipping his bottom lip. Hungering for each other, we kissed ferociously, delving into the familiar wet spaces. Dancing between mine, I sucked on his tongue, relishing the lingering traces of his champagne.

We pulled into each other, writhing and gliding over the silky sheets. Our legs entwined like the twisted blue vipers tattooed onto his skin. Floating like a ship on an endless sea, I undulated and drifted over the currents of him.

He caressed my ass. "I wanna eat you!"

"Yes, please!"

"Lie down and grab your knees," he commanded.

I obeyed, facing the colossal floor-to-ceiling mirror by the bed, and smiled at the reflection. Positioned this way, I was completely open.

It was such a turn-on to watch us fuck *and* see his head disappear into my legs while his sexy ass swayed and flexed in the breeze. I was a voyeur, and we were like the stars in our sex tape.

Moving his hands to my ankles, he caressed my legs from my knees to my mound, rubbing his firm palm against my dripping pussy. With his fingertips, he spread my labia, exploring the dewy folds of my flesh from bottom to top, ending just below my clit.

He opened his mouth and hummed into my gaping slit.

"So goood!" I uttered, trembling as the sound waves from his sweet moans reverberated along my pelvic walls.

Continuing his journey, he ended at my nether hole, where he licked and blew his warm breath over it. Sucking and darting, he swirled his taster, round and round, tickling and bathing my pulsing rosebud with his saliva. He darted his tongue into my ass, twisting it like a drill bit, driving me absolutely wild.

"Butt play is so dirty, but I love it when you lick me. It's so erotic!"

Though I couldn't see him, I knew he was smiling; his moans were his approval. "Don't forget, *la mia figa*. She needs you too!"

"*my pussy*"

His laughter sent more mind-blowing, pussy-stirring vibrations through me. I let go of my knees. "Be inside me," I begged.

Climbing over me, he leaned in and double-penetrated me: two fingers up my ass and his long shaft buried deep in my tight snatch.

"Oh God, Darling! That combination makes me feel so fucking full!"

He guffawed. "I can feel my dick with my fingers, even though they're in separate holes!"

"You're so funny, sweetheart, but I need you to fuck me now!"

He smiled and lifted my hips with one hand while his rigid cock scooped and plowed me.

Slowly.

Deliberately.

And I fucked him back hard, matching his every thrust, propelling him deep into my belly.

My hands and toes burned as blood pulsed through my veins—from my pussy, passing straight toward my belly, then engulfing my entire body.

With my eyes rolling into my head, I saw stars as I came. *"Gianmaaah...."* I giggled as pussy sauce flooded past my ass and spread across my back to pool all over our silky cotton sheets. "Amaaaazing!" I purred, and he exhaled with pride.

He nibbled my ear and whispered. "I wanna cum in your ass."

Nodding, I rolled onto my knees, planting the side of my face onto a pillow. I wiggled my bum in the air for his pleasure since he adored butts and couldn't resist playfully swatting mine.

"Lube. In my purse!" I directed him.

"No olive oil?" he joked, rummaging around my handbag until he grabbed the tube and squirted globs onto his cock. *"Apri, apri, apri... per me!"*
  "Open, open, open... for me!"

I giggled at his joke and loved it when he talked dirty to me in his native tongue. His wish to *open* was my command as I reached behind to grab my ass cheeks with both hands, prising them wide apart. My asshole twitched and quivered with excitement.

My lover continued to open me up in so many ways. Like a

rosebud in bloom, I was ripe and ready to fulfill more and more of his and my incorrigible sexual fantasies.

After climaxing, my muscles must have been so relaxed that, surprisingly, his cockhead easily slipped into my backdoor.

"Aaahh! Oh God! OH GOD!" My moans crashed like thunder.

He grasped my hips, slowly guiding them back and forth along his thick shaft. Slipping and sliding, balls deep, he groaned. "You're so tight! I love it!"

The lube helped, but the friction burned since he was so wide. I gasped and whimpered as he picked up the tempo of his thumping, opening me up even more.

He paused. "You OK?"

"Uh-huh," I nodded. "Go ahead! Shoot your load!"

Dolloping on another blob of lube, he slathered and rubbed it along the length of his shaft.

He was mid-cum, thrusting deeper. Pausing as his orgasm peaked, he plunged himself again and again into me. Right before he climaxed, he grunted and groaned like a caveman. *"Sto... ugghhhh... sto venendo!"*

"I'm... ugghhhh... I'm cumming!"

Spent, he leaned into me and rubbed his bearded cheek on my back while cinching my waist in a tight embrace.

"It tickles, Darling! But don't stop! I adore feeling your body next to mine." I gasped as he pulled out, and his cum dribbled out of my ass. "Leaving me so soon?" I pouted.

He reached into my bag and surprised me by stuffing my ice-cold, gunmetal butt plug into my hot, lubricated asshole. The sudden contrast in temperature made me gasp. "You're so kinky! I love it!" I purred at him like a thoroughly satisfied minx.

He smiled naughtily. "My hot cum—only for you!"

"I love it. I do!" I pushed the plug deeper with my fingers, not wanting to lose a single drop of his precious gift. "I love everything about you."

"Yes, I know!"

We laughed together. Gianmarco turned me over and caressed my hair and face as I pet his chest, shoulders, and face, smiling at each other, fucked to utter exhaustion.

Lying in his arms, I was as relaxed as a wet noodle. I wanted to keep gazing into his gorgeous, mesmerizing eyes, but I was bushed—it was almost 3:00 am.

Before I dozed off, I saw him smiling, watching me fall asleep cradled in his loving arms. His lush lips kissed my forehead, and the last thing I heard was his whisper. "Sweet dreams, my Sabi."

24

SLICE OF SICILY

With elbows propped on the bathroom sink counter and my chin cradled in my hands, I couldn't help but smile in delight, watching Gianmarco as he readied himself. Freshly shaven and radiating sexiness, his alluring scent of Dior filled the air. His outfits were always so fashionably coordinated. Clad in cerulean blue Bermuda shorts, a camel-colored T-shirt, and crisp white tennis shoes, my lover looked every bit the Italian playboy. I could spend the entire day gazing at my handsome man and still crave more of him.

Unfortunately, I had never been a strategic packer; besides one ultra-sexy black dress, I only had a pair of jeans and an ivory sleeveless blouse left, which I had planned to wear on the plane home but had to use today. Perhaps after breakfast, we could go window shopping in town. Maybe Gianmarco could help me select a cute outfit to match his style since the villa staff was dry-cleaning the two garments I wore to his family's big day, Antonio's wedding, yesterday.

My eyes grew as large as silver dollars at the realization. "Family! The wedding! Oh my gosh! I was so distracted by you and everything that happened yesterday that I forgot to let Cyril know I was OK after I landed at the airport."

"Just call him now."

"He thinks I'm meeting with a realtor today." I rummaged around my purse for my cell phone and turned it on; no messages from Cyril. "I should check in and call home. I'm sure my little Kally is missing me."

"Yeah, I should let Mamma know as well, although she was more worried about *you* than me!"

"What?" I laughed, pleasantly surprised at the revelation. "Mamma was worried about *me*?"

"Everyone at the wedding was concerned after I told them you vomited in the bathroom, and I had to clean it up."

"Oh God! You told Mamma that?"

"I had to make sure she bought the excuse why we had to leave so quickly."

"Did she?"

"Mamma looked at me sideways and said, 'Nothing is wrong with the food we made. Why is she sick? Did you get that girl pregnant, Gianma?' Then I laughed nervously," my lover recounted.

"Girl!" I laughed, too, shaking my head at being referred to as a *girl* and possibly being a mother for the third time.

"Mamma and all her friends dream of becoming grandmothers someday soon!"

"Your mamma has no idea how old I am, does she?"

He smiled and shook his head. "Mamma went gray early and noticed the few platinum strands in your hair. She asked how old you were, trying to figure out if we were a good match, but I didn't answer. She probably thinks you're a tiny bit older than me. I didn't correct her."

"Good. Let's keep her in the dark about the truth of our little affair, OK?"

"OK, but I think you're wrong about her not accepting you. You're being judgmental; if she didn't like you, she wouldn't have been concerned about your health."

"You're right. Your mamma may get over our age difference, but the adultery part might not square so well with her and your family's strict Catholic upbringing. No one in your family, not even Niko, knows I'm already married."

Gianmarco's tone turned icy cold. "Niko is no saint. He has no right to pass judgment over another soul."

Whatever went down between Niko and Gianmarco was an unhealed wound between them. Now was not the moment to dig or take sides.

I placed a gentle hand on my Darling's thigh and caressed it to soothe his untempered rage toward his younger brother.

"Hmm, no answer at home, just voicemail. I guess it's past Cyril's bedtime. I'll leave a text message and tell him my phone needed charging, so I couldn't reach him until now."

"Oh, what a tangled web we are weaving, you and I!"

I nodded. "I know. We have to be careful about keeping our stories straight. Well, you'd better call Mamma before she hunts down her favorite son!"

He laughed. "She'll kill me if I don't check in with her at least once a day!" Gianmarco whipped out his phone and stepped onto the veranda to get a better signal. I heard his excited voice. *"Ciao Mamma!"*

Sitting on one of the armchairs in our suite, I finished the text to Cyril and took a smiling picture of myself.

Since my baby couldn't read yet, I attached a voice message for my little Kally. "Missing you lots and lots here in Italy. What should Mommy bring back home for you? I love you, Kally! Bigger than the world! See you soon, my love!"

Just then, a text arrived.

> **NIKO**
>
> Are you OK?
>
> I'm worried about you!
>
> Call me please!
>
> I need to hear from you

I rose from my chair, glanced outside to see Gianmarco still talking to Mamma, and headed to the bathroom. My finger hovered over the CALL button. *Should I call Niko?* Instead, I recorded a message so he could hear my voice and know I was fine.

As soon as I pressed SEND, I felt my lover sidling behind me, kissing my bare shoulder. I stared at our reflection in the mirror and felt hot and aroused, remembering how we loved *playing* in the bathroom.

"Mmm," I sighed. "I like that very much! Thank you, my Darling!"

"Everything OK at home?"

"I think so, but I left a voice message all the same."

"Sabi, what are you doing in the bathroom?"

"Getting beautified for you!"

He nibbled on my ear. "You're already beautiful to me!"

"Mmm, you know just what to say to make a girl hot for you, my sexy romantic man!"

"Oh yeah?" He spun me around, held my waist, and lifted me, placing my ass on the sink counter. "Wanna *play?*"

"So tempting, Darling, but I need breakfast first!"

"*Ay*, you Americans and your love of big breakfasts!"

Gianmarco needed only a coffee and maybe a *cornetto*, an Italian croissant, to start his day, but I needed more!

One never knew what the following meal situation would be like! Most importantly, the word breakfast implied breaking a fast. I had always been a gal who indulged in big, hearty British breakfasts whenever possible; if coddled eggs and spicy sausage were on offer, they always got a *yes* from me.

I hopped off the ledge, grabbed his hand, and dragged him to the exit. "Hierarchy of needs, Darling. Food first, then sex!"

We laughed, heading downstairs to the lounge for our morning repast.

As predicted, Gianmarco wanted only an espresso and a croissant with *marmellata* jam, while I opted for a cup of herbal tea and fresh-cut fruit. Ripe golden Sicilian melon and juicy rose-pink *fichi d'India,* misnamed Indian figs, actually cactus prickly pears, were my faves. Surprisingly, Sicily was the principal place it was grown, with almost 7,000 acres dedicated to its cultivation.

AFTER OUR SATISFYING start to the day, we did the *touristy-couple thing* and aimlessly ambled down Corso Umberto to window shop. We entered an elegant wine shop called La Cantina del Sole. My sommelier smiled, looking impressed as he perused the wine selection, treating every bottle as if it were a rare book.

The store manager approached us and asked if we needed help. She was short, buxom, and fair-haired, with light blue eyes hidden behind large eyeglass frames that extended beyond her face, making her look like a stereotypical librarian.

When she first engaged with us, she was shy. But as she spoke about her beloved wines from Sicily, her voice became more animated, pitching a high, mousey squeak.

If only I understood everything those two said; they were conversing too quickly and in animated Italian. But I loved seeing him hobnob and talk shop with another wine aficionado, absorbing her every word. Finally, they shook hands, and she handed him her business card.

Gianmarco grinned as he read her name, *"Bianca Rossi."*
"White Red"

She chuckled. "I know! My name makes people laugh or smile. My parents love jokes, but I don't know if they knew I would end up selling *white* and *red* wine."

Gianmarco smiled and said he would contact the wineries she suggested to augment his restaurant's wine list.

Since we were already near the Etna wine region, I thought asking Bianca about signing up for a must-see winery tour on Mt. Etna might be fun.

"I'm sorry, madam," Bianca said. "October is harvest time. Wineries are very busy. All hands are picking and crushing grapes." Offering to accommodate us, she made a few calls but came up empty-handed. "Return next season. Easter is beautiful, too."

I was learning to ask for permission before overwhelming him with more gifts. "Gianmarco, I want to pick up some wine for our picnic. What do you think? Would that be OK with you?"

He nodded, and I went momentarily weak as he tenderly pressed his lips to my forehead. "Thank you for asking."

Bianca selected a Sicilian Chardonnay, a Donnafugata Chiaranda Contessa Entellina, and my sommelier concurred.

Before leaving the store, I turned to my partner and apologized. "I hope you're not too disappointed that we won't be able to take even one wine tour. There's so much to do here, but so little time."

"No problem; next time. But I enjoyed meeting Bianca. She's quite wine-smart. I'm sure the wineries I'm interested in can ship samples directly to Lumos."

I reached over to clasp his hand and flashed my eyebrows at him. "I bet she fancied you!"

He smirked, shaking his head at my teasing.

"Young, dirty blonde, blue-eyed, passionate about wine—she'd be a good match for you."

"I much prefer brunettes," he said without the pretense of being interested. "She's nice but not my type, Sabi."

I had no idea why I kept needling him. "Are you sure? She had huge *tits!*"

"My insecure one!" Gianmarco sighed as he put our shopping down on the sidewalk and folded me into his arms. "A woman's appeal to me is more than the size of her bra!"

I pursed my lips as my hands traveled to cover my bosom, whereupon he whispered, "*Your* tits are perfect for me!" He placed his hands over mine and gave my pair a firm squeeze, making me snicker and bury my head in his chest with embarrassment.

"Nevertheless," he paused. "I may be on a diet, but that doesn't mean I can't look at the menu!" Then he winked at me, teasing me back.

I laughed at his funny but true admission, and he laughed along with me.

"So, what *is* your type?" I fearlessly inquired.

Enveloping me in an embrace, Gianmarco tickled my sides until I screamed and giggled uncontrollably. "Don't you know? Sabayon is my favorite dish to eat!" Then he beamed a joyful smile at me.

I blushed and wiggled happily in his arms. Inhaling his intoxicating, pheromone-laced scent, I rubbed my nose into his chest. "So, what do you want to do next?" I was happy to go anywhere as long as I stayed by his side.

"Let's go see the mosaics, Sabi!"

As we walked together, his hand scooted down my back, his fingertips caressing my bottom.

I smiled wide at his attention. "Sure, but it's in the middle of Sicily, and it's a bit of a drive to get there."

"No problem. I'm gonna take every chance I can get to drive my Ferrari, 'cuz I absolutely fucking *love* it!"

I laughed, ecstatic that he loved my gift.

The sweltering noonday sun forced Gianmarco to don his sunglasses.

"My God, you look so enigmatically sexy in your shades!"

"Yes, I know," he said with a suave grin in perfect James Bond style.

Laughing all the way, we ran back to the villa to retrieve *his* beloved ride.

AFTER A ONE-AND-A-HALF-HOUR DRIVE along the Autostrada A19 to the island's interior, we arrived at Piazza Armerina, a stunning archaeological marvel and historic summer holiday house built by a Roman nobleman. Though parts of the site remained under excavation, the villa tour was spectacular.

We walked along a maze of covered, raised platforms to view

the decorated floors. Intricate geometric designs, epic sea and land battle scenes, a menagerie of animals, scantily clad athletic women exercising, and intimate lovers in an erotic embrace were on display.

The tour guide reckoned that teams of Roman captives worked on the stunning mosaic floors for decades. They painstakingly placed millions of tiny ceramic tiles no bigger than a thumbnail to transform the mud subfloors into magnificent murals that had withstood the test of time.

I could sense his excitement, palpable by his quickened pulse. His mouth was agape, with eyes transfixed in wonder, the wheels of his mind turning at full speed. How I loved seeing his inquisitive side blossom!

"I wish we could do the same for the recently uncovered mosaics in *my* hometown. Ours would look stunning at night if we put a raised glass walkway above and illuminated them from below."

"That's a brilliant idea! I love that you want your city's treasure to be accessible and enjoyed by everyone."

"Like so many other Italian *borghi,* towns like ours are depopulating and stagnating; we desperately need something new like this to attract tourists and create much-needed jobs for our community."

"Even though you live in Milan now, I see how strong your connection remains to your hometown."

"Of course, I'm tied to my roots! Most of my family and friends I love are still there."

"Family and home are always first with you!" I said, gazing with love at my Darling.

He folded me under his wing. "You are my home too." He kissed my temple sweetly. "Always."

. . .

At the end of the exhibition, my eyes were immediately drawn to an intriguing carnival contraption that I couldn't resist trying. With excitement bubbling inside me, I jumped up and down, pointing at the machine, and turned to Gianmarco with my hands clasped in prayer. "Oh, sweetheart! I don't have any change! Do you? I really want to do this!"

Gianmarco raised an eyebrow, his expression a mix of surprise and curiosity. "You're still a little girl, aren't you?"

"Darling, for just one euro, I can press a little one-cent piece and transform it into a beautifully flattened medallion embossed with the naked lady from the mosaics we admired earlier."

He dug his fist into his pocket and fished out a handful of loose change. Sorting through the coins, he found the ones I needed, teasingly remarking, "Here you go, my sweet Sabi. One euro and a humble *centesimo* just for you."

I beamed at him, nodding vigorously with my hands outstretched, ready to receive his precious gift. "Thank you, my Darling!"

Placing his two coins in the slot of the machine, I eagerly cranked the handle, and to my surprise, a shiny copper souvenir emerged, burning hot to the touch!

After admiring my simple yet treasured memento, we decided to bypass the lackluster dining options of frostbitten gelato in industrial tubs and reheated pepperoni pizza slices, mummifying under the harsh glare of the food warming lamps —certainly not picnic-worthy to pair with Bianca's exceptional Chardonnay. Although our stomachs growled with hunger, we agreed to hold out for something more and drove southeast on Strada Statale 117 toward the coast and Noto's famous Sicilia Caffe.

25

INTO THE BLUE

As we stepped into the welcoming brick building of Sicilia Caffe, I had high hopes for finding respite after the long, sweltering drive in our *chariot of fire* under the scorching Mediterranean sun. Hot and hangry, I was hankering for a hearty meal with at least a glass of thirst-quenching Sicilian wine for lunch. Alas, the restaurant was so jam-packed with patrons that, with the high humidity, it felt hotter inside than out. Seeking solace, I leaned against the counter and enjoyed the cool relief of standing next to the refrigerated display case, brimming with colorful, beautifully glazed artisanal desserts.

"Darn! They only have sweet offerings, nothing savory!" I lamented, for I was ravenous for something closer to a simple mortadella and pecorino panini and maybe an accompanying glass of hearty Nero d'Avola. However, such options eluded me on this day. I turned to Gianmarco, my voice tinged with disappointment, and asked, "Will a sweet pastry tide you over until dinner?"

"As long as I have an espresso!" I was amazed that this man ran on at least ten shots of caffeinated jet fuel a day!

Glancing at the handwritten menu on the billboard above the pastry case, I noticed a most unusual offering. "Ooh! Have you ever tried Jamaican Blue Mountain coffee?"

"No, why?"

"Oh, Darling! It's one of the world's finest, smoothest, and rarest coffees, and they have it here! Interested?"

His eyes lit up, and he rubbed his hands together in anticipation. "Sure!" Asking him if he would like a world-class coffee was as rhetorical as a question could get. Still, his eagerness gave me a tickle of pleasure.

Spying on what the others were having, our culinary curiosity was piqued, and we ordered the same: an unusual combination of a warm brioche bun filled with a scoop of frozen lemon granita and another with pistachio gelato on the side.

Our server also recommended we try the house's specialty, a Sicilian *cassatina*. This tiny ricotta cake was laden with chocolate, candied fruit, and almond marzipan. For me, we added a carafe of sparkling mineral water and one cup of Jamaican Blue for my java lover.

WHILE WAITING FOR OUR ORDER, Gianmarco noticed a flyer on the table for an action-adventure film. "Hey, wanna go on a date and see this Denzel flick with me?"

"I love his movies! Sure, I'll go on a date with you!" I innocently pecked his lips. "But is it dubbed in Italian?"

He passed me the circular. "We're in Italy! Of course, it's in

Italian!" Then he smiled. "Besides, it will be good practice for you."

I frowned upon closer inspection of the ad. "Hmm, it looks a little too violent for me."

"It's like *Training Day*—my favorite—with lots of action and twists!"

"Yeah, that was good, but a bit bloody."

"OK, Sabi, you say you're into Denzel. What's a good one of his that you like?"

"Well, he was brilliant in *Glory* as Army Private Silas Trip, an enslaved runaway who volunteered to fight for the Union in the Civil War."

"And you think a war documentary isn't violent or bloody?"

"It's not a documentary; it's a highly acclaimed, accurate dramatization of the historical events. Not only does it have a great plot, but it's also full of action and adventure!"

"I don't know," he said, unconvinced.

"Listen, though I saw it over twenty years ago, there's one unforgettable scene in *Glory*. It's the moment where Denzel silently endured a brutal whipping, his stoic bravery shining through. With every strike, tears jumped from his eyes, and it was this powerful scene that earned him his first Oscar win. And the second one he earned was for your favorite, *Training Day!*"

Gianmarco raised his brows in surprise. I played with the sugar packets on the table and let out a little chuckle.

"What's so funny, Sabi?"

"Just a memory from a long time ago."

"Tell me."

"I didn't realize it was him until many years later, but I saw Denzel Washington in a Shakespearean play in San Francisco."

"Cool!"

"He wasn't famous yet, but he was so talented that he made his character come to life that I still remember that performance. Even then, he stood out from the crowd." I paused and looked at him. "Kind of like you, Darling."

He snorted. "Nah, I'm no actor."

"Your talent differs from his. Yours is in your tongue and your mouth."

"Because I can make you cum every time we play?"

I lowered my eyes and blushed. "Yes, there's that, but—"

The server placed our food and drinks on the table. Gianmarco approached his cup of coffee as if blind-tasting wine. He inhaled a noseful and took a tiny sip, letting it linger on his tongue to activate his taste buds, then swallowed.

With my fingers crossed, I hoped it lived up to its billing.

He smiled. "Wow! That's unbelievably rich and smooth. I can taste chocolate and sweet spice. No bitterness at all."

"Look at you! Even when you're sipping coffee, you're analyzing its components!"

He shook his head. "My silly Sabi!"

"You think I'm joking! I'm not. I'm blown away by how you can dissect food and drink to identify all the flavors you encounter with only your tongue."

He blushed.

"I love watching you work because I can see how being a sommelier is your passion, your forte."

He reached for my hand and squeezed it.

"Believe me when I say that Mr. Washington reminds me of you, Mr. Romano!"

He smirked, raising an eyebrow in disbelief.

"Denzel gave a motivational commencement speech where he saw himself as stuck and poor. By chance, he met someone who predicted that people would watch him. She pointed out his innate talent—something special that he couldn't yet see in himself."

Gianmarco snorted again. "A fortune teller!"

My fingers toyed with the edge of the table. "Oh, my Darling." I took a deep breath, hesitant if I should continue. "I honestly don't know if it's a crazy made-up story, but it set Denzel on a path different from the one where he thought he was *nothing*. It inspired and allowed him the freedom to *dream big*."

He lowered his eyes, uncertain how to respond. Reaching over, he brushed the pastry crumbs from my lips with his napkin and kissed my forehead.

Finishing the last drop of his java, he nodded in what I assumed was silent approval.

I frowned, puzzled by his fidgeting. He looked uncomfortable, stacking the plates like he wanted to clear the table and go. "Would you care for anything else?" How strange that his tone reverted to impersonal, formal *waiter-speak*.

Saddened that my message was lost on him, I lowered my eyes. I didn't understand, but we both knew he was deflecting. I lovingly touched his beautiful, bearded face and tenderly brushed his cheek with my lips.

A tiny smile cracked on his face.

If only you could see what I see, my love.

At a loss for what to say next, I drank the last of the sparkling water and put my glass down. Dejected, I half-heartedly small-talked. "No, thank you. The desserts were filling. Was this place, at least, worth the drive?"

"Yeah, it's nice! The brioche dipped into the gelato was fun.

Simply Sicilian." He picked up the empty cup and buried his nose to sniff the lingering, rich aroma. "Aaahh! But this coffee!" He smiled. "*Che bello!* Now, *that* alone was worth the trip!"
"How beautiful!"

My eyes softened, content that I had delivered a new touch of pleasure to this man who had given me so much.

I savored the last morsel of the still-warm brioche with my melting gelato and stifled a chuckle. "A tantalizingly familiar sensation." A tingly warmth rushed over my body as I remembered Niko's handmade gelato and his booming, playful laughter in the kitchen after the wedding. "Like hot and cold dancing in my mouth!" I reminisced aloud. Blushing, I bit my bottom lip.

Perhaps my surge of energy had rubbed off on Gianmarco because he leaned over and kissed my ear, whispering, "Let's go back to our hotel room, Sabayon. I wanna show you my *forte*. It *also* wants to dance in your mouth."

I brushed my parted lips against his, sighed into his mouth, and nodded yes.

26

WALK ON THE WILD SIDE

The warm afternoon breeze ruffled my hair as we drove with the top down, steering the Ferrari back to the main road. Yet, even with the onboard GPS, I somehow managed to get us lost—*again*. This time, it was due to the hypnotic scenery of the fast-moving, billowy white and gray clouds set against the brilliant Sicilian sky.

"Oh, dear. I'm so sorry."

He shrugged. "No problem."

But all was not lost as we rounded the corner and discovered a hidden fortress.

"That's impressive!" he remarked upon seeing the ruins. "I didn't see that giant tower from the road."

I placed my hand on his thigh. "Darling, I know you're eager to *play* at the villa, but would you mind if we had a quick look around, please?"

"Sure." He slowed the car, taking the road toward the fortress.

"It's like I'm Indiana Jones on an adventure with you!" I announced.

He leaned into me with a smile. "Technically, I'd be Indy, and you'd be Marion Ravenwood."

I chuckled and flashed my eyes at him. "You should hope not! Marion was a scorned girlfriend jilted by Indy, and he might have feared her more than snakes!"

He was silent as he parked adjacent to the path leading to the ruins. A curious response to my playful banter, *but did I just cross an invisible line with him?*

"You know," he said, killing the engine. "Indiana Jones always got the treasure or the girl—but with you, I have both!"

I broke out with a broad smile and kissed him on the cheek. My beloved's spontaneous romantic declarations struck me so profoundly that I lost my words. My eyes sparkled as my heart did somersaults—I was a girl excited to prospect and play. The ever-curious amateur archaeologist inside me was jumping up and down at stumbling upon this stunning Norman fortress. Built almost a thousand years ago, it stoically withstood the most destructive earthquake in Italian history.

We locked the car, although it was unnecessary since it seemed like we were the only souls around for miles. Hand in hand, we followed the overgrown trail to a stone gateway leading into an open courtyard, beyond which was a gate. I grasped the iron bars that protected the entrance to the *keep*, the central core of the fortress where besieged soldiers would have hunkered down before a battle. My heart sank, saddened that it was now chained shut to protect it from modern-day vandals.

Continuing our exploration, I ran my hand against the uniform white and cream-colored limestone blocks, easily twelve inches thick. It was as if I had traveled back in time as I touched the marks where the laborers' hand tools had struck the stone.

My jaw dropped in awe as I traced my finger between the blocks, marveling at how the masons hardly used mortar to cement the slabs together. How many thousands of symmetrical cubes must those ancient craftsmen have cut to build this monumental edifice? It was a mind-boggling achievement in an age without the aid of today's modern tools!

I was sure we were alone until two giant, fluffy white dogs bounded out from behind a thicket of trees. Their thick fur gleamed in the sunlight, bushy tails held high. Dark eyes, like large black glass beads, sparkled with curiosity as they padded toward us. Drawing closer, with their wet black noses twitching in the air, it was clear they were hungry, perhaps hoping for some food scraps.

My body tensed as I froze. Trembling, I grabbed Gianmarco's hand and pulled back. "Let's go home!"

"But I thought you wanted to explore?"

"Dogs scare me. I was bitten by one on my knee when I was little, and they've frightened me since!"

"Dogs are sensitive. They can smell when you're afraid, and they react to that." He explained with tender empathy in his voice.

I shook my head. "I've changed my mind."

"They're OK, Sabi. Samoyeds are a gentle breed. But what the heck are these Siberian pups doing here, who knows?" With a reassuring arm around my shoulder, he said, "Look! See how they're tilting their heads and raising their eyebrows? That's a sign of friendly curiosity. They're just trying to figure out if we're safe and approachable."

"You're so brave! I wish I were as courageous and trusting as you!"

He extended his open palm to me. "Do you trust me?"

I slipped my hand into his and grasped it. "Yes."

He was steadfast and would not let me run away from my fears. "I will protect you."

I squeezed his hand, holding on for dear life. "OK."

"We only need to give them the opportunity to gain our trust."

"Sounds a lot like falling in love!" I pulled myself closer to him.

He gave me that smile of his when responding to my quirky thoughts on life.

"Watch, Sabi."

Crouching to their eye level, he turned his hand skyward and waited for them to come. As they slowly approached, he offered an open hand toward their manes. The dogs sniffed his palm and lowered their heads as he tenderly pet them under their chins. He rubbed their fur with a playful tussle as they soaked up the attention, rubbing their faces and bodies against him. The dogs instinctively sensed his gentle, animal-loving soul. "You try it, Sabi. Put your palm out. It's OK."

He guided me as I timidly held out my hand. The dogs brushed their faces against it, and I gently stroked them back.

"You see! Easy."

"Easy for you!" I said, still racked with nerves. As one dog licked my fingers, I gasped in surprise at how warm his tongue felt. "He likes me!" I giggled with glee at their enthusiastic acceptance of me.

Gianmarco offered his hand to the other *doggo*, which immediately adorned his fingers with slobbery canine affection. He kissed the side of my temple. "I like you too!"

"I like you a lot too!" I craned my neck to smile at him, relaxing a little. "You love dogs, and dogs love you! You're a natural around them."

"Yeah, I love 'em. My best friend growing up was my pal, Romo. We went on so many hikes and adventures together. I remember how much he loved it when I cradled him upside down in my arms like a baby. I loved that mutt so much; it was tough saying goodbye to him."

"I'm sorry." I paused. "Would you like to get another?"

"No, he was my one and only buddy. Irreplaceable."

"But these two are beautiful. Do you think they're strays? Maybe you could adopt them, the mated pair?"

He laughed.

"Why are you laughing?" I asked, not sensing any humor passing between us.

"Sabi, look closely. They're males, probably brothers."

I giggled, trying to peer underneath. "Oh! Well, they're so furry, it's hard to see!"

He looked at the shaggy hounds, then at me; his expression changed. With sad eyes, he caressed the side of my face. "No, I can't take something that doesn't belong to me."

Is he referring to the dogs or me?

"This is their home, and they are the guardians of this fortress!"

A flock of birds taking off from the trees distracted the pups, and they ran to investigate. With our canine companions gone, we lapped around the magnificent but deserted fortress. It was amazing how so many significant historical sites were left unguarded across the country that we could explore and touch everything without concern.

. . .

Gianmarco spied a hidden stone alcove, backtracked, and looked around to see if the coast was clear. He excitedly whispered to me as though he had stumbled upon a secret. "Come here. I wanna show you something!"

With that familiar naughty twinkle in his eye, he grabbed my leather belt and pulled me in for a deep kiss at the enclosure of the stone sentry. I loved how he passionately moaned when he kissed me full on the mouth. Being near him, I couldn't help but stroke the front of his shorts.

His cock stirred.

"Is the offer you texted me from the train still good?" he asked.

I had to think. "You want to make our movie here?"

His eyes flared wide with anticipation. "Yeah!"

Playing to distract his focus, I pointed to the heavens. "It's almost sunset, and the light from the red-orange sky is so beautiful!"

He smiled lasciviously at me, nipping the tip of my nose. "I'm not focusing on *that* sky, Ms. Sabina Argento Skye!"

I laughed and smiled back, nodding. "Since we're alone, OK."

He pulled out his phone from the front pocket of his Bermuda shorts, turned it on, and pulled up the camera app. "How many takes do I get?"

"One."

"Aww... only one?"

I looked at him like an umpire strictly enforcing the rules. "You have to earn the others."

"Another challenge!" His eyes grew as big and round as a couple of soccer balls. "How do I win?"

"I'm going to grade you!"

"Pass/Fail?"

"Nope. Only a goal wins the prize!"

"So, how do I score?"

"If I get horny and want to fuck you again after watching your video, you get a bonus."

"You'll do anything I tell you, Sabayon?"

Curious to see how far he would take this, I nodded. "Anything."

"I'm gonna film your face as I fuck it."

"I trust this will stay between you and me. I am a married woman, after all."

"*Sì. D'accordo!*" With our pact, we concretized our agreement.

"Yes, I agree!"

I felt my anxiety fade into eagerness. "OK. Tell me what you want."

A wicked smile crossed his face. "Strip for me!" He switched to recording mode. *Click, click, click... bing!*

"I'm not sure how. I've never done it before." Truthfully, I had never intentionally made a sexy striptease for Cyril or *any* man. Still, I smiled wickedly and giggled. "Except...."

"Tell me!"

"As a teen, I worked at a clothing store selling Levi's jeans. Customers asked me what the difference was between 501s and 505s. So, I demonstrated by wiggling my hips as I pretended to unbutton a super-tight imaginary pair from my belly button down to my crotch."

His eyebrows rose as he giggled. "You didn't!"

I nodded and grinned, biting my bottom lip. "I did!"

Taken aback by my confirmation, he pretended to cover his mouth with his hand as he chuckled. "You were already an exhibitionist minx, even then!"

"Uh-huh." I giggled. "I said, '501s are button flies. Then I squeezed my ass and thrust my pelvis forward as I pretended to zip myself up. Whereas 505s have zips!'"

"*Troia!*" he yelled in playful, mock-shock at his whore.

I threw him a wink. "I sold lots of jeans to guys that summer!"

He cracked up with laughter, making his phone shake in his hand.

"Hey, keep the camera level!" I said to my cinematographer. "I'm about to demo my awesome skills over here!" He shook his head and tried to keep a straight face, stepping back to capture the striptease scene unfolding before him. "Strip for me, Sabayon!"

Whenever he commanded, I obeyed.

I took the clip out of my hair to shake free my mane, and my long, dark tresses cascaded past my shoulders. Placing my hands behind my neck, I drew them slowly across my chest. Pulling off my top, I threw it at my lover, teasing him sensuously, swaying my hips and shoulders, and exposing my sexy see-through bra.

"LOVE YOUR TITS!" he whooped.

In appreciation, I gave my sheathed pair a little shimmy. "Thank you!" Letting go of my inhibitions, I smiled and leaned forward. Cupping my hands underneath my bosom, I offered him my breasts. "You wanna cum on them—or my face, *Gian-Mar-Co?*" I sang his name in three sexy syllables.

"Hey, that's my line!" He boomed with laughter, feigning to be insulted. "God, I love your mouth, Sabi. Talk dirty to me."

"I'm so lit imagining your powerful hands groping me, playing with my pert nipples, squeezing them hard, and turning them into stiff pokies."

"Yesss!"

"You're incredibly sexy, my Darling!" I gazed hungrily at him, licking my lips like a hungry wolf. "I could cum just from staring into your gorgeous, mesmerizing eyes."

"Not yet. I wanna see more."

Slowly, I unbuttoned my jeans, exposing the top of my panties. I placed my hands in front of my pelvis and circled my hips. My fingers dove toward my belly button, continuing between my thighs to massage my hairless mound through my knickers. "I love it when you touch and play with me here."

"Mmm-hmm." His appreciative sounds encouraged me to keep going.

I sighed, provocatively reaching lower to find my full, round pearl and stroke its side. "Holy shit, when you do that flicking thing with your tongue…"

"Yesss!" He hissed for more.

I shut my eyes and threw my head back as my tongue circled the rim of my mouth as if flicking an imaginary cockhead floating in the air.

Sneaking a peek, I could tell he was so turned on by his guttural groans and the giant bulge tenting in his shorts. "When you suck on my pearl," I said, bringing my fingertip to my O-shaped mouth and lapping the point, "you make me melt and scream in ecstasy."

He stroked his hand up and down along his shaft. *"Aaahh, sì, sì, sìii!"*

"It's so hot watching you touch yourself!"

We sighed together. I swayed my hips, resting my hands on my knees, pushing my ass far behind me. "Right now, I want your hard cock in my wet pussy!"

"Aaahh, sìiii!"

Once more, I turned so my rear faced his phone. Shimmying my tush at him, I slowly wiggled my jeans down to mid-thigh. I turned to look back at him over my shoulder while groping my ass.

He beamed a pearly smile at me.

I split my legs into a V and bent over, reaching for my ankles, showing him how flexible I was. "And now your favorite!"

He howled like a werewolf. *"Mio Dio, sììììì!"*
"My God, yesss!"

I plucked the string of my thong.

Still my werewolf, he growled, panting hard.

Whipping my hair back, I turned around and stepped out of my jeans. "I love that you're an ass-man." Then, looking directly into his camera, I said, "I want you!"

His breath rolled out like thunder. "I wanna fuck you so hard you'll break in half, Sabi!"

I gasped as his raunchy words sent an electric jolt to my already pulsating pussy.

"Put a finger inside," he directed.

I obeyed, slipping it deep and swirling it around my warm, luscious folds. It felt so inviting to slip and slide in my pillowy softness, running over my maze of fleshy gills as if his cock were thrashing inside me. "Goddamn, I'm so hot for you, finger fucking myself!" Pulling that same glistening digit out of me, I beckoned him over. "Taste me!"

He reached for my fist and swallowed my finger, licking it, making yummy, smacking sounds, and sucking it clean. "Mmm, a little tangy, good creamy body, with a hint of freshly baked salt bread."

I laughed at how he deconstructed my flavor profile. "Master sommelier, you describe me like a heady sparkling wine!"

"Pussy juice of the finest vintage!"

I smiled, opening my arms to invite him in. "Be with me."

He grinned, and with only his thumb and forefinger, he grabbed his T-shirt from behind and ripped it off his back.

Catching his sweaty shirt one-handed, I buried my nose in it. "Mmm... I love your manly, sweet smell, you sexy thing."

He rewarded me with a chuckle at another one of my zany remarks.

I sighed and marveled while staring at his naked, well-toned body. "You are so young and beautiful... and you belong to me!" I splayed my hands over his chest as he planted his lips upon mine, feeding my hungry mouth with his scrumptious tongue, wanting to devour him all.

His hand traveled to caress my backside. Through the string of my thong, he plunged and pumped one of his thick fingers into my muff, and I gasped.

"Want more, Sabi?" he asked devilishly.

"Yesss!" I answered breathlessly, nodding. "Always *more* with you!"

He slid a second finger inside, moving them in the same summoning motion I used to draw him to me. My walls clenched and contracted around them. My eyes watered, tearing. "Don't stop!" I begged.

"So tight and inviting!"

"Well, what are you waiting for, love? A formal invitation from your *troia*?"

He glanced at his free hand and waved it about. "I need a third hand to hold the camera!" Then he tossed his still-recording phone onto the soft grass.

Together, we tore open his shorts, pulled down his black briefs, and out sprang his tower.

"Oh my God! I love your fucking, veiny monster!" I lunged for his cock, shoving it in my mouth, making him howl. "Now fill me up!" I moaned as I couldn't get enough of him.

Before diving into me, Gianmarco grabbed his phone and then clutched my ass, groping and grinding hard against my bare body.

"Uh... uhh... ahhh!" We moaned to the exact timing of his thrusts, pushing all of him into me.

I raised and tilted my hips so he could reach deeper, crushing our pelvises into each other and bruising my cervix. I was sweating, so close, and panting like a Samoyed baking in the sun.

He grunted in my ear. "Cum for me! I wanna feel you pulse all around me." His voice was hypnotic, and I obeyed.

Beads of perspiration formed on my nose, accumulating above my lips; so consumed was I by my lover's desire for me that I lost control. I couldn't stop cumming on him, gushing pussy cream all over his hairy balls. As he thrust faster, I held onto his arms for leverage. After I finished climaxing, I locked my pussy around his cock. My body was shaking as I breathed raggedly. "Oh God, I'm gonna cum again!"

Thrust for thrust, groan for groan, he and I came together, our *ughhs* mixing and *sì, sì, aah, sììs* filling the air as our fluids blended together.

I moved my hand to cradle his balls and catch his slippery cock as it popped out of me. It was beautiful to behold, glistening with my pussy liquor and his warm cum. "I need *Gran*-Marco in my mouth!"

My *big* nickname for him always elicited a hearty laugh.

He gasped as I swallowed his sensitive, slick cock and sucked him squeaky clean. "Yum, I love how you and I taste. I adore ice cream, but our combo is WAY better, sweetheart!"

He blushed.

"Want to taste our sex cocktail?" I offered.

Not convinced, he leaned away slightly, his laughter fading to a hum as I kissed him full on the mouth, eager for him to try our mix. Then he licked his lips and chuckled. "We're more like a highly-malted Talisker Single Malt Scotch Whisky on the rocks, tangy and briny with hints of honeyed sweetness. Not quite a G&T, but good in its own way!"

I laughed with glee at his analysis of my flavor profile. "Your tongue amazes me, my Darling—in so many ways!" And then he laughed with me.

He turned off the recording. "Wanna watch us, Sabi?"

"Hell, yeah!" I whooped.

WE SAT on the grass of our private little haven. Leaning against the stone wall, Gianmarco cuddled me as I sat cradled on the throne of his lap. My back was against his solid chest, arms embracing me as we viewed the video on his phone.

I turned my head to him and smiled. "It's a good thing no one is here. So vocal—the two of us—we're like wild animals!"

He traced the contours of my chin with his fingertip. "I love that about you, Sabi. Your desire for me is untamed, and it shows!"

I pivoted to straddle and face him fully, overwhelmed by the compulsion to run my fingers through his dark, curly chest hair. The texture and sensation of his pelt reminded me of the soft fur of my most cherished Steiff teddy bear from childhood. "I am so addicted to you!"

"Me too!"

Pressing my nose against his torso, I breathed him in, loving the essence of his sweaty armpits. *Am I weird? I can't seem to get enough of the smell of his sex!* His unique aroma, mixed with his favorite cologne, was distinctively captivating and irresistible. "Mmm, Darling! I'm incredibly turned on watching us!"

"Does that mean I made a goal?"

"Do you even need to ask? You scored, babe! Simultaneous orgasms are like unicorns for me—mythically rare! But you are at the TOP! The best I've ever had."

He beamed proudly.

"We should call our sex tape, *Naughty at Noto!*"

He bellowed with laughter at my inspired suggestion.

Suddenly, it began to drizzle. We were giggling as we hurriedly grabbed our scattered belongings. Half-naked and wet, we raced to our Spider convertible.

With a flick of the switch, the metal hardtop hidden under the trunk rose and unfolded like origami. Now, we were protected from the downpour in less than fifteen seconds and could finish dressing with ease.

The gravel road was slippery as we made our way onto the SS114. Once on the Coastal Highway, driving the Ferrari back to Taormina was a blast.

27
PUSH

Back in our room at Villa Bellagio, I threw open the terrace doors to let in a cool breeze. I noticed the hotel pool was empty. "Darling, want to go for a swim? No one is in there now!" I hoped he caught the naughty glint in my eye.

He smiled back at me. "Sure!"

We quickly changed into our swimming suits. Gianmarco looked so sexy in his skintight Speedos. His thick cock and heavy balls were front and center, making me want to touch them. I bent over and knelt to kiss them gently through the fabric. "My lord, you mesmerize me!" I looked like a novitiate genuflecting in front of the holiest of holy relics. "I can never get enough of you!"

He threw his head back with laughter. "You are insatiable, my Sabayon!"

"I wish you had three cocks, one to fill every hole of mine!"

He shouted in playful surprise, "What happened to the demure woman I met at Mirabella last year?"

"She's gone, Darling. Do you like your hungry cougar, the new and improved Sabina?"

"Very much so!" He French kissed me, which turned me into putty in his hands. "But let's swim first while no one else is there. We can play here afterward, OK?"

I nodded, and my sexy sommelier in Speedos took my hand while draping a fluffy white towel over his forearm, like the waiter he once was.

It was deserted outdoors, with not a soul milling around. Even the poolside bar, usually buzzing, was closed. Italians had a phobia about being outdoors and getting their hair wet, superstitiously believing it could make them sick.

That wasn't a problem for me since I wasn't Italian. Although, when we fucked, I joked that I was more Italian *inside*. Besides, his head was shaved, so there were no worries or unfounded fears about wet hair.

Gianmarco was an accomplished swimmer, and I enjoyed watching him effortlessly do laps, powering through the water like an Olympian. I preferred the less strenuous backstroke, staring up at the gray storm clouds above. It seemed decadent to swim while raindrops tickled my face.

"Darling, I'm curious. Have you ever done it in a pool?"

"Yes. You?"

"No. Is it like sex in the shower?"

"Different. You're in the water instead of the water being on you. Plus, it's more risqué."

My heart sang at the wickedness of the idea. "Mmm, I like risqué!"

"I know you do!" A naughty smile crossed his face. "Is that a request, Sabayon?"

"Yes, please!" I begged, and my hams instantly wet whenever he called me by my sexy Pavlovian nickname.

Draping my arms over his shoulders, my hands clasped tightly around his nape. I felt heavy, waterlogged, yet he was so strong that he effortlessly lifted me. Cradled in his embrace, he looked around and carried me to a secluded corner. The wide, low-hanging canopy of the mature olive tree beside the pool shielded us from prying eyes on balconies high above.

As he nibbled my neck, I threw my head back and howled like a she-wolf. He released me and put his index finger over my lips. "Shh!" That was a tall order, given that we were both vocal, enthusiastic lovers.

His fingers raced down to my pussy, discovering where my clit hid, like a pearl inside its shell. He rubbed my little button through my swimsuit while fondling my erect nipple.

"Take me!" I whimpered.

He pulled down his Speedos, and I grasped his cock, sliding my hand up and down his shaft. Following his lead, I freed one leg from my bikini bottom, lifting my knee so he had a clear path.

As I floated, he grabbed me by my sides, ramming me onto his erect cock. Crossing my legs like a little rock lobster, I locked my ankles and held him inside me. The water splashed about my face to the same tempo as his thrusts.

I closed my eyes; a silly thought crept into my mind that made me giggle. *How do humpback whales rut weightlessly underwater? They don't have hands or fingers to grasp hold of each other!*

"So close," I exhaled in barely a whisper.

"Me too," he whispered back with a loud exhale.

While he humped me, I wedged my hand between us to place a finger on my pearl, furiously pushing it to send me over the edge. I let myself go as wave after wave of pleasure pulsed inside me.

Grunting and groaning, he came soon after me; his face glowed with happiness and peace. I loved feeling connected to him and wished he could linger and stay inside me. But all this was new, so I had to ask. "Darling, if you pull out, will your cum float? Will we be found out?"

He laughed. "Sabi, we're not the only ones who've ever had sex in this pool. That's why they have filters."

I laughed with him.

So many firsts with this fantastic man! Like a koala bear hugging a eucalyptus tree, I clung to him with my whole body, embracing him with my arms and legs as we kissed.

Though our bare asses were exposed, with my bikini bottoms at my ankle and his Speedos around his knees, I didn't care who saw. I wanted everyone to be jealous that I just got good and properly fucked by my gorgeous lover with the sexiest ass in the world!

"I've never fucked so many times in one day! You?"

He smiled. "I don't kiss and tell, my dear Sabayon."

"Good. So, my secret affair is safe with you."

"But are *you* all fucked out?" he asked with a tinge of genuine concern.

I laughed. "Never! I'm always ready for *more* with you."

He smiled. "Good. But if you want *more*, I need to eat something first."

"You want to eat me now?"

He laughed. "For dessert, perhaps."

Lowering my eyes, I pursed my lips. "Ah, you mean *dinner*." I pulled up my bikini bottoms, lay on my back, and floated away from him.

He followed me. "Where are you going, Sabi?"

. . .

I STOOD up when I reached the other side. "I, um, want to take you somewhere, but..." My shoulders nervously rose toward my ears.

Slowly, he closed the distance between us. "But what?"

"I don't want you to be mad at me. Ever." I lowered my eyes again and placed a finger like a gate across my lips.

He leaned forward, his brow furrowed, clearly confused by my mood change. "Tell me!" He turned his hands out, palms up as he did with the Samoyeds at the fortress.

My shoulders lowered, and I knew I could trust him and that he wouldn't become angry with what I wanted to say. "I promised not to push you or overwhelm you with too much extravagance."

He inched toward me. A gentle, understanding smile crossed his face. "The Malvasia and the trip to Sicily?"

I gave a slight nod. He remembered our fight about the Malvasia wine and spoiling him with a lavish holiday to Taormina. Yet, here we were in Sicily because he asked me to accompany him to his brother Antonio's wedding. "I'm afraid I've already pushed you to the limit with the Ferrari."

His arms were outstretched, requesting to come closer. "May I?"

I nodded in assent.

My animal whisperer tenderly cupped his gentle hand on the side of my face, and I leaned my cheek into it. "You know a car means life—freedom—to me. I've never felt more alive than I do now behind the wheel of *my* Ferrari. I absolutely love your gift of this experience of a lifetime. It's one to remember!"

Glancing up at him through my eyelashes, my heart filled

with joy. I smiled timidly and meekly offered, "But I don't know if you're OK with a little more indulgence."

He lifted my chin so I could see his eyes, patiently listening. "No problem. Tell me."

"I think you would thoroughly enjoy dinner at the Michelin restaurant where I got your Malvasia, the one we paired with your favorite dessert, the *pizza dolce*."

He stroked my hair and moved a wet tendril behind my ear. "Yes, I would like that very much, Sabi. Thank you."

I breathed a sigh of relief.

He rubbed his nose on mine. "Wasn't that easy? You see, I don't bite."

I bared my teeth and grazed his nose, pretending to bite it. "But I do!"

He yelped, falling onto the water as he backstroked away. But he let me catch him. I leaped onto his front as if he were a human raft upon which I could float.

We sank and bobbed with our bodies entwined, ebbing and flowing on the surface of the pool, riding the carefree tides of passion and life.

Standing in the water, I wrapped my arms around his waist, sliding my fingertips inside the back of his Speedos. Resting them on the tops of his sexy bum, I nuzzled and playfully scuffed his bare skin, nipping his bare chest with my teeth.

"You visited my world, and now I want to try *your* world." Those words from his heart flowed into mine; we had come full circle as I lingered in his arms. "But I had better not get used to it, Sabi, since I can't afford it just yet."

"Thank you for letting me be *selfish*."

He shook his head, not fully understanding. "Selfish?"

"It makes me so happy to share with you what I have, but I

don't want to tread on your need to earn it yourself to enjoy it. You are so fiercely proud of your independence."

He kissed my forehead. "You don't understand how different your life is from mine, you starry-eyed girl. Our time together is like a fantasy. Unreal."

My eyes sparkled and shone whenever I gazed at him. "If you let me, it could be real." I gently touched his cheek and quoted my favorite line from my favorite book. "All my fortunes at thy foot I'll lay, and follow thee, my lord, throughout the world."

"I'm not Romeo," he quietly replied, shaking his head. "I don't deserve a Juliet."

"It's a good thing I'm not Ms. Capulet, because their story doesn't end well." I nuzzled his beard with my nose. "I am hopelessly and absolutely in love with you, my Romeo! You've worked so hard to become an amazingly talented, experienced sommelier. You already have what it takes to be a Montague."

He lowered his head, his eyes staring into the water between us.

I lovingly kissed his glistening crown. "You are what *you* believe yourself to be, my love."

Before he had a chance to deflect or reject the offer of *me*, I turned away from him, playfully splashing him with a tidal wave of water. "Dinner?" I shrieked with delight as I tried to escape, reaching for the metal railing to climb out of the pool. Pausing at the first step, I turned to look at him, patting and wiggling my backside in his face. "Or dessert, first?"

Like a famished shark behind me, he lunged so quickly, biting my ass hard and sinking his teeth into my flesh.

"Ouch!" I turned and smiled. "I deserved that for teasing you, my sexy thing."

"Oh, Sabayon! That's for more than teasing, and you know it!"

I pursed my lips, shaking my head.

A wicked smile curled on his lips. "That was just your first down payment!" His piercing eyes turned into nefarious slits. "Now, I want the rest."

I screamed with glee as he grabbed my bikini bottoms to yank me back into the pool. He wanted to *play* some more.

Rough.

How I loved *more* with this man!

28

MORE

Dashing and hopping over muddy puddles on Corso Umberto, we laughed when we reached the first of the several dozen steps of Vicolo Stretto, the narrowest street in the world. Gianmarco's shoulders were so broad that he had to climb the steep steps *sideways*, and it seemed unbelievable that at the top lay our destination. But as soon as we traversed through the entry arch, it expanded as if by magic, like Harry Potter's Room of Requirement, into a wondrous little hidden gem, Ristorante Ristretto.

After stepping into Ristretto's wine shop, the maître d' ushered us to our cozy rooftop table, treating us to a fabulous, breathtaking spectacle of the ominous storm clouds on the horizon juxtaposed against the protected bay. The panoramic vista looked like a giant shimmering octopus tentacle reaching out into the deep blue Ionian Sea.

Seated across from each other, I playfully wiggled out of my heels and secretly caressed his leg with my big toe, *sub rosa,* under the table. He reached for my foot and rested it on his lap, pressing his thumb into its arch to massage it.

UNLIKE MY LOVER, my husband, Cyril, recoiled whenever I brushed against him. What a shame, for I loved to touch and be touched. But it wasn't always this way. We used to be such fun, daring lovers before things changed. Now, we were like night and day, two ships passing in the night, and every other cliché attached to a marriage with a dead bedroom at its heart.

I had tried to make him find intimacy with me again. But whenever I playfully ran my fingers over the top of his hand, he jerked it away, saying he didn't like it. I attempted other ways, like kissing his breast and gently flicking my tongue against his nipple, yet he winced, looking pained.

But with persistence come rewards.

And so I moved lower.

I had always loved a man's cock with a passion, nuzzling my cheeks, lips, and closed eyelids against it while holding it in my hand, feeling it grow from soft to hard as I worshiped him. When I sucked cock, a man knew how hungry and desperately I wanted him.

But Cyril pushed me away, telling me to stop because it was too much. I think what he actually meant was that *I* was too much. *I* was wretched to excess, and my depravity repulsed him.

If only I could throw away my wanton desires in a trash bin and forget what my wicked heart and body craved, perhaps Cyril could be happier with me. But then I would be unhappy with myself, living a lie, burying alive an integral part of me that yearned to live, breathe, and be free.

To quash my sexuality was to deny who I was: a passionate woman who longed to fuck and get fucked, to be manhandled by her lover, and to get pounded from here to kingdom *cum*. But I also loved making sweet love to a man's mind as much as I lusted after his hard body.

I couldn't forget or ignore who I was or what I felt any more than a skunk could remove the offending white stripe from its jet-black tail.

And so, I met my match with Gianmarco, my beloved Italian. From the start, I was addicted to him because he responded in kind to my touch and thrilled whenever I explored every erotic inch of his sensual, hairy body.

STARING INTO HIS CHESTNUT-BROWN EYES, I reached for my lover's beautiful hand and skimmed its surface with a fingertip. His ardent eyes sparkled for me as he sighed with hot desire. It was evident; he felt what I felt and wanted what I wanted.

More.

And so, I explored further, tracing the arch around his neatly trimmed nails, and with him this close, I could feel the weight of his breath—a slow yet excited exhale, heavy with joy.

I followed the zigzagging contours between each digit, gliding past the ridges of his knuckles. Up and down, my tingling finger traveled the cartography of his hand; his eyes rolled into the back of his head; mouth slightly agape.

Stumbling upon a fault line—the scar upon his thumb—I tilted my head and winced as I caressed the mark. The thought of him enduring such agony made me lean forward and press my lips together, kissing his pain away.

He reached out to cradle my head, and I leaned into it.

"It's OK. It doesn't hurt anymore, Sabi."

I smiled and blushed when he sent me a seductive sidelong glance; the gusset of my panties dampened as I dripped with desire for him.

Emboldened, I affixed my fiery gaze upon him and scampered the side of my index finger along the crease of my smile. Moving my digit languorously back and forth did nothing to hide its provocative intention.

I rolled one shoulder toward him and triumphantly smiled when he restrained my frisky foot. My flirty toes, nudged into his lap, felt the desired effect I was having on him. Clearing his throat and swallowing, Gianmarco adjusted himself in his seat.

With a lick of my lips, I slipped my naughty pointer into the fold of his hand. His fist squeezed it as I sank it deeper into the hollow of his palm's warm, inviting embrace, teasing his sweaty hand tunnel for some fun, finger-fucking friction.

From across the table, he exhaled through parted lips; his blood-hot gust reached my cheek, igniting me. My foot, still lodged between his thighs, sensed that his flames matched mine. My knees uncontrollably jittered, and I bit my quivering lip to stifle my need.

Shutting my eyes, I arched my back, overwhelmed by the surging joules of electricity zipping through my bones. With my mouth ajar, I inaudibly panted and silently mouthed, *I want you!*

He read my lips and smiled wickedly, sending an air kiss my way.

As the waiter approached, Gianmarco straightened himself, arresting my wayward hand. I felt a crimson rush, from my nape to my ears.

. . .

Our gracious host, Massimo, greeted us with complimentary glasses of sparkling *aperitivo* and presented us with leather-bound menus.

I briefly glanced at the hefty tome and closed it.

With a steamy stare, I said to Gianmarco, "Surprise me!"

"Another challenge?"

I smiled and willingly gave him control. "Not at all. Order whatever you think looks good. I trust you, my master sommelier."

He studied the offerings, and I watched Gianmarco in profound concentration, running his pointer finger back and forth along the line of his closed lips. He abruptly halted, his eyes narrowing into thin slits. "Interesting," he gleefully mused aloud as if having an epiphany.

I took another sip of my fruity, sparkling elixir. "What's up, Darling?"

After tapping the side of his nose twice, he shook his head and sent me a dastardly, wicked smile. "A surprise!"

Since he wasn't going to tell me, I pinched his cheek. "*O, il mio bastardo furbo!*"
"Oh, my cheeky bastard!"

He reached for my hand and kissed it while winking at me. "*Sì, lo sono io!*"
"Yup, that I am!"

Massimo returned to our table, standing at attention with his hands behind his back, ready to memorize our order. I motioned for my partner to take the lead.

"For starters, we'll have the *Tuna Carpaccio* and the *Seared*

Octopus Salad, followed by the *Ravioli Stuffed…*" Pausing, Gianmarco sought our waiter's advice. "*Astice o gamberi?*"
<small>"Rock lobster or prawns?"</small>

Massimo leaned in, offering a confident suggestion. "*L'astice è migliore!*"
<small>"The lobster is outstanding!"</small>

My Darling nodded in agreement. "*Va be, l'astice, allora.*"
<small>"OK, the lobster it is, then."</small>

Continuing, Gianmarco added, "And for the entree, also split, we want the *Sicilian Rabbit served with Saffron Potatoes* and the accompanying *Black Olive, Pine Nut, Sun-dried Tomato, and Raisin Sauce.*"

"Excellent choices, sir. Would you care to order anything to drink?"

Gianmarco was generally on the other side of that exchange, so I enjoyed watching my sommelier take command and control of the role reversal. His dazzling eyes confidently smiled, grilling our waiter. "What would you recommend?"

"I highly recommend the Alta Mora Palmares Etna Bianco DOC for the seafood courses, sir. It is a surprising wine of contrasts: citrus, mineral flavors like crushed stone, beautifully crisp yet balanced against the white peach and tropical fruit aromas."

Nodding for Massimo to continue, Gianmarco observed and listened intently, like a sly cat measuring a mouse approaching a cheese-laden trap.

"And for the main course, the Tasca Tenuta Regaleali Rosso del Conte DOC Contea di Sclafani. It's a vibrant, full-bodied red with essence of plum and chocolate."

Gianmarco massaged his chin in contemplation. "What do you think, Sabi, *vino bianco o rosso?*"
<small>"white or red wine?"</small>

"Well, you love whites, so definitely the Alta Mora. And I love big reds, so the Tasca sounds like my kind of wine!"

"Ahahaha!" Gianmarco boasted, "To wretched excess!"

My heart jumped at the sound of his laughter. But my soul glowed with his remembering and using my over-the-top motto.

He handed back our menus. "Let's go with both!"

"Thank you, sweetheart!"

He raised an eyebrow. "For what?"

I wiggled buoyantly in my chair. "For allowing me to spoil you!"

"No problem." A devilish smirk crossed his visage as he entwined his fingers between mine. "You prepaid for your transgressions earlier in the pool."

I squeezed his hand and grinned while squirming in my seat; my bottom *was* a tad sore. I didn't realize how vital lubrication was with rough water *play*.

He cupped his hand over mine, his expression clouded with mischief. Something was afoot, but I couldn't discern what was up his sleeve.

Ducking my chin lower, I gave him a searching stare. "I know that look! You're planning something!"

"No, not planning! Done something already!"

"What are you up to, *signor Romano?*"

He shrugged. "It's an old trick of restaurants, and we will see if my nose is right!"

Half-panicked and partly amused, I furrowed my brow, expecting a more thorough explanation. "Don't be coy. Tell me!"

He leaned into me and lowered his voice. "Every restaurant has an item on the menu that is an utter failure, a catastrophe, but they have to sell it for one reason or another. It could be the owner's favorite dish or something the chef's grandmother fed him as a child, but on a menu in a top kitchen? No. It doesn't work."

Picking up steam, I could see the boyish excitement twinkling in his eyes, as though he had found the clue to a long-unsolved mystery. I listened with eager ears.

"So then, the question is, what do you do about the hideous boil? You mask it! You find a clever sommelier willing to cover up this hairy wart!"

I giggled at his fascinatingly vivid description of an uncharacteristic blemish on the stellar menu. "How?"

"By pairing the best wine with the worst dish! So, instead of patrons on the edge of revolt with the failed serving, they are astonished and distracted by the excellent vino!"

Thoroughly captivated, I realized how truly talented my man was.

My Darling concluded his culinary lesson. "After all, not every entrée can be a winner, but a superb bottle of wine can become a masterpiece in comparison!"

Puzzled, I tilted my head, furrowing my brow. "But which one?"

"Ah!" His smile revealed how immensely pleased he was with himself. "Now that is my challenge to you!"

MASSIMO ARRIVED with the chilled Etna Bianco. He uncorked the bottle and poured a small measure to taste, seeking our approval.

My sommelier's broad smile signaled his excitement. Wine was his passion, and I loved witnessing his pure pleasure as he discovered new gems.

He swirled the crystal goblet as legs of golden liquid

cascaded down its sides, indicating its rich viscosity. He slipped his expert nose inside the glass, closed his captivated eyes, and inhaled deeply, extracting the wine's essence.

Concentrating.

Analyzing.

Next, he sipped and rolled the straw-colored wine around his tongue, coating every tastebud and deconstructing the elemental flavors of this vintage.

He swallowed and nodded his verdict of surprisingly few words. "Nice!"

I marveled at how Massimo served us with the bottle cradled in his palm, his thumb embedded in the punt—the hollow indentation at the bottom of the wine bottle.

Our waiter didn't spill a drop of wine, despite the height from which he poured the precious elixir into our glasses.

"Cheers!" we said in unison.

I took a sip; it was as beautiful as described and more.

A PARADE of dishes began with our servers simultaneously presenting our first course with a flourish. The kitchen graciously split it into two half-servings, so we didn't have to pass the plates awkwardly across the table.

The Etna Bianca was a superb match with the three seafood dishes, but with each bite, I searched for the shortcomings of the dish before washing the taste down with the wine. When the waitstaff cleared the plates, I looked to Gianmarco for a clue, but he sat stoic and silent, giving nothing away.

"Was it the *astice?*" I asked. "The menu highlighted, *from the Ionian Sea*. But the lobster ravioli was fantastic, though I doubt I can tell the flavor difference a lobster carries from sea to sea."

"Nope." In a theatrical fashion, Gianmarco brought his fingertips to his lips, pressing them gently as if savoring the moment. Then, like a magician revealing a grand finale, he released the kiss into the air, his hand extending outward to me in a chef's kiss. *"I ravioli all'astice erano eccezionali!"*
"The lobster ravioli was outstanding!"

I laughed and clapped, thoroughly amused by my lover's dramatic performance.

Our waiter appeared moments later with the Tasca Rosso, which paired perfectly with the tender rabbit.

Perhaps it was the copious sex to blame or traveling the countryside with my lover, but my appetite for everything seemed insatiable. I dove into the food with gusto.

Stefano, our second server, and Massimo cleared the table at the end of the savory courses and asked if we would like dessert.

"Yes!" We answered simultaneously since we both had a sweet tooth.

"Excellent!" Massimo said, with a bow. "I will return with the menu."

Finally, Gianmarco spoke. "Well, Sabina, we've finished our dinner. Now tell me if you've discovered the atrocity."

I carefully considered each course and its wine pairing, but I couldn't detect any faults in the food. "Atrocity? I haven't a clue. I found everything perfect!"

"Ha!" He snorted. "*Everything*? Really? How could you have found *everything* when they lost the entire rabbit?"

My head lowered as I leaned forward, staring confusedly at my prince of palates.

"Tell me. Where did you taste the rabbit? Was it under the black olives? Maybe it was hiding under the nest of sun-dried tomatoes and pine nuts? It sure as hell wasn't sitting atop those damn raisins!"

I was smiling, amused, and shocked that Gianmarco seemed genuinely offended! "You remain an enigma, and I realize I still have much to learn about you. For example, I didn't know you don't like raisins, olives, or pine nuts!"

"You're missing the point. I love all those things, especially rabbit: delicate of flavor, subtle, tender, and juicy." With a hitch of his eyebrow and a wink, he added, "Like something else I love to have in my mouth!"

I blushed and felt that needy throbbing between my thighs.

"Like my Sabayon, the rabbit needs a knowing touch. The saffron potatoes were a perfect start, but that wretched sauce ruined the dish. The heavy, sharp olive; the tart tang of the tomato; and the too-sweet, grainy raisins—and what was the point of the pine nuts? The mess of ingredients murdered the mellow flavor! Between them all, it was a chaotic battle of textures. The rabbit should have been the star of the show. Instead, it was nothing more than the supporting act."

As I listened to his critique, my eyes were as wide as our entree platters. With each description, the remnants of the rabbit on my palate immediately changed my impression of the dish. Wrinkling my nose, I agreed with Gianmarco, a man with a cultured, refined tongue. He was right; it was not as perfect a dish as I had initially thought.

MASSIMO RETURNED to our table with the dessert menu. "If you have a sweet tooth, we have a rich, beautifully fragrant Donnafugata Ben Rye Passito di Pantelleria DOC by the glass. Robert Parker of the Wine Advocate gave it a stellar ninety-six out of one hundred points!"

We raised our eyebrows in unison, the corners of our lips curving into broad smiles as we nodded our indulgent assent.

"Thank you," I said.

As Massimo bowed and left us to peruse the choices, I turned to Gianmarco, my eyes sparkling with anticipation. "Darling, I know *tiramisù* is ordinary to you, but it's one of my absolute favorites!"

"OK, let's get it for you! There's a reason that classic is a top seller and exists on every Italian restaurant's line-up. It's because it's good! But I'm curious about this *Deconstructed Cannoli*."

"I saw that, too, but I didn't want to be greedy and order two desserts just for myself."

"What happened to your motto of *wretched excess?*"

I grinned. "Well, because it's our favorite, I thought we should order two glasses of the *infamous* Malvasia."

He raised an eyebrow in surprise and amusement, then asked, "Two?"

I smiled unabashedly. "I love you, sweetheart, but I don't want to share mine."

He burst into laughter, the sound infectious. "Ahahaha! Fair enough!"

In a spirit of compromise, I offered, "But I'll be generous and gladly split a glass of the Passito with you!"

"No problem!" He continued laughing. "Two desserts and three glasses of wine!" Gianmarco relayed this to our waiter.

As our smorgasbord of sweets arrived, we moved our chairs closer together such that our thighs touched. It was so adorably corny and romantic how Gianmarco fed me a bite of his creamy cannoli while I fed him some of my tempting tiramisù.

Ristretto's special cannoli was clever. The chefs had taken elements of the original tube-filled dessert but presented it to look like it artfully fell and broke onto the dish. The honey-sweetened ricotta sat dolloped in the center. Scattered on the plate were golden shards of the crisp, candied cannoli shell.

Finely chopped pistachio nuts and pebble-sized pieces of dark chocolate embellished the top.

Surprisingly, our selections were not cloyingly sweet, pairing well with the unctuous, honeyed Malvasia and the Passito. Yet, both wines were so rich that they were like desserts unto themselves.

After emptying our wine glasses, we licked our spoons, shiny-clean. We reveled in our wretched excess, fully sated by the feast and wonderfully buzzing on the equivalence of two-and-a-half bottles of wine shared between us.

"Master sommelier, you look like you've been benchmarking Ristretto, taking mental notes. So, what do you think? How does it compare to your restaurant?"

He grinned. "The service and timing were excellent, spot-on, like at Lumos. Comparing the cuisines is unfair; they're so different in style."

"Worth the experience, my Darling?"

"Well worth the experience, Sabi!" He beamed as I glowed at his approval.

"Now you're sounding like me, dissecting our meal like that!"

He chuckled, recalling the first time I met him at Mirabella. As a chef-wannabe, I delighted in deconstructing dishes to recreate innovative restaurant meals we've encountered. Since he was our waiter, I bombarded Gianmarco with rapid-fire questions about the precise details of the ingredients used, then grilled him on the meticulous preparation of every recipe on the mind-blowing tasting menu he presented to our table.

He was polite, but behind his eyes, a slight sneer looked like he wanted to playfully slap me for being a bad girl by giving him such a hard time. But the rebellion I saw in him intrigued and excited me.

He placed a kiss on my nose. "You were as naughty then as you are now!"

"Worse!" I added.

He smacked his lips in agreement. "Absolutely, yes!" He leaned into me and brushed his soft lips against my neck, whispering, "But I prefer you that way!"

I lowered my eyes and blushed. "Me too."

Gianmarco picked up the empty wine glass and inhaled the residual traces of the Passito's fleeting aroma. "The star of the evening was discovering those exquisite Sicilian wines. And again, this Malvasia was out-of-this-world fantastic! I wish we could carry that wine at Lumos, but I don't think it would meet code without a label."

"It's a bit like the wild, wild west here; in Sicily, anything goes!"

He laughed. "At the very least, we should add the Ben Rye to our lineup. That wine was sublime, buttery, full of caramel, apricot, and lemon flavors, with hints of sage and sea salt aromas. It deserves its ninety-six-point rating."

"So, if you had to choose only one, which wine would be your favorite?"

"All!" he answered emphatically.

"Am I converting you to my hedonistic lifestyle?" I teased.

He shook his head. "Only a little." He took my hand in his again, and we laughed together.

Massimo returned. "Would you care for anything else? Coffee or tea?"

"Coffee, please."

"For you, madam?"

"I need to ask for permission first." I pivoted to Gianmarco, catching Massimo looking perplexed. "I'm going to add four bottles of wine to the tab to bring home, and I would like to gift the same ones to you. If I may?" His mouth opened, but before he could object, I continued. "So, when you drink the wine later with your friends, you'll think of me and remember our special time together."

He quietly agreed and kissed my forehead. "OK, but I don't need a wine to remind me of you."

My heart was drumming as I slipped my hand into his and squeezed it. *"Grazie mille, tesoro mio!"*
  "Thank you very much, my Darling!"

"Prego."

He brought my hand to his face and rubbed his parted lips against the side of my index finger. I lowered my eyes briefly. I was mesmerized and couldn't stop gazing at my Darling, even when addressing Massimo. "Could you add eight bottles of wine to the tally? I want two sets of the ones we had tonight. And could you please send it to Villa Bellagio?"

"Of course, madam."

With the bill, Massimo brought us two shot glasses of amaretto, a digestive. I couldn't eat or drink anything else but managed a tiny sip.

"Waste not, want not!" Gianmarco said, downing his and mine.

"I forgot to ask what you thought of the *tiramisù*."

"It was wonderful, but—"

I finished his sentence. "Not as good as Mamma's!" My lover's robust laughter filled my heart with joy.

AFTER DINNER, the heavens opened with a sudden downpour. We ran to find shelter in a nearby church, a beautiful, simple stone medieval edifice. The glow from the offertory candles warmed the interior.

I rested my head on his shoulder as we sat on a wooden pew, cringing when lightning flashed across the round stained glass windows high above us. Gazing into his eyes, I met his reassuring smile. He tightened his grip around my right shoulder and squeezed my left hand.

"I know I am safe when you are beside me," I said, my words a hushed whisper.

He smiled at me as we rubbed noses. I hardly noticed the sound of the rumbling thunder as raindrops tapped out tinkled musical notes on the terracotta roof.

Before we left, Gianmarco wanted to light a candle at the offertory; he dropped two coins in the collection box, one votive for each of us. Clasping his hands, he bowed, closed his eyes, and said a silent prayer.

I watched him, though, with some difficulty. My vision was fuzzy, and my brain throbbed from drinking too much.

What should I pray for? Should I even be here?

Staring at the flickering flames of the votive candles, I bowed my head and followed his silent lead.

Hello, God. I can't believe I'm in Your house again. Two days in a row. Is that a sign? Do You remember me? We spoke yesterday at a wedding.

I hiccuped loudly, which echoed throughout the empty building. Embarrassed, I clasped my hands to my lips and gave Gianmarco a sheepish smile. He looked at me and stifled a snort.

Of course, You remember. You're the Lord Almighty! But, given what I said to You yesterday, I'm not sure You care to hear from me.

My mouth was dry, and I cleared my throat. I glanced at my Darling and swallowed my pride.

I have no right to request anything for myself. And yet, I ask a wish for another—I, um—my love.

I gazed at my love, unable to help but smile when I was near him. It was he who had opened my soul and filled my heart with love and strength. I could face anything when I was with him.

Dear Lord, I pray that You will help Gianmarco Romano find a way to become complete and achieve his dream. Grant him a path to success. Thank you.

In closing, I crossed myself. "In the name of the Father, the Son, and the Holy Spirit. Amen."

"Ready?" he asked quietly.

"Yes, please! Take me away from here before *He* strikes me down!" I said, playfully attempting to pass off my guilt.

My beloved kissed my crown, tucking me under his arm.

THE STORM HAD LET up as we exited, and the rain had washed the streets of the daily buildup from the tourists' detritus. The moon's reflection on the wet, glassy cobblestones along Corso Umberto made the town sparkle like magic.

Stores stayed open late in the summer since Italians, after enjoying a hearty lunch, liked to nap in the afternoon during the hottest part of the day, emerging to rejoin society in the evening around 5:00 pm when it felt cooler.

As we passed by my favorite store, Canali, a sophisticated Italian men's designer collective, I admired the elegant, dark charcoal-gray suit on display made of the finest *Loro Piana* wool.

"You would look so handsome in that!" I mused aloud, pointing at the jacket.

The shopkeeper saw my interest through the glass window

and removed the coat from the mannequin, motioning for us to come inside and try it on.

Gianmarco studied me. He was silent, waiting.

Remembering to respect his hard limit of not overwhelming him with expensive gifts, I slipped my hand in his, smiled, waved my hand to say, *no thanks,* and walked away from the display.

He knew my internal struggle with using gifts as a form of control.

Smiling proudly at me, I felt like I had passed a test. He stopped and turned to cup my face with both hands. I closed my eyes as he pressed his lips upon my temple, letting it linger lovingly for what seemed like an eternity.

Opening them, I blinked at the storefront behind his back and laughed. "What are the chances we'd end up in front of a fun, sexy lingerie shop?"

He looked at me and caught my eyes drifting to the windows over his shoulder. Turning to follow my line of sight, he saw the mannequin on display and pointed at the glass. "I wanna see *that* on you, my sexy Sabayon!"

I smiled because I knew his tastes. "Funny that you should pick *that* one."

He shook his head and laughed loudly. "You already have it, don't you?"

I smiled and purred at him like the minx I had become around him. He knew me so well—the surprise lay hidden in my valise.

"Tonight. Show me!" he commanded.

29

BITTERSWEET TRUTHS AND HARD CONFESSIONS OF THE HEART

With no destination in mind, we meandered the streets of Old Town Taormina, ending up at a spectacular vista point overlooking the bay against the nearly cloudless, moonlit sky. Holding one of the rusted locks chained along the metal railing, I rubbed its surface to read the couple's names and engraved wedding dates.

The memory of the dream during my train ride to Florence replayed in my mind. *He said, "Kiss me. When we close this, and you throw the key into the river, it will lock our love forever." I could almost hear a quiet plop of the metal hitting the water, locking our love together for life.*

Gianmarco looked at me, grinning like he knew what I was thinking.

"Am I that transparent?"

He grinned. "You prayed for me in the church."

"Yes."

Playfully, he nudged his arm against mine. "You wanna marry me, Sabi?"

With his penetrating stare and his mischievous grin, I couldn't tell if Gianmarco was teasing me or being serious. I blushed that he could read my deepest desire; I played it off as a tease. "Are you asking?"

"What a shame that bigamy is illegal, even in my country," he said matter-of-factly, winking at me.

"That is a bit of a problem."

"Not for me; I have nothing to lose." He put an arm over my shoulder and pulled me into an embrace. "Ah, our worlds are so different, but... to be with you forever."

I melted into his arms as he kissed my lips. "I don't care that you're not wealthy. I'm more like *you* than you realize."

A skeptical look crossed his face. "How so?"

"I wasn't born rich."

"And Cyril?"

"No, he came from a humble background. We met at university as poor students and later became partners driven to succeed. Being consultants, we were like hunters, only eating what we could kill. Those early days were lean, hard years."

I paused, unsure if he wanted to hear the nitty-gritty details of my marriage. Still, he stood there, patiently, in his professional posture, as though waiting for a patron's order.

Staring out into the distance, I monologued my way through the past. "They say all boats rise when the tide comes in, and Silicon Valley was booming. We were at the right place and time to tap into that mother lode."

"If you were such brilliant partners, why are you here with *me?*"

"You want to know if I am a serial cheater?" I answered, knowing where his mind was.

He quizzed me in my own words. "Am I a notch on your belt, Sabayon?"

"You are not a notch on my belt. I had one boyfriend before my husband. And then... *you*. There is *only* you."

"*Mamma mia!*" he howled. "Only three men for a woman like you? So, what happened to your marriage?"

"We grew apart after I accidentally got pregnant."

Gianmarco's eyes grew large, looking concerned since we liked unprotected sex.

"Don't worry, you're safe, Darling! I've had my tubes tied. Cyril insisted after the whoopsie."

Standing behind me, he buried his nose into my long, dark hair, and I leaned into him.

"The irony is that I'm all *talk* and no action." I looked over my shoulder at him as the words left my lips. "Until I met you. You know, my nature is to be friendly and flirty, but I had never crossed the line. Not even close. But even so, Cyril accused me of cheating."

I turned to face him, laying my hands on his broad shoulders. "There was no one else. Throughout my marriage, I had remained a faithful wife, but at the same time, the moment I looked into your eyes, that line vanished."

Biting his thumbnail, my lover looked suddenly uncomfortable. Perhaps the subject was hitting too close to home.

"You are not Cyril," I emphasized. "You believed me when I told you nothing happened between your brother and me." I cupped my hand under his cheek.

He leaned against my shoulder and placed a reassuring hand over mine. I smiled. Turning to grasp the railing, I stared into the past, confronting the problems that haunted my marriage.

With a lump in my throat, I continued, "Even if he said nothing, Cyril pulled away because there was always this doubt in his mind. I could see it in his eyes every time he looked at me; I felt it when he looked at our daughter. So, I pulled away from him too."

Gianmarco stood still, listening.

"We came to Italy to salvage what remained of our marriage—a romantic Italian tour to heal our dead bedroom. You have no idea how lonely it feels to sleep in a bed so thick with contempt—like laying against a cold brick wall." I paused and gave him a great, big, giant bear hug. "But then I found you... and you make me so happy, sweetheart!"

Though he joshed, gentleness and love shone from his eyes. "Do I?"

I grinned at him. "You know you do!"

He laughed. "You're right! Now tell me how!"

"With you, I don't have to pretend to be something I'm not. I'm a simple, messy girl who enjoys having fun taking midnight strolls along deserted beaches."

He snorted and grinned, trying to contain a smile.

"I enjoy eating damn good pizza and drinking Italian beer on the sidewalk with my lover and dancing with him to cheesy romantic 80s music on a jukebox."

He flashed his megawatt smile. "So, you enjoyed pizza at Marì with me?"

"Very much so! I've burned those memories into my brain, like those I had growing up riding rusty bikes around abandoned dirt lots."

He shook his head. "I can't picture you on a dirt bike!"

I chuckled. "Riding without a helmet, brushing off my banged knees after falling. Yup, I was a tomboy in the good ol' days!"

He crossed his arms over his chest in disbelief.

"Or driving south to Los Angeles to meet my cousins, who won tickets to Universal Studios on a radio contest and offered to take us to Hollywood."

"Hollywood. I've always wanted to go to America, especially when I was a kid, but," he added with sad eyes, "other than visiting my uncle in England to work at his Italian deli, I've never been outside of the country."

"But Italy is so close to other great European countries! EasyJet tickets are so cheap! Cheaper than bus fare!" My blurted-out response was a consequence of having a problem-solving personality.

"It's too far if you're busy working or don't have the money to live while traveling."

"I'm sorry. That was insensitive—"

"No problem." His harsh voice cut me off.

Not wanting to inflame or poke the tiger, I took a calming breath before replying. "I understand what it means *to want*. I took odd jobs to get by."

"I had many jobs, too, but mainly in my parent's restaurant."

"Did you know I worked in a restaurant like you?" I asked.

He clutched my hand in his, turning it over as if searching for calluses on my smooth palm. "Never getting your hands dirty, always working in the back office?"

"No, I worked the line and made hamburgers in a fast-food joint one summer. I also worked for a massage parlor."

A wicked grin crossed his face. "Deep, *penetrating* massages, your specialty?"

"As far as I knew, they were a legit, no-hanky-panky business."

"Uh-huh," he said skeptically.

"They hired me to answer the phone and book appointments, but who knows what got negotiated *off the books* behind closed doors!"

We laughed softly.

"Sir, will there be a cross-examination after my confessions?" I asked, hoping to steer our conversation back to safe ground.

"Nah, go on. I'm curious; I wanna know more."

"Oh my God, I feel so old, but thirty years ago, I also worked for a jewelry store at the local small-town shopping mall, where I pierced customers' ears for free if they bought a pair of earrings."

He grimaced at the idea. "Piercings?"

"Strictly earlobes. No bellies, nipples, or penises."

"How d'ya do it?"

"So, there's this plastic gun, like a hole punch for ears, and you load the studs with the sharp bit pointing downward. Next, you center it and squeeze the trigger. I messed up the first one I ever did. It made such a loud crack that we both flinched."

He winced as if it had punctured him vicariously. "Ouch!"

"Yeah! The poor girl jumped a mile off the chair and ran away. I guess she didn't trust me with the second one. Luckily, she paid before I started."

He laughed nervously.

"I knew if I didn't change something, I'd face a lifetime of dead-end jobs like those. Going to university was my ticket to a better life because I wanted more."

"*More!*" he snorted. "Your favorite word."

My soft eyes lovingly gazed at him. "I only want that kind of *more* with *you*."

He smirked.

"Darling, what you see is a seemingly cultured, monied

Sabina who attends Italian operas she doesn't understand. I'm a woman who dines at fine Michelin-rated restaurants when she would rather sink her teeth into a juicy, flame-broiled burger with cheese."

"I love hamburgers!" he said. "But you and fast food? I don't believe it!"

I laughed and smacked his shoulder. "American girls love cheeseburgers!"

He took a step away from me, his face somber.

I stared into his eyes, trying to understand the source of his melancholy. "And what about you, Darling?"

"That's what I thought. Do you want to interview me now? See my CV?"

"No need," I said in a playful voice, hoping to lighten his mood. "I had you investigated before I banged you."

He snapped back at me. "What? You don't trust me?"

I had clearly hit a nerve since he clenched his jaw shut, his eyes narrowing in suspicion.

My heart was pounding a mile a minute; his demeanor had shifted to someplace dark; a red flag waved in the recesses of my mind.

Leaning into me, he wrapped one hand tightly around my neck and stroked my skin with his thumb. "And what did you find out about me? Or my family?" His voice was menacing.

I took a deep breath, put my hands over his, and kissed his knuckles. "Gianmarco. You're scaring me."

As though unaware of it, he released his grip. "There's nothing to tell," he said dryly. "My life was ordinary, boring, and banal until you."

Placing both hands on his cheeks, I looked into his burning eyes to reach his soul. "I'm sorry. I was only making a joke, and a poor one at that. I only know what you tell me, so I'm asking now."

He dismissed me. "Another time."

"You know you can tell me anything. I am on your side; I accept you and whatever it is that's troubling you."

He nodded, but from his succinct answers, it was evident that he had erected a wall between us.

Like a relentless prosecutor, I was determined to break through. "Are you content with your life?"

His eyes glazed over, shot through me, and settled on something far away. "No!"

"Is it fame or fortune you crave?"

"Both," he answered half-heartedly.

"Is the *bar* a pie-in-the-sky fantasy or an actual goal you want to achieve?"

He looked down at his feet, lost in thought.

"Gianmarco!" Calling his name snapped him back to attention; his eyes met mine, earnest but vulnerable.

"I don't want you to look back at the end of your life—a heartbroken man—because you regret what could have been!"

He remained stoic.

"You have the desire and the skill set; you only need the opportunity."

Finally, his voice broke. "I want it all, but I'm *frustrated!*" He balled his hands into tight fists and banged them against his forehead.

"Frustrated with *what*?"

"I *hate* being poor, like I'm *nothing*. Even if I have a dream, I'm so busy just getting by. I'm getting older every year, yet I'm falling behind. I'm treading water to stay afloat. I don't even know where or how to make it happen."

"It hurts me when I hear you say you're *nothing*."

"You live a fucking charmed life, Sabina!" He looked at me with piercing, accusing eyes. "You don't know *hurt* the way I do."

My ears were ringing; my body was shaking. "Tell me. I want to know about your *hurt*."

"I *hate* when those young managers boss me around and command and treat me like I'm *useless*. They think they know better than me when *I* have more experience than them!"

I kept a calm demeanor, listening with an open mind and heart.

"I *hate* serving arrogant patrons who treat me like an object, a worthless thing, being asked endless questions or requests to fill, smiling as though we are friends. Pretending to be happy even when I'm dying inside, but I must because it's my fucking job!"

"So, the look I saw in your eyes when I arrogantly *challenged* you in Mirabella—it looked like you wanted to slap me."

"That and so much more. You were one of the worst, shamelessly flirting with me in front of your husband at Tutto Mare. I wanted to punish you."

"I thought you found me interesting when you flirted back," I whispered. My eyes narrowed into slits. "I didn't realize it was part of your job description because you looked like you enjoyed fucking me in the bathroom. And in Milan. You didn't have to let me visit you. Twice."

"No, it wasn't, and yes, I enjoyed it all."

"So did I." I paused, confused. "But sometimes, when it's rough—we're not playing anymore, are we? You want to hurt me; punish me by violently rage-fucking me when I displease you. Am I right?"

He didn't answer.

I was melting down inside like molten lava on the verge of

breaching the volcano's vent. I wanted to bolt. But I closed my eyes and remembered the loving advice of Niko, my wise owl, that *love is a choice, an act of faith, not an exchange.* I couldn't bear to throw it all away, so I took a deep breath.

To taste your sweetness,
I must face your bitter pain.

"But why are you so angry with *me*?" Then I softened my tone. "I'm not your enemy."

"At the drop of a hat, you can parachute in and do whatever the fuck you want. Spend one, two, or three months of the year on vacation anywhere in the world. You didn't even inspect the bill at the restaurant or ask how much each bottle of wine was. The dinner tonight cost more than my *rent!*"

I lowered my eyes as he rubbed my lifestyle of wretched excess in my face.

"I can't even get Friday or Saturday off because those are the busiest restaurant nights of the week. So, sick or family is the only acceptable excuse for being absent."

My pursed lips quivered. I was helpless since I had no answer or solution for the gross inequalities between our worlds.

"You're rich, and I'm not. So, what do *you people* have that makes you so much better than me?"

"Nothing. I'm *not* better than you, only more fortunate; luckier, I guess."

His eyes burned with fury. "Are you enjoying getting lucky, slumming with me?"

Hurting, I returned fire with fire. "Yes. I want you hard all the time because I like fucking you like I'm an animal. You make me feel alive, you goddamn sexy thi—"

"That's all I am to you—*a thing*," he murmured, then looked down at the ground, forlorn.

"It's a pet name. That's all."

I despaired for him. For me. For us.

"I'm not your pet—at your beck and call—to play with whenever you're horny!"

"I'm sorry. I didn't realize you didn't like it when I called you that. I will stop."

"Or to visit every three months when convenient for you."

"You know my situation!" I argued back.

"Do you know how empty I feel every time you leave?"

"I miss you, too; believe me!"

"You miss me like a drug addict coming off a high and not knowing when or how to get the next hit? 'Cuz that's how it feels to me."

I clapped back at him, annoyed at feeling attacked. "You don't tell me this until now, and then it explodes out of you!"

"When you are away, I fall into a lifeless black hole until you return, and then it starts all over again. I'm like your fucking yo-yo!"

I sobbed, choking for words.

"You have a family you can go home to, but I'm stuck. So even though I'm alone and have nothing, I don't want you to see me—*weak*."

"That's not weakness. You're lonely; I'm lonely. You and I reached out and crossed a line because we needed companionship. It's called being *human*, not weakness."

"But it is, to me."

"If *this* is too painful...." I was shaking. I paused and took a deep breath. With a quivering voice, I offered him the nuclear option. "Do you want me to stop seeing you?"

"Noooo!" he protested. "Never seeing you again would be the greatest nightmare of my life."

His voice was hoarse and pained, like revealing a sliver of weakness was torturous, and *I* was the one beating it out of him. The scene from *Glory*—Denzel's expression of being mercilessly whipped—flashed across my mind, so I backed down. "Oh, my Darling! I wish I could be with you all the time! You are so much more than *a thing* to me!"

"Really? What *am* I to you?"

"A wise lover values not so much the gift of the lover as the love of the giver—that's what Thomas à Kempis said."

He boomed at me. "*Gift?* What gift? I am *nothing*. I have nothing to give you. Compared to you, I am *bankrupt!* And who the fuck is Thomas-a-camp-piss?"

"A wise, medieval monk." A single tear rolled down my cheek. "It doesn't matter. Your anger is too loud; you're not hearing me."

Did those words escape from my lips?

"*Why* are you even with *me?*" He spat the question at me.

"When not seething with anger, you are gentle and kind. You make me feel loved and desired like no other."

Was this the end? If so, I wanted to know the truth. I threw the same question back at him. "Why are *you* with *me?*"

"Because you are gentle and kind to me, even when I'm the angry one. You listen to me and make me feel loved and desired like no other."

"So, why the fuck are we fighting?" I screamed.

"Because I want *more* with you, but I know I'll never have that!" he shouted back. His shoulders slumped forward; head bent low. I sighed and reached for his beautiful beard, wet with the rare stoic tears that fell from his eyes—his beautiful, mesmerizing, soulful eyes.

Approaching him, I wrapped his clenched fist around my waist. He snaked his other hand to envelop me, lowering his forehead to my shoulders in defeat. I cradled and caressed his head as if I were holding a baby. My forearm became a pillow for his weary neck.

"Oh, my beloved Gianmarco! We are like two rivers that cross, flowing but once this way. Your water is emptying into a seemingly endless cavern. Let me help fill the grim void so you can flow free over the land again. Evermore. Where once there was a hollow, now a beautiful lake can exist."

He sobbed in my embrace.

"I know nothing about bars or how to run restaurants. But you do. You don't have to play the game all on your own."

He raised his eyes to meet mine.

"Team Gianmarco. Remember? Your dream can be *our* dream if you want."

He was wide-eyed, staring at me.

"We can build it together. And once you're successful, you can become *that guy* who gives others a hand. Maybe, fund the project to restore the mosaics in your hometown and make them come to life. After that, the sky's the limit!"

"That's easy for you to say, Mrs. Sabina Skye."

"This weekend, I am *signora Sabina Argento Romano*. Yours. I will do *whatever* you want, *amore mio*. Just ask."

I could feel his heart racing as he embraced me.

He has no idea the gravity of my offer. I would leave my husband and start life anew with Gianmarco if only he were to ask me.

Or maybe that's what he wants, and it scares him.

"Ah, my dear *signora Romano*. That's a dangerous offer to make."

"Why? I trust you won't screw me." I paused, and we both laughed at my Freudian slip. "I mean, I trust you. Period."

He tenderly kissed my ear, and my eyes grew large at the seductive wish he whispered into it.

I lost this battle, but I refused to lose the war. I had to pivot.

"You're incorrigible, Gianmarco!" I smiled wickedly at him.

He winked at me. "But so are you, Sabayon."

Arm in arm, we laughed, racing excitedly back to the villa because we knew it was the truth.

30
MARVELOUS MISFITS

Walking arm in arm, Gianmarco stopped mid-stride and raised his nose. Sniffing, he inhaled deeply, drawn to the smoky aroma of roasting coffee beans wafting through the breeze. "Aahhh, I love that smell of fresh coffee!" Comically, with knees locked together and raised arms held out stiff, my coffee monster mimicked a zombie, following the scent toward the cafe.

I laughed. "Searching for a quickie? Cuppa Joe, that is."

"Mmm-hmm!" He grunted like a monosyllabic Frankenstein awakened, making me laugh even more.

"Sweetheart, I'm amazed at how you can ingest so much, especially this late at night! Caffeine now would have me wired until sunrise!"

Returning to his usual charming self, he said, "Not me. But

I think you might need the boost if you wanna stay awake and keep up with me."

We sauntered up to the counter, and he ordered two espresso shots for us, then gulped his down in one go. "Ah, freshly roasted makes all the difference. That was the TOP!"

I shook my head, marveling at my java-addict. To meet the cravings of my own addiction, I added three sugar packets to my tiny serving and slowly sipped it.

He joked. "Are you gonna have a little coffee with your sugar?"

I grinned back at him. "I hope I get some shut-eye tonight. I have a long flight tomorrow."

"Sleep on the plane."

"I will." I passed him my cup, which he drained.

He licked my lips; I was unsure if he was being sexual or merely trying to extract the last droplet of java from them.

Like Rodin's sculpture, *The Thinker*, he rubbed his thumb and forefinger, stroking his bearded chin, which was sprouting a few adorable gray hairs. "I can think of several ways to tire you out, like fucking you into a coma, so you'll sleep soundly on your flight, Sabayon."

My head bobbed happily, nodding at his suggestion. "Mmm... I'm already looking forward to a nap on the airplane." I poked the tip of my tongue into his espresso-flavored mouth —the only caffeine jolt I needed lay on the tip of his. "You make me so horny, Darling."

"It's the coffee. It helps with circulation."

"So that's what keeps your cock rock-hard?" I squealed.

"Ten cups a day, baby."

I giggled. "Show me," I said, taunting my Italian stud.

He rose to the challenge. "OK, let's go!"

As we exited the cafe, a beguiling aroma piqued my interest. "What is that delectable smell?"

He gestured with his head, pointing out a gentleman seated at the outdoor table in the far corner. "I think the trail is coming from that direction." The guy was enjoying a romantic date with his *ragazza*, his arm draped lazily over his girlfriend's shoulder.

We approached the chap and asked about the fragrant smell; he showed us his pack of Toscanello Bianco cigars. The tobacco leaves were imported from America, and the company soaked them in grappa before hand-rolling them.

He took one of the dark brown, pencil-thin, half-length cigars out of the box and offered it to us.

I raised my hand and waved it away. "Oh, I'm not a smoker."

Gianmarco inhaled deeply. "Me neither, but don't you love that perfumed smell, Sabi?" I'm sure he could almost taste the aroma with only his well-trained nose. "Mmm... smoky, sweet, fruity, floral."

"What the hell! We only live once. Be bad with me, Darling!"

Shaking his head at me with the hint of a smirk, he reached for the complimentary cigar and thanked the gentleman. Then, holding it for me, he borrowed the man's lighter and struck a flame to the cigar. Gianmarco offered me the first drag. I inhaled and blew smoke out from between my pursed lips. He draped his arm around my shoulders as we strolled around town, hip to hip, passing the cigarillo between us.

I wasn't sure if I was smoking it correctly, rolling the mini stogie between my fingers and puffing away like a hip teen rebel, but it was still fun pretending. However, I couldn't get the hang of flicking the ash away without getting it all over myself. Gianmarco was better at it—another vice he had hidden? Or perhaps he remembered how Niko smoked, demonstrating the proper technique.

I gazed up at him in wonder. "Do you know that when you blow smoke from your nose, you look like a fire-breathing dragon?"

He embraced me, kissing the top of my head. "Oh, you starry-eyed girl, still dreaming of rainbows and chasing unicorns."

"You're so funny!" I giggled as his teasing cracked me up.

Though it was dark, he donned his shades like a cool cat, flashing a sly grin while leisurely puffing on the Toscanello. "Oh, Sabi. How you make me feel like I'm a child again and can do anything when I'm with you!"

My heart felt like a lost helium-filled balloon soaring high into the sky, and I could see he felt the same from the giddy, cheery look on his face. I handed him my phone. "Freeze this moment in time for us, sweetheart!"

Click.

In the photo, Gianmarco looked like a fun-loving, carefree gangster on top of the world, a cigar clenched between his pearly whites, and I was his adoring moll, wrapped protectively under his arm. Like Bonnie and Clyde, a couple of wayward, marvelous misfits. It was the perfect shot.

HOPING FOR NO FURTHER DISTRACTIONS, we pranced back to Villa Bellagio with my fingers entwined in his effervescent touch. With the spring in his step, I felt something had changed inside my beloved, like a switch had flipped on.

"What's going on in that mind of yours, Darling?" I asked,

peering into his beautiful, dusky brown, elated eyes as he led me along the cobblestoned road.

Gianmarco glanced at me for a split second, his peaceful face glowing with a broad, serene smile. "You make me so happy, Sabi! You continue to show me that not everything has to be how I thought!"

"What do you mean?"

He grinned at me, hatching a secret plan. With his eyes shooting a darting glance over my shoulder, he bent down and scooped me into his arms. Cradling me like a bride, he set me down on a terrace ledge overlooking a stunning bay view of the narrow land bridge connecting tiny Isola Bella to the main island of Sicily.

From my perch, I could see a strip of private gardens beside me. My heart skipped a beat as Gianmarco leaped over the stone wall and moved stealthily among the flower beds.

Bending low and moving as quietly as a sly bunny, he hopped from one patch to another, his hands darting into the terracotta pots and back to his chest. I couldn't see what he was up to in the dim light, but he reminded me of Peter Rabbit pinching vegetables from Mr. McGregor's garden.

What the devil is he doing rummaging around people's yards?

He scampered his way back toward me, and I could see his brilliant smile, beaming with mission-accomplished pride. Leaning against the stone wall, he looked left and right before jumping back over the barricade, his treasures hidden beneath his coat.

"What are you doing?" I whispered loudly.

His mischievous expression, feigning innocence, made me giggle. Shrugging, he opened his jacket. Atop the ledge, he laid out his sneaked harvest of mini butter-yellow sunflowers and daisies, fragrant pink and white plumeria blossoms, lilac rhododendrons, and orange and white lilies. The jewel of the bunch was a large, rare *blue* rose.

My fingers rose to my lips, and I felt my eyes water as I watched his beautiful, clever hands weave the stems together.

He's not making me a wedding bouquet, is he? Did he take the confession of my bleak marriage as a call to action for him to make my secret wish come true? Oh God! What should I do if he goes down on one knee to propose?

His fingers tied the stems together deftly. "A crown fit for a queen!" My brilliant lover had fashioned a beautiful floral garland, which he bestowed upon my head.

Tears tumbled down my cheeks. Showered in the scent of my flower crown, the door to my memories flashed open. I sat just so in the nursery, with its warm yellow walls, peering out of the large double windows overlooking our vast floral garden filled with similar blossoms. My playful Kally and I gathered them into beautiful bouquets, giving them to each other.

But Gianmarco's royal wreath was the most beautiful gift I had ever worn.

The sensory recall overwhelmed me so intensely that I felt my bosom swell as if summoning me to nurse my darling daughter once more. I had an impossible feeling of engorgement I couldn't possibly have, and yet it felt so real that I brushed my fingers across my chest to check my full breasts, feeling hot and on the verge of letting down my milk.

As I rubbed my nipples through my top, it was as if I were home again—a young mother with a happy baby girl cooing in my lap. Rocking her in my Danish wooden rocking chair upholstered in black, brown, and white spotted leather pony hide, I allowed myself to fall into a pool of pure bliss, merrily swimming in the memories returned to me by a new love.

. . .

"Sabina," he called my name with gentleness and weight, summoning me back to him.

"Yes?" At that moment, I was prepared to say *yes* to any question he asked. My heart was whole in the presence of this man, and nothing of logic or reason remained.

There was only love.

"When we first began," he said, "I didn't know what *this* was between you and me. I felt stuck in a room with one door. One way in. One way out. Only one direction to go, but you have changed everything."

I closed my eyes as his lips kissed the teardrops tracking down my cheeks.

"Sabi, when I am with you, that closed room has changed, and now I see open doors everywhere. I believe now. In you. In me. In us."

My tears ran freely. Sobbing, I fell into his embrace. The fragrant flowers I wore on my head bathed me in such an emotional cloud that my heart could burst with another utterance from his lips.

He took my hand, and I leaned into him as we strolled up the avenue toward the villa.

"Sabi, be silly with me!" he said out of the blue.

How funny, but those whimsical words were the same sweet nothings I asked of him long ago when he looked so very serious! But I liked this playful side of him emerging. "Let's do something fun. Will you do what I ask?"

"Anything!" I purred.

"You see the shops?" He pointed up the street. "Let's race! We each have twenty minutes to find a gift for each other. It doesn't matter what, but when we see it, we will know. Then we return to this corner and exchange our treasures. What do you say?"

I was giddy, with an enormous smile on my face. "Oh, Darling! You're asking a girl if she wants to shop? Challenging me to spoil you? You have chosen the right girl for this game!"

We scurried to opposite sides of the store-lined streets. Looking up and down the road, I spied my first destination.

Meanwhile, Gianmarco had found his target and pointed to a little store with a big T above it: a *Tabacchi*, the Italian version of a 7-11 convenience store, selling everything from cigarettes to train tickets and tourist trinkets.

"That's mine!" he called, and with a peck on my forehead and a quick swat of my behind, he scurried off, wishing me luck on my scavenger hunt.

Gianmarco had underestimated my skills as a shopper as I returned to the appointed spot ten minutes ahead of schedule with a stylish, reusable canvas tote bag in hand. My gifts for him practically jumped through the window display as I passed it.

Inside the gift bag was a football uniform from Inter Milan, his favorite team. Its twin blue vipers adorned the shiny blue snakeskin jersey and matching black shorts. Completing the ensemble were a pair of footballer's cleats and team socks.

I remembered how his eyes lit up looking at all the legendary football jerseys while waiting for our pizza at Marì. I was confident that my surprise would score me a winning goal.

Patience was not my strongest virtue, and after waiting a minute at the corner, I turned down the lane, following his invisible footsteps.

He did not say anything about spying.

To my surprise, he was not inside the tiny Tabacchi store. I stepped back outside, unsure of where to go, when I spotted Gianmarco in a jewelry store on the other side of the street.

Even from this distance, I recognized his height, broad shoulders and back, and shaven head through the window.

I snuck across the road.

Gianmarco was hunched over the counter, examining something small. On the other side of the counter stood a stout, elderly Italian shopkeeper wearing a fine dress shirt buttoned to the collar and a black apron over the top. The two men conversed, nodded, and shook hands. Then I witnessed my Darling slip something into the pocket of his trousers.

My heart fluttered at the implications.

I turned and dashed across the street, trying to compose myself, pretending to walk casually back to our meeting place at the corner.

My gorgeous Italian arrived moments later, holding a bag in one hand while the other was casually tucked inside his pants pocket.

"I knew you'd be first, Sabi. I'm out of my league with you—in shopping!" He winked. His insecurities had vanished; instead, he was coy and playful without a hint of uncertainty.

"I should have warned you! You may be the master of the wine cellar, but I am the queen of retail therapy!"

He threw his head back with loud laughter at my comparison.

Suddenly, a familiar aroma wafted past his nose. His eyes lit up, and pointing to the sky, he said, "Ah! A short coffee break would be perfect!"

Following the scent like a bloodhound, he whisked us around the corner to a quaint cafe responsible for the enticing smells of fresh java. A waitress seated us at one of the outdoor tables.

Having ordered a coffee and a glass of sparkling mineral water, we set our surprises on the tabletop. We teased each other about who should reveal first, agreeing to exchange our gifts simultaneously. Smiling proudly and jubilantly, our hands removed boxes from the gift bags, which fell onto our laps.

Upon opening our parcels, words failed us. I looked at him, and he looked at me.

He cleared his throat. "For my Little Pink Kitten," he said softly, and from his expression, he looked pleased with his perfect find. Gianmarco had learned that the way to his woman's heart was through her child.

His surprise was a pair of little girl's ballerina shoes, pink and dainty; each had the face of a kitten with its slanted eyes, whiskers, a small button nose, and a tiny mouth. And the pink leather lip over the top of the open foot was cleverly cut to display a pair of cat ears, making the little pink kitty-cat face perfect and adorable.

"I don't know if it will fit, so I got Kally a big girl size."

So touched and teary-eyed was I by his thoughtfulness that I gasped, barely managing to properly thank him and tell him that Kally would love them! "Oh, sweetheart!"

The irony of the situation did not escape me. My stomach churned as I beheld Gianmarco's beautiful gift for his Little Pink Kitten, and I choked guiltily, winded by a punch in the gut. I didn't want to spoil this beautiful moment, yet my thoughts turned to my six-year-old daughter, waiting for me at home while I was here, gallivanting around Sicily, frolicking with my Italian lover.

"Your turn," I murmured, pointing to my gift for him.

Without looking, he reached in and found a little music box that played *Eternamente Ora*. He lovingly kissed my forehead. "You really like that song, don't you?"

"I do! I love it—our song!" I blushed at the utterance of the words, *our song*.

"Hand me your phone, Sabi."

After unlocking it with my thumbprint, he flicked through the options, customizing the settings. He dialed his phone, and my heart melted when I heard my cellphone playing *our song*, now his personalized ringtone.

"Thank you, Darling! I love it! You know I hate answering my phone, but I'll always pick up when I hear that because I'll know it's you calling."

"Good! You better pick up because I want to hear from you anytime, anywhere, *tesoro*."
"darling."

I nuzzled my cheek against his soft, bearded face in gratitude for his quiet, loving acts of service, then pointed back to the tote. "There's *more*, sweetheart!"

He peered inside and saw the black and blue *Nerazzurri* stripes of an Inter Milan football jersey emblazoned with the team's mascots. "Ahahaha!" He placed the shirt against his chest. "It seems you have forgotten how *big* I am, Sabayon!" His eyebrows flashed at me. "I'll need at least an extra large," he razzed me, and I lovingly swatted his arm.

"There's *still* more!" I said.

Gianmarco laid the jersey across his lap. Reaching the bottom of the bag, he pulled out a pair of shiny, black footballers' cleats, filling the palm of his hands and completing a baby boy's first soccer uniform for a child destined to be a devout Inter fan as much as his father was.

"Sabi? Are you saying we have a...." His hand raced to his mouth to stop the next word.

I felt rather mischievous following his cheeky teasing, so I recounted an Italian saying while flaring my eyebrows at him. "*Tutto è possibile, amore mio!*"
"Everything is possible, my love!"

A shocked Gianmarco replied in English, so there was no misunderstanding. "What do you mean, *anything is possible?*" Still confused, he asked, "How? You said you had the *tubal-thingy*, no?"

I winked at him and smiled naughtily. "Very few things are impossible, *il mio bastardo furbo!*"

"my cheeky bastard!"

That was when Gianmarco realized I was joking and growled at me in mock anger, shaking his head and wagging his index finger. *"Ay, Sabayon!"*

"I'm not pregnant," I clarified, reassuring him by taking his hand in mine.

"Grrr! You know, naughty mammas get spanked!"

"Mmm!" I wondered what other delicious *fun-ishments* he was going to dole out later. I lowered my bashful eyes and then cast my gaze onto his beautiful browns, smiling at him with a heart full of hope. "It's not impossible to reverse the surgery. Difficult? Yes. And there's no guarantee."

His jaw hung limply, saying nothing.

I watched him gingerly return the baby cleats to the gift bag, followed by the infant's uniform, which he folded neatly.

I cannot stop myself from going further, even though I fear I will overwhelm him with what I am about to offer...

"But if you wanted one, my Darling," I paused. "I would do all I could to give you a baby."

... for I believe that a gift of life is the greatest legacy one can give and receive!

His eyes grew into giant disks, finally understanding how much I genuinely loved him.

Having a child with him would destroy the remnants of my marriage and break up my family for good. But then Gianmarco, Kally, our baby, and I could become a new family—his family.

"What do you think my son would look like?" he asked curiously.

"I can already see him, my Darling! An energetic boy, full of life and promise, blessed with a shock of thick, wavy black hair like I imagine his handsome father's head was before he shaved it!"

Gianmarco chuckled, running his palm over his clean-shaven pate. I kissed the top of his smooth crown to reassure him that, hair or no hair, I found him incredibly sexy.

"What else, Sabi?" he asked, intrigued by our imaginary son.

"Well, our son will have your beautiful dimples when he smiles, and he will love to smile because he will be a happy, loved baby. But he will have his mother's complexion of soft cinnamon skin, thick brows, long lashes like peacock feathers, and beautiful cobalt blue eyes."

Gianmarco grinned from ear to ear, listening to my description of our baby boy with all his heart and soul. "And I hope he'll have an adorable button nose like yours!" he added, making me smile.

"Our son will grow big and strong, like you, because he will eat like a horse. Since he knows we love him so, he will flourish without fail and grow like a weed, unimpeded by rock or asphalt. Nothing will stop him because he will be smart like his papà and determined like his mama, stubbornly rising above any obstacle!"

As we imagined our son and carved him into existence, Gianmarco's face glowed with utter happiness, shining through the wet twinkle of his eyes gazing into mine.

"And he will have the most charming laugh and be a lady killer, like his daddy, because he will have the same kind, generous heart. And Daddy will teach him how to treat a woman respectfully, adoring her properly like a queen." Then I drew his fingers to my lips, kissing each one. "And she will love him back as if he were her one and only king."

We leaned into one another, foreheads touching so close that our eyelashes brushed as we blinked; our gaze saw past everything, directly into each other's souls.

"Come with me, Sabi," he whispered.

With our parcels in tow, he entwined his hands in mine. I followed his steps until we reached the same point overlooking the bay where we stood before. At the center of the vista spot, we stopped at the rows of padlocks fastened to the metal railing.

He leaned back, slid his hand into his tight-fitting trouser pocket, and fished out a small brass luggage lock with a key in the slot. Unlocking it, he placed it in my palm. I gasped when I saw our names on the face of the lock's shiny surface, freshly engraved by the jeweler moments earlier.

Sabina Argento + Gianmarco Romano
14 October 2019

Gianmarco gently took my hand in his, his eyes filled with unwavering love and sincerity that resonated profoundly within my soul.

"Sabina Argento, I wish I could be with you forever."

Squeezing his hand as if I would never let him go, my voice

trembled in reply. "Gianmarco Romano, how I wish I could be with you forever, too!"

Before God and a million heavenly stars as witnesses, we sealed our pledge to one another with a kiss.

Neither trivial nor corny, to me, this was the grandest gesture of love from my beautiful, beloved romantic.

Hand in hand, we slipped the lock over the thin bar of the metal railing and closed it. I tossed the key over my shoulder and listened for the splash in the bay far below. My fantastical dream on the train to Florence had become a reality.

Miracles happened all the time, and perhaps my happily ever after had arrived.

Gianmarco lifted me into an embrace, and without a word spoken between us, my legs wrapped around his waist, my bottom balancing on the rail. His hand raised my skirt and slipped my panties to my knees.

In the open night air, under a Sicilian moon, Gianmarco slid inside me, filling me with his beautiful manhood. Our mouths met, and our tongues danced as we made love. It was raw and real, powerful, and glistening with intimacy.

The tenderness of his touch turned to fierce passion; our hungry kisses became needy bites. My hands caressed his smooth head as his greedy mouth swallowed my breast.

I welcomed his solid cock, filling my quivering pussy in a fury of passion and lust. He slammed into me, thrusting over and over and over again until he flowed into me.

So much. So deep. So warm.

As he finished giving me all he had, I gazed into his eyes—calm, beautiful, and perfect.

Tears of joy sparkled on my lashes.

Yes, I knew I could love this man forever.

SHOW AND TELL

31

FLAWLESS SEDUCTION

Tuesday, October 15, 2019

As the church bell struck twelve, I silently lamented, *Where does the time go?* Though we were just on the other side, leaning against the door to the room of our pleasure palace, Gianmarco and I could not wait; his tender lips traced the outline of my neck, and his breath on my skin made me sizzle.

I pulled him closer, aching as I whispered, "Darling," I hesitated and bit my lip. "I love when we play, but...." Slowly, I arched away from him.

He paused, pinning me in his embrace, gazing into my eyes, and whispering back, "But what?"

Sorrow languished in my eyes. "It's our last night together, and—"

"Yes, I know," he said in quiet acceptance.

"I want you, but—"

"You don't want to?" His striking, black eyebrows knitted together as his wide eyes shot a confused look at me.

"Oh, I *want* to do so much *more*. But I must do one last thing with you, something I've never done before."

Intrigued, he smiled with wide eyes. "Tell me."

Nervously, I bit my lip again. "Take me clubbing? Please?"

He snorted, laughing at my unexpected request. "Clubbing?"

My face turned pink from embarrassment. "I know. It's a silly wish." I wanted to stop, but I was goal-bound. "Indulge me now, and we will play as rough and hard as you like afterward. No limits."

Though a wicked smile crossed his face, he gently cupped mine with his hand. "Sure, sweetheart."

My heart soared because he didn't refuse my offer. "Oh, thank you! Thank you, my Darling!" I squealed with delight, giving him a great big bear hug and finishing with a giant grin.

He rubbed his chin, tapped his lips, and, with a frown, looked at me, perplexed by my overreaction. "Wanna go now?"

"First, let me put on my war paint."

"War paint?" One of his eyebrows arched up. "Should I be worried?"

"Not at all, my dear," I giggled. "It won't take long!" I smiled and winked mischievously at him. "I promise it will be fun!"

From my valise, I discreetly retrieved the dress and accoutrements I had saved for tonight. Slipping into the bathroom, I began my transformation.

Threading my arms through the bra straps, I fastened the metal buckles of my silver-studded, black leather brassiere that Gianmarco admired in the store window. The quarter-bra pushed up my bosom, exposing the points of my pink nipples protruding over the top.

Cupping my breasts, I lowered my eyes and flushed pink, picturing my Darling's firm hands fondling and caressing my petite pair. I hoped he would be pleased with this tailor-made-to-titillate balconette.

I glanced at my silly, playful reflection and giggled again. My firm, bite-sized orbs reminded me of delectable, golden, honey-glazed profiteroles filled with pastry cream, ready for my voracious lover to devour. But now I had to focus since there was very little time, and I wanted to look perfect for him.

Flaring open the top of the matching black leather harness, I stepped each leg through the opening, snapping the waistband high over my hips. Next, I unfurled the garter-less, black silk stockings over my pointed toes and drew them up to rest them securely at mid-thigh.

After wiggling and shimmying the tight black bodycon dress over my head, I checked myself in the full-length mirror, turning around and around. The outfit was brazen and shockingly short, with the hem barely skimming past my bottom; if I bent over, one could spy my bare lips.

While gliding my hands from my bosom to my bum, I caught sight of my visible pokies. Naughty me, I circled them sensuously, and my abdomen flexed, quivering into a curl. As a rivulet trickled down my thigh, I wanted to finger myself, but the clock was ticking.

Normally, I didn't wear makeup, but that night, I wanted to be Sabina the Seductress, his dangerous temptress.

First, I lacquered my nails in his favorite color, a glossy Inter

Milan *Nerazzurri* blue, which dried in sixty seconds. Next, I framed my eyes with black kohl and mascara, turning them into dramatic cat eyes. For contrast, I added brown, shimmery eye shadow to my lids to accentuate my deep cobalt blue-violet irises.

A wickedly decadent idea popped into my head as I colored my lips and cheekbones with a *sex blush* made from crushed rose petals and carmine. I slid the dress off my shoulders, revealing my bosom, highlighting each nipple and halo with the same soft red stain to match my lips, giving my areolas a provocative rosy-pink tint.

Brushing my long, straight, black hair, I pulled it back into a high ponytail to repose on my crown.

For a final flourish, I raided his toiletry bag, found his favorite fragrance, and sprayed some behind my earlobes. With a spritz to the pulse points on my wrist, I added another to the hollow of my throat and between my breasts. Finally, I twisted and reached behind my plunging, backless dress to deploy a measure between the cleft of my derriere. The evaporating alcohol down my nether cleavage made my skin tingle.

For jewelry, I locked a two-inch-thick, black leather collar around my neck. Before gifting myself to my beloved, I slipped my feet into a pair of red-soled, sky-high, fuck-me black leather Louboutin heels, enhancing the overall curvature of my form.

Taking a long, final survey before my unveiling, I mused, *Who is this stranger before me?* I gazed in awe at the reflection staring back at me.

Dressed to thrill, I was ready—perfect for him—a sinful box of decadent dark chocolates, ready to melt in his mouth.

. . .

GIANMARCO HAD BEEN WAITING PATIENTLY, listening to songs in the other room. I heard one of my favorites, *Wonderful Tonight,* playing on his phone.

"I love that one! You have such great taste in music, Darling."

Our eyes met, and I smiled when his jaw dropped as I catwalked into his domain.

"You like?" I purred at him, turning slowly like a runway model trying to impress the paparazzi.

I loved how he stared, eye-fucking me, devouring me from top to bottom. His look of desire made me want to orgasm!

"Che bel regalo per me!"
"What a beautiful gift for me!"

He smiled and kissed my hand, licking his lips as I *presented* myself to him.

Bathed in his affectionate attention, I melted as if standing next to a blazing fire on a cold winter's eve.

"Your blue eyes are always so beautiful, but tonight, how they sparkle even more, like rare violet sapphires!"

Here, by his side, he revered me as the most beautiful woman in the world. If it was possible, I blushed even more.

"Grazie, tesoro mio!"

Gingerly, he reached for the dog collar and hooked his finger around the silver D-ring, shaking his head. "You don't need this." He unlocked it, letting it fall to the floor with a dead thud. "I like seeing your bare neck and kissing it, because I know how much it excites you."

Bracing his palm against the small of my back, he pressed his lips firmly against my throat, making me swoon.

"Yesss!" I sighed with parted lips.

"We'll save the choker for when we play later."

I nodded, entirely at my master's mercy.

Ever stylish, Gianmarco had changed into something snazzier and was now wearing a well-tailored, midnight-blue, Italian wool suit with a crisp white shirt. His black leather shoes were polished to a high gloss. Complementing his ensemble, he proudly wore his grandfather's gold wristwatch.

A smile adorned my lips as I caught sight of the iridescent tangerine tie gracing his collar. Its subtle scallop design drew my fingers to trace along its silky length, savoring the exquisite craftsmanship. It was a token of affection woven on 100-year-old looms near Lake Como, a gift from me to him. The shimmery shade of orange served as a perfect foil, juxtaposed against the deep blue of his suit. Placing my hands over his chest, I settled into his loving arms. "You look absolutely stunning!"

A giant grin beamed across his face. His touch was electric as he ran his hands over my bare back, continuing downward to caress my tush. I sighed as he kissed me at the base of my throat, behind my ear, and just under the lobe. He inhaled, caught my scent, and grinned. "Dior Homme?"

"I love your fragrance, and I want to smell of you—like when you mark me after we've just fucked."

He laughed. "You look so fuckable, Sabayon! I'm hard just thinking about how every man in the room will want you!"

"Thank you, Darling." I threw my head back and laughed. "You know exactly what to say to make a woman fall in love with you."

"That's why only *I* get you tonight."

"That's right, my sexy Italian lover."

He pressed his body into mine. "Feel me, Sabayon," he growled.

"I feel you," I sighed, whisking my hand against the bulge growing in his trousers.

"*Ti voglio!*" He exhaled with longing.

"Yes, I know!" Though I tried to reply calmly, my heart was thumping loudly in my chest. I didn't kiss him but teased his mouth with my tongue, trying not to smudge my makeup.

"Keep teasing me, and I'm gonna explode and fuck you in the club."

"Mmm! I'm so excited! The last time I had bathroom sex was with a horny waiter—"

He could not contain his laughter. "Horny sommelier, please!" He corrected me.

"I remember! It was delectable, *Sir!*" I gently guided him toward the exit, our hands intertwined. Side by side, we sashayed to *his* Ferrari. He grinned as I serenaded him. *"Unforgettable, that's what you are..."*

Brushing his fingers against my backside, he gave it a playful squeeze; I couldn't help but squeal with delight at his affectionate touch. Then, like a perfect gentleman, he opened the car door for me.

After we were both securely strapped in, I turned to face him, tenderly placing my hand on his thigh. "Gianmarco, do you prefer I look this way for you all the time?"

Seemingly puzzled by my question, he frowned. "What?"

"The way your eyes are riveted on me, reacting to me—my war paint. I think you like me better this way. A seductress." *Like Ravenna, his ex, at the wedding,* I purposely omitted to say.

"Variety is sexy—the spice of life!"

Quietly, I forced a smile as a wave of disappointment washed over me.

"It's just that I've never seen you this made up. Sexier than normal, like a different person. I almost don't recognize you."

Unable to meet his gaze, I lowered my eyes.

"Don't get me wrong; I like your natural look too!" He

lifted my chin, and I gazed into his earnest eyes. "You are a beautiful, sexy woman, Sabina. I have eyes only for you."

I tilted my head to the side and blushed.

"With or without makeup, I desire *you*."

"Thank you." I glowed, loving how this man wanted me just the way I was.

"Where to?" He fired up the engine and boasted, "I'll never tire of *my* beast's sexy roar!"

"Paradiso!"

32

PARADISE FOUND

On the outskirts of town, Paradiso sat atop a hill with a breathtaking sea view. Unfortunately, the parking lot was at capacity, so we had to park off the road under a tree and trek a little to the modern glass and chrome after-hours disco.

Modern, hip, loud music penetrated my eardrums. It was surprising how brightly lit the bar was. It seemed *this* was where the in-crowd came to *see* and *be* seen.

The guests sat on pink-and-white-striped plush sofas, drinking French champagne. The bubbly flowed freely from the bottles packed into the ice buckets at each table.

The atmosphere was frenetic, and the men were like ship-bound sailors finally landing on a Caribbean Island, ready to celebrate with the local, exotic women to lurid excess after being isolated for months at sea. Couples wild with lust were unabashedly dirty-dancing all around.

It was standing room only, with no place to sit at the bar. While Gianmarco perused the menu, the bartender cast his gaze up and down my body. I pressed my lips together and, with a mischievous twinkle in my eyes, smiled at this curious man. He grinned and gave my Darling a knowing look. *Is this stranger imagining the filthy fornications my lover and I will enjoy before the night's end?*

With a flourish, our mixologist slid our orders across the bar: a G&T for my date and a Cosmopolitan made with pomegranate juice for me. I took a sip of Gianmarco's cocktail—a faint outline of my red stain remained on the rim of his martini glass. I winked at him. "Yours is better," I whispered.

He smiled proudly, then kissed my ear, whispering matter-of-factly, "I use better gins."

Serendipitously, the DJ played *Eternamente Ora,* the first song we heard on the car radio after having our fiery make-up sex session by the beach. We recognized it instantly and grinned ear to ear.

"Dance with me?" I asked seductively.

He looked hesitant.

Reluctant.

Shaking his head, he pulled back against my hand. Gianmarco was not into public displays of affection, including suggestive dancing in front of others. Ignoring his standoffishness, I shackled his hands in mine and walked backward, dragging him to the dance floor.

"Our last night together! Our favorite song! Be wild with me tonight." I begged him with fire in my eyes, gazing at him as I sang the line, *"Mi perderò se ti perderai."*
"I'll lose myself if you lose yourself."

Then I asked him, "Do you lose yourself in me? Because every time we are together, I lose myself in you!"

He nodded. "I'm lost without you."

"Then, be with me," I invited him, and he followed as I placed his hands on the small of my back, and his palms instinctively traveled down to caress my derriere. We joined the most daring couples in the spotlight, seemingly copulating to the throb of the bass.

Side to side, I swayed my pelvis against him, chanting his name, *"Gian-mar-co, Gian-mar-co..."*

As his cock stirred, he yelled breathily over the music, "If you keep teasing me, I'm gonna lift your dress so everyone can see your panties while I fuck you on this dance floor. Right here and now."

"They're not gonna see any," I called out in reply, "because I'm wearing only a crotchless leather harness!"

He tilted his head toward me as his eyes bulged in surprise. Forehead to forehead, I gave him a wide, wicked smile, grabbed his ass cheeks, and rammed his pelvis into mine.

"You're asking for it, Sabayon!"

"Begging you, more like it," I said. "Now take me somewhere so you can spank your slutty, bad girl."

Gianmarco erupted with delight and conceded. "Right!"

I could barely contain my fervor. "I'm so aroused! Bathroom or car?"

He growled, "Need you ask, *mia troia!*"

Gianmarco grabbed me, his obedient slut-whore, and practically dragged me outside.

"Is sex in public allowed in Sicily?" I mischievously purred, and he laughed.

He turned to face me and nuzzled my ear. "You told me to be wild with you tonight!"

Giddy with anticipation, I added, "I suppose we've already had sex *on* the car; we might as well have sex *in* the car!"

He chuckled.

"And if we both end up as criminals in jail tonight?" I asked.

He smiled wickedly. "Who cares! I love *fuorileggi!*"
"*outlaws!*"

WE SCURRIED THROUGH THE CROWD, out the doors, and down the street to the waiting Ferrari.

He paused before opening the car door for me, both of us still laughing at his joke about outlaws. Unbelievably, we laughed even louder, staring at the impossible layout in front of us—too compact for us both to occupy the same space.

"Who's on top?" I asked him.

"You!" he commanded, reclining the passenger seat. He yanked down his trousers and briefs as he slid in.

It was a tight squeeze, but I managed to swing my knee to climb over and straddle his lap. As my dress rolled up, exposing my harness, he grabbed my pussy.

"So wet!" he roared with delight.

I licked his lips. "*You* make me wet!"

"Yes, I know," he wickedly replied.

He held my hips while I guided his throbbing cock, dancing at my entrance.

"Yes, right there." I nodded my head vigorously and gazed into his eyes. "I need you!"

He grunted as I impaled myself on him.

"Unghh, I love how you fill me up!" I exclaimed, delirious with pleasure, as I ground against his erection.

"Ohh, yesss!"

He grasped my butt cheeks and kneaded them, crushing my pussy into his groin and burnishing me to the beat of the loud club music thundering from the DJ's Tannoy speaker towers.

Mouths open, lips barely touching, I breathed in the life-giving air that was just inside him. I felt our souls connect as one body, one breath. And like grain and millstone, we moved together, smashing and pushing against each other, melding our passions and desires into an intoxicating mix.

"Aahh! So good!" I shuddered as he nibbled my neck and fondled my bosom through my dress. His girthy cock stretched me profoundly, even more so when I made loud, enthusiastic bedroom noises to match his every thrust.

Tilting my hips up, we pulverized each other's pelvises, squeezing my engorged pearl against him; I loved the tight clitoris sandwich we made. And the wet smacks of our flesh slapping against each other made me giggle.

Parked under a tree by the side of the road, we were well hidden, but I lost focus, nervous that someone would notice our conspicuous red racecar and catch us in the act.

"Relax, Sabi! It's only us here," Gianmarco said. The man was in tune with my body and mind. Luckily, the traffic was primarily patrons heading to Paradiso since it was the only establishment on this road for miles.

I gasped in surprise as he ripped the top of my dress off my shoulders. He roared and smiled from ear to ear when he noticed my exposed bra was the same as the one on display at the lingerie shop.

He caressed my chest. "Oh, I love this!"

"I knew you would!" I purred.

He scooped out my bosom, releasing it from its leather cage, and finger-teased my erect nipples, making them tingle with excitement. The full moon's reflection bathed us in scattered strobes filtered through the tree's canopy. Nature's disco lights made us look even sexier.

"Wow! Your nipples are so pink and rosy, like ripe, juicy raspberries ready for devouring!" he called out at his discovery.

"I painted them, especially for you!" I shimmied my perky pink pair in his face.

He marveled. "Painted!"

I nodded.

"Grrr... love it!" he howled.

We laughed, then he rubbed my points, and I yelped as he surprised me again by sinking his teeth into my breast.

"Aaahh, yesss!" I exhaled huskily.

Wild wolf howls burst from his chest. He glanced up at me, with my breast filling his mouth.

"What a beautiful sight! Mark me! Bite me!" I yowled in glorious glee. His lascivious smile widened before he sucked me harder, taking small nips of my flesh.

"Like that?" he asked with a beastly snarl.

"Mmm, I love it, Darling!"

He beamed as I admired my new purple, butterfly-shaped hickey.

"God, I want to bite you too," I said, nearly breathless with lust.

"Gently, Sabi."

"Where?"

"On my neck, but no marks. I have to go back to work tomorrow."

Obeying his request, I answered, "I promise. Relax."

He closed his eyes and held his breath in anticipation as I kissed his soft skin and tasted the salt of his savory sweat, licking him up and down and sucking only below the top of his shirt collar. I had to control my urge to suck harder and mark him. So instead, I lightly grazed my teeth against his flesh.

He yelped.

I lowered my neck and offered it to him. He kissed the side, and my eyes shut as I threw my head back. His soft lips traveled, planting wet kisses from the hollow of my clavicle up to my throat. The whiskers on his beard tickled like crazy, and I curled into a ball as I giggled uncontrollably.

"I'll never forget fucking you in a Ferrari!" I confessed.

He smiled. "Me too! Never!"

I could not resist his beautiful mouth, so I brushed against it. His tongue, asking for entry, flicked at my lips. Conditioned to his touch, it unfurled like flower petals kissed by sunlight, opening in auto-response. I loved how he Frenched me, our tongues exploring and parrying like crossed swords. Eye to eye, we breathed and panted in syncopation to the club's rhythms carried across the evening air.

His gaze was intense with concentration. With his whole being, he seeded me, body and soul, more intimately than ever before as we abraded harder against each other. Hammering me from below, we howled in erotic bliss until we reached orgasmic oblivion together.

"*Cazzo!*" he groaned, while I moaned, "Unghh!" squirting my juices over his thighs and onto the leather upholstery.

Then he commanded, "Doggy!"

Happily, I obeyed.

We hopped out of the car to switch places. As he passed by, I gasped as he playfully swatted my ass, gently caressing it afterward. Pausing, I looked over my shoulder and smiled at him. "Only one?" I asked. Holding the door, I leaned forward, pushing my ass toward his body.

"Well, if you want more, Sabayon—"

"I always want *more*."

"Rough?"

"Yes, but only with *you*."

"Good!" He smacked my other cheek. Hard.

I cried out delightedly, loving the vibrations that coursed straight to my pussy with each blow.

He held my hand like a perfect gentleman and led me to my seat. "Madame, would you care to step inside my carriage, *perché voglio essere dentro la tua dolce figa e scoparti!*"

"'cuz I wanna be inside your sweet pussy and fuck you!"

"I love it when you talk dirty to me in Italian. Did you know that total immersion is my favorite way to learn a foreign language?"

He laughed. *"Allora, immersione totale, è!"*

"Well, then, total immersion, it is!"

I nodded then climbed into the car, moving in first with my knees pressed firmly against the back of the bucket seat to make more room for his long legs; my head and arms dangled over, facing the rear of the car.

Then he climbed in and followed, kneeling behind me. It was a good thing we were in a convertible, as my head was free to sway without the constraints of a roof. I was completely open as he pushed his rock-hard cock into my dripping pussy.

"Oh my God, I can feel we're both so turned on! You're bigger than you've ever been before!"

His panting punctuated his laughter.

"It's like you're tickling my tonsils from the bottom up, love!"

He laughed at my silly, sexy words.

Being taken doggy was one of my favorites. I shuddered at

the exquisite sensation of his rigid cock slamming deep inside my belly.

"You were made to be inside me!" I panted.

He grunted as he grabbed the sides of my hips, ramming me harder into his pelvis. I ground and pushed against him. His moans became louder, and his cock thickened as I contracted my slippery walls around his hardness.

"*Aahh! Sì, così... ahh, sììì!*"
"*Aah! Yes, like so... ahh, yesss!*"

Deep, thunderous growls emanated from his diaphragm. His breathing quickened, and within moments, he came, grunting and groaning, sending his welcome sweet seed into me. "Aahh, Sabayon!" He beamed a beautiful, sweaty afterglow across his face.

"I'm beaming proudly like you," I said.

We laughed and straightened ourselves out. My considerate neatnik handed me his matching silk pocket square, but I shook my head and declined his kind offer.

"I love it when your *crema* trickles out of me!" I rubbed my thighs to spread his cum between my legs. "Your cum is the best lotion ever!" I shouted.

He grinned at me, shaking his head.

I tilted my head to the side and asked, "Do you have enough energy for another, Darling?"

"*Another* round of pounding, Sabayon?"

I laughed. "I do LOVE your cock! You're like an insatiable teenager with a hair-trigger piece that won't quit!"

He burst into a peal of rich belly laughter. "I'm old, Sabi!"

"Never! Not with a rifle like yours that stands at attention like he's trained in the military."

"Ahahaha! I was in the Italian Army for a minute."

"Well, soldier boy, I thought you might enjoy another adventure at another bar."

He saluted me. "Yes, ma'am!" And I winked at him.

"Where to next?" He fired up the Ferrari, running his hands over the steering wheel as if he were tenderly caressing his lover's cheek. He sighed. "I'm gonna miss my baby!"

"Onward to Andaluz!"

33
ALL THE TIME IN THE WORLD

Perched on a cliff, Andaluz was an exclusive nightclub with another unobstructed, multi-million-dollar view of the bay below. As we pulled up to the entrance, two valets approached. The first eagerly took our keys, while the second, moving in perfect choreography, courteously opened the car door for me as if performing a ballet of impeccable service.

Our eyes widened, mirroring the shine of the polished wheel rims that adorned the car lot. Among the luxurious vehicles, we spotted not only another Ferrari but also a Bentley, an Aston Martin, and two Maseratis—a truly distinguished collection in this *stable* of opulence.

Walking hand in hand, Gianmarco intertwined his fingers with mine, and together we stepped onto the plush red carpet. Greeted by two doormen donning crimson fez hats, they graciously opened the double glass doors, instantly transporting us into a realm reminiscent of a Moroccan harem, complete with Moorish-styled arches. The air was infused with an aura of tranquil elegance and charm—a stark contrast to the frenetic vibe of Paradiso.

Since I was still jittery from the mini-cigar adventure earlier, we skipped the hookah lounge filled with patrons smoking flavored tobacco through a communal water pipe. Instead, we headed to the bar, which offered an after-hours adult play area with a dozen couches arranged around the dance floor to maximize one's privacy. In the back was an exclusive, roped-off section for VIPs.

We sat on one of the sumptuous, comfy red leather sofas. When the hostess approached, Gianmarco ordered a G&T. I declined more alcohol, choosing sparkling water instead since I was dehydrated from our energetic escapades earlier.

He took a sip of his cocktail. "Not bad." He slid the drink over to me.

I took a sip. "Your version is still better," I whispered over the mellow music.

He proudly grinned. "They use good ingredients, but see how it's cloudy and tastes a tad too bitter? That's because of their technique. They should barely stir it." He pretended to shake an imaginary cocktail shaker up and down in the air. "Too heavy-handed, and it bruises the gin."

I smiled. "Despite your love of savage sex, your hands have such an amazing technique that you never bruise me!"

"Only my hands?" He breathed the words lasciviously into my ear.

"No, not only your hands, Darling!"

He leaned over. With one hand cradling my nape, he tickled my ear with his tongue, making me laugh.

His eyes scanned the room, soaking it all in: the richness,

the subtle music, the less frenetic atmosphere, and the caliber of the drinks. He was on a scouting expedition, benchmarking and making mental notes for the future.

I was happy, content to bop and sway to the music while crunching on the ice cubes from my refreshingly cold glass of San Pellegrino.

"You'll chip your teeth and ruin your beautiful smile if you keep chewing on ice, Sabi."

"I can't help it. I have a biting fetish."

He massaged his tender neck, where he had allowed me to give him a markless love bite. "Yes, I know!"

"I'd bite your tight ass right now if you'd let me, Darling!"

"Wrong venue, my dirty girl. At Paradiso, I'd have said yes. But here..." He shook his head. "Tsk-tsk."

I laughed.

"Wanna dance instead, Sabi?"

"I was hoping you'd ask. We didn't finish our first one."

"Nope." He beamed a wicked smile at me. "We finished something else."

Taking my hand, he curled his fingers around mine and led me to a private corner of the dance hall. Slowly, we swayed to an old recording of *We Have All the Time in the World*.

Draping my hands around his neck while wrapped in his embrace, I gazed into his mesmerizing brown eyes, wishing... if only we had more time. With so many precious things that I still wanted us to do, every second had to count as two.

"Are you having fun, Darling?" I asked.

"Yes, I love your world so very much. Thank you for sharing it with me."

"You're welcome." I confessed, "But really, I'm being selfish."

"Again, with *selfish?*"

"Spoiling *you* makes *me* happy. But it's selfish because I see how uncomfortable you are with my extravagance. And yet I push and push, attempting to cram a lifetime into an evening."

He nodded in understanding, hugged me even tighter, and kissed my forehead. "Thank you, Sabi. I appreciate everything you do for me."

I hugged him back, loving how his perfume matched mine. He laid his head on my shoulder as I leaned into his chest to hear his heart thumping, letting the lyrics of the song carry the mood.

As I listened, I finally understood that trite saying that the most important things in life aren't *things!* All I ever wanted was Gianmarco. With him by my side, I needed nothing more... only his love.

He nuzzled the tip of his nose against the side of mine. "I know why you asked me to bring you clubbing tonight."

With stars in my eyes, I gazed into his. "Oh yeah, why?"

"You weren't being selfish. It was for me; show me new ideas, inspire me."

He was smart and figured out my ploy. I placed my finger over my lips to cover my smile.

"Let me see for myself how my concept, *my bar*, can be better than what's already out there."

He took my hand that was covering my face and kissed it. Like pure sunshine, I glowed at him.

"Help me envision my big dream; make me believe that maybe, just maybe..." His voice trailed off as he folded his hand into mine and pressed it to his chest. I felt his strong heart beating wildly through his shirt.

"Am I that transparent, sweetheart?"

He laughed. "Absolutely, yes!"

"Words alone weren't working; show, don't tell." I repeated a piece of advice I once received.

He laughed again, nodding in agreement.

As the jazz singer's gravelly voice continued its serenade, I beamed happily at my beloved. He finally saw what I could see in him, and peace settled on his face as if the cares of the world were falling far behind us.

"So, tell me. What do you envision *your bar* looking like?" I asked.

"Perhaps something between classy and ritzy Andaluz, but exuding the modern vibe and sex appeal of Paradiso."

"Mmm, *un dolce paradiso*—the best of both worlds!"
"a sweet paradise—"

"Exactly! In my luxury bar of *wretched excess,* I want every guest to feel like a pampered star, basking in the warm glow of the spotlight, wherever it shines!"

"*Wretched excess,* huh?" I teased him, chuckling with delight at his audacity to embrace my mantra.

He blushed because we both knew that now that he had caught a glimpse of my world, he was dancing at its edges and reveling in its opulence.

"It's perfect! I love your bold concept, my Darling!"

"Oh yeah?"

"Uh-huh! And here, in your arms, I feel it, see it, like I am already there with you!"

A mischievous smile curled on the corners of his lips. "You have a vivid imagination, my starry-eyed girl! And I don't know what she sees in me, but she never gave up on me."

"Never." I kissed the valley of his chest, where his heart lay. "Never ever."

"You knew that words were not enough, that I had to see it

with my own eyes." A precious teardrop escaped from the confines of my stoic's eye. "That I am enough."

"You have always been enough for me, my Darling love." Now, tears were welling in my eyes. "Let me be there with you, as your big dream comes to life?"

"What about you and your dreams? Why always about *me?*" he asked.

"You know why," I replied. *"You* are the dream."

"Yes, I know." He cupped my face with his hands. "I feel the same," he whispered.

He didn't need to say those three little words. His love for me was clear and unmistakable as my shy guy passionately kissed me publicly, tongue and all, for the whole world to see.

Unlike the song, we didn't have all the time in the world. At the final stanza, which ran too close to home, I shut my eyes in a desperate attempt to stop my uncontrollable, hot tears from streaking my face, fearing I looked like a raccoon as a river of black kohl trailed down its sides. "My war paint is running! I'm going to be ugly."

My Darling wiped away the smudges with the pad of his thumb. "With or without war paint, *il mio bellisimo dolce paradiso,* you could never be ugly to me!"
"*my beautiful sweet paradise*"

He lifted my chin and cradled my face, kissing me softly on the lips.

"Ti amo."
"*I love you.*"

Gianmarco left me speechless. Words caught in my throat; I kissed him back, dissolving into his embrace.

Never had I ever felt so loved and accepted as I did now. If this was paradise, I was loathed to leave it and wanted to spend eternity with him.

34
THE CLOSER I GET TO YOU

Cuddled in bed, spooned in my lover's embrace, I felt his chest rise and fall while watching the indigo sky dissolve into the soft *blue hour* just before sunrise. Magenta-pink and orange light painted the horizon like watercolors splashed across a fresh canvas, washing away the old and heralding the birth of a new me.

I smiled as my glorious morning reverie was distracted by my lover's wood knocking at my backside. Was he dreaming of me? I wondered. I hated the thought of wasting an opportunity to taste his precious essence, especially since these were our final hours together. So I turned around and pressed my face into the curls of his hairy chest, gently suckling and circling my tongue around his tender nipple.

Gianmarco squirmed a little as I buried the tip of my nose into his ticklish armpits. I breathed in his earthy scent of java and cedar; the man smelled like a coffee plantation after a fresh rain shower.

Cloaking a trail of kisses from his heart, down his abdomen, then landing at his sexy shaven mound, I brushed my cheek against the soft, smooth foreskin of his beautiful cock.

Gazing up at him, I asked, "Want to *play?*"

"Whatever you want, dear Sabi," he sleepily replied.

"Let's make slow, simmering love together, Darling."

"You prefer it over rough sex?"

"Start sweet, finish savage," I answered, kissing my way along his shaft. "Teach me to talk dirty... *ma in italiano!*"
"Teach me to talk dirty... *but in Italian!*"

"Silly girl!" He chuckled. "Dirty talk *è lo stesso in qualsiasi lingua.*"
"Dirty talk *is the same in any tongue.*"

"I still want to hear you make love to me in Italian. *Per favore?*"
"*Please?*"

"*Scopare o fare l'amore con te?*"
"*Fuck or make love to you?*"

"*Fai l'amore con me, Gianmarco!*"
"*Make love to me, Gianmarco!*"

He nodded and kissed my nose. "*Va be.*"
"*OK.*"

Reaching for my purse, I found my pink Moroccan rose oil bottle and dropped a trail of its liquid where I first covered him with kisses—his heart.

His sultry bedroom eyes followed me.

Slowly rubbing it into his skin, my oil-infused hands traveled north to his sculpted shoulders and muscular arms.

A smile and a deep, relaxing sigh escaped from his mouth. "*Mmm... è così piacevole!*"

"*Mmm... so nice!*"

Pleased by my effect on him, I skimmed my palms over his broad chest and the valley between his pecs. My slick fingers fanned adoration over his sumptuous six-pack.

"*Aaahh, mi fai sentire bene!*"
"*Aaahh, you make me feel so good!*"

A peaceful, satisfied smile grew on his face, encouraging me to continue. I playfully circled my finger like a vortex going around his belly button; then, I naughtily poked it inside, making his eyes shoot open. He shook his head and grinned.

"*Sei una cattiva ragazza, Sabayon!*"
"*You are a bad girl, Sabayon!*"

I loved being his naughty girl and continued on my journey south, exploring his gorgeous body, and he inhaled, holding his breath in anticipation. But I skirted his pelvis as my hand hopped to his inner thighs, continuing down his long, muscular legs.

"What game are you playing, Sabi?"

"Uh-uh!" I wagged my finger at him. "Only in Italian, Darling!

"*Solo se mi rispondi in italiano.*"
"*Only if you answer me in Italian.*"

A wicked smile parted his lips. "*Cosa vuoi che ti faccia?*"
"*What do you want me to do to you?*"

My beloved *bastardo* had changed the rules of our game, making it more challenging. Thinking, I bit down on my lip, not expecting to have to reply in Italian too!

I desperately wanted him inside me, so I climbed back up his body. Lying above him, I rubbed myself over his torso, transferring the oil from his chest to mine.

"*Voglio le tue dita dentro di me!*"
"*I want your fingers inside me!*"

He drummed his fingers in the air to tease me. *"Questi mignoli?"*
"These little fingers?"

I giggled when he placed two of his fingers on my lips and traced their outline; my mouth opened at his touch. Circling my tongue around his fingertips, I sucked them in as he slowly pushed them in and out of me.

I released a thrilled sigh as his other hand moved to my glossy chest; his pointer pressed and rolled my erect nipple around the circumference of my pink areolae. As Gianmarco lowered his mouth to swallow my breast, his hand moved to the swell of my mound, gliding beyond the groove and pushing his middle finger into my dripping pussy.

"Voglio farti venire solo con queste due dita."
"I wanna make you cum with just these two fingers."

I shook my head, desperately wanting to cum with more than just fingers.

"Di più! Ho bisogno di più per favore! Farmi venire, tesoro mio!"
"More! I need more, please! Make me cum, my Darling!"

He pulled out and hooked me with two. Taking control, he effortlessly flipped me over from an embrace, then swung me underneath him. *"Ti farò bagnare così tanto che sborrerai come mai prima d'ora!"* He promised.
"I'm gonna make you so wet, you're gonna cum like never before!"

"Mmm-hmm!" I moaned. He didn't have to do much more to make my pussy wetter, as I was already drenched and enjoying everything he was doing. Luckily, *mmm* was universal in all languages. *"Gianmmmaaahh..."*

While gazing up at him, a deep exhalation escaped my mouth as he nipped and kissed the base of my throat, sending a shower of sparks over my front and making me shiver with delight.

"*Ah, sìììì!*" I wailed while arching my back and pushing my pair skyward into him.

Reaching for the bottle of rose oil, he squirted the liquid between the valley of my bosom, swirling and massaging the sweet fragrance on my skin, moving his slick palms from my clavicle to my shoulders, then back to my chest.

I loved how he manhandled my breasts, rubbing and squeezing my rigid nipples with even more force. The oil was both a lubricant and a desensitizer. What would have been painful without it now seemed erotically titillating.

Taking a proverbial pulse check, he asked, *"Ti piace così?"*
"*Do you like this?*"

"Yes, I do. But harder," I begged. "Grab me harder!" And he smiled as I moaned and arched my back even more.

"God, I love your stiff pokies!" he declared to the universe, and I giggled with delight.

Probing for his penchant for delivering pain with pleasure, I had no idea how to translate my following thought into Italian, so I blurted it out in English. "Want to try nipple clamps on them next time?"

He grinned, clearly amused at my suggestion. "I love how you're as kinky as I am!"

"Oh, Darling! Keep talking to me in Italian, please!"

"Only if you do too, Sabayon!"

He pecked the tip of my nose, spurting the oil into the well of my belly button and rubbing it around my abdomen.

"Aaahh!" I groaned in elation and frustration at his touch since I still couldn't fully express myself in Italian, despite being immersed in him.

Silly me! Gianmarco and I had been so inordinately

close this weekend that he had seen every inch of my body, yet I self-consciously placed an arm across my tiger-striped stomach. My beloved lowered his head and kissed the top of my fist, moving my trembling hand aside as he worshiped my belly with his lips, poking his tongue into my navel. *"Il tuo ombelico è così carino! È come un delizioso tortellino!"*

"Your belly button is so cute! It's like a delicious tortellini!"

"What?" I giggled, confused. "The ring-shaped filled pasta stuffed with meat and cheese?"

"Esatto!"

"Exactly!"

He nodded, then buried his face into my tummy, playfully French kissing my belly button. It tickled, so I tried to push his face away, but he was persistent in his amorousness.

The stretch marks of childbirth streaked my middle, and I sighed as he tenderly feather-brushed kisses across it, resting his head on my tummy as though it were a cuddly pillow. *"È così morbida e calda!"*

"It's so soft and warm!"

Though it tickled, I loved it when he rubbed his beautiful, bearded face against my skin. Kissing me there once more, he playfully blew a raspberry on it, and we laughed.

My face was aglow from Gianmarco's gentleness. His simple, loving act of acceptance gave yet another example of his affection for me, tying my soul to his even more closely.

He bent his head low, his mouth inching down past my mound. *"Adoro il tuo sapore!"*

"I love how you taste!"

With two fingers in a V, he spread my labia apart and sucked on my hidden pearl, drinking me in as if I were sucking the best cocktail from a straw. "Mmm!"

I shuddered at how much he loved my taste. "Lord, have mercy!"

Slowly, he swept my slit with his tongue before gliding his long finger between my wet lower lips.

"Ungh!" I sighed. *"Lo so che—um..."*
"I know that—um..."

I laughed. "Shit! I can't translate fast enough in Italian *and* fuck you at the same time!"

"Ahahaha! I feel the same, but in reverse!" We rolled in laughter together.

"Fuck it!" I said. "Do you know how much you turn me on?"

He nodded, and I was deliriously faint as he hummed his answer, "Mmm-hmm!" while vibrating against my entrance.

My knees shook uncontrollably as my body hummed for him. "Like no one else!"

He curled his tongue along the underside of my clit, lashing the tip from side to side in a quick flicking motion.

I grasped his head, pushed his shaven scalp against me, and pressed his face closer. "Damn, how your tongue never ceases to amaze me!"

Absorbed by his passion, Gianmarco moved his hand to my chest while his vocalizations rumbled from below. His punctuated moans echoing deep inside me were so good that I could hardly speak.

"Ah—ahh—*ahhh!"* I exhaled in rapid, staccato bursts of pleasure, matching the tempo of his fingertips strumming my nipples. I was the instrument, and he was the savant.

"You like that, Sabayon?"

I nodded vigorously. "Don't stop!"

Though I could not see it, my pussy felt his mouth smiling.

He lapped me faster, and the forceful pressure of his tongue flat against my pearl sent me over the precipice. I quaked and convulsed, cumming and exploding over all of him like a volcano; hot nectar squirted into his mouth and onto his beard and chin. Through it all, he continued sucking me, moaning with me, thoroughly enjoying swallowing my overflowing elixir while I orgasmed.

"You are so fucking amazing, oh, beloved passion master of my pussy!"

He beamed triumphantly.

"I want to pleasure you the same way, please. May I try something new with you, for both of us?"

"OK."

I reached for the bottle of rose oil and opened it.

"Lie on your back," I commanded.

Sitting cross-legged in front of him, I raised his knees so his feet lay flat on the bed and set his legs wide apart.

Scooching myself into the gap and resting my knees against his ass cheeks, I bent over and brushed his shaft with my cheek and half-open lips.

"It's so beautiful! I can never get enough of you!" A wicked smile crossed my face. "I'm dying to suck your cock... but I have something else in mind."

He smiled just as wickedly back at me. *"Ah, Sabayon! Amo il modo in cui mi assaggi!"*

"I love the way you taste me!"

"I'm not just tasting you, Darling; I love fucking devouring you!"

We laughed together at this truth.

"Allora, Sabi, dimmi cosa c'è di meglio del tuo pompino perfetto?"

"So, Sabi, tell me what's better than your perfect blowjob?"

"*Pompino!*" I giggled. "What a wonderfully descriptive Italian word for blowjob!"

Bending my head low, I cradled his seriously sexy shaft and licked the pre-cum glistening from his snake eye; then, I locked my gaze onto his mesmerizing eyes. "I *love* swallowing you whole, but I want to *milk* you!" I reached for his firm ass and rested my pointer finger on its rim. "Here."

He arched his eyebrow. "*Milk*, my *asshole?*"

I confirmed by wiggling my finger at his entrance. "Yes, the prostate gland. In there."

His wild, hesitant eyes looked at me sideways. Nervous.

"You know I'd never hurt you, my Darling."

"Yes, I know." He nodded me onward. "*Ti fido.*"
"*I trust you.*"

"Thank you for being *open* and adventurous with me, my love!"

"*Open!*" He burst into laughter when I tickled his pucker and repeated the words he had used earlier on me: "*Apri, apri, apri... per me!*" I teased.
"*Open, open, open... for me!*"

I smiled and laughed with him when he said, "*Ti voglio così incredibilmente, mia ragazza cattiva!*"
"*I want you so incredibly much, my bad girl!*"

Still holding our gaze, I bent over him and French kissed his cock. I drizzled a generous amount of the rose oil onto the top of his smooth mound, letting it drip past his balls to bathe every ridge and fold of his sac.

"Aaahh!" He exhaled with exhilaration as the cool liquid trickled over his skin toward his butt crack.

Refilling my cupped hand with the scented oil, I dumped a generous palmful over his cockhead to thoroughly drench it.

Grasping his shiny shaft with one hand, I stroked it, up and down, along its coated length. The hollow of my palm twirled over the top of his bell in a circular, twisting motion, as if I were chalking a pool cue.

"Good?" I inquired, as I had never done this before.

He moaned in approval, "Mmm-hmm! *Bene! Aaahhaa, behhhh!*"

"Good! Aaahhaa, so good!"

My hands traveled down, reaching between his thighs to fondle his firm balls. Gathering more liquid, I slathered it along his base, clasping his stones with the other hand until they disappeared into his body. "God, your walnut sac looks so sexy when scrunched up tight like that!"

Panting, he laughed as I wrapped my fingers around his balls, gently squeezing them while gripping and pumping his glistening shaft with my other hand.

I watched him writhe with pleasure and loved that he hadn't stopped making yummy bedroom sounds the entire time, such that I could not help but moan along with him.

Slowly, I moved my fingers to the rim of his tight pucker. I stroked it with my oil-slathered fingers, first with my left thumb, followed by my right, alternating my dainty digits in a rhythmical, upward motion.

"*Siiii!*" he howled as his body shuddered in response.

I placed my generously lubricated finger at his entrance and asked him, "Are you ready?"

"*Si!*" His breath dripped with excitement as I slowly penetrated his asshole, one knuckle at a time. I pushed deeper into him, curling my digit toward his navel, searching for his walnut-sized gland.

I paused as he throbbed around my finger. "Are you OK?"

He hissed breathlessly. "Yesss…"

I gently pressed, in an upward, back-and-forth, *come hither* motion, against his prostate, making his legs tremble and quake. Writhing. His eyes were ablaze with desire. "Oh God, what are you doing to me, Sabi?"

"Just pleasuring you, my love!"

Jagged, panting, eyes closed in ecstasy, Gianmarco looked like a magnificent beast, his wildness expertly broken.

A milky liquid flowed from his snake eye, covering my fist. "Are you cumming?"

"I don't think so. But it feels so good!" With his head thrown back into the pillow, he gave a guttural command. "Whatever you're doing, don't stop!"

I gripped his rigid shaft with my free hand, twisting and constricting my grasp, stroking it from the base to the tip.

"My God, I love the way your veiny cock strains toward me! Guide me! Show me what you want, Darling!"

He grasped his hand over mine, and together as one, we stroked his throbbing monster, pumping it up and down like a well-oiled piston.

At the same time, my finger, buried deep within his canal, stimulated his p-spot in the same quick back-and-forth motion, trying to tickle him from inside.

Grunting and growling even louder, his anal ring of muscles spasmed and squeezed tighter around my finger. His breathing was heavy. "Aaahh... so close!" His legs stiffened and straightened the faster that I pulsed on the spot. He crushed me at my waist between the grip of his powerful thighs.

"*CAZZO!*" he yelled as his body quivered and convulsed as he came.

Now, jets of his milky-white spunk shot straight into the air. His seed spurted out as I kept milking him. "*O mio Dio, sto venendo!*"

"*Oh my God, I'm cumming!*"

I laughed as his jizz hit my face, narrowly missing my silky raven hair. Then, I leaned forward to lick his glistening tip. "I love how you taste! Decadent in your own deliciousness!"

He roared. *"Che emozione!"*
"How emotional! I'm so moved!"

His powerful arms dragged my body across himself, wiping his thick cream along my front. "Oh my God, I saw stars! That was fucking amazing, Sabayon!"

"Yes, I know!" I chuckled at my reply; usually, I complimented him on his impressive sexual prowess.

He giggled giddily. "So insanely intense, like my whole body was cumming, not just my cock!"

My face hurt from smiling. I was positively beaming, ecstatic at his thorough enjoyment. "We aim to please!" I wiped his cumshot from my forehead, licking his creamy goodness off my fingers. "Yummy!" I purred.

With half-closed eyes, his laughter turned to giggles, and his gorgeous, radiant face was basking in a beautiful, carefree afterglow.

My head, cheek on his chest, rose and fell with his every breath; I felt his heartbeat, strong and true. Inching forward, I tenderly kissed his soft, succulent lips. Nuzzling my head against the crook of his neck, I whispered, "I love you!"

He raised my chin, kissed my forehead, and rested his cheek on my crown. *"Sì, lo so."*
"Yes, I know."

At that moment, I realized that, all along, when he told me, "Yes, I know," it was his way of saying, "I love you!"

Relaxed and thoroughly sated, we fell asleep, safe in each other's arms.

35

UNTIL IT'S TIME FOR ME TO GO

Mid-morning
Tuesday, October 15, 2019

Knock, knock, knock! A booming voice from the other side of the door jarred us awake. "Room Service!"

"Uh-oh!" I gasped, remembering, then jumped up, ripped the top sheet off the bed, and wrapped it around myself. "It's our breakfast wake-up call!"

Gianmarco grabbed one of the fluffy pillows to cover himself. "Hey!"

I raced to open the door in my impromptu gown, fastened securely under my arms. Holding two of my freshly pressed dresses hooked over his fingers, the bellhop stepped inside without batting an eye at my attire. "Shall I place these on the hook, madam?"

"Yes, please. Thank God! Something clean to wear today. Could you place the tray just there, please?" I pointed toward the terrace and, rummaging around in my purse, found a coin and pressed it into his palm. "Thank you!"

The porter bowed farewell and took his leave.

After dropping the bedsheet toga, I shimmied into my clean linen frock and sat on the edge of the bed, gazing lasciviously at my lover. "I'm not sure what I should eat first." I stared at my favorite —his gorgeous cock. Sighing, I placed my interlaced fingers under my chin as I watched him pull on a pair of black briefs from his valise. "If only the world could see what I see, my god!"

He snorted and shook his head at me for how I revered him.

Drawn, I knelt before him and gently bit his equipment through the fabric; I snuck a peek behind his legs to grope him. "You have the most beautiful ass in the world!"

Chuckling, he lifted me by my arms, turned me around, and playfully swatted my ass, making me giggle.

He sniffed the air, and his eyes lit up—his favorite smell. "Coffee!" Grinning, he headed to the veranda.

I followed, shaking my head. "Oh, my incurable caffeine addict!"

On our terrace overlooking the glorious view, it was difficult to tell where the sea ended and the beautiful cloudless azure sky began. The hotel pool and the bay below were postcard-worthy, framed by the bright magenta bougainvilleas and the evergreen trees growing low.

Another new day and a new cruise ship awaited to dock and unload the hordes of tourists upon Taormina. We were heading to Mt. Etna today for a picnic to avoid the worst of the crowds.

"Wow!" He looked flabbergasted at the feast. "Is all that just for the two of us?"

I smiled and nodded.

The table was laden with a little of everything. Gianmarco's favorite indulgence was *spremuta d'arancia,* so I pre-ordered a massive jug of freshly squeezed orange juice, and his beloved coffee and croissants with jam.

There was herbal tea for me; to share was toast, a plain omelet, bacon, and prosciutto wrapped around batons of Pecorino cheese.

The fruit consisted of freshly cut melon and peeled, shocking-pink cactus pear. Next to a bottle of sparkling Prosecco chilling in a silver ice bucket were some chocolates on the side.

"Hey, Darling! Did you know that I only drink Prosecco on two occasions?"

"Oh yeah?" He sounded surprised.

"When it's my birthday, and when it's not!" I smiled after delivering the punchline. It was so adorable how he roared with laughter at my corny joke while opening our bottle of bubbly.

"Sabi!" He shook his head in disbelief. "This spread could feed an entire army!"

I laughed. "I wanted to celebrate, so I ordered a big breakfast from room service before we checked out. We have a great day ahead of us, Darling!"

"What are we celebrating?"

"You. Me. Us. Life. I'm just so happy to be here with you!"

We raised and clinked our glass flutes together. *"Salute!"*
"Cheers!"

"Nice!" he said while I said, "yummy!"

Gallantly, he pulled a chair out for me. "Shall we?"

"Thank you." I smiled at him, and he smiled back at me.

We sat together as I served him coffee, like an ordinary

couple having our usual lovely, leisurely Sunday breakfast. Except, it was Tuesday, and we had only a few hours left together.

Sipping my chamomile tea, I watched him scan the headlines of *La Gazzetta dello Sport*. He folded the newspaper into four to read the football section.

I gazed at my Darling, wishing this could last forever, but I knew to savor the moment.

Carpe diem.

After the feast, I rubbed my tummy. "I'm so stuffed!"

"Me too. I don't need lunch after all this!"

"Aww, but what's a picnic without food? Can't we get just a few of our favorites, please?"

"OK." He relented, chuckling at my wretched excess.

I pocketed the untouched chocolates in my purse for later.

IN HIS RACECAR, snaking up the eerily deserted roads to the top of Mt. Etna, Gianmarco was giddy and whooped as he accelerated into every hairpin turn.

The concentration on his face was mesmerizing as he went hand-over-hand upon the steering wheel, wrestling control of the beast to reach the apex of the most active volcano in Europe.

We zipped past the new layers overlying the old black lava flows that had swallowed up houses, and now only the moss-covered adobe roofs remained. It was strange to see the top of a still-recognizable STOP sign poking out of the solidified volcanic rock, with the wooden post devoured long ago.

And it was surprising how much cooler it seemed at 11,000 feet above sea level, given how hot it was at the visible shore below.

At the top, we were the only Ferrari in the parking lot. The other vehicles were mainly giant double-decker coaches, unloading tourists herded around by a female guide holding up a sign. Outside the tour bus, she shouted at the group so stragglers could hear her memorized spiel.

Seeking warmth and protection from the cold, the visitors marched toward the kitschy souvenir shop. On sale in the shelter were sweatshirts, postcards, trinkets, and the cloyingly sweet, neon-yellow bottles of Limoncello liqueur.

We scurried from the ridge to escape the crowd, stepping carefully to avoid the thousands of hibernating ladybugs resting in thick patches amongst the craggy steam vents.

Suddenly, an adventurous ladybug with distinctive brown wings and gold spots landed on my hand, and Gianmarco quickly abutted his palm next to mine. It was strange to experience this tiny, graceful creature's trek across our palms, tickling our skin. My Darling had the cutest chuckle, sounding like a delighted little boy.

"I wonder what they eat," I mused aloud, "as nothing grows at the top of the crater."

"You're such a foodie, Sabi, wondering what *le coccinelle* eat!" He kissed my nose, and I laughed at his keen observation of me. Then we watched as our little friend flew away.

WE RECLINED side by side against a giant black boulder, enjoying our lunch on the volcano. My sommelier was as prepared as a well-trained scout, easily handling the uncorking with a wine opener pulled from his pocket.

The Donnafugata Chardonnay, recommended by Bianca Rossi at the wine shop in Taormina, complemented our picnic perfectly: minerally, salty, and briny, yet beautifully aromatic and floral.

We sat cross-legged, and I faced Gianmarco as we fed each other. We had grown fond of Sicilian *arancini*, pointy, breast-shaped, fried risotto balls filled with mozzarella cheese and tomato ragù. The pickled langoustines and the thinly sliced octopus antipasti were favorites too.

For dessert, we had delicate mini cannoli no bigger than the size of his charming thumb. The pastry chefs had stuffed the classic chocolate cannoli with honey-sweetened sheep's milk ricotta. We shared one bite of each.

Often a bit of a messy eater, it was so sweet when Gianmarco used his tongue like a napkin to lick the sides of my lips clean.

I took the tiny surprise from my purse and hid it behind my back. *"Baci?"* I offered.

"You want a *kiss*, Sabi?"

"Sure!" I closed my eyes and puckered my lips at him. He pecked mine chastely, making a loud, smacking sound as I laughed.

"Would you like this *kiss* instead, my Darling?"

I opened my palm, revealing a nipple-shaped chocolate and hazelnut confection, wrapped in silver foil and embossed with blue stars, called Baci, a little *mignardise* to sugarcoat our last bittersweet meal together.

A smile of recognition crossed his face. Opening mine, I fed him the bonbon and felt the wetness of his lips, his mouth sensually enveloping my fingers. I licked my lips and sighed.

Gianmarco put his hand up to stop me as I was about to toss the wrapper. "Wait. There's a saying inside!"

"A saying?" I opened my palm, and he retrieved the semi-crumpled foil. Sure enough, a tiny piece of parchment printed in blue ink was hidden inside, like an Italian version of a fortune cookie.

In his deep, rich, sexy Italian voice, melodic and warm, he read, *"Rapita nello specchio dei tuoi occhi, respiro il tuo respiro. E vivo."* Translating, "Enraptured in the mirror of your eyes—"

But I finished the phrase, "I breathe your breath, Gianmarco, and I live." It tore my heart to pieces to leave, for he had become the breath of life to me.

"I'm glad you came to Sicily with me!"

I gasped and closed my eyes.

With his thumb upon my eyelids, he wiped the tears clinging to my eyelashes. "Your world is magical, my dearest Sabi."

"It's magical because of you!" A lump stuck in my throat, such that I could hardly speak.

He spread his arms wide to invite me in, and I crawled into his lap, yearning to lose myself in his embrace. I nuzzled my nose against his beautiful, soft beard and kissed his neck, eyes, and face. Snaking my arms between his, I cuddled him, rubbing my face into his chest, breathing him in, and storing his scent in the memory banks of my very soul. And then I kissed him with all the love and passion I could give, worshiping him, the most beautiful man in the world. My love for him had no limits; it had no bounds. Gianmarco made me feel more loved and adored than anyone else *ever* had!

I glanced down at his watch.

He did too.

"Do we have time?" I asked.

He shook his head. "No time."

We both knew it was almost time to go to the airport.

My heart was bursting as I serenaded him with a fitting final song, for I knew without a shadow of a doubt that without him, I would hunger endlessly for his touch.

"Wait for me. I will come back for you!" I whispered my solemn promise to him, and eye to eye, he nodded once as his reply.

Showered in the raindrops of reality, we drank the other in with endless kisses, holding each other as we held back time, trying to meld our souls; a love, remaining now and always...

One.

MiLFY NEEDS YOU

Did you know that over 11,000 new books are published *every* day? And on Amazon, alone, over 4,000 new book titles are released, *daily!*

Debut authors, like myself, face challenges in distinguishing themselves amidst the crowd, making your support even more valuable. Thank you for taking a chance on MiLFY and embarking on this sensuous adventure with me.

If you've savored the tantalizing world of Gianmarco + Sabina's torrid love affair, please consider leaving a review and sharing this enticing secret with your friends who might also crave an unforgettably fun and explicit escape.

Once tasted... never forgotten!

♡

The Italian Affair 2

A NOVEL

Have you 🤍 MiLFY on Facebook, X-Twitter & Instagram?

Be the first to know about MiLFY's upcoming books, access to exclusive content and contests, and stay in touch with news about Sabina + Gianmarco's world.

facebook.com/TheRealMiLFY
https://twitter.com/StarryEyedGirrl
instagram.com/milfy.writes

ACKNOWLEDGMENTS

Many hands make light work

This book could not have been born without the invaluable guidance and ardent support of numerous individuals to whom I owe my deepest gratitude.

First, I extend heartfelt thanks to my incredible team of editors: Teresa J. Conway, who showed me how to craft compelling erotica, and Victoria Wise, whose brutal honesty challenged me to improve. Special appreciation goes to Ben and Christopher Keith, for their boundless patience as we meticulously combed through every line of the text, filling gaps and polishing the story until it dazzled brilliantly, like lithium combusting in air.

I'm also grateful to my fearless editor, Arpad Nagy. When faced with a scathing review, suggesting that I only had half a story, I was ready to chuck it all, but you never lost faith and remained a guardian angel, guiding me through moments of self-doubt. Your unfaltering belief in me and my little story, along with your patience and grace, encouraged me to persevere. Even if I write only one book in my lifetime, I'm exceedingly proud of this one—so beautifully nuanced and authentic that this would be enough for me.

I express my undying thanks to my fantastic Avatar Readers, who enthusiastically devoured every word I presented to them: Ava & Michael, Jason & Mary, Bridget, caro Gianluigi, Noor, Rhobeau, Reef Baby, Shelley, Steve, Sophy, and Peach & Monette. Your invaluable feedback and insights breathed life and authenticity into the story.

To SimonX, for enlightening me to find clarity from chaos, and to m'dear B, for guiding my hand and training me in the finer points of branding… in marketing, lol. Thank you. I'm chuffed that we are on this journey together!

A special thank you goes to Roland Helerand for generously allowing me to use his sensually provocative photograph for the book cover—Perfect! I must acknowledge my super creative Graphics Design Artist, Dragoslav Andjelkovic. Thank you for your immense patience with the countless niggly little changes I asked of you. Readers' eyes popped out and were drawn to your stunning cover so much that they couldn't *not* look!

Lastly, but most importantly, I would like to express my profound gratitude to my family. At times, I was lost in my world, yet you gave me the opportunity, the time, and the space to follow my dream. This odyssey of mine would not have been possible without your love, encouragement, and steadfast belief in me. I love you.

From the bottom of my heart, thank you all. I'm eternally grateful for your fierce support.

With love and utter gratitude,
    M

ABOUT THE AUTHOR

MiLFY is an American author indulging in a world of exotic escapades. With an insatiable curiosity for diverse cultures and cuisines, she weaves tales of passion, discovery, and lifelong connections with extraordinary people.

As she delves into the creation of *The Italian Affair's* steamy sequel, she invites you to stay connected and be among the first to receive updates and exciting news. Don't miss out!

Subscribe to her email list at TheRealMiLFY@gmail.com for exclusive access to her latest work.

www.the-italian-affair.com

Milton Keynes UK
Ingram Content Group UK Ltd.
UKHW031014170924
448459UK00007B/439